On the Edge of the Loch

Dear Reader . . .

One late-summer evening a long time ago,
in a little picturesque train station,
I noticed a graceful young woman sitting alone;
she looked to be waiting for someone.
Over the next week I re-visited the station on
five occasions to photograph it in different light.
The woman was there every time,
still waiting.
On the day I was leaving, our eyes engaged,
a moment of silent conversation;
she smiled, seemed about to say something.
Then her head dropped, she turned away.
I never saw her again.
Never knew why she was there or who she longed for.
But she inspired this novel.

I couldn't make her the main character,
she's too much of a mystery.
So I wrote a bigger story around a driven man,
and married the two.

Thanks for reading it – Enjoy!
Joseph Éamon Cummins

May 2016

International Praise for *On the Edge of the Loch*

New, unmistakably Irish, this is a social and psychological cosmos of evocative writing, the authenticity of J.M. Synge, the thuggery of Brendan Behan . . . one exquisite insight after another into the mind of the protagonist, what it is like to be lost and flawed, maybe insane.

I found it compelling, each chapter a literary or visceral delight; I could neither wait for nor predict the sublime outcome. I commend this work in the strongest way. It has epic qualities.

Jack Engelhard
International Best-Selling Author of *Indecent Proposal*

A taut, richly atmospheric tale of romance and redemption set amid the wild grandeur of Ireland's Atlantic coast. At its heart *On the Edge of the Loch* is an exploration of hope, the shining possibilities, the harsh limits. Hope is the strand that runs through the lives of almost every character, binding them one to the other, a silvery thread reflecting light in shadow.

Geography is a full-blooded character here, a rejuvenating, life-giving force, and Cummins' gift for describing it, alternately solemn and resplendent, is as cinematic as the sweep of the land itself.

James Rutherford
Author of *Trumped! The Inside Story of the Real Donald Trump* (2016)

This story is dark and frightening and brilliantly bright, with twists and turns like the back roads of its west of Ireland setting.

Just when the author gives you enough to let you think you have figured out the two lead characters, here comes another of those perplexing but pleasing turns, and heart-pounding action scenes to increase the stakes and your nervousness. On my second read I will take more time to appreciate the creative turns of phrase that seem the gift of the Irish. And I'll listen again for rhythms of other Dubliners, like James Joyce. Yes, it will be worth the second read.

Dick Noble
Author of *The Adventures of Mousco Polo*

A story as inspiring as it is original, full of brooding, suspense, tension, complex character relationships, the superiority of new dreams. But it's also a romance. In many scenes the music of Riverdance played in my head, words dancing off the page, beautiful poetic language, nothing short of startling at times; and the scene at the cottage with Lenny and her mother is haunting.

This is simply a beautifully crafted story, compelling and original. I was transported back in time to many happy visits to Ireland.

Amanda Clowes
Cambridge, England

I read a book with the anticipation of a journey that will take me out of the ordinariness of life, into places unknown. *On The Edge Of The Loch* gifted me this and so much more. I feel fortunate to be asked to read an advance copy. The reader is introduced to characters who immediately feel alive; you truly care about them. I found very early that I had become a part of the story, continually imagining the climax (with anxiety), hoping I had foreseen what lay ahead. I hadn't!

The book lived up to all the big expectations it built up in me – it's a journey of heart-stopping moments, not without romance and tenderness. What a great movie or TV series this would make!

Emma Feix Alberts
Author of *All That Is Familiar*

On the Edge of the Loch builds its deeply focused qualities around one seemingly simple concept: Leave the reader wanting more. This is what each chapter accomplishes as the plot becomes more complicated with each new psychological twist. Cummins' gift lies not only in his ability to weave a theme through intricate wording and exquisite characterisation, he presents layer upon layer to force the reader to constantly question. What appears at first as conventional perspectives on love, moves far beyond cliché with surprising results. In the tradition of Thomas Hardy, Cummins blends the Irish landscape with psychological intrigue to produce a truly compelling read.

Daniel R. Flinn
Author of *Dancing with the Ants*

A vivid picture of the human condition, it left me wondering what became of the characters as their lives went on. Many aspects of human life are alluded to: the utter inhumanity of war, the hopelessness of incarceration, unbridled self-sacrifice, etc.

The author draws upon powerful imagery to illustrate challenges that can seldom be altered. References to Mweelrea, the enchanting yet foreboding mountain, reinforce the enormity of the task facing protagonists Tony and Lenny. But Leo and Cilla's selfless qualities lift the novel. This examination of loss and its impact upon those who have yet to fully understand how their lives have been affected by it, provides the reader with many layers to ponder.

Nigel Castle
Ely, Cambridgeshire, UK

From start to finish I was captivated – by the main characters, the scenes in Dublin, western Ireland and America, all presented in such vivid terms. I loved how the writer describes the emotions of the characters; I felt I was almost part of their souls.

At times you think you know where the writer is bringing you, then you realise you don't have a clue! It's a compelling love story, with a backdrop of the complexity of relationships and life experiences. If you love a novel full of raw emotion and fantastic characters, this is for you!

Janet Mooney
Dublin, Ireland

Cummins delivers at a forceful pace the near cursedly indomitable spirit at the very essence of what it is to be Irish. His characters range from the living souls of its city streets to the mercurial, earthy and embracing denizens of its rugged coastline. This 'hero's journey' is a tapestry woven from themes jagged and brutal, forgiving and abiding. You can touch the texture of the thoughts and feelings of Cummins' characters. Above all, though, it's honest, unpretentious, and unapologetic. A very good read . . . one very memorable tale.

Robert S. Galasso
Vancouver, Canada

These excerpts are from longer reviews. To read the full reviews visit the author's website: JosephEamonCummins.com, or the author's book page on Amazon.com

On the Edge of the Loch

A Psychological Novel set in Ireland

Joseph Éamon Cummins

MOON ABBEY MEDIA

On the Edge of the Loch: *A Psychological Novel set in Ireland*
by Joseph Éamon Cummins

First published in 2016 by Moon Abbey Media
Moon Abbey is an imprint of MindWave Limited, (Ireland)
Trade enquiries: JEamon1998@gmail.com

PB 1: 0: 0:

A CIP catalogue record for this title is available from the British Library.
Trade Paperback ISBN 978-0-9935452-0-7
ASIN:
eBook ISBN 978-0-9935452-1-4
Audio Book for release in autumn 2016

Cover design by Estella Vukovic, Zagreb, Croatia.
Cover image, Plitvice Lakes National Park, Croatia (Photo: Estella Vukovic).
Book design by Maureen Cutajar.

Poetry quoted is from *Eyes of Mine*, a forthcoming book by this author.

Codes 1-5: P2234 P3345 P4456 P5567 P6678

Extras in this book . . .

A Guide for Book Clubs, Teachers and Writing Students
and an Interview with Joseph Éamon Cummins

For more author interviews, stories, articles and Q&A visit author website:
JosephEamonCummins.com

To book author for media interviews, conferences or speaking engagements:
JEamon1998@gmail.com

** Reader Review Request **

I'd be very grateful to you if you'd write a short review of this book on Amazon, GoodReads, Barnes & Noble, or other distributor website. It really will make a difference. Many thanks: JÉC

Dedicated to my wife, Kathleen Argenti Cummins,
a light that never fades.

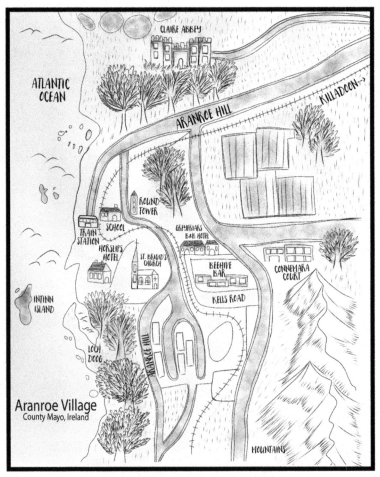

('Loch' is the Gaelic word for lake.)

PROLOGUE

A lifetime had died since Tony MacNeill took to the streets fists up. Even now, that feeling hadn't changed. On Newark's concrete turf he had found an arena to flaunt his Irish working-class toughness, his fast hands. What he gave away in size to his new-world peers he more than made up with guile and courage. From when he was fifteen until he was almost eighteen these had made him king, peerless among all who had challenged him unarmed. Though alienated and brazenly immigrant, his only hard-core loathing was for the sluggers whose courage came from blades and guns.

Now, at twenty-seven, after nine years in maximum-security prisons, he was free, confronting again the outside world, battling to disassemble, finally, his street brain. And believe he had choices. Nine years of blue-sky days had been taken from him, throughout which he had fought relentlessly to save his mind. But what was done was done, he accepted; building a new life would demand more.

When his compulsion to move ahead caused him to reflect, it was clear he had been drowning in one abyss after another. Ever since he descended into New Jersey: February 27th 1980, one day after his fourteenth birthday, the day his parents abandoned Ireland, as he saw it, for the American dream, and traded his green world for a grey maze that sent him to hell.

Despite all that had happened, though, and what he had been forced to become, he'd survived. So too had the memories of his childhood and who he once had been.

It wasn't that he could escape what had happened, he knew too well, or recapture the youth Newark had stolen. Nor wash away the blood of Jesus Pomental, or close those dead sixteen-year-old Latino eyes.

No, there'd be no such escape. But he had in the years since then, in certain ways, re-sculpted his brain, grown up, grown wiser. What was left, he believed, was to blot out the stain of death, the stench and violation of prison cells, and defuse his sometimes still fiery mind. And one day, if he could, exit Jesus' gaze.

Already, five months had passed since he stumbled out to face a new world. Now, washing cars in corporate parking lots and writing a weekly column on schools-soccer for the *Arizona News Sentinel*, Tony MacNeill allowed himself to believe he was forging a new sanity. Each morning he re-fired his determination and replayed the wisdom of prison psychologist Joel Vida. Neither the forces that had derailed him at fourteen, nor the survival code that had sustained him through incarceration, were any longer relevant.

Eva Kohler had helped, initially on his release by renting him a room in her boarding house. And then her influence within her pool of intimates had landed him a half-dozen minimum-wage jobs, all brief stepping stones. From the beginning, tuning out her flaunting of her on-going affairs had caused him only slight dis-comfort. Of late though, that had changed. Now it was the things she said, how she looked at him, how she touched and brushed too close, that increased his isolation. Yet, as his confidence built he was biding his time, stashing away fives and tens for the day when he'd high-wire away. For he accepted now that he had paid in full for his sins, those for which he could atone. It was time to stop paying. No ghosts, no guilt, he swore, and no parole terms, would keep him imprisoned. Or keep the prison in him.

Each passing day, in his solitudes, his mind abandoned the Arizona desert for something he'd once had, a boyhood, with badges to prove it: playground woods and endless fields, the rhapsody of rivers and streams, the tiny home where he was always safe and its scorching turf fires. A time when he belonged. When he wished for no more than to live in each breath. When he knew who he was. When who he was was never a question. When days were escapades and sleep simply interludes.

Could he regain such peace, he needed to know, belong again to something, to someone? His vow was solemn, to find out if his soul might still be alive in Ireland, place of his only remembered comfort. Anthony Xavier MacNeill, the self he was meant to be, was anything left of it? Had the boy survived exile? All that had happened on the unforgiving streets? And what of the cost of nine years penal servitude and everything it entailed? Could he, this still obsessive ex-convict he had somehow become, resurrect the spirit that had once been his?

Soon he'd find out. Thirteen years after watching its green pastures fade into mist he'd go back for the first time, a short visit made possible by just two people still with faith in him.

He could ask nothing of the world, he accepted that, only of himself. If the gods were against him still, what then? He wouldn't let himself imagine such a fate, not with a past so dark, or a mind now so fired.

He'd never be more ready, whatever lay ahead . . .

1

1993

For three days in the heather-purpled mountains, he had hiked and climbed with the isolation to which he feared he was becoming addicted. On this, the day of his impending departure, his mind jumped between two worlds. Life in America: parole, washing cars, lying low, struggling to write. In this other world all of that felt foreign, unreal: these highlands, the islands, the pounding Atlantic, this bare country colluding with the ascetic he'd long embraced within himself. Yet now, as much as he could make himself be, he was ready to depart, to leave an unthinkable adventure made possible by Joel Vida's string-pulling, and funded largely by Kate, eldest and closest of his sisters.

He strolled toward the tiny flower-trimmed station looking forward only to seeing Kate again, in Dublin, with whom he'd stay for five more days, then head back to Arizona and parole orders. But the station's chalkboard timetable confirmed his suspicion: he was two hours early for the Dublin train. His wait would not be without consolation, however. Beyond the station's half-glassed canopy towered Mweelrea, dark and intimidating, the great mountain that had won his respect and awe, which he would one day climb. How exhilarating his time here had been, he reflected, and how nurtured and fortunate it made him feel.

For over an hour he switched between *For Whom the Bell Tolls* and his meditations. At that point he was befriended by Aranroe's old station master, an Einstein look-alike, an unexpected but welcome diversion. William, in his shiny-blue uniform and de Gaulle cap, was soon monologuing freely. By now, though, Tony MacNeill had few reservations about these people and their ways, for weren't they his own, he thought, the salt of the earth, even when they didn't recognise that his blood was as green as theirs. The old man recited with the sureness of age through a rosary of incidents, opinions and local lore. To Tony, the mutuality felt therapeutic; he'd been much too long away, a fact that wounded him now.

On this, his first return to Ireland, he'd come to know his father's love of this land, a love he'd long been told was unrequited. Still, this would always be his father's home. His home, too. He drifted into William's wrinkles and whiskers, consumed his culture, felt the man merge with the air about and the bog underfoot, with the mountain below which he laboured, saw him become one with the strange air that enveloped everything – William, him, Ireland.

Then, in the evening sunlight, his gaze found a sole figure, a woman, on the opposite platform. Everything about her said she could not belong to a place like Aranroe: her style, her long flowing hair, her light-grey figured coat, which in itself seemed out-of-place on an evening he thought of as mild. She stood alone, staring alternately out to the meadows and back into the black tunnel chiselled out of rock. Her movements seemed edgy, he thought, or maybe it was just the thrill over someone due to arrive.

She expanded the arc of her eyes, taking in where Tony sat. He fought to draw away his gaze. But it was no longer his to control. Her glow felt warm, hypnotizing. His hand halted William.

'Who is she?' he asked.

'Oh, her ladyship? *Is fear ná bac lei.*'

'I don't follow. What are you saying?'

'Lady Leonora Quin.' He spoke her name as if announcing her arrival at a grand ball. 'If you're a smart boyo you'll mind your own business. That's all I have to say.'

'A lady? You mean she's knighted, like a lord?'

'Not at all, aren't I only acting the eejit on you. I call her that because that's how she goes on, the way she talks. Lenny Quin, that's her name. One of them rich folks from up at the Abbey.'

'Beautiful. Totally.' Tony lingered in his own whispering, as if savouring an apparition. 'Who's she waiting for, do you know? Bet you know most of what happens around here.'

'Get yourself into all manner of trouble and strife, keeping the company of gentry like that.' William's words bristled. 'Especially the Quin clan.'

Beams of sunlight broke into the station's interior. The woman paraded: tall, resplendent, rimmed in warm light. Tony's mind was already made up. This was his time, his turn, he was only starting, feeling for once still young. An old man's caution wouldn't limit this opportunity, or take the lustre off risk.

'Mind what I tell you, young American, for your own good. There's trouble there.'

No, no, he wouldn't, the voice inside him insisted. He could handle William's idea of trouble. 'I'm a Dub, William,' he said, his eyes still on the woman. 'Born in the heart of Dublin. Just happen to live in America. Tell me about her, anything.'

'You don't sound Dublin to me. All me life haven't I been meeting all manner and creed, from red Russians to red Indians, and that's not . . .'

Tony disengaged. Some previously vague part of him was responding, moving with her, with each sway and step and swish as she strode to and fro, to and fro, along the opposite platform, her high heels kicking clicks into the quiet of the evening. She was godly and mysterious, stylish, Hollywoodish, confident, alien. But it was something else about her, he caught himself thinking, something beyond words, that made him not afraid of her, which in itself caused him wonder.

'William, introduce me!' No sooner had the words rushed from him when a blare pierced through the station.

'The Westport express,' the train master said. 'Late again.'

The coming of September was always like this, William went on, finding no urgency to rise off his ancient wooden bench. By this time every autumn nearly all the visitors were gone, he said, all but the late climbers and the Irish Language students. This year the rain had come early, some days hiding the peaks and valleys the tourists came to see, some even to paint. And the Atlantic itself, it was too rough now, though not for the old currach men, fellas born with sea water in their veins. September was good for one thing though: making things quiet, the way he liked it, not that he was past doing a jig or a reel at the odd *céili*. And right enough, the old saying still stood: one year in four September brought the devil's weather, and that spoiled everything.

The Tony MacNeill of late had been fighting to see life in a new light. Fog and rain and wind and the scent of fresh wet countryside meant he was living again, and he cherished that. Such things as William might wish away, he had wished for and done without for too long in his twenty-seven years.

Then, at 5.58pm, eight minutes behind schedule, William declared, the old train groaned to a stop.

The woman leaned and strained, searching through the first wave of passengers disembarking. All streamed past her and out through the narrow, iron side-gate leading onto Aranroe Hill.

Tony noted her uncertainty, the impression that she might not easily recognise whomever it was she expected. Twice her interest had risen to particular men, but both times died as they got nearer and swept past.

Still, she held her vigil, showing signs of unease, drawing occasional nods from the final group of passengers.

Then, the platform empty again, she returned to pacing either side of the spot she had claimed earlier, scouring the carriage windows. Three or four times she stopped, remained still momentarily, then searched on into the emptiness of the station.

'William, introduce me,' Tony said. 'I'm serious.'

'Here she comes. You'll not need me.'

Tony turned. The woman was coming alright, crossing over the railinged bridge, hair swaying, legs dancing out of her flapping coat. He sat motionless. What would he say, he asked himself; he'd zero experience at this kind of thing. He'd screw up. Perfect body, perfect legs. Fuck it, he couldn't screw up. Only yards from him now, nicer, taller than he'd imagined, confident, sexy, slim. What did she want? Not him. She wanted William, train information. Calm down, he commanded himself. Fake it. Have a smile ready, something to say. What could he say: Hi, good-night, warm night, lovely evening, cold evening, grand day, chilly night, lots of frogs out, hello there, looks like rain, lovely night for rain.

'Hi, I didn't bring matches,' the woman said, smiling down at him, much too close for his nerves, sweeping a hot storm over him. He felt himself gawking up at her. His smile was gone, words gone, mouth half open. Idiot! he cursed himself. He tried to speak but uttered nothing. Now his head would not move. The woman seemed to be floating. Was it all in a half-second, this paralysis? Then her puzzled expression gripped him. She was playing with his scrambled brain, that was it. A witch casting a spell over him, waving her white wand in his face. Then the noise came back.

'You're American?' she said. 'I'm guessing.'

'Eh . . . well, em – '

'He's a yank,' declared William.

'I love Americans.' The woman's smile unglued his stuck face.

'Well, I'm not, I'm not really, I'm . . . born in Dublin.'

'So was I – here in Ireland, I mean.' She extended a slim unlit cigarette and asked with her smile for a light. 'Didn't bring matches,' she said.

Tony rose up, but when erect he found himself too close to her, the bench behind allowing no retreat. As much as he could, he forced his body and face into casualness. He patted his denim jacket pockets, then his shirt pocket, then his jeans and jacket again and back to his shirt.

The woman held firm. 'I bet you don't even smoke. Do you smoke?' Her voice was gentle, teasing. She radiated an I-found-you-out smile that pulled from him a laugh that went on too long and became what they were sharing.

'I'm sorry,' he said. 'I'm, you're right, I don't. It's just that I – I don't see, you know, see many people – '

'Like me?'

'No, no, I don't mean that. I mean, I don't smoke. But I usually do, carry matches, with me, just in case, to light a fire. But I don't have any, right now. I do a lot of hiking; that's why I usually have them, matches, but I don't..'

'Not to worry. Truth is I don't smoke either – when I'm feeling down I do.'

'You're . . . meeting a friend?'

'Kind of. Not now. Where are you travelling to?'

Her intensity muddled his brain, roamed around inside him, saw all he was thinking, he was certain; she was being entertained by his fantasies and there was no way he could stop them, or her.

'Actually, just before, just now, I was thinking of getting coffee, or tea. I have about an hour to fill – free, I mean, an hour free. You feel like – '

'Coffee? Are you serious? Around here that's not easy.'

'In the village, I thought, got to be some place open.'

Lenny's manner of half-smiling had become a trap that caused him to stumble among words he knew nothing of until they had escaped from him. Now she looked at him as though carrying out an intimate assessment, a sensual examination of all that was private in him, his darkest secrets, at least that's how it felt to him. His mind yelled again at him to say something sensible that would halt her invasion, enable him to hide. But he could not, dared not, speak his thoughts. Yet all other words, the polite words, felt wrong, foolish even, as he simultaneously endured and took pleasure in what she was doing to him.

He found comfort eventually in the realisation that they were both aware that what they were doing was no longer accidental. They were choosing this, whatever it was, each was knowingly expressing something: a need, a beginning, a longing, an interest, an emptiness. He didn't know what it was. Nothing in his past had felt so compelling. In this moment was hope as he had never defined it. A rope lowering into the grey yard of his life. Perhaps.

'Anything sounds good,' she said, after what was probably only moments but not to him. 'Remember though, we might be on to a lost cause – the coffee, I mean; we might not get any this late in the day.'

He smiled, shrugged his shoulders. She mimicked his gesture, which sparked them both into laughter.

She offered her hand. 'Hi, I'm Lenny, Lenny Quin.'

'Great. I'm Tony – ' The silk off her fingers tripped his words. 'MacNeill. Tony MacNeill. Like I said, from Dublin.' Her grip tightened: soft, sensual, firm. 'Right now from Phoenix, Arizona. Actually, Tempe, south of Phoenix.' On his second try her hand released, left a tingling.

'Tony MacNeill. So nice to bump into you.'

The way she said his name sounded like music, like the fire of the pipes, carrying intonations of things he found too deep to indulge, things almost terrifying.

'I'm from here, this place, County Mayo,' she said, 'from Claire Abbey.'

'You're a monk?'

Her outburst of laughter, loud and undisciplined, echoed through the station, then tamed into radiance that stole from him even greater devotion.

'No, I'm not a monk. Really I'm not. I think I'd know if I was. Someone would have told me.'

He sighed. 'Glad to hear that.'

'Far from being a monk, believe me. Claire Abbey is where I live, a three-hundred-year-old castle, just a mile and a bit up the hill, overlooks the water.'

'Sounds nice. I'd like to hear about it.'

'You would? You mean it? Then what are we doing here?'

They started off, pursued by William's troubled stare.

'I'm looking forward to this,' she said. 'Should I link you – or pretend we're strangers?'

For a moment he lost her in the worship of his eyes. 'Sure you're not a monk? Or a witch? I heard there's witches in these parts.' His arm opened out. Her hand slipped through.

At the station's gated exit she passed through first, Tony close behind. As he emerged, a hand pushed hard into his chest. In front of him stood a rough-looking man, red-faced, heavy body pressed into a tightly-buttoned suit. Tony's senses kicked in: five-nine, near his own height, a heavyweight but not a fighter, a hard-man face much too close, chin exposed. In his past he permitted himself only an instant for this, the weighing up of an opponent, rarely the pause he was allowing now, even when it was sensible. But those days were over; he was no longer the old Anto MacNeill, as he was once known, but the new one he'd learned to control. Yet still it lurked inside, what he had been, what he had paid for. In need, it would never be far away. Right now he had to remember: it was Ireland, the 90s, not Newark, not the peniten-tiary. Hands down, cool head, feet balanced. If he was forced to deal with this so-far-lucky moron, he would. Parole or no parole. He had the fucker's number, no problem, power wound, release one command away.

'Y'hear me or what? Push off. That way!' The man's bulky head jerked toward the village.

Tony's neutral stare held. This was enemy flesh, so close he could smell him, within range: straight left, right cross.

'Dominic! That's enough,' Lenny yelled.

'What's the problem?' Tony asked.

The man sneered. 'Can you fucking hear? You bollox. Fuck off, get outa here. Right?'

Tony entered hair-trigger mode. The unconscious guile of the street fighter had taken his hip through a slow rear rotation, dropped his right shoulder and lengthened his first-strike arm. The body he was reading had made no such preparation, was standing flat-footed, square to him, a big soft mark, he'd go down fast.

'Tell you what,' Tony said in a steely monotone. 'Get out of my face or they'll be picking you up in pieces.'

'Yeah?' The man's face warped. 'You'll put me down?'

'Count on it.' Tony's attention glued to the small muscles around the man's face, for the sign that would set fire to fists pleading for release.

'Stop this!' Lenny cried. 'Dominic!'

The man flicked a look at her.

'Stop! You hear me! Stop this now or you will not have a job tomorrow.'

The man retreated one step, then a second. Tony's stare followed him, until it was broken by a burst of sobbing from Lenny. He moved to her, guided her aside.

'You alright?' he asked. 'What's this about?'

Head down, she clutched him, shaking.

'Who's this guy to you? If he's giving you a problem let me sort it out right now.'

'You can't. You can't.'

'Why? What's wrong? Tell me. You in trouble?'

She shook her head. 'There's nothing you can do. I have to go, please.'

'No you don't! You don't. Listen, let me help. I want to help you.'

'You can't hope to understand. Just let me go.' She tried unsuccessfully to pull away. 'I'm okay. Really, I'm okay. Thank you so much, thank you.' She followed the man to a white Mercedes.

Tony watched, cold sweat sticking his shirt to his flesh, a double-pulse in his heart. But he didn't move. Just berated this new him for not being sure what to do. No other time had he been like this, no other time would it have cost him a thought. But ex-cons couldn't expect breaks, anywhere in the world.

As he watched, her anguish built in his mind. He could still intervene, he told himself. But she had seemed so resigned. For her sake, much less for his own, he'd let her go. For now. But it was not over.

From the car, the man stabbed an index finger at him, mouthed silent words. The Mercedes sped off into the approaching dusk.

*   *   *

'I warned you, young fella. Loud and clear I told you.' William's voice bellowed from inside the closed gate. 'That bucko; you need to keep away from his sort. A boxer he was once, so they say. And that's his name, Boxer. Wait there and I'll get the key and you can come back in; I locked it up when that blackguard started.' The old man waddled down the path, his shoes squeaking.

In the near noiselessness of the Mayo night, Tony MacNeill gripped the cold bars, reliving the incident. It didn't make sense, he told himself. Her class, with a fat swine like that, they didn't go together, not as partners. And how she threatened him, made him back off; what gave her such power over him? Then leaving with him. Just when it was all feeling like a new dream, new hope, for minutes, then over, taken away. Why? What if she was being abused. Bad marriage. Mixed up in political trouble. What could he do anyway? One thing was sure, Boxer didn't scare him. He'd beaten plenty of brawlers, not worth anything against a fighter. Whatever the story, he wasn't accepting defeat, wasn't walking away. He'd find out, he'd talk to Lenny Quin again, some way.

'You can come back in now.' William rattled his keys, pulled open the gate. 'Twenty minutes your train'll be in. Loads of time to tell you what you asked me before. I'll tell you as much of it that's good for you to know. Then off you'll head for Dublin, then off to America, like all before you, all them other Irish boys and girls that are never coming home again.'

On the same bench they had shared earlier, William slipped into his tale of Lady Leonora Quin, as he had referred to her.

For three years now, he explained, she had been coming into his station to wait for the evening train from Dublin. But only in September, hardly ever saw her at any other time of year. Nobody could tell who it was she was expecting, or if there was anybody at all. These days nobody bothered to ask, not any longer. He'd heard talk in the village, he said, of other goings-on, a whole different class of trouble altogether, not that he knew a thing about what they were talking about on that score. One thing he did know, though, she lived up at Claire Abbey, top of Aranroe Hill, an old castle now a posh hotel. The Abbey, all the locals called it, for golfers and tourists. Rich people. And she never married, far as he'd been told, and never went to any of the local *céilis*. Just the same, she came to his station, hail, rain, snow or storm, every evening of a September. Always alone. Once in a blue moon the Boxer Dunne fella would wait outside, snoring in the car or acting the big man with the lassies. Besides all that there was always the gossip, hard-to-believe things that he'd not repeat, that he'd heard tell were said to account for the woman's odd ways, but his lips were sealed and that's the way they were staying.

Tony let him babble on, words that would not tell. Then he stopped listening. He'd heard enough to be scared, but not scared off. He wasn't ready anymore to leave Aranroe. His mind had turned. Now he had a mission.

'Here she is!' William bellowed.

Tony's head spun around, he twisted quickly to his feet, searching about. No one. Then a blast pierced the night.

'The Dublin train,' William said, then into his aged face came a realisation of what his words had done.

As the train shuddered to a stop, the old man stared with deliberateness into Tony's distress. 'Go back to America, son. There's nought but trouble for you here, grand young fella like you.'

Tony dug out a smile, slung his backpack over one shoulder, and walked away from the train.

William sighed. Then he wobbled forward to greet his full-service express from Heuston Station in Dublin. This night, he'd have not one passenger departing.

Tony exited the station, back into the stone-saturated country-side.

*   *   *

He drifted beyond the ancient round tower, through the village streets, back to the boarding house where he had stayed since his arrival three days earlier, and re-rented the same sparse room. He phoned Claire Abbey, gave a message to the receptionist: Lenny was to call him as soon as possible.

By 3pm next day no response had come. He called again, left the same message. And again at 8pm, stressing urgency. Earlier in the day he had set out for Claire Abbey, only half prepared for what he might find. Part way there something had halted him. It felt like fear. Not the fear he knew, something different. What was it? What was he to be afraid of, he deliberated. After further stops and starts he turned back. He was a stranger in a new world, pushing into someone else's privacy, he told himself, into who knows what, into lives where he did not belong, into money.

Later, the day almost over, he rambled out again, this time to the station, where he sat for two hours. She was nowhere to be seen.

Saturday arrived wrapped in vapour and brought still no contact. Just more waiting, hoping, staring at bare walls. Waiting and boredom. Hope fading into afternoon and dusk, then late evening and another empty station. Then Sunday came, grey again, crazy sky, and it crawled by, slowed by emptiness and silence and more emptiness. And now it was feeling harder to go to her, maybe impossible, despite the urge. Had she abandoned everything, the station, whomever she had been waiting for? No way to know, but he wasn't willing to be beaten.

Monday morning, the receptionist reported again there was no response from Lenny's apartment. She'd pass along his message, when she saw her, if she saw her.

At mid-afternoon it ended. He'd go there, he decided, find guts. He'd walk through the town, up the hill to Claire Abbey. Find out. In person. He was through fucking around, no more fear, ex-con or not, working class or not, out of place or not.

The room phone screeched; he grabbed it.

'Tony. I'm sorry . . . about Thursday night. I – '

'No. Listen, listen, that's okay, it's okay, are you alright?'

'I am, I truly am, I'm so sorry. And Tony – '

'Sure you're okay? You sound tired, your voice, what's – '

'I'm fine, I'm fine. Tony, look, it's not what you're thinking, it's – '

'I'm not, I'm not thinking anything, nothing. Can I see you, now? Now? You free now?'

'No, I can't. I can't now, but . . .' Her voice died off into silence.

'Lenny? Lenny? What's wrong? Lenny.'

'Look, I can't! I just can't. I'm very sorry. That's all.'

'You're married, right? That it? Living with someone who's hurting you? Say it.'

'That's not it. It's not. Anyway, Tony, look . . . I'm thrilled we met. I so enjoyed the time with you. I've not laughed like that since, since I don't know, since in another life.'

'Lenny, listen. It's Monday. I've been calling you since Thursday. Do you get your messages? Do you?'

'Monday. Monday? What messages?'

'The phone messages I left, five messages. They didn't give them to you, did they?'

'Phone messages.' Her voice faded, became indistinct. 'That's what. . . I have to go.'

'Lenny, no, don't, please, don't go. Hold on, hold on. I have to see you. Listen to me, Lenny, you know the Horslips Hotel?'

'I'm not . . . What?'

'Horslips. Horslips. The hotel. Beside Loch Doog. Meet me there, please, at eight o'clock? It's ten after six now. Can you do that, can you?'

He waited. Not even her breathing broke through.

'Lenny! Are you – '

'Horslips. I'll try, I'll try. Tony, no!'

'What's wrong? Tell me. Trust me. What's going on there?'

'I am, I am fine now, I'm fine, fine.'

'You're not fine. What was – '

'Tony, can you forget we met? Can you do that? You have family in America, people you care about?'

'I'm not married, if that's what you mean. I'm leaving for America in a few days. Meet me, please.'

'I'd like to. I would like to. I don't think so, I . . . I don't think.'

'Lenny, I'm not following what you are saying. Let me help. Listen, meet me at the Horslips at eight o'clock. Tonight. We'll just talk, that's all, I promise. Okay?'

'Well . . . fine, fine.'

'You're sure now, right? Horslips Hotel, eight o'clock?'

'Loch Doog. Dark water.'

'Dark water? Is someone listening? Is that it? You sound, you sound – '

'Always listening, Tony. Listening to me. Looking to find me. You don't know that.'

'I don't follow, Lenny. But it doesn't matter; we can talk in less than two hours, about whatever you like. Eight o'clock, right? You'll be there? OK?'

'Fine. Bye.' The line went dead.

He switched to his best jeans and pulled a white shirt from the bottom of his pack. The boarding house's old clothes iron did as good a job as his shaking hands would allow. By 7.30 he was ready.

On the road toward Loch Doog, with over twenty minutes to spare and a fresh sea breeze blowing in, he allowed his senses to escape to the peaks running three sides around him. Along Main Street, Aranroe's rainbow shopfronts gleamed, people passing by, leaving nods and smiles. This was a bright world, he felt, he was seeing it this way now despite his circumstances, an almost deserted world compared with the busyness of life in Phoenix.

At Concannon's Bar he climbed the hill, up to a lookout over Loch Doog. From nearby, traditional music floated, reminding him of a never forgotten life he once had. This, and the late sun in his face, carried him back to beach days and bottles of lemonade. How he'd loved Ireland back then, never-ending days bright until 10.30pm, even later, during school holidays, something he'd hated losing; playing street games at a time when most of the world was in dark, and the people in far-off countries, his sisters would tell him, even the head-hunters in Borneo, were already fast asleep; and he hadn't even gone to bed yet the night before. He was lucky then, young and happy. Life was great, Ireland the best country in the world, and the last to go asleep. Everything was good until Ronan died. Little Ronan, ten years alive. Then not long after that, moving to America, to Newark, when he knew that Ireland, like Ronan, was never coming back. That's when it all changed. Maybe that was why the blues came to dwell in him, the gloom so few suspected, out of what had happened in those long-ago days. But perhaps not, perhaps his troubles were bigger than loss or sadness or belonging.

Suddenly he caught his drifting thoughts, drew his mind out of what was lost, forced it into what was to come. He needed nothing more, for how easily he drifted into reveries of the beautiful Lenny Quin, into wonder and hope, and things that scared him, those feelings he had never before felt, not in the real world. But now he needed to be practical, grounded; there were problems here to be sorted. He could handle it.

Outside Horslips Hotel he chastened his inner chatter, slicked back his hair, and marched in through the big timber doors. It was still only 7.45. Plenty of time.

From his seat in the lounge his stare swung between the deepening greys of the loch and the arched entrance through which she would soon make her appearance.

Two hours later the loch was black, a void. The velour lounge seat was hard. He sat alone, his third coffee stale on the table. Still hoping for Lenny Quin. Another half-hour dragged past, then more. At 10.30 he left. Collar up, hands deep in his jeans pockets, he walked to the lookout over the water, then down the hill to his room.

*   *   *

Tuesday morning's mist had descended before dawn and now greyed away the whole world. He fought out from under heavy blankets, shivering at the chill in the air. He dialled Dublin, willed himself to sound brighter than he felt. Kate would be disappointed, he knew that.

'Tony! You're not in trouble? Are you? I'd almost – '

'No, I'm not. I'm on my way. See you around ten-thirty.'

'I was so worried. I didn't know what to think. I was expecting you – '

'I know, Kate, I know. Stop worrying, I'm fine. Psychologists are not supposed to stress out. I'm not who I was; I told you that. I'll see you soon.'

'I'll keep Ferdia up. He's been asking the whole time: Is Uncle Tony coming today? You won't get over how big he's grown. Don't get lost, Tony.'

'I won't get lost. And Kate, next time I get home, I promise, I'll get to see you for much longer.'

'Where did you get to anyway? I was expecting you before the weekend.'

'Hiking. The mountains. Have to go now, Kate. The train will get me to Dublin around ten. I just have one thing to do here first.'

Connecting with Kate always lifted him; this time was no exception. She never changed: strong, smart, spiritual, able to understand. A refuge still, as she had always been for him. Cutting his time with her wasn't fair. Especially now, her marriage gone. But always a warrior, big sister, winning even when losing. One to emulate, not that he ever would. Ireland's gain against the odds, America's loss.

The blur ceased. He had drifted, not been listening. 'See you tonight, Kate, definitely, around ten-thirty.'

'I can't wait to see you, Tony. It's been a long time.'

He grabbed the water-proof cape and sou'wester he thoroughly disliked, and threw on his backpack. This day he'd be baptised in County Mayo rain, the first he'd seen. On Aranroe Hill the climb offered no vistas. Colours previously alive now hid, and sea and sky mixed into grey union. Intermittently his melancholy deepened, sank his thoughts into this fog of oneness that he could so easily belong to. But his mind denied him reflection; he had a pressing purpose in front of him, at the top of the hill.

Shrouded in vapour, Claire Abbey looked like an old photograph, colourless except for smudges of amber in the Tudor-style windows. It was his first time to see it. It was a castle alright, that much was fact. Inside the portico he paused on the weather mat. An ornate world: antique furniture, tapestry sofas, oriental rugs, paintings, sculptures, a log fire scenting the air, and everywhere the look of wealth. A set to which he would never belong, he felt. So removed from the poor streets of his early life, from the land and the people it shaped; he'd take the unspoilt Sheffrey Hills and craggy Nephin Begs, any day.

'Gloomy day out there,' a friendly female voice said. 'But we can't complain.' From beyond the marble-topped reception desk a young woman's green eyes stared, black ringlets framing her bone-white face.

He tried to hide his reaction but was already returning her warmth. 'I'm here to see Miss Quin, please.'

The woman smiled with unease, as though offering an apology.

'Leonora Quin.' He inflected the words with as native an accent as he was able.

She leaned toward him, but pulled back as voices filtered out from an open office behind her. 'I'll just get the manager. Won't be a moment.' She paused conspicuosly, then left.

'Something we can do for you?' A tall, middle-aged woman spoke with a you-shouldn't-be-here tone. 'Is there something we can do for you?' On her navy blazer a gold badge read: Ms C VanSant, Manager.

'Yes, there is,' he said, his voice an octave higher than he intended. 'I'm Tony MacNeill, from the U.S. I'm here to see Miss Quin.'

'She's not in town today. Is there something else we can do?'

He paused. 'She's due back?'

'I have no way of knowing. A while, I would think.'

'What does a while mean? Minutes? Hours?'

'Sir, I've told you what I know. Now if there's nothing else?'

'Nah. Know what? I'll wait. Here.' He switched his gaze to the girl, her countenance still troubled.

'Time to get back to your duties, Miss deBurca,' the woman said, prompting the girl to move away, but not before her hand half-gestured to him.

He removed his rain gear and sat onto the edge of a paisley sofa. In an open area to his left three elderly women reclined before a log fire. And from somewhere within earshot the buzz of celebration filtered through. He set out to investigate, finding a large group of well-attired revellers. None Lenny.

He returned to the lobby. But soon the sleepless nights began exacting a toll. And he had yet another journey ahead of him, down to Dublin, to Kate. He opened the adjacent credenza and found what he wanted, Claire Abbey notepaper and envelopes. His third battle with the words satisfied him, as much as satisfaction was possible:

Tuesday, October 5 1993. 5.45pm

Dear Lenny:

I have not been able to stop thinking about you. Please call me: Dublin 830 4744, just to talk. I'll be there until 7am tomorrow, then I leave for America.

If I could put off going, I would. I can't. If you cannot call me (please try) call me in Arizona, 602 231 3490.

Or write me, 7070 North Wesleyan Drive, Phoenix, Arizona 85281, USA.

I'd love to hear from you. I really would.

Tony MacNeill.

He wrote *Lenny Quin – Personal* on the envelope and placed it on the inner counter of the untended reception desk. Just then his glance diverted; in the distance the young, green-eyed girl caught his eye; once again she seemed to gesture toward him. At that moment a train of shuffling bodies spilled between them, headed by the celebrating couple. When it passed, the girl was gone. He waited another minute, confused, torn for time, and left.

At 6.17pm he trudged into Aranroe train station, sent a half-wave to William, and boarded the 6.20pm express to Dublin. As the train started, his eyes met William's through the open window. The old station master tipped his tattered de Gaulle cap. An instant later they both waved. Tony watched until William was no more.

After the blackness of the tunnel, an almost-hidden Mweelrea barely showed. He pledged to climb to the summit, just like at fourteen he pledged to come back home, and here he was, thirteen years after, good to his word. Soon again another good-bye, he thought, another forced departure. He pulled his mind from the passing countryside, into reflection. Some things, he had learned, could be lost, even the sacred, and other things, he knew only too well, persisted and persecuted. He needed to learn how to let go, how to discard, and what to save. Yet even when he tried hard, as he had done since he got out, there were always pools to drown in, as Joel Vida had cautioned him; for him it was Jesus Pomental, then the unbearable trial, then Shift Commander King Kong Yablonski's vile reign and bloody end, and his father's death, and stinking prisons; these were the things that wallpapered his mind, he had to deal with them, put them each in their place, and move on.

*   *   *

Though Kate tried a number of times to get inside his head, he did not accede. To him the facts of his own life were not worthy of the few hours they would share.

He said nothing of Lenny. They spent time reminiscing about growing up in the heart of Dublin. Birthplace of Shaw, O'Casey and Behan, as their father had always boasted. The city that of the five emigrant MacNeills only Kate had reclaimed, a decade earlier as a twenty-nine-year-old with a new counselling qualification. They recounted their exodus as children from the city centre to the north shore, five miles out, to woods and hills and Bull Island, all bunched together in one previously impossible-to-imagine place, and how soon they grew to love the wonders of never-ending fields, and lakes and tree-swings and apple- and pear-orchards ripe for robbing, and old haunted mansions and chestnuts, plus their first house of their own, which they never stopped prizing. They talked about sisters Violet and Patricia, now both settled in America, the middle two between Kate at the top and him at the bottom, about Ronan's dying and how warmly they remembered him, short life that he'd had. And mother, now in Florida, in her mid-sixties, buying a new condominium and doing very well according to her infrequent letters. And poor dead father's gambling: horses, greyhounds, anything that kept the bookies in big cars, and his life-long battle for trade union solidarity on the docks. They recalled warmly, too, occasional trips to their maternal grandparents' tiny farm in Sligo, and watching the countryside roll by out of dirty bus windows.

Kate and Tony's spirits mixed easily, the closeness that had long tied them as strong as ever. In these hours his darkness became a lie he'd been telling himself. It seemed certain, as it always did with Kate, that he could start over, neutralise the catastrophic events of Newark and prison, chart a new life through the wisdom that comes out of dark experience. After everything, all the horror, he could do that. Through losing he could win.

Then, all too soon, it ended, conceding only to time.

That morning, without sleep, Tony MacNeill departed for America, reliving every instant of the fifteen minutes spent with Lenny Quin. Just the beginning, he pledged, there was more to come. For no fear inside him and no danger outside was bigger than her imprint on his mind. He'd pursue it to the end.

2

1994
LATE SUMMER, PHOENIX, ARIZONA

The sun prowled compassionless, baked pavements and paint, turned car metal fry pan hot, and exiled humans to pools and climate-controlled interiors.

In the large rooming house on Wesleyan Drive spears of light lanced past the edges of the opaque window shades. Noticeably braless under a white CSNY T-shirt, Eva Kohler glared from the bed, her towel-turbaned head propped against pillows.

Jorge Ravarro's fingers had stopped flicking the pages, his attention now fixed on the handwritten notebook.

'Jorge, Jorge, come here,' Eva sighed. 'That shit's more interesting than me? You look cute in a white shirt, big Mr Parole Man.'

He ignored her, as though lost in the words he was reading. Then he started reciting, rhythmless, in a hard Latino accent:

'The seeds we've sewn still bloom in silence
as each new day begins and ends –'

She sniggered. 'Come here, I said.' She stretched her arms wide.

'Your problem, you know what, is you are not educated.' he said. 'You try listen, you hear? You listen:

The seeds we've sewn still bloom in silence
as each new day begins and ends
though Arizona nights never seem easy
to navigate single-handed
without even a stranger on a pier
or a flock of seabirds in the air
– or you.'

She screwed up her face. 'Shakespeare?'

'Shakespeare? He knew about Arizona, you think, eh?'

'How the hell do I know? You go to Catholic school to learn that shit.' Her voice turned breathy. 'Like you, mister big, tough Catholic, Me-hi-cano officer.'

He ignored her, and continued:

'Some create suicides by jumping from bridges
or rolling under trains.
Others by blasting bridges of thought
or derailing trains of communication.'

'Morbiddd!' Eva snarled, putting on a face. 'Mr Jor-ge baby, come, come.'

'It's sad, very sad. I know it's right what this man says.' He paused, then went on:

'Loneliness is so punctual now;
It arrives on Sunday morning
and stays the whole week through.
I try to fight it off
with poems and prayers
when I can find someone
to pray to,
but not even – '

The door opened in.

'Tony!' Eva scurried off the bed. 'You're home early.'

'What are you doing in my room?!' Tony powered toward Ravarro.

'Gringo, you sit!' Ravarro thrust out his hand, behind it a

rough stare. 'This,' he said, holding the notebook out of reach, 'is better than I seen my whole life.'

Tony grabbed for the book.

Ravarro thrust his hand into Tony's chest. 'Back up! You watch it, you hear, Irishman. Back up!'

Tony knocked his hand aside.

Ravarro hardened his pocked face, stood square. 'I read because I respect you; you write beautiful things. And is true what you say.'

Tony's swipe knocked the book to the floor. Their hands locked into each other's shirt.

'You want to fight me, your parole officer, eh? You loco. You get killed. I kill you. Or you get back for another ten years. You want that, eh?'

'Fuck you, we'll see who kills who,' Tony said.

'You make trouble, gringo, I shoot you. You die, you not die, bad trouble for you. You let go. Sit down now, eh? Eh?'

'Hey guys, guys, for fuck's sake, it's cool, it's cool. Come on!' Eva shouted.

Tony released his grip, pushed Ravarro's hands away. He bent to pick the book from the floor; Ravarro kicked it aside. They grabbed each other again, faces inches apart. Ravarro pushed hard, backed Tony across the room, forced him down onto a chair.

'Son of a bitch. You are a smart man, but you don't act like no smart man, you act like a dumbass. I say I like how you write, you want to fight me.' Ravarro backed away. As he picked up the book he glanced at the open page and shook his head. '*This day, in losing and finding you I have become you, and all before the sun.* Very beautiful.' He handed the book to Tony.

'*This day, in losing and finding you I have become you, and all before the sun,*' Ravarro recited again. 'I will remember. I will say to a friend: the loco Irishman, he write this. But when I say to a woman, I say Jorge he write these beautiful words.'

On no response from Tony except an unbroken stare, Ravarro turned to Eva. 'Muchacha, adios,' he said and made to give her a lip kiss. She offered her cheek. He hesitated, then accepted, firing a look at Tony. 'You watch what you do here, gringo. And you put ice on your temper, eh? Or one day maybe I shoot you.'

'Barrio pig,' Eva said when he had left. 'No class, doing a thing like that.' She approached Tony, arms crossed to opposite shoulders. 'I told him twice, I told him stop, when he was going through your shit, before you got here, but you know the fuck-ass he is.'

He remained seated in the chair, said nothing.

Eva's expression changed, her arms fell away from her chest. Her well-preserved middle-aged body moved toward him, breasts swaying under her cotton shirt. 'I said you were very, very, very satisfactory, to all his questions: what you do, your work, all that shit.'

He ignored her. She moved closer and without warning pulled his head to her breasts. He yanked back. She dropped to her knees in front of him.

'Tony, screw that dickhead wetback. Don't let him bum you out,' she said. 'Snap out of it. You're too good. Okay?' With that, her hands were groping at him through his work shorts. He swore, swept her away roughly. She persisted. He sprang up, started to move away. She hooked her fingers into his waistband.

'Y'know I adore you; you're strong. I watch you on the weight bench all the time.' He wrenched hard. She held tighter. 'Y'don't have to be scared of me, you little shit.' Her arms encircled him, face jammed to his back, and she groped again at his groin.

'Eva! Lay off!' He forced open her grip, pushed her away. 'My letters!' he said, standing over the bureau. 'They're gone! The letters, the papers, where – '

'Cool it, will you, fuck's sake. They're stashed. Real safe. I hid them from Ravarro. See I figured out what you're scheming, weeks back.' She spoke now with the conceit of perceived advantage.

Junk put away, pictures taken down, shit like that. Figured you were hauling ass.'

His hand demanded the items.

'Could've told him. Be dick deep in shit now, wouldn't you. Parole violation big time. Bum city, fleeing the jurisdiction, no authorisation.'

'Joel Vida got clearance for me.'

'No shit, Antoin. Fucking Antoin? On your passport, the new one. You a frog now?'

He demanded again what she had taken.

'I feel for you, Tony. I'm serious. Always did, you know that. I would never never never rat you out. Your shit's under the locker, safe; y'have to stick your hand under.'

He lifted the locker aside, grabbed the papers.

'See, I protected you. Wasn't for me you'd be riding the DOC Cadillac, back to the country club. Soooo.' She cast off her turban, shook out her hair, and with the confidence of a woman submitted to by men she swaggered toward him.

'Quit it!' he said, his voice full of threat, trying to push her back. She bored forward, head lowered. 'Stop it, fuck it!' he yelled.

'Whyyy!? You don't have to love me, you jerk.'

'Just quit it, will you. We're friends.'

'Friends?' She spit out the word and bulldozed inside his guard. 'What's wrong, cat got your dick?' He forced her head back. Until suddenly she let him go, stepped away, looking upset. 'I'm sorry, Tony. I'm being very unfair. Amigos always, always amigos. We cool? I apologise. That was wrong of me, I know. You're a gentleman. I care about you; you know how special you are to me.' She turned aside, eyes to the floor. 'I'm a schmuck.'

He did nothing but observe, realising that there was a side to her that he admired: this brusque, sometimes humorous woman who went after what she wanted, the men she wanted, and rarely suffered defeat. But the warning signs had been there from the beginning: her lustful staring, open sex talk, her pressing her breasts and pelvis to him at greetings and good-byes, things a raw teenager would have objected to, but not him, he thought, not soon enough. All he wanted now was to avoid trouble, bide his time, just five days left, then go.

He accepted her atoning hands, a brief touch. But instantly, her arms jammed her body to his again, head buried into his chest, and she let out a loud libidinous sigh. 'Come on, come on, come on, Mr Ireland; it'll be dynamite, you and me.'

'I'm warning you, Eva. Last time, let go.'

'Wanted to screw you since you got here. Y'must've known, stuck-up little prick.'

His hands found her throat, fingers and thumbs sank into her flesh, deeper in, until he made himself stop; he forced her chin up, glared into her face. 'You want a real fucking problem?! I told you it's not on!'

She let go, a look of imminent retribution in her face. 'Y'don't get it, do you? Think it's weird: man fucks woman? Huh? Can't talk, can't fuck, huh? You ungrateful faggot, you don't get to say no to me. Know what I'm saying? Get it? We have one killer of the time, or I talk to Jorge, your buddy. Now you get it?'

His explosion of power knocked her back, a two-handed thrust to her chest. Power he had not allowed himself to use since he'd left prison.

Her plump face froze, flushed. 'Tough-guy! Fucking faggot! Car washer con – '

'Get out! Fucking now!'

'Out?! Get out?! You forget, sucker, I'm on your parole team. You were a stray mutt; I took you in. This is my house, all twelve rooms. You get the fuck out, jerk!'

His eyes scoured the room for anything to anchor to, a memory, a meaning, a thing to come.

'And take your third-grade poems with you. Think I don't know? I read them. All of them. She must be a dork to hang with a dumb fuck, double-killer, loooooserrr – '

He burst toward her, rammed both hands into her hair.

'Gonna kill me too, faggot, like you did those other people? I'll put you back in for life, fucker.'

In a sea of obscenities, he ran her across the room, heaved her out into the hall. She thudded against the wall, crashed to the floor and quickly sat up, speechless. He kicked the door shut, sent a thud through the house. Then, shaking, he listened. At first, there was just ruffling, muttering.

'Going down, sucker,' she shouted moments later, her voice hoarse, sounding venomous. 'Real quick, real quick. Fried fucking meat, dumb Irish jerk. Jorge'll nail your fucking ass good.'

Her slapping footsteps grew fainter and fainter, until he could hear them no longer, then all he could hear was an incessant replaying in his head, over and over and over.

Eyes shut, he braced against the room door. The quiet spooked him, more than her raving and ranting. Spooked him this much, he knew, because of the favours she could call in, the quick damage she could do. But more immediately because of Ravarro, tough and dangerous, yellow-eyed mercenary, crazy man. A maze of thoughts flummoxed his brain. What should he do now, he asked, what could he do? Five days, nearly a week, to go.

He started packing away the few small items still on the bureau top: Kate's letter, his half-read copy of *Borstal Boy*, father's watch, his journal, hand-written poems, parole papers, new Irish passport; he then retrieved his ticket from Los Angeles International Airport to Dublin, undisturbed inside a sealed envelope he'd hidden well.

Minutes later a fit of doom choked him. He sat hard onto the floor. Felt the room become a cell, walls closing in, ceiling coming down, suffocating him. No bars to grip or steel to see, but that's what it was, how it felt, how it smelt, another rotten cell. The darkness he thought he'd beaten, that he had beaten, it was still alive in him, coming back, and he had to make it stop, make the buzzing stop, make it all stop, find something, anything in his screwed-up life to hold on to.

He plunged his face into a sink full of cold water. Left it sub-merged as the air in his lungs grew scarce. Then a burst of air roared out of him and became a whine. His head went under again; he could go mad, he thought, maybe he had gone mad; same choice he'd had for nine years, give up, go mad; he'd fought it off every day for all that time; now pain like a knife in his lungs; but he could leave Arizona right now, go for good; he could do that, before the sirens came, before Ravarro came, because then he'd be dead again, and he wasn't going back inside, insane or not, never going back, the one thing he could swear to; just get out now.

His face came up out of the water, blood-filled, coughing out a drool that splattered the glass, melted his reflection, until it all seeped away and left a man recognisable again. Had to stay sane, he warned himself, stay sane. She'd be crazy to call Ravarro. Or the cops. He had too much on her: cops, attorneys, politicians, councillors, in her bed. And she knew he knew. Too many would fall, big wigs in high places. The twosomes and threesomes he'd stumbled over, in the pool, the gazebo, inside the house. All moral crusaders. These were the fuckers to fear, who'd kill to stop him identifying their faces and license plates, soldiers against grass, gas chamber salesmen, smug hypocrites. Dangerous peo-ple. Make murder look like suicide: unstable ex-con takes own life, falls down mountain, drowns drunk in pool, puts bullet in brain. Eva's boys.

Nah, he was losing it, he thought, imagining shit, turning into a screwball. No, he wasn't. He'd nearly killed her, maybe he had killed her, banged her head, she could be dead. Felony murder, prison, lethal injection, odourless gas. No, she wasn't dead. But she knew about Ireland, figured he was jumping out for good; she'd try to stop him, that's how she worked: blackmail, make him stay, become her gigolo. And that would be that. No escape. No home. No Lenny Quin. Nothing. Couldn't let that happen.

Maybe right now she was on the phone, spilling everything to Ravarro. But Ravarro would be miles away by now, abusing other ex-cons. Which meant he had time, a little. When Ravarro found out, he'd come for him; Ravarro would come. Calm down, he told himself. Think. Stay sane. Remember Joel Vida's advice. Keep control, find options, choose. He'd slip away quietly.

Suddenly, a sound. Somewhere in the house. Someone. Couldn't be Ravarro. Had to be her, he thought. Doing what? His head dropped into his hands. She wasn't dead. He could make it, all set now, set to go. Everything he could call his, that had any value, was stuffed into two bags in readiness for this moment, five days premature as it now was. Five days to lie low, somewhere, anywhere but here. That was it. He was leaving Arizona, for good.

He freed the window shade, exposed his shaking self to glare and heat. A big, hot, perilous outside that was once a world of green fields and boyhood freedom. A life lost, he thought. But maybe not forever. He'd make his break through the rear garden.

Outside, yellow grapefruits hung still and glistening; beyond them the rich blue of the Arizona sky, the cool blue of the pool, treasures he'd basked in in the eighteen months he'd been here. Under the acrylic canopy, his weight bench sat loaded. He whispered farewell to his time in this desert, this half-way house to nowhere. And then it was gone, this phase of his life over. His gut was ready for different air, different sky, for fields and mountains, a new life. One good chance to come, and what he would make of himself.

He manoeuvred through the yard, bags in hand, out through the side gate and past the yellow public utility truck parked next to his old white Mustang. As he placed his backpack in the trunk a blow from behind thudded into his shoulder, knocked his head against the lid. His reflexes pivoted him aside. Instantly, he was pumped up, ready to call on everything he had. The only way they'd get him, he vowed, was dead. As he spun back he recognised his attacker, Rip Wundt! Not Ravarro! Rip Wundt, a large roustabout type he'd seen about the place, utility company boss man, one of Eva's boys. The blow had been meant for his head. Sucker punch. Designed to pulverise. Instead, it shot a spark into him, provided license, the rush he had once loved, that he had learned to un-love but had never dismantled.

His hard-hatted opponent shuffled and sparred, mouthing profanities, work-belt dancing around his middle, big frame leveraging for another strike.

Loose and focused, Tony timed his duck perfectly. The man's fist tore through the air inches away, leaving his front unguarded. An instant was all the Anto MacNeill of old had ever needed. He shot forward, uncoiled a lightning right hand, shoulder behind it. It thudded into the utility man's chest. Solid strike. Tony felt it all the way down in his thighs, and now he moved like old times, doing what he did well, already a second shot revving in his fighter's brain, just like in Witchell Heights. But the man was still backing away, reddened, wrinkled. Tony had him. But no, no pursuit, he decided, his single strike was still working its poison. The man's bulk had kept him upright; now his knees buckled, mouth and eyes askew, as he danced drunkenly. Tony suppressed the impulse in his fists, satisfied by the fact that he was still this good. No second or third hits. As he unwired he tried not to like how it felt, not like it quite so much. He hadn't lost everything, he told himself.

The man didn't fall as much as crumple in a heap of noise on-to hot concrete, hard-hatless.

Tony slammed the trunk lid, climbed into the Mustang. Just then, Eva appeared on the garden path in her shorts and CSNY T-shirt, looking older than he'd ever seen her. Alive at least, he thought. Not another corpse he'd carry and curse and plead with for the rest of his long or short life. She glanced at the man on the ground, then back at the Mustang.

The car backed out of the driveway, braked hard. She gestured his doom. He rammed the stick into gear, stared once more at her, then he revved the engine until it obliterated Eva Kohler, until fear turned to power. Five days to go. He braced erect, locked onto the wheel, sank the gas. The Mustang roared free, out of Eva Kohler's world, out of Jorge Ravarro's world. For all time, he swore.

3

1963

<small>Outside Aranroe Village, County Mayo, Western Ireland</small>

Once more her gaze broke from the frosted-glass door. She drilled the end of her third Woodbine into the damp pavement, and through a cloud of blue fog she trudged up the rectory path, petite feet hop-scotching in her wake. Her insipid ring tolled the bells within the holy house and drew a hobbling shadow up the hall. The aged housekeeper led her and the child into a parlour of clashing patterns and lemon-polish air.

'You'll have to speak up, love. The old hearing is not what it was.' The woman bent closer. 'Who did you say will I tell Father is here to see him?'

'Róisín Doyle. From Gorse Hill.'

'Wee one's full of go, isn't she?' The old woman's warm eyes danced after the skipping child. 'Speedy Gonzales, what? What age is she, love?'

'She's four now. Has me jaded.'

'Gorgeous blue eyes, God bless her. A new pair of hips now and I'd be keeping up with her. Mind she doesn't smash into Fr Coy's crystal, or he'll have one of his fits. I'll go now and get him for you.'

The young woman pulled off her paisley head-scarf and shoved it into her raincoat pocket. In the glass of the cabinet she frowned, pressed into place errant wisps of her tight red hair and wiped a wet finger under both eyes. Five minutes passed before the room door creaked in.

She jumped to her feet. The curate, a large, not un-handsome man in his late twenties with a coal-black mane, stood before her, expressionless.

'Hello, Father.'

The priest's attention dropped to the child, still lost in play on the buffed linoleum.

'Shh, shh, shhhh!' His outburst silenced the room. The child ran to her mother, who struggled to lift her.

'Fr Coy,' the priest announced, yanking a chair away from the table and flopping onto it. 'So. You're here about the bingo.'

'Oh no, Father, no. No, I want to get married, Father, here in Aranroe, in June, in St Brigid's, to an American man.' Her words poured out as though otherwise they might go unspoken.

'An American?' He picked a pen and a small black notebook from his inside pocket. 'How long have you been seeing him, this American?'

'We've been going serious since before Christmas, father, but I knew him before then but we didn't – '

'The child?'

'The child. She's my daughter. Leonora Marie.'

'So. You're Róisín Doyle, widow?'

'Oh no. No, Father, I'm not. I was never married. And the man, he's not Catholic, Father, not at the minute, but he promised me he'll convert over for me.'

'This man: name, date of birth?'

'Charles Kenneth Quin, with one n, Father, in the Quin, I mean. He's a few years older than myself. Can't remember right now what his date of birth is. I think it's – '

'How older? What's this "a few years"?'

'He's I think thirty-four now. Thirty-four or thirty-five. His father owns a big ranch, Father, in Texas, in America.

'That's it? Nothing else you know about him?'

'He's tall, and he's nice looking.' She stalled, almost smiling, as though drifting into her thoughts. 'He went to college and got letters after his name. And he climbs mountains, Father; that's why he came here the first time, in '58; he wanted to be the first American person to get to the top of Carrantuohill and he nearly got all the way up except that it started lashing rain and he had to come down. And he stuck the American flag up there, and we think it's still there. He's got one brother and no – '

'Your age?' The priest's eyes remained in his notebook.

'Age. Twenty-two, nearly twenty-three. Charles is very well-to-do, Father. He'll give Leonora a good home, and send her to good schools. He'll do that. He wants to buy a hotel here. He wants to buy Claire Abbey; he has his own big apartment up there now, so we'll be staying in St Brigid's parish.'

'Why isn't this man with you? Or does he not think the Church is important enough?'

'Ah no, no, he does, Father, he does definitely. He's good like that, except he's in America at the minute. He goes lots of places on business. But he comes here all the time, to the Abbey. That's where we met, Father.'

'That a fact now? So. And you believe this is a union God will bless? Meeting in a bar, a public house? Did no one teach you anything at home about the evils of drink?'

'Claire Abbey? It's a fancy hotel, Father, for rich people from America and places like that, and golfers. I'm there part-time since I was in secondary school and I'm full-time now, ever since I came home from Liverpool. It's really posh, you should – '

'Unmarried. Female child born out of wedlock. Hid away in pagan England. And I take it this older, absentee, non-Catholic, millionaire American is the father?'

Her body tensed.

'I won't ask again.'

Still she said nothing.

The priest slapped the table. 'I asked you a question, Miss Doyle.' He lunged his large face at her. 'Is he, or is he not, the man responsible for this, this individual?'

'Sorry. Sorry, Father, I can't answer. Sorry.'

'So, so, so. The father could be him. Or maybe any of a number of other men you've sinned with. And you have the nerve to come – '

'No! No, that's not it, Father. That's not what I mean.' Her fingers coursed through the child's wild auburn locks. 'There was only one. Only one. Just that I don't want to say.'

'Oh, you will. You'll say alright, mark my words, if you're to hold any hope of being married in my parish.' He gavelled his pen against the table. 'I'll warn you again, my patience is not inexhaustible. Father's name?'

'Would it, would it be okay for me to think about it, Father? For a day, or a couple of days?'

'There'll be no thinking about it. You'll tell me this instant.' He positioned his pen on his notebook and glared at her.

'I can't, Father. I'm sorry. I can't.' She hugged the child to her, their bodies swaying gently. Then her gaunt face firmed. 'No, can't,' she whispered into the child's hair.

'Then that's it. Over! Won't be happening in my parish; you can put that in your drum and beat it.' He reached for the housekeeper's bell. 'Mrs McEvoy will show you out.'

'What I mean, father, is – '

'No! I'll tell you what you mean. You're protecting the fornicator and yourself from rightful indignation, which you both earned, the sinfulness of the lewd and the lecherous who lost Paradise for all mankind through your very same sins of the flesh.' He sprang up, red-faced, pocketed his pen and notebook. 'Off with you.'

'But my little girl, Father, please. She'll need a proper home. She's only four, and – ' Her voice gave way to tears. 'She needs a family, that's all I'm saying, to look after her. Truth is I'm not blessed with the best of health.'

'The very things you should have been thinking before you conceived in sin another suffering unfortunate.'

'I know that. I know what you're saying is the truth, Father. It was, just, just – '

'Selfishness! Carnal selfishness, pure and simple, that's what it was. So. You think you can cover it up by marrying this American millionaire; probably old enough to be your father. Who nobody knows one iota about, who doesn't even live in the parish, isn't even a Catholic.' He thumped the chair into place at the table. 'Not at all, woman, not here you don't. Off you go.'

Her damp cheeks turned ghostlike, haloed by her tight carrot-red hair. She stood up, cradling the child. 'I'm begging you, please. Please.'

The priest clacked the door handle, swept his arm toward the dark hallway. Trembling, but with a look of defiance, she remained where she stood. He clacked harder at the handle, eyebrows arched.

'I'll tell you. You can have your way,' she said, disdain in her voice. 'My baby, my little girl, Leonora Marie, the man, her father – '

The noise of a door opening halted her. At the far end of the room a black-suited priest in his late-thirties was already at the cocktail cabinet, Jameson Whiskey bottle in hand, without seem-ing to realise he wasn't alone.

'Oops, I beg your pardon,' he said with an exaggerated startle. 'Sleep-walking again. Too much tea, I believe.' He went to leave with the bottle in hand, then stopped, stared back at Róisín's spent bearing. 'Anything I can help with? Fr Coy?'

'Nothing at all, Father. Few minutes here, we'll be gone.'

'Wait a minute! Wait a minute!' His face lit up. 'You're Tommy Doyle's wee lassie! That's who you are!'

Róisín nodded.

'I'm Liam Foley,' he said, as though she should recognise his name. He captured her hand between his palms and guided her into a soft chair. 'Holy God, you're all grown up. Your da and meself – God rest your poor father's soul; it was a terrible thing that happened – we played on the Westport team, right up into the fifties. You must've heard him talk about Kicker. Me! Kicker Foley?'

Róisín nodded. With her hand still in his, he focused his gaze in the manner of one perceiving beyond what was being spoken.

'Right, I'll see you out now, young lady,' the younger priest said. 'The parishioner was just leaving, Father.'

'And who's this gorgeous little scallywag, what?' The older priest leaned forward and beamed directly at the child. The girl spun back to her mother. 'Oh, I see, I see, said the blind man; that's how it is, is it? Well, well, look what I've got.' His fingers held up a Flash Bar, which he painted with a delicious fixation. 'I've been saving this yummy shokkolat for the prettiest six-year-old girl in Aranroe, whenever I find her.'

'I'm four.' The muffled reprimand was immediate.

'Ooohhh, well then, I'll just have to give it to a pretty wee lassie who is not six, not even five; I'll have to give it to a wee lassie who's four.' His animated gazing searched left and right. 'Does anybody here know, is there a pretty, four-year-old girl anywhere in this house?'

'Me!' Leonora's reflexive response came with a big blue-eyed smile. She climbed down from her mother, reached a tiny hand for the waiting chocolate. Suddenly, it disappeared. Then long magician fingers fluttered over the empty hand, beckoned it back, fluttered a second time, beckoned again, and a third time. 'Abracadabra, abracadabra,' the priest recited, then magically the top of the Flash Bar reappeared, crept higher and higher, up from behind up-standing fingers, until all of it was back and it tipped over and pointed directly toward the child, drawing a shriek of delight from her. 'I bet I'm the first real live magician you ever met,' he said, placing the prize into her outstretched hands.

With the child occupied, his aspect darkened. '*A mhuirnín,*' he said, turning to Róisín, 'tell me what the trouble is. I see the bother all over you.'

Her glance swept to the younger priest then fell to her lap.

'I've been clear with the parishioner, Fr Foley,' the younger man said, 'about what the Church can and cannot do.'

'Do about what?'

'The parishioner had been hoping – '

'Róisín! That's it! Róisín,' Fr Foley exclaimed, ignoring the curate's hanging face. 'How could I forget.' He eased closer to her. 'I was so fond of your da. He'd be telling me all about you, when you were only knee-high to a grasshopper. His *Beautiful Dreamer* he called you; you slept day and night non-stop.' He journeyed off behind a private smile then was quickly back, graver. 'What is it, girl? Tell me.'

She quickly recounted her desire to be married in the parish in June, withstanding the grimaces of Fr Coy.

'Ó *cailín caoine dearg*, settle yourself, will you. You've not a thing to worry about as long as I have health in me. But look at you, you're like a skeleton. Get some meat on your bones; will you try do that for me? The clinic's looking after you and the wee one?'

'Aye, Father, 'tis. And Dr Lappin, one of the best.'

'He is that,' he said, drawing the large brown journal across the table. 'Dr Lappin. One of the best, all right, but not an ounce of humour in the poor man, God bless him.'

'Fr Foley, I must speak with you. Now, please, if I may,' the curate said.

'Speak.'

'In private, if I may.'

'No.' The older man shook his head. 'Right here.'

'Bishop Buckley has been very clear on this sort of thing. The Church's rulings are not to be flouted, Father, not for – '

'Enough! That'll do, Fr Coy. I see no reason not to write it in the book,' he said. 'What date in June, Róisín, were you hoping for?'

'Excuse me, Father, excuse me, I must insist. My vocation compels me to object in the strongest terms. An altar ceremony would not be proper, not in the eyes of the Church, nor according to – '

'Proper! Proper, you say!' He jumped up, glared at his challenger. 'In my book, Father, my book,' he said, jabbing his thumb into his chest, 'and in the book I follow, living the faith comes first and last. Proper is for smug bishops and the tally-ho set, who've both bedevilled this poor country.' He swept back his prematurely-greying hair and turned to Róisín.

'Now, *mo chuisle,* let's see what June looks like and we'll put your details in.'

'Parish priest you might be,' the flushed curate cried, 'but there's no call to be disrespectful. You yourself know this is going against diocesan directives. Bishop Buckley is most adamant about this kind of thing.'

'Right, Father! Enough! As long as I'm in charge here, I'll decide. Not you. And I'll deal with Bishop Buckley if it comes to that.' He whipped off his collar and flung it against the mahogany table, along which it bounced and at the end tumbled to the floor. 'The man doesn't know one friggin thing about this little piece of Mayo bogland, never laid eyes on Loch Doog, or Mweelrea. He wouldn't know Aranroe if it bit him in his arse, whether it's east or west of the Shannon or north or south of the friggin equator. So, cut the Bishop bulldust, Dick!'

Fr Coy smirked, exhaling loudly.

'Thanks,' Róisín whispered. 'It's Leonora I care about. I want her, I want her to have a good healthy life.' She grasped the priest's hand.

'Curate I might be.' The younger priest approached. 'But Dick Coy has his duty and do it he will.' He snatched up his black serge overcoat and swerved into the hall. 'The Bishop will hear about this post haste. This priest will see that he does.'

'Fr Coy, don't leave this house! I want a word with you.' The senior man's tone bore no hint of concession. His blood-shot eyes swung back to Róisín, then heavenward. 'Wants to be Pope,' he whispered, 'and not a wet day out of the seminary.' He pressed a finger to his lips and winked back at her before pulling the door behind him.

In the hallway Fr Coy presented a cold face. 'Don't try talk me out of this. My decision is made and it's final. I'll be respected, Father, and by those in higher places than you. You've gone against me for the last time.'

'Tell me this, Dick: What made you put on that collar? I'm asking you; think about it if you need to. Was it for the love of Jesus Christ and His flock? To heal? Comfort? Help those in need? Or was it power? Or the status that comes with the cloth? Or do you know yet?'

'Oh, no. Not a chance you'll bamboozle me with your liberation psychology. It's priests like me that'll restore the Church in Ireland, in this very parish, and not too long from now. And not with cry-baby Christianity; you can count on that too. So.'

'Calm down, Father. I'm offering you an opportunity to take back your threat.'

'An opportunity? You are offering me an opportunity? Ridiculous, man, the shoe's on the other foot this time. The bad blood between yourself and Bishop Buckley, it'll get you shifted before the summer's out, back to Finglas, or Kilburn.' A smirk kinked the curate's lips. 'Nothing better than a bit of curate's work, I believe, to re-focus a vocation. I'll do what's needed here, have no fear of that, as parish priest.'

'Listen to me, Dick, there's – '

'Nothing more to say, Liam. Sorry.' He snapped open the door latch. 'Dick Coy's duty is neither deniable nor negotiable. Remember that.'

'The words of Saint Thomas Aquinas, Father. For a different time and place.'

'And true, still. I'm off.'

'Hold your friggin horses!' the senior priest thundered.

The curate poked his head back into the dimly-lit hall. 'I've spoken, the talking is over. I should have done this months ago, when I got here; I see that now. Good night.'

'Question, Father! Before you fall off your pedastal: Where did you go last night?'

'What last night? What do you mean, last night?'

'You heard me. Step back inside, please. Now.'

Fr Coy complied, awkwardly.

'Well? Where were you?'

'Last night, Father?'

'And the previous Thursday night, and the Thursday before that.'

'Different places. Seeking out my congregation. Doing parish work. I'm not the cleric who keeps spirits in the house.'

'No, that you're certainly not. Now answer my question.'

'This is nonsense. Three, four calls. Of no concern. Parish duties. I'm off now.' He stepped outside once again into the night air and started to pull the door after him.

'Between nine o'clock and eleven o'clock p.m.'

'As I told you, various different duties. I don't work to my watch.' He held on to the half-closed door, out of sight of his questioner, his voice tamer now. 'Anyway, it's nobody's, it's really nobody's – '

'Well, I do know.' Fr Foley pulled the door in. 'Force my hand and your purple-hatted pals will know too. Inside, Father.'

'This is ridiculous, Liam. Really downright ridic – '

'No, it's not. And you know that. You were down at The Terraces. In the company, let's say, of certain parties I won't be naming. Unless you leave me no choice. Things going on, Father. Things the good bishop would see you de-frocked for.' The older priest's voice cut with a savage ruthlessness. 'Count on this, Dick: Whisper a word in the wrong place against Róisín Doyle and her wedding – and your collar's mine. Clear enough?'

'Yes, Fr Foley.' The curate mulled back into the hall, his fingers fumbling with the door until the brass bolt drove home.

'I want what's going on down there to stop. D'you understand that too? I'll help you any way I can, but if you're seen within the vicinity of The Terraces, there'll be ructions in this holy house. We'll talk in the morning. Eleven o'clock?'

The curate nodded, then trudged up the unlit staircase.

'And mark your calendar for June 2nd!' the parish priest boomed up into the darkness, shattering the rectory's quiet.

He then sat on the stairs and leaned back with a smile. 'Kicker Foley to be the celebrant of record,' he said heavenward. 'D'you hear that, Tommy? You do, I know you do, y'boyo.' After a brief lull his words took up again in quiet recitation. 'The morning of the second of June, Tommy Doyle, in the year of our Lord, nineteen hundred and sixty-three, your old pal Kicker Foley will marry your Beautiful Dreamer to her American beau, and watch out the cleric of any colour who tries to stop me.'

4

1994
IRELAND

Despite persistent catastrophising, he'd made good his escape to California and his departure out of Los Angeles International Airport. Now, one day later, leaving Dublin on a train bound for County Mayo, Tony MacNeill propped his feet on the opposite seat and stretched out.

These were the colours of his memory, he recalled, this country, the tints and tones of an infinite palette, all carved up and spread out and casting spells upon him once again. Like he'd never left. Crowds of grey and white clouds rolled with him, past the greens and yellows of patterned countryside. Then out of the heavens burst a light that stole his soul, a different sun than that in Arizona, a different sky. He was home, for sure. To try again. Tracking the same journey he had made one year ago. This time he'd indulge or escape the woman who had haunted him every day since.

The land imprinted its earthiness on the air flowing through the carriage: mountain mixed with bog and farm, earth and heather and hay, turf and rain; he could smell them all, the land that had provided hope through his solitude. Ireland, again. His too rarely. Now his to explore. What would it hold this time?

About him danced stars of sun-lit dust; and soon the clacking of the near-empty carriage found rhythm in his thoughts. Harmonies, somehow, that bound him to Lenny Quin, a woman he did not yet understand, who had usurped his mind, altered the beating of his days and nights, and now compelled his return to her stony world of sheer cliffs and bottomless lochs, mistshrouded mountains and soft bogs.

Before him lay wonder and doubt. Danger too, he suspected. As well as he knew this, he knew too that her face and voice had not left him in this endless year. A face that each morning had smiled on him and each evening kissed him, a face that had followed him, implored him, seduced him. Eyes of hope and hurt that left him with nothing except their pursuit of him, and their lure of him into pursuit of her.

This time he had skipped through Dublin, where he'd landed hours earlier. He'd seen little of the city of his birth, just fleeting streetscapes as the airport bus lurched along the Liffey to Heuston Station. There he had boarded the train, a train feeling sometimes like a cave, sometimes a chariot, rolling coast to coast, east to west, across the land. He had wanted earlier to call Kate but needed even more this sense of independence, of navigating solo his own, old country, for a day, maybe two.

His snatched glimpses of Dublin replayed now in his thoughts and an older nostalgia took over, re-immersed him in his childhood. But not even the jangle and glee of those times could detain him long from thoughts of Lenny Quin and what she had done to him.

Meeting her had coincided with a time when he was at last erasing the spectre of Newark, wasteland of his teens. Not that his life had been in any sense sane since at fourteen he'd watched his green island disappear beneath him. But in the last year and a half, in Arizona, virtues he didn't know he had salvaged, didn't remember ever owning, had firmed inside him. Now there was more to win, a future, perhaps close, that he wouldn't miss. Whatever the price.

Gone was his job at the *News Sentinel,* weekend soccer reporter, so be it, he thought. Gone was America, so be it too. No job, no country, could extinguish this flame, his chance to re-find his spirit, light his soul. He would accept what was to come, what it asked of him, for nothing he could imagine could keep him from whatever it was in her that made joy seem attainable. Worth a life. And if it all proved foolish, if this road twisted back to hell, he'd deal with that too. No, no retreat.

*   *   *

Aranroe, the village where Lenny had appeared, where his obsession started one year ago, lay still three hours to the west. Time for too many replays, and doubts. Despite his fears, he had not the way nor the will to stop his thoughts of her, or of what it was he'd found in her that was always beyond words, this passion possessing him.

Over the windy flatness of the midlands the speeding train swayed side to side, offering him thrills and distraction. He struggled to save faith in his future, beat away dark thoughts. But now his mind blanked out the image of Lenny Quin, blanked out her geometry of curves, the sound of her voice. He re-questioned his being here, locked in this carriage, heading once more for a hilly village beneath great mountains.

Then she re-emerged, teasing his senses, floated into him, and vanished once more. He wrestled his mind down, back to earth, Ireland, his homeland, blood and culture, history, wars on sacred soil, what he and she were part of, those elements they shared: Irishness, roots in this land of suffering that might unite their otherwise foreign lives.

Soon the bogs and meadows of the Midlands gave way to fields of dancing barley and everywhere cattle idling on great green squares. Then came the water, Loch Rea, mile after mile, silver, rippling to the wind. And then Claremorris and the Nephin

Begs, purple apogees atop a massive fence. A little later, out of this tapestry Mweelrea shot up, sovereign and welcoming. His heart skipped.

After Westport the train headed west, past rocks and islands being battered by surf. And like a sailor saved, a prodigal forgiven, he found a new belongingness taking hold.

Then Aranroe train station re-entered his reality, one difficult year after he'd first been here. He stepped down onto the flagstone platform. The old bowing bench, still unpainted, sat empty, no William to admonish or entertain him. Somehow it didn't feel right to go in search of the old man.

'*Dia is Mhuire dhuit.*'

A voice calling. From behind him. He couldn't turn.

'*Dia is Mhuire dhuit.*'

The voice took form. A woman, approaching, wearing William's de Gaulle cap, middle-aged, chaotic charcoal mane, magenta face.

'Don't speak Gaelic. Sorry.'

'Can't say I do myself, ha-ha. A few words I collected,' the woman said. 'Impresses the tourists like mad, especially the Germans. And no better way to shame the Brits; pay them back any way you can; that's what I say. You look lost; you're American, are you; do you know where it is at all you are?'

'No. I mean yes, I do know. I've been here before.'

'You look lost to me. Was it looking for William you were?'

'Is he here?'

'Well, he is, you could say, and he isn't. Isn't his spirit all over the place, looking at us this minute, I wouldn't doubt. And where else would he be, and him looking after his trains going on sixty-one years.'

'You mean, he passed away?'

'In a way he did, but away couldn't be far for himself. I'd wager he walks about here all the time, and sits next to his old stove inside. He's here alright, for his trains, and all his friends.'

'Sorry to hear . . . When did he pass away?'

'Christmas day. In the chapel after Mass he left us, the morning of his eighty-ninth birthday. He planned it that way, I'd say, natural as it was. He was like that. Did everything his own way in living, so why not in dying.'

'You knew him, knew him well, I mean?'

'Well as any daughter knows her father – '

'Your father?'

'Didn't we live under the same roof these last twenty-eight years, since the mother died. Now there was a woman for you, the mother; she'd have sixteen cows washed and milked before you'd – '

'Sorry, I'm not being rude but I need to check into my B&B; they might rent the room to someone else.'

'Not at all they won't. Tons of rooms this time of year. So, tell me, who is it you're here to visit: man or woman? You wouldn't be one of them agricultural fellas from Boston?'

'No, nothing like that. Just like this part of the country. The mountains.'

'Sure that isn't what's in you at all. Who is it, tell me? Romance, I'd say; that's why a lot of them come, for the matchmakers, find a nice Irish cailín. And sure why not. I'm not spoken for myself, if you follow me, and me half past fifty and never been kissed, if you can believe that.'

'Have to hurry, or I'll be late.'

'Aren't you a nice man now, nice pleasant young man. You're married yourself, you are?'

'Soon to be. Soon. Very soon.'

'You're spoken for so. Lucky divil.

'Would you know the Quins, from Clare Abbey?'

'And who wouldn't. It's Lady Leonora you're here to see so. Could look like that meself if I had her money. Fine woman. Still, if I was in your shoes, I'd be careful, if you don't mind me speaking my mind.'

'You see her around?'

'Can't say I do these days. She'll be here the day after tomorrow, for certain. First day of September. Nearly every evening of a September she waits here for somebody off the late train from Dublin. A body that never gets here. Poor soul must be lonely, like the lot of us, I suppose. And that's all I have to tell.'

Outside the station the earth posed for him, at peace, almost people-less, white-cotton clouds in a pale-blue sky, the dropping fuchsia of Aranroe Hill a carpet of crimson and scarlet bells. Out of everywhere poured memories. Up in the distance, Clare Abbey lorded over the land. One half-mile in the opposite direction sat the village, its few thatched roofs shining in the sharp light of the day. And thirty feet below, the green ocean raged, infusing the air with spray and scent.

Yes, he affirmed, standing at the low stone wall bearing the carved letters of Aranroe. He closed his eyes, listened to the water, relished the wind whipping through his hair. He was ready this time, really ready, he reassured himself. Whatever it demanded.

'Grand day, sir, sorry to be disturbing your rest.'

Tony jumped.

'Could I be dropping you somewhere to your liking?' said a large rotund man with floppy hair and an apologetic smile. 'Paddy McCann, sir. McCann's taxi service.' The man spoke with a softness that belied his size. 'This is me right here.' He nodded toward a tired yellow station wagon with a removable roof sign.

'You know Greyfriars; it's a B&B hostel-hotel?'

'Certainly, sir, not too far away at all. Not a farmhouse in these parts I couldn't take you to.' The man's generous face stretched and swung with his words. 'I'll look after those for you, no problem,' he said, reaching for both bags.

Tony grabbed his backpack 'Just the one,' he said, stepping back from his duffel bag.

'Here for a bit of climbing, sir? Grand bit of weather we're having for it.'

'Looks good, Mr – '

'Paddy – that's how I'm known far and wide. Now, before I run you up to Greyfriars could I interest you in a little tour of the village, and maybe a short hop up to see Loch Doog? Everything's within two or three or four or at most five or six miles of where we're breathing God's holy air this minute. Tons of history all over: druid stones, Celtic crosses, round tower, St Colm's well, even the oratory where St Brendan said his last Hail Mary before discovering America over a thousand years ago in a goat-skin boat. Will we give it a go?'

Tony accepted, smiling covertly at the man's manner of speaking, which seemed reminiscent of an old time that he as a city kid had heard only in films or on the radio.

'I'm not a tourist, Paddy,' he said.

'Sure aren't we all tourists, in a sort of a way, here on a short visit.'

After stopping by Greyfriars B&B he resumed his liaison with Aranroe. The taxi cruised through the narrow streets around the village, slowing occasionally so that he could savour particular remembrances. Leaving Aranroe, they weaved through farmlands to the east then circled around the loch. Everywhere wild hedges divided roads from fields and ditches, and hugged stone walls. At notable spots Paddy recounted local folklore or struggled through tales of supernatural happenings, which usually imprinted a terror in his face and caused his jowls to puff and tremble. The bumpy roads bounced his bulk about the seat, yet he managed still to exchange waves with almost every person who came into view, even some whose presence he seemed to anticipate.

'Well, here we are: back safe and well, thank God,' Paddy said as the taxi cruised along Market Street in the centre of Aranroe village. 'Anything else I can show you now, sir? Still a couple of hours brightness in the day.'

'You can forget the sir, Paddy. It's Tony. What about castles?'

'The very thing! Why didn't I think of that. Americans go mad for the castles. Ah, Holy God; there, I did it again. You told me you're not a Yank at all. Anyhow, I can run you up to Murrisk Castle, seventeen miles from here. Or Rockfleet Castle, ten miles beyond that. And I'll tell you something now that most people never hear. Both them castles belonged to Queen Granuaile, in the 1500s. The Pirate Queen, they called her. Came from just down the road from here. High Queen of the whole of Ireland. Tough woman to live with, I believe, not the type to go for the groceries or cook you a nice omelette. And not the best-living woman either. But she robbed the English blind and not one of them could catch her. Queen Granuaile. Distant relative of me own on me mother's side, from the O'Malley-Melia clan. So there y'are now, you're with royalty.'

'Very impressed. I'll take your word for it. What about Clare Abbey?'

'Top of the hill. We could take a run up but it's not one of them castles you can tour around; more a hotel and golf course for well-to-do people, lots of foreigners.'

'You know the people who own it?'

'I do. Do a bit of business up there, run the guests wherever they want to go. Sometimes Mr Quin himself – Charles, that's the owner – I drive him down to Galway; has a private plane there. You know Mr Quin, you do?'

'Never heard of him.'

'Free to speak me mind so. Between yourself and meself and not another soul, he's a bit of a troubled man. But isn't that how most of them poor millionaires are. Helter-skelter lives brimmed up with problems that people like ourselves never need to bother with. Should never stop thanking God we're not like that.'

'You know Leonora then, Leonora Quin?'

'Miss Lenny, Charles' daughter, grand girl altogether. Doesn't drive anymore. Not since; well, what I mean is not now, so I take her around, places, wherever she wants.'

Tony recorded Paddy's poorly concealed stumblings.

'Gorgeous woman altogether.' For a moment, Paddy's thoughts seemed to drift. 'Different from most people. Littlest bit unusual. Never the same since the war, God bless her.'

'War? What war? And what do you mean – unusual?'

'Gulf war, would have to be.'

'You said unusual?'

'I wouldn't be saying anything against her good self, y'understand. But times I'll be driving her, telling her all kinds of stories, make her forget what might be ailing her, and she wouldn't be with me, be thinking her thoughts, much more important things I suppose. Sad things, by the look of it, sometimes.'

'Married?'

'I am. A good wife and two disobedient teenagers.'

'I meant Leonora.'

'Ah, no, no, never married. Told me herself. Plenty of chances, you can be sure, a woman like that. If I can put a word in your ear, and I don't mean to poke me big nose into your business, but if you're keen on the lady – and what man wouldn't be – you're bound to bump into a nasty lump of a bucko they call Boxer Dunne. Acts like he's her chaperone.'

'I know him.'

Paddy's mouth fell open. 'Friend of the lad, you are?'

'Far from it.'

'Thanks be to God again. Thought I put me big foot in it that time.'

'Not friends. And not going to be.'

'Nothing lost for that. The bucko's a bully, nothing more. From Dublin, a jackeen. And the mouth on him.'

'I'm a jackeen too, Paddy, remember? But that's alright.'

'Ah, no, no. You might be from Dublin but you're a different cut of a man. I could tell the minute I laid eyes on you. Always know a gentleman. Were you saying you want me to run you up to the Abbey? I won't be charging you a penny extra, I'm heading up there anyway.'

'No. It's late. I'll get out at Greyfriars. Look up at it from there. Tomorrow.'

*   *   *

In the ensuing hours he submerged in contemplation, foraging for certainties, rejecting old frauds and self-deceptions, planning his next move and the fallback for when it failed, as life had taught him it would. Now mature, and free, could he think his way past trouble, he asked, outsmart danger? But the biggest question kept intruding: Why hadn't she called him, ever, or written back to him? Maybe she never got the note he left for her a year ago. Maybe she did. But he was certain he'd seen honesty in her eyes, unless he was a fool and blind, heading into more serious trouble.

He'd psych-up his fight energy just in case, the old thrill he now feared; it felt like instinct, dulled but not dead. Ready for Boxer Dunne, or whatever else. He sensed he might need it, hoped he wouldn't. Just days since Rip Wundt went down in Arizona, seven years since Shift Commander King Kong Yablonski died naked and roaring; both big men, just bulk; like so many others, no skill. The adrenaline was tingling now; it had always been this way, he thought, a drug in his veins. Could he ever not enjoy it?

He could no longer afford a street mentality, he thought, it could lose him the freedom he'd won back. But failing with Lenny wasn't going to happen; he wouldn't let it. This was his time, a new life, new place, and no alternative he could imagine. The caution he'd heard from Paddy didn't change a thing. And of Boxer Dunne he had no fear, but also no need to prove anything. Charles Quin, though, something about him felt threatening.

It was past ten. He stretched out, sank into the bareness of the room, which took him back to the seventies, a world that was fascinating to him, when being poor, desiring nothing but pennies, had the feel of being rich, which he was. The flight from Los

Angeles to New York, then New York to Dublin, had been long. But here he was, at last, back in Aranroe. Nineteen-ninety-four, twenty-eight years of age, breathing Irish country air, ecstatic that Lenny, though she wouldn't know it till morning, was so close that his exhilaration might reach her. What was she doing, he wondered. Lying alone in her bed desiring Tony MacNeill? Feeling him next to her? Feeling for him what he was feeling for her? Tomorrow, he would not be dispossessed, stood up or scared off.

* * *

It was 10.30am, after a night of little sleep. His shaking hand gripped the receiver. Like a diviner's rod his index finger sought each of the numbered holes in the chrome dial. He was calling, he explained, for Ms Leonora Quin; it was urgent and confidential. In that case, the receptionist responded, he should be dialling Miss Quin's private number: 66038.

He stared at the telephone. This was going to be different, he told himself, minder or no minder. Maybe now the pain was over and there was such a thing as luck, or God, after all.

After aborting two attempts, he picked out 6-6-0-3-8.

'Hello.'

The voice! It came too fast, halted his breathing.

'Hello, who is it? Hello.'

It was a heart beating across darkness. And it broke his courage. No words came, not a syllable would breathe out of him.

'Hello, hello. I can hear you breathing. Who is it?'

All at once it tore through him, what he had gone through in the year since he'd heard that voice. Now he didn't belong in her world. Eva's words returned: double-killer, ex-con, gas pumper, car polisher, loser.

'I'm still waiting. Are you going to talk to me?'

The self he had re-invented, had believed in, was paralysed, a sham, hopes trapped in a heart that couldn't speak.

'Can't wait forever. Hellooo-oo.'

He smashed the receiver down. Fool, no fucking guts, he cursed. He deserved nothing. On the street he had it every time, could always perform. But her world was different: fancy, false, not for him. He dropped back onto the bed, fighting his thoughts. He'd held his own, he told himself, in the housing projects at fifteen, sixteen, seventeen; in prison, every day up against scum; he'd learned well that you paid for guts, he had paid; the price for fear was always higher. Here, as Joel would tell him, he needed to defeat fear, not make excuses for failing. He sat up, dialled again: 6-6-0-3-8.

'Tony?! Tony MacNeill? Is it you?'

'Lenny. Hi, how are you? Hi.'

'Tony! I felt it was you. I just felt it. Where are you? You're not here, in Ireland?'

'Just down the hill.'

'Oh, my God. You serious? You can't be.'

'I am. Are you able to get away, today, I mean right now?'

'Yes, yes. God, it's so good to hear your voice. I can't believe it. I really can't. Where have you been, where? Twelve months.'

'Twelve months,' he repeated. But now it felt like he had looked into her eyes just yesterday, and in a sense, he had, in each of the yesterdays.

'I did write to you,' he said. 'One note and five letters. But don't think about that now. Can you get to the Beehive Bar at eleven-thirty? It's a really nice day; I thought we could sit outside, have lunch, if you'd like.'

'Like?! Like?! Of course, I'd like. Half-eleven I can be anywhere you say. This is so wonderful. I am so excited. I'm just, I'm – '

'Have you got transport?'

'I'll walk. It's a lovely day, a lovely day.'

'Okay. Great.'

'I can't believe you're here, Tony. I'm, I'm shocked, nicely shocked.'

'I can't believe it either. I'll see you at the Beehive, eleven-thirty, forty-five minutes from now. You will definitely be there, right? At 11.30?'

'Be there? I can hardly wait. Do you look the same?'

'The same? Pretty much, I guess. See you real soon.'

As he put down the phone the world bloomed again. The fear and failure of minutes earlier seemed juvenile, crazy. From his backpack he extracted the small box he'd placed there weeks earlier and had opened a dozen times since. He inspected its contents and slipped it into his back pocket. Time to spare; no way he could sit around in his present state of mind. He'd walk to the village. Maybe sing along the way to the green Atlantic, songs he'd sung silently in American prisons, songs his father sang: *The Foggy Dew, She Moves Through the Fair, The Old Bog Road.* At the end of the hill he'd turn right at Concannon's Bar, into Kells Road, and there, on the right, at the Beehive Bar, Lenny Quin would be waiting for him.

The walk took less than fifteen minutes, taking in a stop at the newsagent's for a packet of Silvermints, the Holy Communion of kissers, as his sisters used to call them. Near the end of the hill he slowed. How would he greet her, he pondered. Throw his arms around her and kiss her? On the lips? Sounded good, but no. Place his arms gently on her shoulders, maybe a light hug? A kiss on the cheek? Offer his hand, hold on to hers as she had done to him when they met? Better wait, see what she does, take his cue from her. After all, though the thought seemed incredible, he'd been in her company just once. Out of their whole lives, all their combined years on earth, they'd shared only fifteen minutes. Intense minutes. And before today he had talked to her by phone just one time, when he sensed the upset and confusion in her, the day she was to meet him at the Horslips Hotel. No, he should play it cool, like the year just gone hadn't been a year obsessed, of frequent despair, and worse at times. But none of that mattered now. He could hold it together; he always could.

At the village, lower down, the ocean beat a rhythm into the air. He turned into Kells Road, a narrow avenue of people drifting into and out of cafes and small shops, smelling like one great bakery. The warm morning had brought out the Beehive's green-and-white umbrellas, lined along the footpath. He had six minutes to spare. Each step mattered now, because she was here, somewhere, in this freedom. Somewhere. Face after face auditioned for him, sun-bright faces, passing, standing, sitting.

He scrutinised the three Beehive tables occupied: four young women, shopping bags by their feet, huddled in chatter; two older men behind pints of black stout; two younger men in hiking jackets flanking an attractive blond woman over an opened-out map.

He checked. Only 11.27. Twenty yards beyond the Beehive he turned back, weighing all events within his compass. Not one dark-haired, thirtyish female anywhere. The two hikers, map in hand, were moving off. The blond woman, wearing oversize sunglasses, was seated now, chin resting on her hands. Was she watching him? He caught himself staring, looked away, assumed a casualness of wellbeing. Then his eyes flashed back. She was definitely staring, offering a half-smile. He reciprocated, began moving away. Then he turned. She was on her feet, as though about to signal. Five-six-ish, blond hair clipped back above both ears, long calico dress billowing in the breeze. Not brunette like Lenny. She was moving toward him.

'Tony,' she said quietly, as though in full confirmation.

The voice that had never gone away.

She whipped off her sunglasses.

Eyes that could only be hers. Just as he saw her from William's bench, one year earlier.

'Tony! I don't believe it.'

His body stilled. She appeared lit by a thousand candles, fingers probing through the air to touch him.

'It is you,' she said, as though verifying. Their arms wrapped each other in a gentle hold that became a firm wordless embrace.

'How are you?' he asked. Then leaning away he admired her from her blond crown to her canvas sandals, then back.

'I want to kiss you,' she said with no hint of request, eyes already closed.

Their lips touched, brushed apart, and met again and parted, and a moment later engaged more deeply, then broke once again until the waiting was too long and the full kiss consummated, firm and still, drawing attention from passers-by.

As the afternoon pressed on they talked over streams of tea, reminisced in disbelief about the sheer chance of how they had met, and dismissed the episodes of their separate lives since then, their year apart. He wanted to ask why she had let him down at the Horslips Hotel, wanted to tell her of the eternity of waiting for her. And he wanted to know why, on the phone that day, she had sounded disturbed, and hard to understand. For such questions, though, the moment felt wrong. Instead, he listened to her telling that she was not brunette to begin with, but light auburn. And no, she said with anguish, she had received none of his five letters, or his note, whoever was conspiring against her; even so, she would not let that cheat them of this day.

Hour after hour their chatter flowed, long after it was obvious to him that she was deflecting his enquiries. For too long he himself had hid like this, and too often still did, secrets hiding beneath what he showed and told. Better to be ready, she said, to grasp the grandness that comes in rare moments, because real joy seldom visits. He understood, for he knew well stigmata. But here he felt wiser, so he went along with her celebration of the moment, was pulled along, was coloured in by her, by everything about her.

Later, he probed again, cautiously, into her life. Again she brushed it aside. Why, he could not guess. He needed to know her. And the questions would not go away. What fear was in the hidden part of her, her life beyond this here and now? To him, she seemed at times like a teenager shielding a dysfunctional other life. This woman who, as Paddy had told it, had survived war, and all that that suggested. Or maybe none of that was true, just story. Not that any of it mattered, for he was already won by her mystique, her promise. Even her secrets. His curiosity could wait. They had saved all this out of fifteen minutes of thrill and conflict and a year of nothingness. Each had defeated something, no doubt very different things, to make it to this moment.

He moved closer to her. She was real, touchable, near enough to count her eyelashes, which he played with doing until he found himself hypnotised in the blue of her eyes. His heart had come alive, he felt, after adolescent despair and nine years of brutality in American prisons; his sign was truly rising once again in this new existence he had sworn to.

'I could stay here forever, couldn't you?' she said.

His attention went to her hands cradled within his own. Was that it, he wondered, what she meant, love? Could it be?

'Well?' she said. 'What do you think?'

'Stay here?' He lifted a strand of hair from her brow, let his touch linger on her forehead. 'Forever? Why not.'

'You believe in ideas like spirit? And feelings that never die?'

'Moving in that direction.'

'Or is it that we merely invent to make glorious mysteries plausible?'

'Bright mind. Sceptical soul.'

'I have a soul? You sure? If you believe that, I want to know what it's like. What do you see in me? Apart from my being bright or sceptical.'

'Blue eyes. Maybe blue soul.' He smiled awkwardly.

'I'm serious, Tony. Look at me. Who am I? What do you see? Tell me. Tell me.'

'Who are you?' His eyes broke from hers. 'On the outside, a very attractive woman, which you know. On the inside, the same. Bit mysterious too. What do you think?'

'Hardly. First, physical beauty is an accident of genes, has no meaning. Second, everyone has secrets, even you. Zero marks.' Amid shared amusement she drew his face closer and kissed him. 'Want me to tell you what I see inside Tony MacNeill?'

He suggested ordering another pot of tea instead. She pressed for his compliance and won it, then drew back in regard of him. 'Denim shirt, jeans, climbing boots, brown-red hair, smart, resilient, big fire burning inside, doesn't trust, been betrayed, made a big mistake or two. Yes?'

'No comment,' he said, hoping it was over.

'Nothing is permanent, Tony,' she said. 'Today's truth is tomorrow's lie. Everything goes on changing. Not even the past can be trusted, history of any kind.'

'Wouldn't go that far. We direct our own lives. Some parts of what we are are always changing, but some parts – '

'But even so, even if we do direct our own lives, it's still in a random universe. That's my point. Look at how we met – accident! Fate is not a matchmaker; it didn't bring you and me to that station to meet each other. Things just happen. Good or bad, all change comes out of chaos. Control is a construct, a philosophical illusion. If we had control, we'd all change our inner worlds.'

'We can change what we decide to change. Most things. Takes time and belief. Most people never try hard enough to get what they say they want.'

'You sound like a counsellor,' she said with a touch of angst.

He smiled dismissively.

'Things that happened years ago; tell me, who can change those?'

'Day comes we decide. We say this or that is not going to haunt us any longer. We leave the past behind. Why look back, even to good times? Life is this very minute.'

Lenny reclined in silence. Then it struck him, their exchanges had an intensity that comes only out of personal pain, and neither was trying to hide that fact.

'Sounds fine, in theory,' she said flatly. 'When all the good times are in the past, what do you do then? Tell me.'

His mind juggled how he might avoid her fervour. Clearly, she had contemplated these questions. The irony was that he had long shared her perspective, but he dared not tell her so. And despite alluding to her happiness being in the past, she hadn't once in their hours together mentioned her own past. But his best escape, for now, he decided, was retreat.

'The one thing I'm sure of, absolutely certain of, is that I must, immediately, if I am to defeat an accident of genes, go to the bathroom.' He hobbled away clownishly, moving only from the knees down, then turned to her. 'I'll have all the theories figured out by the time I get back.'

On his return he found her reflective. She took his hand and studied it: palms, back and fingers. The sense of her he had already absorbed set him on alert. Whatever was on her mind now was about to find voice.

'I love, really love, how you think,' she said, 'about the past, what it can do to you if you let it. The present is what matters, and the future. I'm learning that. Slowly.' Her fingers pressed along his jaw, then across his lips, as if authenticating his carnal actuality. 'I'm thrilled you're here,' she whispered in his ear. 'I don't care about anything else.'

On the approach of evening they left the Beehive, strolled hand in hand through the buzz of Market Street, down to the ocean, where at the end of the steps they sat staring out to the restless water, sharing each other's warmth, and talking hardly at all.

In time, the sun slipped down, colouring their world with its warm light. Then soon the air took on a chill, sending them back to the comfort of the Beehive. There, Lenny's interest caused him to tell of milestones from his fourteen years growing up in Dublin and what America had given to and taken from the MacNeills. He hoped she would reciprocate.

He told of Kate, his eldest sister, Dr Kate MacAnna now, her bravery and perseverance, who had built her own dreams. He spoke little of sisters Pat and Violet, or of his mother, now living contentedly in Florida. And as to why at twenty-eight he had not been seduced into marriage and a mortgage, he responded only with a shrug.

Then his probing of Lenny's past met with the same resistance of earlier. That story, she insisted, were it ever to be told, was for some other day, not worth the price of present time. It was an entirely forgettable past anyway, she said: dead people, old fantasies, immature hopes, nothing of value, a past of no consequence to this moment, drinking merlot by a fire. Yes, she said, his philosophy was sound; that was clear now, the holy present, the only existence, no looking back necessary.

Even more passionately now his mind jumped between fascination with Lenny Quin and thoughts of what this turn in his life portended. Her warmth, her intelligence, her rebel individuality, all gave healing to his long-aching psyche, much as her sensuality tormented his deprived senses. Her mind was not unlike his own, he thought. Yet neither the wealth that refined her nor the poverty that characterised him affected their potential together, a life, perhaps, that lay beyond either of them separately. Hers too was a survivor's mind, rich in the cleverness that comes of failing; he could sense that in her.

What price had she paid? He knew too little to even imagine. What he saw clearly, though, was that in Lenny Quin there lived a particular dimension, a bloom almost touchable, the mystique of those who are unconquerable, who survive because there is no better option. Was he closer now to knowing this woman who had appeared in the nowhere he inhabited? He thought so, and the feeling carried fear. Could he trust in this world, her world? Survive where fast hands and guts counted for little? Would all this unmask him? The dream could end tomorrow, in a week, all hope vanish. But even as he struggled with his thoughts, his fascination with this woman carried him off on great adventures, into a new land.

With these thoughts came a feeling of wholeness, unlike anything he had known, a realm of wonders unseeable in their
singled parts for they existed only as inseparables, like a hillside
of flowers dancing. He had screamed so long for life; now he
wondered if the inciter of his emptiness had finally been subdued.

'You're miles away,' she said. 'What are you thinking?'

Only his glance acknowledged her.

She pressed a double kiss to his cheek. 'We're the last ones
here,' she whispered in his ear. 'What now?'

He foraged for a response. Then she smiled a smile he'd never
met, a smile that required no prior acquaintance.

'Ready?' she asked.

'Think so,' he said, and tried to manage the friction in his
brain.

5

1964
ARANROE FARMLANDS

In the grey of dusk it was an immature wail that stilled him. His senses shot to the house. Then a second cry. The garden fork dropped. He bounded over the potato greens, through the half-open door, took the stairs in leaps. The bedroom door fell away before his soil-encrusted hands. In the bed her tiny face hid behind clutched blankets.

'Leonora, Princess, what is it? Another bad dream, was it?' His arms wrapped around her. 'It's alright, it's alright. Only a dream, Princess, that's all. Uncle Leo is here now, everything's going to be grand.' Back and forth he rocked her, to no avail. 'That big monster you told me was chasing you, he's not real, there's no real monsters, only in stories. Everything's grand now, you're grand now.'

'I want mama,' the child sobbed. 'Mama, mama.'

'*A ghrá mo croi,* mama'll be home tomorrow. Uncle Leo's going down to the big hospital in Galway and he's bringing her home to you. You can come with me; would you like that? And Aunt Peggy. We'll all go down together in the big bus, will we? And we'll buy choc ices; how does that sound?'

With no sign of the girl settling, he called to a pair of young boys in the adjoining field, sent them down to the O'Riain farmhouse with a note. Within minutes Peggy O'Riain arrived, shoulders shawled, her sandy hair rolled in pink plastic curlers. Soon she had Leonora comforted and in peaceful sleep.

In the kitchen, Pope John XXIII and John Fitzgerald Kennedy shared the mantle with the Blessed Virgin, below which a smouldering turf fire sent earthy odours through the cottage. Leo plodded about in his boots, a heavy mood over him. Peggy entered, reflective, knelt with her palms to the pulsing turf.

'What in God's holy name is bothering the poor soul?' she said. 'That's three times this week. Whatever's the matter I pray she's over it for Róisín getting home.'

'Something's not right, nightmares like that,' Leo said. 'Never before seen her that way.'

'Has to be Róisín's nieces. I'd nearly swear to it. They can be a right pair. I hope they didn't say something in front of the poor lamb, those couple of times they minded her. More than once it was that I caught them yapping about things – you know what I'm saying – after me giving them a right telling off.' Peggy's face changed. 'Leo Reffo, will you stop wearing out the lino; stop troubling yourself like that. Are you hearing me at all, man – stop!'

He halted beside her, his half-bare arms outstretched to the mantle. 'Something's turned the little angel; that's all I know. It might be what you say, them nieces. Or something else.'

'Listen to me now: There's no good getting yourself upset. We don't know a thing for sure, whether it's the nieces or not. She'll surely snap out of it as quick as it came on. Childer are like that, the younger ones especially.'

'I never was. At five or any other age.'

'Not at all what I heard.' Peggy rose in the glow of the fire and began uncoiling her rollers. 'Never told a lie or chased a chicken or set fire to a haystack. We all did them things. Anyhow, it's thirty years since you were five; you couldn't remember right. And don't you still go on like you're five when you don't get your way.'

Barely containing her amusement, she crossed the kitchen and stood before him. '*A stóir,* stop letting it trouble you. Things'll be grand when Róisín's here.' She snuggled against him. 'Between this and that you can't rightly relax, I know, no more than me. Few more days, that's all, then you're spoken for, for good; your bachelor days are over.' His arms clutched tighter around her; he kissed her on the lips, then kissed her again, a kiss that migrated along her neck as his hands dropped to her hips. She quickly freed herself and knelt back at the fire.

'You can dampen that look, Mr Reffo. You know the rules.' She set three sods of turf in the hearth and glanced back at his quietness. 'The day can't come soon enough for me either. Isn't it an odd woman you'll be making of me, getting me to give up the grand O'Riain name for a silly Italian one. I can hear them in the village, what they'll be calling me, the old ones: Peggy Mary Dolores O'Riain Reffo. Maybe I should just be Peggy O. What do you think of that?'

Leo approached her, his dourness all but gone.

'Only the good Lord knows,' she said, back in his arms. 'Please God soon we'll have a wee one of our own. A little Leo Reffo, Lord save us from all harm.'

'I'm worried, Peg.' Leo walked to the window, stared out. 'What if the wee nieces told her? It started a week and a half ago, first time they minded her.'

'Whisht, will you. We don't know they said a thing. And even if they did there's nothing to do now. Could be she heard them telling their secrets, the way young girls are at that age. Anyway, Róisín'll be home tomorrow, and with the help of God back to her old self in no time. And Leonora too.'

Leo turned from the window, found Peggy's troubled regard still on him. He threw his cap on the table and made for her, open-armed. 'You're a wise woman,' he said into her de-curlered hair. That's why I'm marrying you. One reason anyhow. The other one's the thing you won't be saying no to after next Saturday.'

Her look of mock disgust was followed by a parting kiss. Then suddenly her hands sprang to her hair, picking and pulling. 'The state of me. God almighty. A head full of rats' tails the night of me own hens' party; it'll be over if I don't gallop now, without the bride-to-be.'

'I heard the word in the village,' he called after her, 'that I'm the luckiest man in Aranroe to be marrying Peggy O.'

'Don't be falling for that old gossip,' she shouted back. 'You're only a big ruffian. Even so, I might love you. *Slán, mo mhíle stór.*'

6

Outside the Beehive they lingered as linked couples stole away under twinkling stars and the ocean beat in all the little streets.

'Well?' Lenny asked again, her hands tucked inside her jacket. 'What will we do?'

'Great night. How about I walk you up to your place? Then I'll head back down to where I'm staying.'

'Fine,' she said curtly. 'Up the hill together, half an hour. That's it?'

No right response came to him, so he said nothing. What was she suggesting? Without the clues of experience he had nothing to tell him. Except fantasy. 'We can do whatever you want,' he said. His words hung in the air.

They walked on under moonlight, out beyond the edge of the village, with no agreed destination. Lenny moved purposelessly, gazing up frequently into the whispering sycamores. Tony halted their advance, coaxed her to look at him.

'Everything okay?'

'Tell me you don't feel it!' she said, as though discarding the politeness of new friendship. 'Is it just me? Is that it?'

'Is what you? What? Tell me what's on your mind, Lenny.'

'On my mind? Well, for one, the Abbey's just ahead. And no-tice I don't call it home.'

For the next minute they walked in separateness and silence. When they reached Claire Abbey's gates her mood seemed less troubled. She led him in under the perimeter trees and leaned against the castle wall.

'Too nice a day to end. I want to stay out. Stay out and play. For a long, long, long time. I know, you don't have to say it: I'm thirty-five sounding fifteen. Whatever that says about me.' She took both of his hands in hers and squeezed. 'Tony, know what I'd like? I want to go back with you, to your place.'

His averted gaze was pulled back by her closeness. 'Lenny, it's, it's – '

Out of the black bogland a spear of light shot across them. The white Mercedes had turned in off Aranroe Hill and now rumbled to a halt just feet away. For a moment nothing stirred but the glimmering of the light beams. Then a door clicked open. A dark figure stepped out, glared across the car roof at their partly hidden outlines.

'Leonora?' the man called and waited for a response. 'Is there a problem?'

'Everything's fine!'

'You're certain? You know it's getting quite – '

'I'm fine, I said. Fine.'

The man remained motionless.

'Quite fine! Thank you.' Her articulated words pierced the ether.

The man said no more; his car continued along the weaving stretch toward the castle.

'My dutiful father. Now can we go?'

'I remember the car. At the station last year.'

'Can we go?'

'Sure. Where can we – '

'Anywhere! That's where. Any damn where. This has been one of the best days of my life. Can you understand that, can you?'

She turned away then quickly back, and held him. 'I'm sorry; I don't want this to end, a kiss against a cold wall. I don't want to be alone tonight.' Their embrace intensified. 'I want you to love me, Tony. I want to love you.'

*   *   *

In the bare room Lenny perched on the edge of a worn sofa. Tony flitted with distractions, certain of nothing but what joining her would mean, before his head was right. In the sanctuary of the bathroom he cursed his hesitancy. Was it fear or street sense or insanity? At twenty-eight, what stopped him? What was wrong with him? With being here? He allowed himself one minute, no more, to get control.

Nine years of incarcerated fantasies, all his dreams of this. And now it wasn't as he envisaged. He wasn't. It wasn't simple or fearless. His unease felt asinine, given how he felt about her. Fuck his crazy mind, he cursed. Fantastic woman, waiting for him, a woman who wanted him as he was: flawed, shaking. And he was dishonouring the moment, and her. He didn't deserve this freedom.

Since he'd laid eyes on her this morning he had not stopped picturing her naked. Hadn't been able to nor wanted to. Nor stopped imagining her next to him, her scent, the feel of her. Through all those hours the body and spirit of this woman had tortured his senses. For a whole year, in fact. A lifetime. Now he had to deal with it.

Through the slightly-ajar door he stole her reflection from the mirror: half-reclining on the double bed, long legs, cotton dress, bare shoulders, her neat rounded breasts high up and distinct. His imaginings put tremors into him, forced him out of hiding. Just then her expression caught him, a face kind, bearing sureness, wiser than he would ever be.

'Tony,' she said, jolting him into the actuality of the moment. 'Come beside me.'

He sat on the edge of the bed, close to her.

'I want to tell you something,' she said.

'No, no, no, you have to tell me nothing.' He stood up. 'Nothing. No.'

She placed a finger to her lips and looked at him with need. Her hand brought him back to her.

'I want to say this; please allow me. I'll be thirty-six in March. I've been in love before, one time. Just in case all this seems some other way to you, I want you to know you are very, very special to me. Being here like this, it's not something I do. I haven't made love with anyone in close to four years.'

'No, you don't have to explain to me. Nothing. Not to me. I wasn't thinking anything – '

'Shhhhh. Darling, no more talk . . . Make love to me.'

His eyes climbed her slim, bare legs and over her curving form, then his hands, delicately, tentatively, and he kissed her sea-fragrant flesh, her shoulders, her chest, her trembling mouth, and a shared glance told that each was pledged, in abandon.

'We can turn out the light,' she whispered, 'if you'd prefer.'

'Can't imagine not seeing you.'

She unloosed both shoulder strings, slipped out of her clothing. 'Then see me, Tony. Love me. Never stop.'

Her smooth, pale flesh, warm to his hands, pushed his throbbing to the edge.

'I want you so much,' she whispered in a whisper full of dreams. 'I love you.'

7

1964

ARANROE VILLAGE

In the icy air rang the chant of carols. And from overhead a shining angel and strings of bulbs gave life to the dark street.

Child tightly by the hand, the gaunt woman hurried past tin-selled shop fronts, avoiding passing faces. Her bulky overcoat, buttoned high, lent substance to her slightness. Outside McCann's Village Hardware her hurry halted. She glared down once again at the wild-haired young girl wrapped in a scarlet raincoat, then struggled in against the weight of the shop door.

'There y'are, Róisín Doyle,' Paddy called out. 'Bit under the weather? Something the matter?'

'Not too bad, Paddy,' she said in a tired voice.

'And how's the wee lassie? Didn't get her mammy's flaming hair.'

'Sure red's a curse, Paddy. Anyway, she's grand. Six in March, wild as a vixen.'

Paddy's big apron-draped frame leaned across the bare-board counter. He poked his thumbs into his ears, stuck out his tongue, and flapped his fingers at the child. Instantly, she mimicked his tease, expelling a blare of spit and air until her breath ran out.

'God in heaven bless us and save us,' he said with alarm.

'Wasn't me that taught you that. I never do things that bold.' He picked a bulls-eye from a big glass jar and dropped it into the girl's waiting palms. Then he turned back to the woman.

'What can I do for you, Róisín?'

'Do you mind if I ask you a sort of a personal question?' she said, leaning closer to him. 'When you were setting up the new shop, did you have to get a solicitor?'

'I did. Sean Breathnach, up the road. If you don't mind me asking: you wouldn't be going into business against me?'

'Don't be silly, Paddy. Nothing like that. Is he a decent sort, Mr Breathnach?'

Paddy brightened. 'Grand lad. I still owe him a few quid and he never says a word.' He drew back his shoulders, assumed an affectation: '"A pound or two, Patrick, in your own good time", that's it, all he says. Be sure you tell him it was me that sent him the business. Say you're on the best of terms with meself and he'll see you right.'

'I'll do that so.'

'I've one shilling off the new artificial Christmas trees, just in from Germany. For yourself, one-and-sixpence off; how's that?'

'Not this year, Paddy. All I need is one of them plastic clothes lines.'

'A line, a line,' he said, searching the shelves behind him, and in a moment slapped two on the counter. 'The twenty-foot's one-and-eleven pence, the thirty-foot's two-and-six pence. And I have the wire ones in the back, thruppence a yard.'

'The cheapest one'll do, with the plastic.'

'Twenty-foot: what if it's not long enough?'

'It'll do.'

'Look, take the longer one. I won't be charging you. Wee Christmas present. If it's too long just snip the end off with a pliers. Now is there anything else I can do for you?'

'You're a good ould soul, Paddy.'

He glanced to both sides then leaned over the counter. 'Y'know what, Róisín Doyle, like I told you before, and I hope you won't take offence at me saying it again; I've often said to meself: if you weren't a married woman I'd be – '

The brass bell over the shop door clanged. He straightened up.

Róisín gave a weak smile, picked up her straw bag, and departed.

On the footpath, the child tugged at her mother's coat. 'Mammy, I want to light another candle, to the Blessed Virgin. Can we? Just one more. I want to.'

'Tomorrow, pet, not today. You have to be very very good today. For mammy, okay?'

'The doctor didn't give me a sweet. Remember you said? And he didn't. And I – '

'Stop it! Stop it! He forgot, Leonora. He forgot.' She yanked the child forward and said nothing for a while. 'I'll buy you sweeties. But you have to promise to be the best girl today, you hear?' Just then a car pulled up beside them.

'Hop in. I'll run you up home.' Paddy reached across the front seat of the maroon Morris Minor and pushed open the door. 'All them clouds mean only one thing.'

'Ah no, Paddy, not at all. I've not far to go. You're very good just the same.'

Paddy scrambled out of the car. 'Tell me what's the matter? If you're short for the Christmas I can lend you a few bob till '65 is well in, up to March, if you want.'

'No, Paddy, thanks, it's not that. I'm just, I'm just a bit worn down. Nothing more.'

'C'mon so, hop in. I'll run you up. And I'll stick the line up for you while I'm there.'

'I wouldn't take you away from the shop. You have – '

'Not a bit of bother. That lazy lump of a brother of mine is well able on his own when he wants. And anyway I've a bit of business up in Westport.'

'No, really, Paddy.' Her dark eyes lowered, and a moment passed before she swept errant auburn locks off the child's forehead. 'But if you wouldn't mind, you could drop her off at Leo and Peggy's. Peg's knitting her an Aran cardigan for Christmas. And you won't have to wait; one of them'll walk her back over after she gets measured.'

'Mam, mam, remember you said you'd buy me sweets, remember? I want a Trigger bar, a Trigger bar and lemonade.'

'That's enough! I told you, not now! Didn't I? Didn't I tell you?'

'I've a brainwave!' Paddy's exuberance defused the moment and captured Róisín's attention. He took Leonora's hand. 'It's half-three now. Why don't I buy her her Trigger bar and lemonade in Ridgeways, then run her up to Leo's, and on me way back from Westport I'll collect her and bring her back over to you. And sure maybe then meself and yourself could have a bottle of stout, or something stronger, for the holidays, if the humour's on you. What do you say to that?'

Róisín's smile strained, then with a vacancy her eyes floated up to the lights and trumpet-bearing angel rattling overhead.

'I want a Flake; I want to get it in Christina's. I don't want a Trigger bar any more, mam; I want a Flake and a bottle of lemonade in Christina's.'

'Flake and lemonade it is. But we have to ask Mammy first.' His attention flashed back to Róisín. 'Are you alright, girl, or what? You're as pale as a ghost and you need to wipe your eyes. D'you want to nip in to the Beehive or Concannon's and have a small one, warm you up, get some life back into you?'

'Not at all, Paddy, thanks, the walk'll warm me. Just drop her off, if you wouldn't mind. She's grand at Leo and Peg's place, and they always make her a bit to eat.'

'If that's what you want, I will. I could knock on your door anyway, later, put the line up for you. Wouldn't take me five minutes.'

'Another day, Paddy. You're always going to trouble for me;

you're too good. Off with you now and do your business; don't be delaying on account of me.'

'Mammy, mam – '

'Whatttt?! Stopppp! What did I tell you? Stop!'

The child's face flushed. She hid behind Paddy's baggy trousers.

'I suppose Charles himself is away foreign?' Paddy asked.

Róisín shrugged distractedly.

Paddy reached for the child, still huddling behind him, but she rotated with him, staying out of his view, and was thrilled at his show of bewilderment. 'You're being a very good wee girl,' he said. 'And you know what? I was told by a fairy princess I met on me way home last night – flying around above John Taylor's Bar she was – that Santa's making a grand big present for Leonora Quin of Aranroe, County Mayo, Ireland, Europe, the World. That's what he wrote on it, and that's what she told me, and he'll be here very soon.'

'Couldn't tell you, Paddy, where the man is,' Róisín said. 'As you already know, I haven't seen trace nor tidings of him this seven months. And don't want to. It isn't for all men, marriage. Not for him.'

'They say God never closes one door unless he opens another. If things were meant to be that way 'twas better it happen in the first year.' After a silent nod from Róisín, Paddy's tone changed. 'And about yourself, girl, what is it you see yourself doing? Eventually, I mean. Edna O'Brien says there's tons of Irish girls getting divorces in England, and marrying again. Anything of that sort cross your mind?'

'I'm lost, Paddy. Lost. Gospel truth. Knowing what's best is the hardest thing. Not for me I don't mean, best for the child, if you understand me. What's best for the child. Putting things right. All the legal stuff.'

'Sean's the man for that. He'll see you right. And tell me this: the young one in the post office, she said you were down with a bad flu.'

'Not flu, Paddy. But what's the use complaining. The child's healthy, there's that to be thankful for. And there's good people here, like Leo and Peg, and Dr Lappin and Fr Foley. But I never like bothering anyone.'

'Good souls every one.'

'And yourself as much as any, Paddy McCann. One of the best. And you should hear that.'

'Ah stop, will you. No better than any other.'

'I mean what I said. Or I wouldn't say it. This day of any.'

His eyes lifted to the strings of glowing lights. Then he regarded her directly. 'Look, maybe a wiser man than me wouldn't say this, but I'm saying it. I never could take to calling you Róisín Quin, so I won't. If you weren't a married woman, Róisín Doyle, I'd be asking you – '

'Married, Paddy? For eight months. Now only in name.'

'I'd be asking you long ago, to go out with me, I would. And I know you know it.'

'Life, Paddy. Desperate hard station.' Her hand squeezed his. 'The right somebody'll come along for you. I know that. A lovely alive girl. Not half-taken like me. Won't she be the lucky one. Fall for your good looks and kind nature.' Her pause brought his regard back to her, whereupon her dark fluid eyes met his. The confluence ended at the blare of a car horn. Beside them Leonora cavorted in the driver's seat, droning out engine sounds and pulling at the steering wheel.

'Put the heart crossways in me,' Paddy said, slapping his chest. 'Time I was off, I suppose.' He nudged the child over and fell into the driver's seat.

'Second thoughts, Paddy.' Róisín hunkered down at the open window, 'Ask Leo and Peg to keep her up there, not to walk her home. I'll fly down and see Mr Breathnach; I could be delayed, could be late, you never know.'

'I'll do that. Any interest in the Christmas Pageant? It's at eight tonight. I could collect you in the Morris. Car's grand in the cold. I bet Leo and Peg won't mind keeping an eye on the lassie.'

Her unfocused stare hung in the divide as she reached in and stroked the child's head.

'You're shaking, look at you,' Paddy said. 'That's it, I'm dropping you up home this minute!' He pushed out the passenger door. 'Get in, girl, we'll get a hot Jameson inside you, warm you up, do you a power of good.'

'No!' she said, a sternness in her white wintry face. Paddy offered no retort. 'Go, Paddy McCann, go on. I need to get walking, that's all. You'll be sure it's Leo you say it to, about keeping her? Wild she is, you know.' Her attention turned to the child. 'Only now and then, pet, not all the time.'

'I will. Y'have to start looking after yourself; that's the last I'll say about it.'

She found Paddy's hand already half-way to her.

'Happy Christmas, Róisín. Róisín Doyle.'

'Thanks, Paddy. For everything. You're a star; you really are.'

His big face flushed.

'Be good, pet,' she said as the Morris pulled off into the ebbing day.

Two hours later the black clouds that had menaced since morning deluged Aranroe and all the western lands.

*   *   *

'She in here with you?' Peggy peeked around the scullery door.

'She's in the small bedroom,' Leo said. 'Playing with the crib figures.'

'She's not! I've just now been in the two bedrooms.'

Leo shouted the child's name above the battering of the weather. 'She's hiding under a bed, or in the loft; you know the way she is.'

'I'm telling you she's not, man! And she couldn't get into the loft, the ladder's down.'

'She's not far. Has to be somewhere.' Leo's demeanour changed. 'Leonora! Leonora, time to put the lights in the window.'

Together they searched the loft, then in each of the cottage's four rooms, inside the big brown suitcase they'd bought for their honeymoon, behind the old wool baskets, under the couch, in dressers and sideboards, even inside the turf boxes. The child was nowhere to be found. Outside, the storm from the north had turned into an Atlantic gale and was now whipping against walls and window panes.

'Jesus, she wouldn't.' Peggy's voice pitched higher. 'She wouldn't have rambled off home through the back field.'

'She'd have no cause to do that, in this weather. Isn't she afraid of the dark anyway.'

'She's done it before. With Róisín away in hospital and you up in the high pastures. I didn't tell you.' Peggy's voice dropped. 'That's it; that's what she's done.'

Leo pulled his raincoat off the rack. 'Needs a good smack; she knows better.'

'I'll go with you. Róisín should be home by now. I'll bring the measure; I promised her I'd finish her cardigan for Christmas.'

'You'll need your boots. It's well flooded.'

They followed the long meadow before stepping down into the squelching softness of the back field, waves of sleet beating against their oilskins. Half-way across, amber room-light beaconed through the dark, then red and green blinking bulbs marking out both front windows of Róisín's cottage, and soon the faint twinkling of Christmas tree lights.

Leo banged on the door. Nobody appeared. No voices, no sign of life. 'Róisín, it's us. Are you in?' he yelled, pushing the door open. The only sound in the main room was the rapping of rain and the wind in the chimney. The fire in the grate was set, but unlit. On the timber floor, Leonora's scarlet raincoat lay in a pool, beside it one small black boot.

'Róisín! Leonora!' Peggy shouted. 'Place is frozen cold. Róisín, darling; Leonora, darling, it's us.'

They entered the kitchen. Empty. Peggy grabbed Leo's sleeve. 'Something's wrong. God forgive me for saying it.'

Jesus Christ, are you here or not? Where are you?' Leo's calls echoed through the cottage.

'The bedroom,' Peggy said, hands covering her face. 'They're fast asleep.'

In the dim hallway he gripped the brass knob, eased the door in slightly. A moving shadow accosted him. Candle flicker. He called out, without response. Only a weak, seesaw creaking stood out from the gale. He pushed the door further. On the bed, a small body, prostrate, lying awkwardly, eyes open, lay completely still.

For a heartbeat, he faltered. 'There you are!' he said. 'You are never – ' Suddenly a cry burst out of him. He sprang to the bed, gripped the child's tiny shoulders, lifted her forward. 'Leonora! Peggy!' Her body sagged in his hands. He shook her, shook her softer, cradled her, then he lowered her to the pillow, talking to her, her face between his palms.

'Please, Jesus!' Peggy barged up against him, pulled the limp body upright. 'Darling, what happened?! Darling, wake up, wake up!' She rubbed vigorously at the child's hands, put her ear to her chest, kept shifting position, kept listening. 'Oh my God, she's breathing, she's alive. Wake up for Aunt Peggy, darling, Aunt Peggy and Uncle Leo, we're here now, wake up, darling.'

'Thank Christ,' Leo said, plucking her into his arms as Peggy tucked a blanket around her. 'She's like ice and she's saturated. We have to get her dry, get some heat into her, find a telephone, get Dr Lappin.' He clutched her to him, rubbing briskly on her back. 'You're grand now, Princess. Uncle Leo's with you now, Uncle Leo's with you. Everything's alright.'

Peggy turned for the door.

And saw Róisín.

'Nooo! Jesus, no.'

Then Leo saw her, behind the half-open door.

Hanging.

No words or sound came out of his deformed face.

Head bent forward, the body swayed with a low rhythmic creaking.

Leo thrust the child toward Peggy. He locked his arms around Róisín's thighs, lifted her weight off the plastic-covered line. 'Not this, not this, no, Róisín Doyle, no, no.'

Peggy edged back into the room, Leonora in her arms.

'The dresser, Peggy. Climb up, cut it, cut it, hurry! Cut it, cut it.'

With the child laid on the bed, she pulled a scissors from a wool basket, climbed on a chair, and cut. Róisín's slight body crumpled into his arms. 'Get the child out, get her out,' he shouted.

As he placed Róisín on the bed her lifeless face caught the light of the candle. He slapped her cheeks, yelled her name over and over, demanded her response, his voice peaking and breaking. 'For me. Wake up for me. Listen to me, you never would, just this once, listen to me. Wake up! Wake up!' He pressed his face against hers and let out a long wail. 'I was here. I was always here, right beside you.' He lifted her forward, rocked her back and forth, back and forth, locked to her.

Suddenly he stopped. He took her ringless left hand in his, and into her ear he recited a prayer and marked her with the sign of the cross.

In the living room he found Peggy cuddling Leonora before kindling burning in the grate, small clothes hanging on the wire screen.

'Get hold of yourself, man,' Peggy's strong, tearful voice ordered. 'You'd no part in this. Not your fault. The truth I'm speaking to you.'

'She's gone.' He fell to his knees alongside Peggy. 'Róisín's gone.'

'Shhh, Leo, Leo! She's gone to God; she's with God now.' Peggy tightened the blanket around the comatose child, and let her own sorrow spill out unchecked. 'We're going home now, darling. Yes, we are, we're all going home. You, me and Uncle Leo, home.'

Leo's heavy hands remained pressed to his eye sockets.

'You hear me, Leo Reffo? We're going home; we're going

home right this minute. There's nothing more you can do here this night.' She linked one arm into his, and when it seemed her voice was failing she spoke more commandingly. 'We'll phone Fr Foley and Dr Lappin, from the kiosk on the hill,' she said. 'Here, you take her; she's always better with you.' He fastened his arms around the child, and together, under blankets and oilskins, they headed away from the cottage.

In their wake they left Róisín at rest in her bed, a solitary bulb burning overhead, and all the Christmas lights extinguished. And against the swamp and darkness of the back field, they battled forward, clutched together.

*   *   *

Under great Celtic crosses the black-clad mourners began moving away from the grave in twos and threes. Fr Liam Foley, with a plaintive countenance, picked his way to higher ground and stretched out his hand to Leo. A moment later Paddy McCann arrived beside them, shoulders stiffened, suit collar up. The three men huddled amid headstones mottled by moss and age.

Fr Foley recounted the day, just two years earlier, as he remembered it, the spring of 1963, when Róisín came to see him to be married and had a bother with a curate, since gone from the parish. She had hinted then to him about her health without saying more. And then her marriage ending after just months. A tragedy, no less, he declared, Charles Quin and his idea of marriage, not deserved at all by such a grand wee lass.

'Have only meself to blame,' Paddy said, eyes red and watery. 'Talking to her on Monday I was. Had a feeling all wasn't what it should be. And what did I do? Sweet fuck all! At twenty-six any gobdaw would've known. Not this gobdaw. Clear as day now, her telling me she was off to see Sean Breathnach and getting me to drop the wee one up to yourself and Peg. Big fat *amadán* is all I am, a dunce. No other way to say it.'

'That's totally nonsensical, Paddy, I'll hear none of it,' Fr Foley said. 'You're not God. No more than I am. No call blaming yourself. She went to see Sean alright – for a reason. Do you know what that reason was? To fix up the will, so the child wouldn't be done out of whatever's rightly hers. Our Róisín was smarter than she let on to any of us. Young Róisín gone, can you believe it, Tommy Doyle's only daughter, poor unfortunate soul.'

'Smart she was. Too good for the likes of me.' Paddy sobbed into his handkerchief. 'One of the best.'

'Come on, Paddy,' Leo said. 'Pull yourself together.'

'That's what she said to me, on Monday, the very words. I was one of the best, if you can credit that.' Paddy's distress broke into his words. 'She put both of you, by your own names, in the same company. Leo and Fr Foley, she said. And Paddy McCann. The best.'

Leo squeezed Paddy's shoulder. 'Too hard on yourself, man. Liam's right, the blame's not yours. Not a soul could've known what lay ahead.'

Leo's crestfallen stare searched both men's faces then travelled to the unfilled hole in the ground. 'Where was her Saviour the day she needed him? Could you explain that to me, Liam?' he asked.

'She was in God's hands all along. Every day. We can count on that.' The priest took both men's arms, drew them closer. 'Dr Lappin called it a miracle, his very words to me. She borrowed five years, he told me, that she shouldn't have had, and she knew it, knew it all along. It was the good doctor himself that broke the news to her, when she was only sixteen. Leukaemia. Not much anyone could do, he told her, except pray for a miracle. She wouldn't accept that, not for a whole year. Told him she'd cure herself, that nothing would stop her getting married, rearing a family. As certain as you like. So on with us she went for another eight whole years. Can you beat that? The spirit.

'She swore the doctor and the ma and da to secrecy that first

day. And held them to it ever after, never relented. She's with the
da now: Tommy, me old pal.' His smile lived only seconds before
he reached to Leo, as though to stem his own distress. 'The grave
is but a hollow tomb,' he said, 'that inherits nought but bones. We
can never let ourselves forget that, men.'

'What about the wee lassie, Leo?' Paddy un-did the knot in his
black tie. 'Any change?'

'No change. Still just staring into space. Won't even cry.
They've a name for it I don't remember. She's up in Harcourt
Street Hospital; supposed to be the best. Peg'll stay with her for as
long as they let her. Could be a while, they said, before she snaps
out of it. Or she might not.'

'If there's a god in heaven she'll be right as rain,' Paddy said.
'Or I'm done with the Church for the rest of me days. Sorry
y'have to hear that, Liam, that's how I feel.'

'And by God's good grace she will turn right,' the priest said.
'She's in the prayers of everyone in the parish, and far beyond.'
He paused, forlorn looking, then took a more stout-hearted
bearing. 'We don't know better than God, men, why he calls
those he does. I've shaken a few sticks at him in my time, but I do
know he has a purpose in giving us the crosses we bear.'

Paddy climbed down from the rise to greet his parents.

'I know how much you're suffering,' Fr Foley said quietly to
Leo. 'I believe I'm free now to tell you what Róisín told me. That
you were always the closest to her heart. Said yourself and her da
were the kindest of all and meant the most to her. A fortnight ago
she confided that to me.'

'Then you know I asked her. More than once. She wouldn't
have me.'

'I do know that. And I know more, being of the cloth, as they
say. The girl knew she wouldn't be staying long with us, despite
her courage. Saying yes to you wouldn't have been fair; she truly
believed that. Hardest decision she ever had to make, saying no
to you; you have my collar on that.'

'But the innocent child. Look at the state she's in. I can't understand, why, why she – '

'*Mo chara dílis*, there's more to living and dying than any of us will ever understand. In fairness to the dead, no one on earth, not Róisín Doyle nor anyone else, could have foreseen the wee lassie crossing the bog in the black of night, in that weather. Could even be she was drawn there by a spiritual connection with the ma; such things have happened.'

Leo nodded, hands in his pockets, his gaze in the distant Atlantic.

'I hear Charles asked yourself and Peggy to look after her till matters get sorted out?'

'Yesterday. Telegram from Australia. How could we not. Róisín's brothers are all emigrated and Granny Doyle's not able for a wee one.'

The cold morning mist had thickened and now it hung heavy and damp over graveyard and mourners. Paddy, puffing clouds of breath, climbed back to the men.

'Have to get inside out of this shagging weather.' He pinched his lapels together under his chin. 'C'mon, Leo, I'll stand you a drink. And yourself, Father. The chill up here would freeze the balls off Satan himself – sorry, Liam.'

The priest shook his head. 'I'll stand us all a large Powers, two apiece. God knows we deserve it. Christmas Eve tomorrow, I'll be on me last legs. Confessions from ten till six then turkey and bulldust with the purple-hat brigade.'

As the trio trudged toward the gates, Leo fell behind. Alone in the watery light, he glared back to the new white cross atop the rise, luminous against the dark dome of Mweelrea.

'Y'all right, boy?' Paddy whispered over Leo's shoulder. 'The Morris is ready when you are, in your own time.' And he departed Leo's farewell.

8

The double knock came again. Tony slipped into his jeans and called out. It was housekeeping, a female voice responded. Lenny let out a gasp and flopped back in the bed. The room was fine, he shouted, and he fell back into waiting arms.

'I could stay here forever,' Lenny said. 'Resign from the world and all its rottenness and indiscriminate pain. Keep it all at bay.' She kissed his cheek. 'But we cannot.'

As she made to rise he pulled her back. 'Let's resign right here for the whole day.'

'You have fire in your hair,' she said, freeing her naked form from his hold. 'The flame of the Celts.'

'When I was fourteen, in Newark, all I wanted was Puerto Rican hair or Dago hair, even Chinese hair, anything but Irish hair.'

'That'd make you a totally different person. Which would not be good.'

'You did it. You changed to blond. Did you become a new person?'

He watched as she stepped into her dress of a thousand tiny flowers, watched her settle it on her hips, raise it over her breasts, then fix the shoulder strings and pat the cotton smooth.

'Too soon to tell,' she said disinterestedly.

'You know, I know zip about you. You realise that? I know you're smart, you're pretty, you're rich, that's it. And one other thing: after last night I know there's no words for some things I know.'

At the oval mirror her hands flicked at her hair. 'A warrior talking to me like a poet. Hard to fathom. Like a dream.'

'Warrior?'

'I saw them. So many scars. Your snoring woke me up. That long purple one inside your thigh.'

'That.' He was caught suddenly by memories, which he suppressed with effort then lay back in the bed, arms spread wide. 'Whoever he was, he's long gone. I'm ready to surrender. To you.'

She pressed a small gold-heart earring into each ear, and didn't answer him.

'Surrender can be better than victory,' he said, as though speaking to himself. He pulled his mind into the present and sat up. 'Now that you know me, scars and all, what are you planning?'

'I don't own you, you don't own me.' Her demeanour seemed stiff. 'I have to go up to the Abbey. One or two errands.'

'Work?'

'Woman of leisure. Remember?'

'Pleasure?'

'Leisure. Opposites, often.'

'I'll go with you. Then we can get something to eat in the village.'

'No!' she said firmly, appearing to strain. 'Better not. I should be through in an hour.'

He suppressed his protest; dissuading her felt impossible.

'I'm going. I'll be one hour, possibly two. Don't look so damn depressed.' She buckled her sandals, bent across the bed, and winced momentarily as she kissed him.

'Everything ok?' he asked.

She kissed him again, lightly, looking as though her thoughts had already left. Then her fingers slipped away, leaving his hand suspended in space. Neither said goodbye, nor gave any goodbye sign.

Now alone, he locked his hands behind his head, wondered how long an hour would feel in this new life. And he thought about how far he had come. From childhood innocence, his original life in this land, to an epoch of ugliness and violence, his life since he left this land. Now time ran back and history paraded in detail: America 1980, the new kid, fourteen, Irish and wild, how most of his peers tagged him, or crazy, tags that stuck as he grew older, taking on all-comers: jocks and toughs eagerly sought out, no size or race or religion rejected, all jerks welcome, scumbags too, big-mouths, punks, slicks, home boys, anyone who thought they could fight; but no hardware, just fists, feet if needed, and all submissions honoured. Then at sixteen, how the code fell apart, rulelessness took over, when blades and wharf hooks and Saturday-night-specials made Goliaths out of worms and wrecked too many unfortunates. And how he, Tony MacNeill, ruled on, fought well, stayed king of Witchell Heights for one more year. And from that time a dark stain burst out:, the face of Jesus Pomental. And the blood. He tried to bury it, because here, he was sensing the first feelings of rebirth, because here his faith in the future felt real, much more than hope, for the first time.

He drew her pillow across his face, inhaled her legacy: subtle and exciting. What part had he played in creating this, he contemplated, being alive and awake and lying here in his own dream? How much should he trust in it, this turn in his life? He was certain it was that, a turn, maybe bigger even than the freedom Joel had opened up for him. Joel Vida, the smartest man he'd ever known. Now his old fantasies felt hollow, juvenile. Crazy how in the year since he'd met her he could not have imagined her passion, the way in which she had loved him, so terrifying, so warm. How wanted he felt. And lonely now. But lonely only for an hour, maybe two, not even that long.

Truth was, he realised, he could not remember anything he had envisioned in the year just gone. Had he even once allowed himself to imagine beyond just seeing her again? Not that any of that mattered now, for nothing could have prepared him for the love of Lenny Quin. If that's what it was, love; if that's what she was feeling for him. It had to be, he told himself, it was in her, how she could sense what was going on in his head, what he was feeling; already she knew him like no one ever had. This time no running away. He'd care for her so well that she'd always be as happy as now, joy the world didn't often give, exactly as she had said. And he'd keep his past to himself, the guilt, the despair, the violence, all the crazy shit.

Then his mind turned again. What if all this was just his own delusion, what if he was assuming, naïve, jumping too fast, dumb, if she felt none of this? He couldn't permit such thoughts. No self-crucifixion, Joel had warned him. He'd rounded the final turn, finally free, that's how he'd see it, the end of an old life, end of pain, end of Newark, end of parole, old ghosts disappearing. And true to his oath to the end, he was never going back.

The sun was up now, shining in his window, sharp autumn sun. When Lenny got back they'd celebrate this first day of September 1994. Lenny and September, somehow they seemed to go together.

He jumped at the blare of the telephone. The clock radio's red digits read 11.05am.

'Tony, it's me.' Her tone sounded stern. 'What are you doing?'

'Nothing. Just thinking. Waiting for you.'

'How long will you be staying in Aranroe?'

'What? Staying in Aranroe? Why? Is something – '

'I need to know. Two days, two weeks, a year, one hundred years, what?'

'I'm not planning to skip town. If that's what you're thinking. We're going to do things together, aren't we, like we said? Climb Mweelrea, row out to Intinn Island, lots of things, whatever you'd like to do.'

The silence was interrupted only by her laboured breathing.

'Lenny? . . .'

'I have to go away. Two, three days.'

'But, hold on – '

'We'll get together soon, as soon as I get back. You'll be here?'

'Of course I'll be here. But where, where are you going? Why?'

'We'll talk.'

'Lenny, I want to know what – '

'Have to go, Tony. It's not, it's not – '

'Is this like before? Is somebody hassling you? I'll, I'll . . . Lenny, tell me!'

'That's not it! Definitely not.' Her assertiveness brought back to him how she had dealt with her father's intrusion the night before.

'Then tell me. What is it? Why?'

'A few days, Tony. Three, maybe. I'll be back on Sunday. That's the – '

'What? That's what? Where are you going? I want to know. I care about you; can you understand that, can you?'

'I understand. But this is not the time. We'll be together very soon. Sunday, I promise. Have to go now.'

'Lenny, wait! Is this about the train, you waiting at the station? Or that guy Boxer?'

'Nothing like that. I'm going now. I'll see you on Sunday. Believe in me, please. I believe in you.'

'Wait! Lenny! Where on Sunday? Lenny! Lenny!'

*   *   *

During the next two hours he called her private number repeatedly with no response. And each time he dialled the front desk he recognised the voice of the brusque woman from last year, whose badge he could still see: Ms C VanSant, Manager, and hung up.

What would he do now? Even asking the question needled him. This was a strange loneliness, not like what he'd known. He flopped back against the door through which he had watched her leave, and slid to the floor. Aranroe was outside, he thought, the mountains and ocean, the meadows over Silver Strand. But such felt beyond him now. Maybe she too was beyond him, gone, with her secrets.

The morning passed, eventually. He'd go to the Beehive, he decided. No, he'd stay in the room in which she was a ghost in scented space.

The whole day passed, and evening into twilight. After a long night and fitful sleep, hunger forced him out, careworn, unshaven, to the Beehive, where close to midday he ordered coffee and a sandwich at the same table where life had come good forty-eight hours earlier. The street was busier now, but with no cause for awe.

Then he sensed he was being watched by two girls standing close by, one in her early twenties, the other a late teenager. The older girl appeared to wave. He looked around; no one was responding. He returned a half smile. Both girls started toward him, smiling. The older one, shorter and more attractive, in denim jacket and jeans, reached him first.

'Hello, sorry for disturbing you,' she said in a perfectly articulated country accent, 'but would your name be Tony?'

He caught himself, in spite of his gloom, admiring her pale complexion and black curls. The younger girl, with a rosy complexion and plum-streaked mane, just watched.

'I met you once before but you probably wouldn't remember, up at the Abbey,' the first girl said. 'I'm Cilla, Cilla deBurca, and this is Magdalena McCann.'

Then his memory clicked. He straightened up. She was the girl from behind the hotel desk, with the angelic face, when he went in search of Lenny, the girl who had acted like she wanted to tell him something but couldn't.

He got to his feet, stretched out his hand. 'One year ago. I do remember. You haven't changed. Would you like to sit down, have something: coffee, tea?'

'Hope you don't think I'm being nosey. Sure we're not bothering you?'

'No, no, sit down, both of you, please.'

'Maggie – Magdalena, I mean – she has to go; she's got to be home. Today's my day off.'

They bade the younger girl farewell. In conversation with Cilla he detected a manner he found puzzling. An Irish country-girl's way of flirting, he imagined. Whether that or not, he needed to be cautious given the trouble of last year. These were his people, he reminded himself, but this was not his turf.

'Sure I'm not disturbing you? I think Americans are really interesting.'

'I'm as Irish as you. A Dubliner.'

'You're one of us so. That's even better. I remember how you stormed into the Abbey. I was trying to warn you to watch out for Mr Quin. He doesn't like anybody calling in to see Lenny. And that Boxer fella floats around the place; I heard you bumped into him; he's a right eejit, an *amadán.*' Her hand jumped to her mouth. 'Sorry, I shouldn't be cursing.'

'Curse away,' he said. 'I knew you were trying to tell me something, that day at the Abbey, but I was running for a train.'

'Nothing really. Except to warn you that it wouldn't be smart for a nice fella like yourself to be getting into trouble with that big fat bucko Boxer Dunne.'

He caught his internal smirk, turned it into a smile of thanks. Minutes later he wondered again about what he was detecting in her; was it infatuation? 'How did you know I was back in Aranroe?' he asked.

'You serious? Everyone here knows everyone's secrets. That's why part of me'd love to move to Dublin. See, Magdalena's da – his name's Paddy, he drives a taxi – he told her you were here, then she told me, and crazy Mairead at the station told Leo – Leo Reffo, he's the manager at the Abbey – and then Leo told me too, so everybody knows by now, nearly. That's Aranroe for you; it's like a living room. No harm in it, I suppose.'

'You know where Lenny is now?' His tone cut against her easy demeanour.

She stared out toward the street then back at him. 'I know she goes away now and then, that's all. But not where. Magdalena's da probably knows but he'd never tell you, one of the few that doesn't go on with the gossip.'

'You and Lenny are good friends?'

'Wouldn't say best friends. I know her three years, since 1991. She's very nice. And can I tell you something else?'

'I won't say a thing to anyone.'

'It's just that she's not like ordinary country people, or city people. She's kind of a special woman, in a good way. She was out in America for a long while. I heard she was a really famous photographer over there. But I heard America didn't do her any good.'

The more Cilla talked, the more her unadorned nature intrigued him. In an endearing way she seemed blessed with unselfconsciousness, despite seeming also to be holding back when answering some of his questions. Nonetheless, she caused him to recall the girls in Dublin, when he was thirteen and just awakening to female graces. But there was even another quality about her, an aura, something inexpressible. In her fresh, unmade-up face resided the earthiness of the West, probably fused with Spanish genes. She might lead him, he thought, to things he needed to learn.

When they'd finished eating she offered to show him around the locale. She could drive him to spots, she said, known to few humans, and some to none but her. Her talky charm and high spirits, which had already granted him escape from his melancholy, ordained his acceptance.

Her command of her forest green Ford Escort made him feel like he was strapped into a fighter jet, which, he imagined, she'd handle with equal confidence. Around narrow twisting roads the Escort sped, up and down stone-walled boreens and into the purple-patched Sheffrey Hills, then on to Aasleagh Falls on the swirling Erriff river, where they left the car and hiked along the water, overlooked all the way by Mweelrea and Croagh Patrick. Along the trail, Cilla's knowledge of the natural environment poured out. She identified plants and birds, and talked about the builders of lairs and nests. She distinguished lichens from mosses and fungi, and described great glacial flows. And in pointing out hard-to-see curiosities she pulled him into her personal perspective.

They crossed on stones above the falls, adjourned briefly to record the river's babbling rush and swirl, its sweep through space to a foamy moss-green pool. And soon they too began descending, this time along the northern bank, dense with ferns and rushes and here and there riverbed boulders rising up out of the shallows. To his continuing amusement, she handled the rugged terrain with ease.

Later, driving back to the village they detoured to the eastern edge of Doolough Valley and the lake – Loch Doog, as an old stone marker identified it – then stopped along the twisting boreen. From there they hiked through scrub to the water's edge, where giant, swaying reeds whispered like crickets in a mirror loch.

These were sacred waters, the waters of the *caointe*, she told him, said to hold the souls of the dead of tens of thousands of years, since man first walked on Ireland. Bottomless waters that turned coal-black in winter, waters that some said were heard to wail, like spirits weeping for all the suffering of Ireland, often frightening livestock and visitors.

He listened.

To the west, outside the loch's pincer headlands, the whitecaps of the Atlantic raged. Still keeping his thoughts to himself, he imprinted this scene on his mind, savoured the balm of woods and meadow and ocean. Meanwhile, Cilla stared out, wide-eyed, as though absorbing everything.

Despite the wonders of the countryside and the distractions of the loch and ocean, the absence of Lenny began to press harder in his mind. At times, he retreated so deeply into thought that he missed whole chunks of Cilla's commentary. He imagined Lenny at his side, the sky in her eyes, hair tumbling, her smile. Every scene that had captured him, every castle ruin and curiosity, each solitary horse in a thistled field, he saved for her.

Still, he could not deny that Cilla's laughter and wit provided respite. Being with her was effortless. He could be himself, without concern. Haggard and unshaven as he was, she appeared not even to notice. Her joy seemed to spring from her being precisely and only who she was. And her moments all seemed happy. His hours with her, he realised, had been more pleasant than he had anticipated.

Back in Aranroe, Friday night activity was winding down. They strolled past the closed-up shops and sat on the sea wall, picking vinegary chips out of a paper wrapper. An hour later they headed back to the Escort and were soon driving again, this time to Old Head, where they watched the gradual purpling of water and sky, and Inishturk and the islands fade.

'You must be tired,' Tony said on the way back to Aranroe, after a period of mutual quiet.

'Me? Not at all.' The definiteness in her tone returned him to silence, which went on until the village lights appeared.

'Up ahead is Aranroe Hill,' she said. 'We go left. Where you're staying is just a couple of fields past my place.'

He broke into laughter. 'Sorry. It's just that I've never heard that expression – fields past.'

With no acknowledgement of him, she revved the engine, down-shifted the gears, then sped out onto the hill.

'I really had a good time,' he said. 'I had fun, thanks to you. I really appreciate – '

'Why are you thanking me? Don't be doing that. Alright for a Friday night, I suppose.'

She whirled the Escort off the road and braked to a stop. 'My house, number 9.' She gestured to a small strip of modern cottages. 'Coming in? Nice cup of tea? It's just me there, no one else, except Duke. Wouldn't worry about him though; he's a dog.' A smile filled her face. 'Oh no, I'm telling a lie. He's not there, I keep forgetting, he's away till Sunday, over at the kennels in Castlebar, trying to, you know; he's on his honeymoon, you could say.' She tried to contain her amusement. 'Don't mind me, I'm mad. I laugh at meself all the time. So c'mon, you coming in?'

Her invitation assumed his compliance, and her stare did not veer from him.

'I think I'm just now feeling the jet lag, I'm drained,' he said unconvincingly. 'But listen, thanks, I mean that. I had a really good time.'

'C'mon out of that; a cup of tea won't kill you. And I promise I won't either. Safe enough?'

He dug a second time for the least hurtful words, which didn't arrive quickly enough.

'You wouldn't have to go back to the B&B later, if you're tired,' she said, 'unless you wanted to. I've tons of room. You could stay in bed in the morning, sleep off your jet lag, go whatever time you want. I'll be gone at seven; I'm on breakfast, but I'll be home at half-ten then back in at half-eleven then off at two. And tomorrow night they're having a big céili in the hall; we could go, if you like céilis. Great craic. C'mon, you're coming in.'

'I don't think I will, Cilla. But thanks. I can walk to the B&B. I can see it from here; you don't have to pull out again.'

'Stay in,' she said without charm. 'Takes a minute, no more.'

He laboured to breathe life into their nearness but all that happened was disconnected small talk. Then to his surprise he discovered himself deep in imagination. Her closeness had lulled him from admiration of her into fantasies he was indulging.

She slung a glance his way and in that instant her smile exposed him. 'I knew you were staring at me!' she said triumphantly. 'Is it because you think I'm nice looking?'

He scrambled mentally for a way out. Before he could utter a word she caught him with a look of reproof. 'Or is it that you take to all girls who aren't afraid to drive fast or climb rocks?'

'I'm really sorry . . . I didn't mean to – '

'Sorry and thanks, thanks and sorry and thanks. Will you stop! What are you sorry for? Don't be a silly man; it doesn't bother me. The woman that doesn't want to be admired wasn't born.'

Outside his B&B she turned to him with an air of softness. 'All I was wondering was, was, if you thought I'm, you know, if I'm pretty, that's all.' She drew in a loud breath and left him alone in silence, for a moment. 'Ah listen, don't pay me any mind. That wasn't a fair question.'

'No, no, I do. It was fair. I mean I think you are, definitely you're pretty, very.'

'Would you, would you say I'm beautiful? Gorgeous like? Not just ordinary pretty? Would you?' Her face waited; eyes watching him twitch and strain. Then her hands shot to her face, she erupted with laughter, her cheeks blushing. It took just a second for him to join her for her glee was a gigantic release from the fix she had put him in. Their convulsions fed off each other, rising and subsiding and rising again, until eventually they settled into calmer merriment.

'You poor thing. I'm really, really a messer. God'll never forgive me. You shouldn't pay me any mind, I'm a silly person.'

'Yes, you are, you're a messer. But I didn't tell a lie.'

'You didn't? You mean you think I am nice looking?'

'Of course.'

'Thanks. And thanks for being a good sport. Fellas around here would never tell girls things like that. You know, I never forgot you from last year, that day at the Abbey, you were drenched, dripping rain all over the place, and Charity Van Sant was fuming. But she didn't frighten you one bit.'

'Oh yes, she did! I was trying not to show it. I remember you too.'

He noticed now that something he had just done or said, he had no idea what, had brought a pleasure-full meditation to her face. Clearly, her thoughts were playing for her a private reverie. He reached for the door handle.

'Wait! Sure you don't feel like a nice cup of tea? Or something stronger?'

'Maybe another time.' As he spoke, his mind travelled a line from the tip of her retrousse nose, down over red lips and bare neck, to her breasts. 'Thanks again for the ride,' he said anxiously.

'Glass of Jameson?' she asked. 'I promise I won't tease you any more. Scout's honour.'

'Another time,' he said, realising that he was still considering her invitation, and that his compliment was not flattery; beautiful she was.

Her smile spilled disappointment. He pushed open the door, stepped out of the car.

'Wait,' she called out, leaning across the passenger seat, chin raised. He hesitated, then kissed her. Light as the kiss was, from both of them, she remained closed-eyed for moments longer, then pulled herself upright. 'I had a brilliant time,' she said in a voice more serious and personal than he had heard from her before. 'Interested in the céili tomorrow night?'

'I'll keep it in mind.'

'You're different. You know that?' she said, thrust the gear stick forward and accelerated away.

*　　*　　*

Next day, Saturday, the day before Lenny would be back, he rose early, tense and un-rested. Maybe she'd surprise him, arrive today, in time for breakfast at the Beehive.

But time crawled by, filled with confusion, too much thinking.

The avocado telephone sat silent to his glare and wish. Sometime in mid-morning he propped himself against the pine headboard for another attempt at reading *Borstal Boy*. Soon he hurled the book at the wall. Reading was impossible, every line derailed. He retrieved the book. Now he allowed passages to float away. Occasionally, Behan's familiar world spirited him off into interludes, only to be drawn back by sounds of doors opening and closing and a compulsion to stare at the phone.

A long while later he dialled the reception desk for the time, which he already knew: 6.24pm. Later he made the same call, asked if anyone had tried to reach him, a message of any kind. Room 17. Tony MacNeill. Anything?

Yes. There was a note, he was told, in his box. A woman, didn't leave her name, telephoned at 4 o'clock, asked the clerk to take down a message for Room 17, for Mr MacNeill. That was it.

Why had no one told him, he asked. He got the note from the desk, read it, crumpled it, flung it across the tiled lobby as the clerk watched. He then retrieved it and re-read it:

Saturday, September 3rd 1994

Dear Tony,
  Will not be returning to Aranroe until Tuesday.
  Sorry. I hope to see you then.

  LQ

*   *   *

Shortly after eight o'clock something stirred outside his room. He listened, waited, pressed his ear to the door. Rustling, moving. He pulled open the door. In front of him, behind dark glasses, smiling, as if awaiting his approval, it was her, for an instant.

But suddenly it wasn't; it wasn't Lenny Quin.

9

1971

<small>Outside Aranroe</small>

Streams of blue chimney smoke billowed from the thatched cottage into an unpredictable sky. Still no one answered the knocks. The uniformed girl and the erect, black-coated man sought refuge by the front door from a crisp November wind.

'See, I told you. They're away in the vegetable beds,' the girl said, her long auburn hair in turmoil. 'When a gable gate is open you've always to go around back; everyone knows that.'

The man tugged at her, talked into her face. 'Watch that tongue of yours, young lady. I've spoken to you about your cheek, haven't I?' He then yanked his collar higher and rapped harder at the wooden door.

'You're a silly person; I bet you don't even know that,' the girl said.

'Listen you! I'm taking no more of your guff; do I make – '

'What is it?' Leo Reffo appeared at the gate by the gable, his earth-stained forearms protruding from tightly-rolled sleeves.

'Good day to you, Mr Quin,' the man said, approaching.

'The name is – ' Leo stopped, left his sentence unfinished. His questioning eyes connected with the girl's, then shifted back to the man. 'What can I do for you?'

'I'm Turlough O'Riordan, the new inspector for St Agnes's. I have an item here to show you.' He pulled outward on his heavy coat and began searching inside. As he did, Leo slipped the girl a knowing nod. 'Appears I've left the papers in the car,' the man said. 'I'll get them.'

'No need,' Leo said. 'Something the matter? Why's this lassie not in school?'

'They wouldn't let me sit in sixth class for English, that's why.' The girl's high-pitched voice flung out the words. 'They wouldn't let me because they said, they said that – '

'Please! Why don't you allow me to explain, young la – '

'No, no harm,' Leo interjected. 'Let Lenny go first, then you can tell me. If that's not a problem with you, Mr O'Riordan.'

The man's face tightened. He said nothing.

'They won't let me sit in sixth class for English any more, and Mr MacMathuna always lets me, and they tried to make me stand in the corner. And I did nothing wrong. Nothing!' She paused, breathing hard, features jumping. 'I don't care, I don't care, I'm not standing in the stupid corner ever, ever, ever, I don't care, I won't!' With a jerk she turned her back to the men and her face up to the mountains.

'You see, Mr Quin? You see?' The man's glare switched from Leo to the child and back to Leo. 'See this? Her behaviour has been a problem for some time, I'm reliably informed. And we have just not been able – '

'Hold your horses there,' Leo said. 'Before you head off on that road, tell me what she did; what's this all about today?'

'I didn't do anything, I, I – '

'Shhh, shhh.' Leo placed a finger to his lips. 'Lenny, dear, let Mr O'Riordan tell me, please. Then'll come your turn again.'

'Thank you.' The man said sharply. 'We just cannot continue allowing Leonora into the higher classes. She seems unwilling to accept that she's twelve; she must stay with the twelve-year-olds, in fifth class, not sixth, for all her subjects.' He turned to Lenny, 'Fifth, not sixth!'

'They're all stupid in fifth. I want to be in sixth. Mr MacMathuna said I could and he – '

'That's enough, young lady. Mr MacMathuna is gone. He won't be setting foot inside St Agnes's ever again, not as long as I'm – '

'Tell me, Mr O'Riordan, what caused this? Was it something Lenny did?'

'Yes, it was. And I might add that Sister was expecting responses to both notes she sent home with the child. Just today, Leonora defiantly refused to return to her class when requested to do so, and she's been having an upsetting effect on her fellow pupils. And if that wasn't enough, she was obstreperous with the principal, Reverend Mother DeLellis.'

'You'll have to explain to me what you mean by that word, about Lenny and the nun.'

'Obstreperous? She was obstreperous, obstreperous, with Reverend Mother. And other teachers. Repeatedly obstreperous; I have that on good authority.'

'I'm still no wiser what you're saying. You're using that same word. Just tell me what you mean.'

'Impertinent. Impudent. Insolent. A half a dozen times or more. It would appear, too, that Leonora believes it's perfectly alright to take items that are the property of other children.'

'I'm not a child! I'm twelve and three quarters. And nobody ever ever calls me Leonora. Nobody! Why can't everybody just let me alone!'

Leo said nothing, just placed a hand on Lenny's shoulder as she locked her arms across her chest and turned away once more.

'Now, about Sister's notes,' the man said to Leo, hiking his eyebrows for a response.

'Aye, the notes.' Leo's words firmed. 'A response is in order alright. But there's no reason I can see not to address matters now, seeing that you're here. You say you're new to the parish; did anyone tell you that Lenny is top of her class in every subject bar one or maybe two, out of eleven subjects?'

'Twelve. Twelve subjects,' Lenny insisted. 'I do religion too.'

'As I was saying, that may or may not be the case – '

'It is the case,' Leo cut in. 'Look, as I see it, it'd be fair if you'd accept that she's not the usual pupil, if you get what I'm saying. Looks to me like you're bent on turning her into something she's not; you're trying to hay-tie her.'

'The rules are the same for every pupil, Mr Quin. Every pupil. Without exception. Not that we're insensitive about the mother being deceased, Lord have mercy on her soul. But despite that, we simply cannot – '

'You can't make an exception. That's what you're saying. Even though she's exceptional and we all agree on that? Why not? She's not thirteen yet, but she's won a medal for the school at the Young Scientist Exhibition in Dublin last year, and two more in the schools competitions, and other awards. What does that tell you, man?'

'Seven medals I won!' Lenny shouted without turning, and held up seven ink-stained fingers, a few bearing only half a finger-nail. 'No other girl in St Agnes's won any.'

'Seven it is,' Leo said.

'Evidently, Mr Quin, you're not willing to see this from St Agnes's point of view. Nor do you appear to appreciate Reverend Mother's difficulties.'

'I'll see it from my own point of view first, Mr O'Riordan. And what manner of difficulties are you meaning?'

'I thought I'd made myself clear. Reverend Mother has reported to me that the child – '

'I'm not a child!'

'That the child – '

'I'm not a child!'

'That she has too many times acted obstreperously with teachers. Plus, she takes what she wants, regardless of whose it is.' The man's increasing emphasis shot arcs of spit into the air. 'And, and, she asserted recently, in front of the full class, that she knows more than Miss Trimble, the maths teacher. All round she's been stubborn and uncooperative. Those are the good Sister's actual words, not mine. Which, if I'm not mistaken, were stated in both her notes.'

'Enough said. I'll have a word with her. On one condition: that you do the same with the school. Tell them take it a bit easier. She's a bright student. Make an exception now and then. Bend your rules. Would harm no one. You don't have to break them. That's what I'm asking.'

'I sympathise, I do, Mr Quin. But school is not like a farm. It's standard policy to treat every child the same, and for as long as I'm the area inspector that's how it shall remain. Good day to you. I'll be driving her back now.'

'No! I'm not going back, ever!' Lenny clung to Leo's jacket. 'They all hate me there. I hate them, I hate them, I hate them.'

'Lenny, listen to me,' Leo said.

'No, I won't go back. I won't!' She spun away, teeth clenched, fists thrown down by her sides.

'Lenny, darling.' She retreated out of Leo's reach. 'You want to be a great scientist, you have to go to school. Everyone – '

She backed farther away, her bearing unchanged.

'There! Just like I've been saying. I'll deal with this.' The man grabbed Lenny's blazer at the shoulder. 'You, are coming with me, right now.'

Leo's right hand thrust forward, grabbed the lapel of the inspector's big black coat. 'Better you'd wait in your car, Mr O'Riordan,' he said. The men's breaths mingled in the air. For a moment neither moved.

'I'll talk to her. Alone. Right?' Leo's words carried conciliation but bore still an expectation of compliance.

In that moment Lenny took off, arms and legs pumping, up through the dandelion field, auburn tresses skying wild behind her, swept back by her abandon and haste, until she crested the closest hillock and merged into the meadow.

A while later, Leo found her hunkered amid the mountain grasses, weaving a string of flowers, consumed. His interruption drew from her an exuberant greeting.

'Look what I made, a necklace,' she said.

'Very nice. Now you should wear it.'

She shook her head. 'It's for you. It's nearly ready.'

'Listen to me, Princess. The inspector's gone, but you can't do that ever again. You can't let on I'm your father and this is where you live. This is very serious. Your father needs to be told what's happening at school. He'll talk to them and sort it out. Is that clear?'

Her indecipherable whispers flowed on, as though she were lost to a world woven by imagination and ink-stained fingers.

'Lenny? Are you listening?'

'Where's Aunt Peg?'

'She's at the market in Louisburg. Did you hear what I said?'

'I'll tell him. When I see him.'

'Better head up to your own place now. Go up by Grimes's field; I don't want you down near the paddock; the bull's there. Off with you now. I'll be watching.'

Lenny held up the flower chain with both hands. He lifted his cap, bowed his head, and accepted it.

'You look nicer now,' she said, bright and smiling. And in a flash she galloped down toward the paddock, where she stopped to fling a clump of earth at the staring beast, then ran along the hedging and all the way up the rise to Claire Abbey.

10

'Hi,' he said, holding the door, his voice energyless.

'You can't be that sad to see me. How do I look? I got all fancied up for you; I thought you'd like this better than muddy jeans.'

'I don't feel up to it, Cilla.' His words grumbled out, devoid of courtesy or pretence.

'Well, myself, I think I look nice. You could ask me in.'

'No. Place is a pig sty.'

'Well c'mon then, get your céili shoes on. You look like a bit of a dance couldn't do you any harm. And you don't have to worry, I won't drive fast. I promise.' She closed one eye and drew a cross on the right side of her chest. 'Or I hope to die.'

'Cilla – '

'Oh c'mon, stop it, will you.'

'I'm not up to it, I told you. Anyway, I can't – '

'You can't dance? If that's what you're trying to say don't bother 'cause neither can I. I never could. Who cares? I just thought – '

As her brightness faded he noted again the unadorned country girl: her paleness and green eyes, the sense of humour of someone who had never had to endure terrible suffering.

'Cilla – '

'Wasn't easy coming here. I wanted to see you, that's all. And I don't give a cow's shite whether your name's Michael Flatley or Tony whatever-it-is!'

The hurt in her disturbed him. Even more, feeling this close to her spirit, her courage to go after what she wanted, a quality he too was committed to in this outside world. He could not deny her his admiration. Neither could he let it get out of hand, become more than it could be.

'Right. Bye!' She started away.

He let her go until she had travelled too far into his pain.

'Cilla. Hold on. Give me ten minutes. Meet you in the lobby. Okay?'

Her face lost its gloom, flashed him a cheeky smirk. She wobbled away as he watched, on clicking heels, her spunk and the swish of her baggy suit infatuating him. Half-way along the corridor she turned. 'Don't have to go dancing. Probably break me neck in these suicide shoes. Then I'd have to sue you for millions.'

In Nalty's Bar on Crispin Street a table carnation and the spill of light from a street-lamp provided atmosphere, augmented by low strains of traditional Irish music. Cilla enquired of the waiter if he might have a full-bodied shiraz or cabernet not shown on the wine list. He had, he reported, a Wolf Blass cabernet-merlot. That would be fine, she told him, and ordered a bottle. Tony just observed.

'It's on me,' she said. 'I hope you like it. It's from Australia. I got very grand working with Leo Reffo; he knows all the wines from everywhere, better than I ever will. I used to think Dom Perignon was the head fella in the mafia.'

She had begun working at Claire Abbey, she told him, in February of 1991, when she was going on twenty, just before Lenny came home from the Middle East. In the three-and-a-half years since then she hadn't once seen Charles and his daughter acting warmly toward each other. They hardly ever sat down for a cup of tea together, not in the hotel anyway. Charles would often be away for weeks, off gallivanting in America, something to do with big mining companies, probably making a fortune. When he was home, she reported, he stayed in his private house on the golf course, and he always carried his portable computer with him, every place he went, and he was very touchy about it, never let it out of his sight, like it was gold or something. One time he forgot it, left it under a table at the Abbey, then all of a sudden he stormed back in, straight through the middle of a whole bunch of nice Japanese tourists, and he grabbed it with a terrible face on him and stormed back out.

And that Charity one, Cilla went on, she'd been the manager, if you could call her that, for four years, since Charles brought her over from cowboy land. She took orders from no one only him. Plenty of times she made a mess of things, even Lenny had to stop her doing daft stuff, real eejity things, had to tell her to do it the way Leo did it, like the set-ups for St Patrick's Day or the races or the holidays, things like that. She hadn't a notion about what's important, only wanted to boss everybody around. But Lenny never got involved with the hotel, or with other people, she just kept to herself. Once in a while she and Leo would have lunch together, or he'd bring coffee and sandwiches into the staff room for the two of them and they'd talk. He asked her loads of times to help him run the place, and she'd have been brilliant at it, but she always said no, she didn't want to be a manager, just to do her own things, and read books, and she always went walking on the beach and up in the hills, even when it was raining, and she brought her camera with her everywhere.

As Cilla talked, the downpour outside began pick-pocking against the window. A little later, with her wine glass in one hand, she held aloft on her fork a single asparagus spear and peered over it at him.

'Now that I filled you in on all the scandal, what'll we talk about?'

He sipped his wine. 'You.'

'Me? I'm only a nice-looking culchie,' she said, her face play-acting. 'Well, I think I'm nice looking. Least, last night that's what you said. But I'm definitely a culchie; I'm sure about that.' She wrinkled her brow. 'Stop staring at me, will you, you're making me nervous. Bet you don't even know what a culchie is?'

''Course I do; didn't I grow up here. It means a country person. It's not a compliment though, right?'

'What's the harm. I'm a culchie, I'm from the bog. You're a jackeen, you're from the big smoke. So what? Except I'm better looking than you. And a better driver. And I can climb better. But you're not too bad. Really, you're kind of an okay climber. I've seen better, though.' She stopped prattling, as though suddenly concerned. 'Listen, I hope you know I'm only messing, I'm pulling your leg, I swear, I'm not serious, about nothing.'

From behind his wine glass he had sunk into her enjoyment of herself, her no-off-switch humour, the delight she took in poking fun at him, her being just who she was and what she was. How free. Now his thoughts returned to her looks, to her lamp-lit features and unedited joys. She had taken of late to drifting off for brief interludes into a smiling quiet. And right now she was gazing into her glass like it were a crystal ball, as though fascinated by what she was finding.

His mind jumped around, in wonder at where she might take him next. She had an unburdened style, tricks, things that held his interest, kept him excited. But moods too, implied more than shown; he could sense that in her. Being with her was like speeding on a river of blind bends, adventures at every turn, new depths, new dangers. Her possibilities stripped him of thoughts he needed to shed, made him feel vulnerable, young, alive, that he was really learning about living. His hand reached distractedly for the newly uncorked bottle of Wolf Blass and almost tipped it over, which drew from her a shriek that turned into uproarious laughter, and he filled both glasses.

'What are you thinking right this second?' she asked with sharp inquisition.

'What? . . . I don't, I mean I wasn't.'

'Yes, you were. I know what you're thinking. You can tell me; I'm brilliant at keeping secrets.'

'Secrets? Wasn't thinking anything like that. You were telling me about you, remember? What life is like living in County Mayo; last back yard before Boston, you said.'

'Me and Mayo? Nothing else to tell. Yours truly is twenty-three going on twenty-three and a half. Think I told you that at least five times. Maybe I told you three times, I don't remember now. Must be the water in this place, probably spiked with poteen. You can't trust poteen.

'Anyway, I'll try to be soberious and tell you a bit more. My step-mam and step-dad run a tiny little farm outside Killadoon; they're getting on now, really old, God bless them. They adopted me really late. Both of them'll be eighty-eight this year, both in the same month, November.'

'Eighty-eight? That's fantastic. And they're well and still run the farm and – '

The first signs of upset entered her face.

'Is everything alright, Cilla. You feeling okay?'

Seconds after covering her face with her hands she lost herself in another outburst of laughter.

'I'm really, really, really sorry. I'm not adopted. I'll stop, I promise, I will. No more. I can't stop. No, I will stop. Holy God'll never forgive me.

'Seriously, Killadoon is where I grew up. I'm being serious now. On the farm, milking cows, feeding sheep, all sorts of sexy things like that. Especially when the bull came to kiss the heifers; will I tell you about that? Will I?'

She was on a roll again. He leaned back, absorbing. A while passed before it burst into his mind, his years in hells they called correctional facilities, all the decent living he'd been deprived of, his own inner hell and the baggage he was carrying. He castigated his brain, refused to go along; wasn't this wet night in Ireland what he had hungered for for all those years, fourteen in all, since he'd first lost the plot in Newark. Hadn't he earned the right to this dream, this wit and conversation, this laughter.

'No, no, it really was,' she said, misreading his face. 'It was great, the farm. When I look back I remember I couldn't wait to get out, go off someplace. That's how I went to work in Galway; I was eighteen. Only forty miles away but me mam and dad wouldn't talk to me. I was away ten months, then I came home. That's when Leo Reffo gave me a job as a waitress. It's him that runs the Abbey, not Chastity Van Superwoman. And now look at me: here I am, merry, not drunk, just merry, on me way to being locked thanks to you topping up my glass when I wasn't looking.'

'Me? I wouldn't – '

She waved away his protest. 'Do you not know me by now?' she said. 'And I forgot to tell you. I have four brothers, no sisters, and I'm the baby. That's it. Told you everything. Now you're laughing at me.'

'No, no, I'm not laughing, not at you. It's just the way you tell it, your life. Some people would die, many would, to have had your life.'

'Never thought of it that way. So, what's good for the goose is good for the gander. Not that I'm a goose. Tell me everything about you, and no lies.' She placed a hand on his arm, spoke with the affectation of a counsellor. Just relax, let everything out, you can trust me. You're in good hands, so to speak.'

'Nah.' He shook his head. 'Your life, you've done a lot more than me. I was born on a cold stormy night in February 1966. Went missing in 1980. That's all I remember. Until eighteen months ago.'

'You were in a coma for fourteen years? Stop messing! I want to know. I'm trying to be serious; it's very hard for me. Go on, I'm waiting.'

'The headlines, that's it: Born in Dublin, loved Dublin. Left Ireland the day after I turned fourteen. Never to be heard from again.' He looked directly into her scrutiny, tried to smile, but couldn't. 'Sorry. I mean the whole family emigrated to America. Newark, New Jersey, big strange city beside New York City. I hated it, and it never got better. Felt like my whole life had been ripped away. Then recently I moved out west, to Arizona, then came home to Ireland to visit, last summer, as you already know, first time back since I was fourteen. Wanted to climb a mountain or two. And here I am.'

'What about your mam and dad, brothers, sisters, cat, dog, goldfish, pet crocodile? Where are they all?'

'My mother lives in Florida. My father died when I was a teenager. Kate, my eldest sister, lives in Dublin; she's a shrink, a psychotherapist. Two other sisters live in Atlantic City, in New Jersey. Look at that rain! I wonder if it means it's too late in the season to climb Mweelrea.'

'Means you're trying to get out of telling me things. You're full of secrets; I can tell. Bet you have a steady girlfriend in America. You could even be married or divorced for all I know.'

'No girlfriend, no wife, no divorce.'

'Asking too many questions, am I?'

'We probably should get moving. It's eleven-forty-five.'

'No, it's not; it's a quarter to twelve. Afraid you'll turn into a frog?'

'You're right, a quarter to twelve. I'm in Ireland. Have to re-member that.'

'We're parked all the way up in the village. We'll get soaked for our sins; I mean skins, shins, soaked to our – ah, feck it, you know what I mean; we'll get drowned, and it's all your fault.'

'If you're willing, I am,' he said, then blushed. 'To get wet, I mean.'

'If I show you mine, you'll show me yours.' Eyes glassy and warm, she tried to smother her giggling. 'Don't mind me, I don't know what I'm saying. Let's walk it, why not. Be a bit of fun getting wet together. I can barely move in these stupid shoes; I'll end up on me arse. Rear-end, I mean. Sorry, sometimes I forget to speak respectable.'

Arms entwined, they huddled first in Nalty's doorway, peering out beyond their security, into a stormy world. Cilla unbuckled her shoes and hooked them over her arm. 'I'll walk barefeeted. I mean footless. Feck it, I mean no shoes on me.' She reached for his hand and found it. 'Now's good a time, want to go for it?'

They sailed along the gleaming pavements in the pouring rain, neither speaking nor hurrying. And the feeling came to him again: home! Out of nowhere, this was home, an epiphany of a different kind than he'd felt before. Here he had no past but an innocent one, no record but that which he chose to reveal; here the brand new him and the original him could combine, minus the terrors he had lived with for too long. So much less to conquer now. Was it Cilla deBurca? What she permitted him to be?

Soon they fell into the car, saturated, lost to the gaiety of it all. Cilla pushed back her dripping black mane, tucked curlicue strands behind her ears, then glanced blissfully at him. 'Nice cup of hot tea?'

'Want me to drive?' he asked.

She was never incapable, she told him, and it was only half-way up the hill they were going. Minutes later they were safely inside Number 9, Connemara Court. 'The bathroom's behind you,' she said. 'There's a big white robe behind the door; you can use that. I'll dump all the wet stuff in the dryer.' Her look questioned him. 'Go on, I won't come in. You don't have to be shy, you're only a wet man! I'll change in the loft; that's where I sleep.'

He didn't move.

'What's wrong? Go on, I'm not messing. Then I'll put the kettle on. We can have scones, if you're hungry. I baked them myself this afternoon; took me hours. I even put cherries from Italy in them, make them taste even better.'

He shuffled backwards, smiling at her cheekiness and lies, knowing she was reading his thoughts. He bolted the bathroom door behind him. She was right, the robe was large. When he had dried off, he wrapped it tightly around his nakedness, triple knotted the belt, and resigned himself to her inevitable teasing.

They arrived in the kitchen simultaneously in matching robes, he in white, she in pink. More than once she bit back a snicker as they sat at opposite sides of the café-style table. And with her humour even more loose and animated, their conversational ease resumed and remained fluid.

A while later she struggled to her feet. 'If I don't get to sleep now I'll be serving breakfast like a zombie. Follow me; I'll show you where I'm putting you.'

He faked nonchalance, tried to conceal his puzzlement. Especially after last night, when she had all but insisted on being kissed. Now though, he could not deny what had been simmering under his enjoyment of her, the excitement that had been pressing him to decide how far he could let things go. In silent observance he followed the shapeful bathrobe through hall and lounge to a sofa made up into a bed.

'You'll be alright here? Isn't Claire Abbey but it's comfy.'

'Perfect. I'll be fine. Great.'

'See,' she said, pointing toward the window. 'The silver moon. I often sit here at night. Looking out at all the eyes in the sky looking back at me.'

Neither said anything, just gazed at the heavens.

'Does that sound kinda too – '

'Poetic?'

'Mushy?'

'No way! No way is it mushy. It's artistic, sensitive; it's nice.'

'If you're true to your word, Tony MacNeill, you must be the only man in Ireland who thinks like that. You aren't having me on, are you?'

'I mean what I said. How many men have you asked?'

'Enough,' she said, still fixed on the stars. 'Enough to know better.'

'Wrong kind of men.'

'I was sure there was only one kind. Up to not that long ago.' She turned abruptly and swept past him, 'Night,' she said, sounding wounded.

'Goodnight, Cilla. And thanks.' His call chased after her through the moonlit room. He cringed, wished he had chosen different words. Then he gave his attention back to the silver moon, the eyes in the sky that looked back in. What might they reveal of her, he wondered, this richer, deeper, different Cilla deBurca?

Behind him he sensed a presence.

'Sorry,' she said matter-of-factly. 'I'll be away in the morning, before seven. Sundays are early starts, but I'll finish at two. Weather's to be fine. Want to take a stab at Mweelrea, part way?'

He said nothing, just stared at her.

'And I forgot to give you your goodnight kiss,' she said without humour, as though a more resolute woman had taken over. She stretched up, and near his mouth placed a slow kiss.

He held her gently, her heavy black hair cool to his skin, still infused with rain. A rarely nurtured part of him urged his arms to clasp her, his mouth to kiss her, his hands to tease her damp curls. No one, save Lenny, ever stoked him so intensely, or made him feel so desired for himself, the youthful uncorrupted him.

They each conspired to hold, as though cautious of what the moment offered. Then his hands tightened around her, while the fight inside his head raged against surrender to the feel of her body against his, her touchable nearness. Then Lenny spoke. And everything in him obeyed. His eyes met Cilla's. Words were not needed. She turned away.

'See you,' she said in a barely audible voice.

11

By early afternoon the next day, Sunday, waiting for Lenny was becoming impossible. At Greyfriars B&B Hotel he paced the small room, more on edge than at any time since the day he tasted freedom. The hours passed into night.

On Monday the shaking in his hands returned. He swore at the affliction, which had not struck since his early days in Rahway State Prison, when he was twenty-one. It had begun suddenly then, one week after he had ended the savage reign of Shift Commander King Kong Yablonski, and didn't give up for 213 days, each scratched into a cell wall.

Right now the greatest good that could come to him was to know Lenny's whereabouts and that she was safe. An hour, she'd first said, maybe two, until she'd be back. Then not till Sunday. Then Tuesday. He wasn't accepting it, not this time, after a day and night that replayed constantly in his mind. Chill out, the voice in him warned, go out, walk, read, just twenty-four hours to go. But how many minutes? How many scratches in a cell wall? Hold off, just wait. No, he wouldn't. There were no rules here, nothing forcing him to wait, no screws, no wolf dogs, no electric fences, no leg chains; he could do anything he wanted; and fuck it, he would! He swiped his jacket from the bed.

As he neared the top of the hill the Atlantic breeze whipped at him. Just then, the green Escort slowed, swung around, drew up alongside him, twenty yards from the entrance to Claire Abbey.

'Let me guess,' Cilla shouted from the car. 'You were coming to meet me getting off work?'

'Can I talk to you? Something serious.'

She nodded, as though with an intuition that what she was agreeing to would cause her strife.

He squatted down by the car window. 'Something's not right with Lenny; I can feel it. She said she'd be back yesterday; then a message said Tuesday. Something crazy is going on. You'd tell me, wouldn't you, if you knew?'

'I don't know. I don't know where she is. What're you doing here?'

'Going inside, talk to her father. What else can I do?'

'He's away, someplace foreign. Charity's there. But you wouldn't – '

'Will you help? As a friend?'

She turned her face away.

'I know it's not fair, Cilla. I know all about that. But you're the only one.'

'We have a key, inside, for her apartment. Not saying that'd be a right thing to do.'

'I swear, Cilla, I won't involve you. You've got my word.'

'And you and me,' she said. 'What d'you think? Anything in that?'

'Cilla – '

'Forget it. Dreaming, that's all. You want the key?'

'Listen, Cilla – '

'Forget it; it's okay. It's your life.'

'I won't forget it.'

'Men are just brilliant at saying things like that.'

'I mean it.'

'You'd have to look like a golfer. That Charity one has eyes in her big fat Maggie Thatcher hairdo.' She pulled repeatedly at a dangling curl.

He watched but didn't intrude.

'Gets into a fit if she sees a tiny little mouse. Even afraid of bumble bees.'

'Cilla . . .'

'Imagine. Bumble bees. Afraid.'

'Cilla . . .'

'Wait here. I'll get you a golf trolley. Colin owes me a favour, the greens-keeper. Pull it after you, in around the back, act like you're a golfer. Her apartment has a birdhouse in front of it. I'll be back, few minutes.'

Staring out, he rode the giant breakers ripping the coast and tried to look inconspicuous to passing traffic. Invariably, he found himself returning waves. Ten minutes passed. It was getting harder to stay calm; his mind flitted with calamities of all kinds. After a while he turned his back on Claire Abbey, gazed south to Mweelrea, purple and brown and bare. Twenty minutes. Something's gone wrong, he suspected. The day was duller now, just a watery sun. Storm brewing, maybe; noisy wind, no gulls crying. He pulled his watch out of his pocket. Twenty-five minutes.

Then it ended. Spitting stones on the shoulder, the Escort pulled up inches from him.

*   *   *

Peering from under the cap Cilla had provided, he hauled the trolley along the path, rounded the castle wall. Suddenly footsteps sounded, approaching, from beyond the border hedging. He froze, in sight of the birdhouse, caught a glimpse of her through a gap. Reflex set him back in stride. From around the turn the figure took form, the VanSant woman, marching toward him. He couldn't run. Maybe she wouldn't even look at him, or notice his climbing boots. If she did, the game was up. He speeded up. Before she got to him his shaking fingers held the peak of his cap, tipped it up and down, obscuring his face. She passed without a nod. He recorded her fading heel-stabs in the cinder. At the next break in the hedging he ducked in, checked, she had vanished.

At his shoulder stood the birdhouse, beyond it the brown door bearing the Liffey God knocker Cilla had described. With the trolley concealed, he reconnoitred his surroundings, then pushed twice on the doorbell, with no response. A minute later he was inside, standing stiff and quiet.

He called out a greeting, expecting no answer, but wondering if someone answered, whose voice it would be. And what he might say, or do. Heart pumping, he crept in. The apartment seemed big. But not noiseless. He called out again, and waited. No answer came. A minute passed. Maybe he should leave, he thought. He had no right. What if he walked in on something that was none of his business? Or was caught inside? Prison, not that he was ever going back. But the thought was unnerving. He should go, get out now; he'd do that, he decided. Then keys rattled. Outside. The scrape of someone at the door, coming in, into Lenny's apartment. The door bolt turned. Seconds earlier he had noticed a bicycle wheel poking out of an alcove. Now he swept the curtain aside, ducked in, lying as he landed, in semi-darkness, hard edges poking into him.

As daylight burst into the hall he steadied the curtain, tried to muffle his breathing. His legs would have to wait, so too whatever was sticking into his back. Through the gap at the floor his eyes followed a pair of men's black polished shoes squeaking into and out of downstairs rooms, sometimes doubling back, then climbing the stairs, no one calling out in expectation of finding anyone home. Then came sounds of drawers being pulled out and pushed back in, and then the man coming back down the stairs, stopping in front of the alcove, an arm's length away, followed by a phone being dialled.

'Dominick, where are you?' the demanding voice asked. 'Leave that. Come over to Leonora's place. Bring my cart.' Then a pause. 'No! I said leave that. Get over here. Now, please.'

The accent sounded American, Tony thought. So the body in the shoes was Charles Quin, probably. And Dominick was Boxer Dunne, now on his way over. It made sense. In another way it made no sense.

Growing achey and with sweat stinging his eyes, he put a picture on every sound, tried to place the footfalls. He braced himself for exposure, how he'd explain his presence, what he'd say, what he'd do. He'd be compelled to act, if only to run, as a last resort. Then the feet creaked the stairs, ascending again, moved about, seemingly searching for something.

He tried to reposition; his muscles had cramped. A slight roll provided some relief and a better view of the hall.

The door knocker clacked twice. New feet appeared.

'Mr Quin, I'm here.' It was a man's voice tainted with the politeness of subservience. He plodded past the curtained alcove, deeper into the apartment, emitting cologne.

'Dominick!' the man upstairs shouted.

The scuffed sneakers scooted back to the front door. 'Right here, boss.'

'Did I tell you to come in?'

'Just standing here, boss, just waiting for you to tell me what you want me to do.'

'You have the cart?'

'All ready to go. Got here rapid, like you said. I brought your clubs in case you might have forgot to remember to tell me.'

'Wait outside. Pull the front door.'

Tony caught sight of the figure exiting: Boxer Dunne. He looked bigger than he remembered, fatter around the middle, still stuffed into a bad suit. The train station shit-head from last year. He'd seen that face only once. He'd see it again, he suspected, soon.

Five minutes passed before the man upstairs descended and moved into Tony's view: Charles Quin. The man in the white Mercedes at the castle gate. In spite of all the rummaging, it seemed he was leaving empty-handed.

The whine of the golf cart had died away before Tony emerged, stiff-legged. It was only then that he noticed the photographs, clusters of small framed prints. Inside the nearest room his eyes ran full circle. At least ten magazine covers in large frames: Vogue, Harpers, Cosmopolitan, Self, and others he hadn't heard of. But it struck him that there was no life in this room, no feel of it being lived in, just a gallery. Nothing seemed touched, no papers, no open books, no sat-on sofas. The second room, farther down the hall, had neither the décor nor the deadness of the first. Instead, colourful paintings, pillowed sofas, ornate rugs.

He had no idea what he was looking for. Nothing seemed conspicuous. He checked his watch; he'd been in the apartment ten minutes. More time brought more risk. Another few minutes, he decided, then he'd get out.

At the top of the staircase he pushed open a door. And froze. His eyes followed an arc. Lenny Quin stared at him. And so too a second pair of eyes, a man, a stranger. All in photographs. Forty or more, all black-and-white, most hanging, a few standing. Four or five of Lenny, maybe seven of the two of them, all the rest of the man alone, portrait studies. In a sculpted heart above the bed their unity was evident, Lenny radiant in all.

Why? His heart thumped, he tried to make sense of it. Beyond what was clear. What did this mean for him? He wasn't the man in her life, obviously. The man in the photos, she was his. Without question. That's where she was gone, to be with him. Cilla knew, he figured, even tried to tell him in a round about way, then helped him learn for himself.

On a wicker stand near the bed lay items of men's clothing neatly folded: shirt, pants, a pair of polished but well-worn boots, an Australian ranch hat with snake-skin band.

A chill cut through him. No need for any more, the voice inside him said. Just leave. Someday meet someone he could trust. Fucking fool. Should have known. He never belonged in this snob class. His face distorted, fists rose up, trembled in the air. He could deal with it better in his core, he thought, from where all his victories had sprung, the resource Joel Vida had shown him. Deep down in his core. The sacred place. Where he had found how to survive. There, he hoped, he could deal with this.

He subdued what he could, regained some composure, picked up a small double-heart frame. She shook in his hands, looking sparkling, joyful. Why not, with her beauty, he said silently, why not exploit the privilege of women beautiful to men.

He pulled open the top bureau drawer. Prescription containers, lots of them, many full. Chemist-shop labels on all: Lenny Quin, Aranroe. Drugs. The names meant nothing to him. White pills, blue pills, small orange ones. Was she ill, or addicted? Was that it? Part of it? Did it even matter now?

His anger at his naivete deepened. Crazy world: the words kept repeating in his head. Harder than fighting on the streets, where he'd never gotten caught out; was always ready, people couldn't fuck with him without facing him, and he was never so dumb to trust. Now life felt dark again, suddenly, the darkness that started with Jesus Pomental's dead eyes. Get away, one voice in him said, go. How could he? No home, no country. He rammed the drawer shut, spun away.

And there she stood. In front of him. Real. Alive. Pallid. Blond, black polo and blue jeans. Wordless. Lenny Quin. He backed away, staring, until he reached the window, then turned his face from her.

Her fingers swept across her full watery eyes. 'Tony . . .' Her voice asked only for his acknowledgement, for an equal intimacy.

He gave neither.

'Tony, Tony.' She made his name sound sad and sweet, like it contained everything they had been and might be. And she waited as if for fate, without forcing him from his withdrawal.

She had a story, no doubt, he decided. He didn't want it. What he thought he had, he never had. Get to Mweelrea, climb. Away from this woman, the only one he'd ever even thought he loved. He tried to stop shaking.

'I'm so sorry, Tony. I should have said something. There's a perfectly good explan – '

'Said something?' His words exploded. 'That you lied? That what you said was a rotten lie? Remember? Do you? Love – was that it?'

'Please listen to me; there is an – '

'You married, that it? Or just this guy's lover? Maybe others' too?'

'No, I'm not! None of those things. I've never been married. And I am not seeing anyone! No I didn't tell you everything. But I did not lie to you, Tony. Not once.'

'Your bodyguard?' he said, gesturing to the intimate portrait over the bed. 'Chauffeur? Daddy's personal chef? The fucking gardener?'

'Stop it! I'll tell you. I'll tell you if you let me. Can we go downstairs now, get a cup of tea, can we? Talk about this calmly?'

'Fuck talk,' he said. 'Fuck talk.' He angled his shoulders to pass her in the door frame. She blocked him, hand reaching to him. He backed away, made to push past her again. She blocked him again, face in pain, arms open to him.

'Tony!' she yelled.

He jumped, then fixed his eyes on her.

'Listen to what I'm saying. Please. You need to hear me. We've each had our own lives up to now. Some things will never go away, good and bad. But we can live for now, today; they're your words. Nothing has changed; I still feel the same for you.'

'Feel? For me? Run off to him. Sham fucking lousy shit life.'

'Stop it, I said! You've been hurt; I know that, and I care. I've been hurt too, in ways you don't realise. But I'm, I'm – '

She tried to go on but seemed to fall into an inner struggle, and then her features firmed into sadness and she just stared at him.

'Think you know what real pain feels like?' he said. 'You're the expert on pain?'

He heard his words only after they had left him, knew them to be shields against his own suffering, and he felt again the solitariness into which he knew he could sink. His hands pressed hard against his temples. He powered past her.

'Tony. Tony, wait! Please.' She continued to call after him, until the thump of the front door sounded.

12

'You look terrible!' Cilla glared at him. 'What the hell happened?'

'Can I come in?'

She poked her head out, scanned in both directions, then followed him into the kitchen. 'Don't tell me she was there? She wasn't there?!'

His look made her cringe.

'Don't worry, she's doing great, better than ever.' He fired a stare at her. 'Ever been in there, in that apartment, upstairs?'

'What reason would I have? Tell me what happened.'

'You said you've known her for years.'

'I didn't say I know her; I just know her in a certain way. I told you, I come from a little sodden farm, not a castle. Leo knows her; I'd say he's the only one. Why are you asking me this anyhow?'

He paused before answering her, sounded less angered. 'Remember you said I was different?'

'Wasn't that long ago that I'd forget.'

'I want to know what you meant. What's different?'

'Don't know. Just different.'

'You must know. You said it. Why would you say it?'

'Hold on. Why are you so bothered? What's got you so upset? Tell me what happened?'

Just tell me what you meant. It's important to me. Or is everyone in Aranroe a fucking liar, including you?'

Cilla's glare imposed a lull between them.

'If it means that much to you, I'll tell you,' she said firmly. 'You're different because you're not like most fellas. Probably other reasons too.' She looked away, then back at him, softer now. 'You're going to think I'm mad but I'll tell you; I started really thinking last night when we were in that restaurant. Things I never thought before. Private things. About me. Then after that, when you were asleep on the couch, my eyes wouldn't close. Just lying there I was, thinking all kinds of stuff. Nice things, different things. I started laughing so hard I was sure you'd wake up and think there was a madwoman in the attic. I could've sworn you were going to try to talk me into bed, you growing up in America and all that. But you didn't, and that made me feel, feel sort of really special.'

He reciprocated her silence, the hard edge of his distress now assuaged. Once again her simplicity was challenging what he believed about himself; her simple openness had just punished him, exposed his narrowness, and in this moment she enriched and complicated his thinking.

'Sorry,' he said with obvious embarrassment. 'An odd time the temper just happens. Hard to stop it; goes back a long way.'

'What's there to be sorry for? I'd love you to tell me about who you are really.'

'I didn't mean what I said. I could never see you as a liar.'

'Don't be a silly man. Aren't all girls liars. You should know that, a fella your age.'

Their eyes connected, and for him underlined what was different in these moments; they had each revealed a chunk of their inner worlds.

'I have to change for work,' Cilla said. 'Stay as long as you want; the key's always under the geranium pot.' Then passing behind him she trailed a hand along his shoulder. 'I finish at ten. See you later tonight, maybe?'

He forced a smile.

*   *   *

After Cilla had left he walked the short distance to his B&B, blocking from his view in every step the great dome lording over the bog and rock and water of this world. And soon, like a man from whom new hope had been too soon taken, he crashed onto his bed, arms across his eyes. America had taken his young years, nobody could give them back, not one day. He'd never know how it felt to be eighteen and nineteen and normal. Or twenty, twenty-one, twenty-two, twenty-three, twenty-four, twenty-five, twenty-six. Except in a sub-world, prey to perverts and psychopaths, a trophy of penitentiary scum. And in all of life no romance that counted, but one. Was this, too, part of what was dragging him down, that he had never learned to understand women, how they thought and functioned, what they sought and needed?

Maybe it was none of that but what the shrinks warned him about. Fit in, they said, stay on guard: depression, conflicts, losing control, giving up. Since he got out eighteen months ago he'd been up and down, but he'd managed, even survived Eva Kohler's madhouse. Now this, end of the dream, her deceit, making love to him, obsessed with someone else, and a room full of drugs. So many holes to fall into, everywhere. So many things he just didn't get. Even Cilla: clever, sexy, strong, just as much a riddle.

How far down did all this bury him, he asked. Could he cope? Honour his oath, re-find his spirit, become himself again, belong, ever? With anyone? Could these people understand only their own? Was he one of them? Or was he lost still, a misfit still, native nowhere, slipping back into the darkness?

Mweelrea was still there; that was all. He'd climb, tomorrow, early, grate once again against stone and earth, rest somewhere along the way, in yellow heather, minus civilisation, minus everything. At dawn.

*   *   *

Hours later it was hunger that awakened him. He split the curtains and was blinded by a bright evening sky. He needed to move, escape, breathe country air.

Outside, Paddy McCann called out, and shuffled toward him. 'I have a wee letter here for you. From her good self. And strict orders to wait and bring a reply back to her.'

Tony took the envelope and glared at Paddy.

'I'll be leaving you to read it in private,' Paddy said. 'Chance for me to get in a little bit of a walk around the driveway. I'll tell Eilis I did half a mile.'

'Hold on, Paddy.'

'Won't be far, just give a shout when you need me.'

'Hold on. There won't be any reply. Take it back.'

'Couldn't do a thing like that,' he said, still retreating. 'Wouldn't be fair on herself. Not in the best of spirits at the minute. Y'know yourself the way the women are.'

Tony watched as Paddy's big out-of-synch frame moved away. Despite his distrust of these people, this was the quality he admired most in Paddy, compassion. But he wouldn't be taken in by it.

'Don't give me any shit, Paddy. Take it back to her!'

'Afraid I couldn't do that, sir . . . wouldn't have the courage.'

'I'll tear it up, right here.'

'No, no, I have it, sir,' Paddy hurried back. 'I could say I talked to your good self, that you were on your way someplace fierce important, the hounds of time were after you, and that you'd not a chance to read it but you took it with you, and, and, you said, you said you would, that you'd read it.'

Tony offered no response.

'Not a right thing to do, make up a lie to tell herself. Could you, could you just – '

Tony threw the letter into the taxi. Paddy reached in, plucked it out.

'Couldn't you just take one peek? The first page. It's probably only – '

'No, I said! The answer is no. You understand?' He moved off along the long driveway.

Paddy followed. 'What if I run you down to the village? You could read it on the way; there'd be no charge, not a red penny. How's that?'

Their eyes engaged. With both hands, Paddy offered the envelope again. Tony shook his head, continued his departure. Paddy scrambled back into his taxi and moments later slowed alongside Tony. 'I'm headed to the village anyway. Give you a free lift for nothing.'

Tony's expression terminated what was happening between them. The taxi drove ahead toward the exit but stopped after twenty yards. The horn blared once, a long, loud blare. Paddy's hand emerged dangling the envelope. It dropped, spun twice, landed flat on the grass border. The taxi drove out through the gate and sped away.

Tony stopped at the spot, stared at the small cream envelope. He watched it transform, become a chute to a time long ago, to a cell at eighteen, nineteen, twenty. It was his father's letters then that had kept him alive; he'd ached every day for them, and for Kate's, and never expected mother's but was glad if one came. For those first three years he could not write back: couldn't or didn't, not once. But his father's letters still came: four or five, at least, every month, sometimes more. Later, he found a way, was able to write one letter, two pages that took weeks to sound right, to send, to say the things he hadn't been able to say, the feelings that saved his sanity every solitary day, that reciprocated the love he received from all of them: Kate and Pat and Violet, mother and father. And then the dark that befell the world, the news that father was gone. He'd never asked, nor been told, if his one letter, his two pages, had arrived in time. Late by a day or two, maybe by hours, or minutes, or maybe not, maybe early, in time; he didn't know. All hope died then, the childhood memories he'd been cherishing became unbearable, some soon unrememberable.

Up to that day his often carved oath had been to build a real life when he got out, as father had insisted he could, just as he had assured him that he would be there for him the day he walked free, that the first thing they'd do was dig a hole together in the back garden, plant a sapling that over time they'd watch grow strong and straight. They'd all be together again, he had preached, a family. But he wasn't there, father, gone long before the gates opened. And they never were again, never could be, a family. His fifty-two-year-old heart couldn't hold on, letters said, or words that said as much, not for one more mail delivery. Just his heart, not the man, who'd always be waiting.

One too-late letter, maybe. A letter that might have held off death. A letter in front of him now.

Claire Abbey
Monday, September 5th 1994

Dearest Tony,

The situation is not how you are seeing it. You have my solemn promise. Please allow me to explain some events of my life which I have told you nothing about.

Tomorrow, they say, will be a beautiful day. Can we walk along Silver Strand, go up the cliffs to Killadoon? It's a good hike, three miles to the summit. I'll wait for you on Station Road beach, at 9am.

My deepest hope is that you'll say yes. If you cannot come, I'll go alone. It's time I did.

Losing you would be unbearable.

All my love, Lenny.

13

He turned off the hill into a sea of charcoal and blue, waves of uniformed school children streaming toward some indiscernible academy. The pageant and banter brought back flashes of his earliest years at Gardiner Street School in the heart of Dublin. These fresh bouncing bodies, enraptured in a young world which he lamented would too soon pass, seemed oblivious of him until he enquired of the location of Station Road beach. In response came a blur of eagerness, alas in a dialect he found incomprehensible. But from all the small hands jabbing in the air, he gleaned he was moving in the right direction, so he pressed on in patchy sunlight.

At the next corner, pedalling toward him came an aged post-man moving barely fast enough to remain upright.

'Station Road beach, I do,' the postman said as though preparing for conversation. Tony was soon consuming the man's life tale, and listening lifted him. He felt his spirit lighten, like this stranger was re-igniting what he believed was lost. Maybe these were his people after all, he thought, maybe he was closer to home than he believed: how they danced all over you, sang to you, felt you worthy of their stories, of their trust and time, and seemed not to doubt you'd feel the same for them; how they made light of the hard outer world at every opportunity, and when there was no opportunity, how they invented one; they played with what others called suffering until it wasn't suffering but something essentially good for you, a redeeming purgatory ordained by God. They seemed at one with the mill of living. And as for those he'd called liars the day before, they now seemed in some way saintly; maybe equally saints and liars. As a race, there was no denying it, these people inhabited a realm beyond him, a holy place that he might rise to, this Irishness.

'Remember now what I told you: go past Macker's field, bear left into Eamon's Lane, and at the end take a sharp left and Station Road beach will be staring at you, and may God go with you because I can't.'

At 8.45 his partnership with the postman ended.

*   *   *

He spotted the figure in the distance, by the water's edge. Uneasiness and doubt ran through him. He was already old in an unfamiliar world, he told himself. She was moving slowly toward him on the rippled sand, sandals in her hands. A woman who had held his destiny, and yet might. Then he noticed the first easing of the anger he'd been holding. What story would she tell today? He was not here to serve Lenny Quin's dreams, nor rescue her from affluence or misfortune; he had troubles of his own. He caught his mind once again: pre-judging, catastrophising, but still living inescapably in her world.

Now she stood just four feet away, bearing kindness and hurt and the promise of reconciliation, clearly joyed by their nearness.

For a moment she was the woman she had been to him days before, the woman he wanted to possess. But she wasn't, just a woman of lies and deceit. His gaze aimed past her. The brush of her hand shot his arms out as wings. She insisted, clasped his hand in both of hers; and she squeezed until the wildness in him abated and his eyes re-opened. In her face he read what had no need for words, that she understood, that she wasn't giving in or giving up.

'I'm so happy you came,' she said. 'We can just walk, if you like. Don't have to talk.' They began moving, divided, along the beach. 'The top of Killadoon takes about three-quarters of an hour, a good walk. Feel up to it?' She tugged at him.

He nodded, as if unconcerned with her joy, but in fact still deifying her while wondering how he'd deal with her absence from his life.

'There's a cosy little tea room up there,' she said. 'You'd like it. They have okay coffee. I used to sit up there. Quite often at one time. And, Tony, I do want to do what I said: tell you some things.'

Their journey by the waterline was silent, marked only by the arbitrariness of a blustery ocean. Hand in hers, he had grown responsive to her touch, sensations still igniting in him a sensuality he had no power over.

He tried to force his thoughts away, but his thoughts would not stay away. She was forbidden and distrustful, magnetic, commanding. But she was someone else's.

Soon they left the beach, turned onto a trail that twisted up through thickets of gorse and heather until eventually a rocky clearing emerged. Above them seabirds glided, powerless against the air currents. Holding tightly to each other, they crossed the bare skull to a stone marker, from where they peered into a lightly-veiled blue universe.

It happened just then, first as Lenny was pointing to something. He said nothing. A half-minute later he noticed it again: her briefly stilled face, a fracture that lasted just seconds and passed without her acknowledging. He still made no comment.

To the south she pointed out Killary Harbour and its rocky headland, where the water glistened beneath green hills and white houses dotted the shoreline. Beyond this, the village of Renvyle stood out, and farther still like hands in prayer the peninsulas of

Connemara. And eight miles out, as though it had fallen from the heavens, the island of Inishturk floated alone. She went on to identify Clare Island's stony scalp and the grey and black cliffs of Achill towering above the foam, and lastly Mweelrea's purples and browns lighting up.

She then retreated surreptitiously, until she stood on the cliff edge, above sea-blackened rocks more than a hundred feet below.

'Lenny! Too close!' Tony yelled, realizing what had taken just moments. He gestured frantically. 'Get back. You're too close!'

She glanced at him, before turning her face back to the ocean.

'Move back! Lennnny! Lennnny!' He began edging toward her, searching for anything to hold on to.

Her upper body swayed forward and back.

'Nooooo! Lennnny! Lennnny!'

14

1980

In Davy Byrne's pub the Friday night racket clattered on. The musk of rain-damp patrons suffused with the fog of tobacco and the aroma of Guinness. In every nook and booth and space, students fraternised while barmaids squeezed and pushed to distribute drinks.

In their favourite corner, Lenny Quin and Emer O'Hare had still one reason to celebrate: each would graduate in six weeks' time, their four years of study over. Tonight though, that didn't make up for their disappointment. Up to two hours earlier they had been planning to escape the city and head to County Mayo for the weekend, a three-hundred mile round trip. But at the last moment a friend's Renault R4L had refused to start. Since then, both girls had been scratching around for someone with a car, a rarity, who they might inveigle with the attractions of Claire Abbey and Ireland's remote west coast. So far, no takers had emerged. Around them now sat their band of a dozen or so associates, mostly fellow UCD students, some well on the road to inebriation.

'Does Hamilton still have his jalopy?' Lenny asked, her tone heavy with the brooding she had taken to.

'Ham? He's gone to Cork with Professor Farrell's daughter,' Jacko said. 'Hands-on research. We can all go back to my gaf after here: few bottles, bit of smoke, sing-song; what d'you say?'

'After last time? You nearly got us all dumped in jail,' Emer said.

All except Lenny fired hoots around the table. 'What about Tidey and Stroker?' she asked into Emer's ear. 'Think they'd be up for it?'

'Them maniacs, are you daft? Wouldn't trust them with me granny. They're down near the door. Stroker's trying to chat up Mary Donnelly. Half-eejit! She could buy him and sell him. He told me I was looking ravishing. Male chauvinist pig.'

'But Tidey's okay. Has he still got his little yellow Mini?'

'Drop it, you're talking dangerous.' Emer glanced around. 'Don't look now; here comes Wolfman Dermot and he's seen you. He's on his ear, can barely walk.'

'Did he bring his Beetle?' Lenny said. 'That's all I want to know.' Both hid their snickering.

'There yous are,' said the big, stumbling, twenty-something man. 'How're yous?'

'Ah, it's yourself, Dermo,' Emer responded as Lenny sent him a promising smile.

'See you brung your snazzy camera, Lenny.' Dermot craned forward. 'Take me snap; are yeh, what?'

'She'd have to be desperate,' Emer said, 'the state of you.'

'It's a Nikon F2, Dermot. And I don't take snaps; I explained that to you before. But I might create a portrait of you. Soon maybe.'

'Do one now. Will I do a pose for yeh?' He folded his arms and bared his teeth.

'Where did they dig you up?' Emer shook her head. 'You should be in films. Anyone ever tell you that? Return of the Abominable Tipperary Plasterer!'

'Y'only take dirty pictures anyway, am I right, Lenny?' Dermot said. 'For museums.'

Lenny returned a demure reprimand, and added a smile.

'Know the best thing about you, Dermot Connolly?' Emer said. 'Your mummy and your dada didn't waste their few shillings trying to educate you. Ever hear of a photography gallery? Museums are for mummies, things that get dug up – like yourself.'

'Nah, you're wrong there. Y'are, you're wrong. I have a ma and she's not in no museum. Least she wasn't when I went to work.'

'You're only hilarious, Connolly; I'm in stitches.' Emer's scorn drew hoots from all around the table. 'And if you want to know, they're not dirty pictures she takes, they're nude studies. Not that you'd qualify.'

Dermot rose to speak but was engulfed by jeers.

He swore at the culprits then turned to Lenny. 'I'll buy yous a gargle, girls – or ladies, birds, youngwans, whatever yous are.'

'Just because you're plastered doesn't mean you can insult us like that,' Emer said. 'We're not ladies. Or girls. Or birds. Or youngwans. We're female arts students, and you've no – '

'You're very kind, Dermot,' Lenny interjected. 'I'll have a vodka and white, please.'

Emer fixed a glare on her.

'Vokka-n-white coming up,' Dermot said. 'Yourself, Emer? Or are you saving your lips for later?'

'Watch your mouth, Connolly. I'm warning you.'

Soon Dermot returned with drinks, barging his way into the booth and crashing down next to Lenny. Over the next hour his hand probed often and was now set firmly around her waist. She raised no objections. Nor did she heed any of Emer's underbreath swearing or elbow digs.

At closing time the group streamed out into Duke Street and loitered in the after-rain freshness. Dermot's attachment to Lenny was now a two-arm lock around her midriff, as much to keep himself steady as a statement to the crowd.

'Who wants to go for a spin?' he shouted, rattling his car keys in the air. 'Are yous on?'

Lenny snuggled closer to him, looped her arms around his neck, and launched into a long kiss. Emer's face became a snarl. Lenny sneaked her a wink and went on.

'I'm bursting for a piss,' Dermot said, and scooted off.

'What the feck are you doing?!' Emer snapped. 'You can't mess like that! Stop it, you hear me? Just quit it.'

'You don't understand. This is our chance. I bet he'd let me photograph him nude.'

'You're loopy, bonkers. He's a big dope. And you don't like naked men. You said so.'

'Lenny glowed. 'Full, fleshy body, little or no hair. Glorious. Think of Steichen's sensual work. Or Weston's luminous human forms, full tonal range, smooth planes – '

'Fecking strait jacket; that's what you need! You'd ask Wolfman Connolly to strip for you? That what you're telling me? You're a lunatic.'

'Shush, Emer, I'm not serious. Listen, here's the plan: when he comes back, tell him I've gone to the toilet. I'm going to buy a small bottle of Jameson.'

'Too late; they're closed.'

Lenny charmed her way past the doorman, back into Davy Byrne's pub, and returned minutes later carrying a brown bag. Into Dermot's ear she whispered that she had decided against driving to the mountains; she and Emer were going back to their flat on Leeson Lane and he was welcome to come along; the only condition, she told him, was that he would let her drive his VW Beetle there.

With a miss-aimed kiss, he handed over the keys. As the purple Beetle cruised along Kildare Street Emer fed Dermot the Jameson, faking her own swigging. The car circled twice around St Stephen's Green, then doubled back along Nassau Street and a couple of times around Merrion Square, adding at least two miles to the one mile journey. At that point Dermot was spread-eagled across the back seat, snoring loudly.

'Men: a means to an end,' Lenny said. 'He promised we'd all head off to Mayo tonight if I made love with him first. You heard him.'

'Liar. I heard no such thing. And don't even say things like that.'

'We'll grab our gear and hit the road. When he wakes up, you say you found him in bed with me in the flat. He won't know any better.'

'That's kidnapping. We'd be in big, big trouble; we'd go to jail.'

'No way. Student prank. And we get what we want – a car.'

'I won't forget this to my dying day. Could be today, if he wakes up. Then both of us will be dead. I hope he kills you first.'

'You're right. We should smother him, bury him in the woods. Nobody would know.'

'Now I am really frightened. Of you.'

'Lenny's fit of laughter pulled Emer into hilarity that went on subsiding and re-igniting.

'What will happen to us, Len, you and me, after we graduate?'

'Don't sound so down. We'll survive.'

At the flat they flung their bags into the boot and shortly after midnight cruised out of Dublin. They had pulled it off. Just as they had done with so many challenges in their four years to-gether at UCD. Now, hands drumming against vinyl, Lenny Quin and Emer O'Hare, like wolves to the moon, crooned in unison to *Band on the Run* as the purple Beetle hummed through the star-less dark of an April night. Bound for County Mayo.

*   *   *

The car moved slowly through the gates and along the side of the darkened Abbey.

'Dermot! Wake up!' Emer slapped him. 'Wake up, you big fat lump.'

'He's not going to,' Lenny said. 'We'll carry him inside.'

They climbed out of the car into a chilly western air and yawned and stretched. Just then a bright moon gave way to clouds blowing in off the Atlantic. Ignoring Dermot's growls, they hauled him out of the car until his feet hit the ground, then hooked his arms over their shoulders. At the apartment door Emer pinned him upright against the entrance.

'Damn it!' Lenny said. 'I left my door key in the kitchen in Dublin.'

'What?! You couldn't, at this hour. Is anyone awake in the hotel?'

'They'd all be in bed. And I am certainly not ringing the bell. Damn!'

'We'll have to sleep in the car. It's half-four.'

'Haul that monster back into the car? No. Anyway, we'd freeze.'

'So, what do we do? I'm banjaxed,' Emer said. 'He's got about fifteen keys on his key ring; one of them might open the door.'

Three keys seemed like good fits; one even turned promisingly. But none would unlock the door. Lenny swore with increasing intensity as she retried the keys.

'Len . . .' Emer's face turned to dread; she grabbed Lenny. 'Len, I heard something. Out there. Coming from over there. I know I did.' Their eyes fixed on the fluttering sycamores. 'Holy God. What is it, Len? Len?'

Lenny listened, scouring the bushes.

'Len, what is it, what's out there? I heard – '

'Shhh, will you! Has to be someone we know.'

'I know nobody. In the middle of the night?'

The noise came again, cinder scraping on the path close by. Emer caught on to Lenny, while trying to hold Dermot in place. Then came the sound of footsteps, growing louder. Both girls held their breaths.

'Watch out!' Lenny shouted. Emer screamed. Dermot was falling forward. They grabbed him, jammed him back against the entrance.

Out of the shadows a person was moving toward them.

They stood clutching Dermot, waiting.

'Is that yourself, darling?' The figure came into light from above the door. 'I thought it might be yourself.'

'Aunt Peg!' Lenny exhaled as Emer gasped noisily. 'Aunt Peg, you wouldn't have a – '

'Right here, darling.' She held up a single key and unlocked the apartment door. 'He looks like a heavy one, let me give you a hand.'

'No, no, we're fine, he's okay, really tired. He'll sleep on the floor,' Lenny said. 'Aunt Peg, this is Emer, my friend.'

Peggy Reffo smiled warmly. 'Leo will be beside himself, darling, knowing you're home. Now, get some rest.'

'Very sorry to wake you, thanks a million,' Emer said, still panting.

'You didn't, love. I was preparing things inside. Breakfast is at a quarter to six for the early tee-offs. Goodnight now.'

'Wait, Aunt Peg. My father, is he here?'

'He is.'

Lenny let out a sigh.

'The Avalon Masters Tournament starts in three hours. The house is full.'

*　　*　　*

Six hours later both girls walked through the chandeliered lobby, into a nearly-empty lounge of plush decor, where they found Peggy.

'I've a nice table all set up for us,' she said. 'It's a lovely surprise both of you coming down from Dublin to see us. Leo just ran over to the house to get something; he'll be here in a tick and we'll all have a bit of breakfast.' She escorted the girls into a smaller, pink-curtained dining room, to a window table set for six.

Just then, Leo appeared.

'Princess!' he said, throwing open his arms. Lenny brightened instantly but responded with a restrained hug and dropped back into her seat. Over breakfast their chatter laboured from time to time under the awkwardness of Lenny's detached bearing. But on each occasion Emer's perceptiveness and timely wit provided relief.

'We have to go now,' Lenny said just minutes after they'd finished eating, and stood up from the table.

'What's your hurry, darling?' Peggy said. 'Charles will be in any minute now; I rang him.'

Emer's stare cut into Lenny, demanded compliance.

'Speak of the divil,' Peggy said.

'Good morning, good morning.' Charles approached briskly, sweeping back his thick greying hair. 'Leonora!' He spoke her name endearingly as he manoeuvred around the table. She gave a dispassionate smile and stayed distant from his embrace. He stepped back and regarded her with pride before sitting into the vacant chair.

'Darling, aren't you . . . ' Peggy's eyes prompted Lenny.

'This is Emer, my friend, Emer O'Hare,' she said. Emer bounced up, bumping against the table, and shot her hand into Charles' two-handed grasp.

'So Leonora, what a day you have coming up. You'll have the lot of us up there at your conferment,' Charles said. 'Leo and Peggy and myself, and a few more, I'd say, from the area. Paddy McCann and Fr Foley for sure; your dear mother thought very highly of them both.'

'Aye, that she did,' Peggy said, as though indulging private thoughts, then took hold of Leo's hand. 'It'll be the grandest day in many a year.'

'That's what they call it, Lenny, is it, a conferment?' Leo asked.

'Halloween's what *we* call it!' Emer interjected, breaking the awkwardness that was mounting and drawing laughter from all.

'Big black capes and silly hats and gallons of black mascara, and that's not – '

'I won't be going,' Lenny said tersely. 'The ceremony isn't till June fourteenth.'

'Why would you not be going, darling?' Peggy asked. 'You've passed all your exams, every one of them, with flying colours. And please God you'll do the same in the ones that are left.'

Lenny straightened herself in her seat and looked askance. 'I'll be in America.'

'America?' Charles said. 'What would take you to America?'

'Work. In Manhattan.'

'What a surprise,' Charles said. 'You're not going alone, I hope. America's not Ireland, not the safest of places, by a long shot, especially New York City.'

'Would you not put it off until after your graduation?' Leo asked. 'That way we could all go up to Dublin, make a day of it. You could fly off then if that's what you still want to do.'

'Can't.' Lenny's head shook decisively.

'But, darling,' Peggy said, 'you've worked so hard, four long years. You deserve your big day, God knows, if anyone does.'

'See, it's because of the visas, the J1 visas for America, that's the problem.' Emer distributed her words around the table. 'See, you have to get one long before, months before, they let you go to work for the summer over there, and if you get one you're really, really lucky, like Len, and if you don't go early, then they can take it back off you; and even if they didn't, after a few months you can't use them any more, so you kinda have to go, really early. Right, Len?'

Silence fell over the group.

Lenny turned to Emer. 'Ready?'

Emer's face objected.

'We have to go,' Lenny said, to no one in particular.

'We're off to Mweelrea,' Emer said, remaining seated. 'Just a little bit up, to see the views. I want to see the Twelve Bens. I never seen them before. When I learned about them in geography class, when I was eleven, I used to think they were twelve fellas named Ben who lived in Mayo.'

'It's to be bitter cold on the mountain today,' Peggy said with reservation in her words. 'Best you stay to the lower parts, the Ballygall pass, no higher.'

'Oh definitely, we will; I've a horrible head for heights anyway,' Emer said. 'When I was small my dad and my sister and me got lost on The Scalp, in Wicklow, for a whole Sunday. I was whispering the Rosary the whole time that we'd be found alive. It took four-and-a-half Rosaries to get us rescued. After that I wanted to be a nun.'

'You'll need money for the States, Leonora?' Charles asked.

'I've been self-sufficient for two years, haven't I?' Lenny said.

'I mean will you need extra money, until you find work, just to – '

'Len's been doing great, Mr Quin,' Emer intruded, 'with the photography, I mean. She gets jobs from big companies now, and sometimes I go with her.'

'You're a photographer too, love?' Peggy asked.

'Ah no, I just put things in the right place, the lights and stuff; it's really hard to get all the things right, but Len knows how.'

'You're going out together? Out to the States, I mean.' Charles asked.

'Part of me'd love to, Mr Quin. But I'm a real chicken; I think America's too big. Anyway, I can't even if I wanted to; I start a job in RTÉ Television in July. Making tea and sambos for all the bigheads. Can't wait. Maybe I'll get discovered and be famous.'

Emer's dramatics drew smiles from all but Lenny.

'No, seriously, I'll be doing programme research for Joe Packard and Des Duggan.'

'Well done; they're very popular fellas,' Leo said.

'A girl who works there told me that both of them think they're rock stars; that's what I heard anyway. I'll find out soon.'

'Never know, darling,' Peggy said. 'They're both young, and grand-looking lads. You could end up marrying one of them, an attractive girl like you, and with your sense of humour.'

'Me, married? Never, ever, ever.' A blush burned Emer's cheeks. 'I was thinking of going into the Convent. My ma said they'd never take me because I curse too much and I only get holy when I'm freezing to death on mountains.'

'Lenny's a lucky girl to have found a nice friend like you.' Leo smiled broadly. 'Why haven't you come up to visit us before?'

Emer stalled. 'Sure Len'll be home in September; won't you, Len?' Lenny didn't respond. 'We'll have tons more time then to do lots of things together. The studying will be over for good. Can't wait.'

'Is something wrong, Leonora?' Charles asked.

'No. Nothing. Just like always.'

Charles ignored what was in her voice. 'You will come back up before you leave for the States, won't you?'

'Can't. Have to study. Last exam is on the eleventh; I'm going on the twelfth.'

Nobody spoke right away.

'Have to be extra careful, Princess,' Leo said. 'America can be a tricky place when you don't know it, especially now with the American hostages in Iran and all that trouble.'

'We have to leave now.' Lenny glowered at Emer. 'All set?'

'We're bringing Dermot out to introduce him to all the moo-cows and sheepses.' Emer blushed, and was clearly amused at her own words. 'Seriously, we want him to see parts of the west. He's never been anywhere outside Dublin. Or inside Dublin either. He thinks the northern hemisphere is upstairs in his house.' Everyone smiled, but not as before; all now seemed distracted.

'Who's this Dermot person?' Charles asked.

'Medical student from Dublin,' Lenny responded immediately. 'We're bringing him to Mweelrea – '

'For a miracle,' Emer said.

'He's Emer's boyfriend,' Lenny said.

'Friend! Not boyfriend.' Emer's tone reprimanded her comrade. 'Actually, he's a friend of a friend of me ma's second cousin, twice removed, but he came back both times.' She broke into a chuckle, then quickly aborted it.

*   *   *

Dermot shuffled out of the apartment, hair hedgehogged, clothes crumpled, and searched his surroundings. Eventually, he found his way to the lobby, to a perfectly attired concierge with a professional face.

'How'r'yeh. Where am I, will you tell me that?'

'Why, certainly, sir.' The concierge sculpted each syllable. 'As we speak, you're in the east wing.'

'The what?'

'Hmm, I see. Late night; missed your tee-off time?'

'Missed me what? Look, all I want to find out is where am I. What's this place?'

'This place? Why, it's Claire Abbey, sir. You're a guest?'

'Might be. Maybe. Don't know. Where's this place anyway, tell me that.'

'I beg your pardon, sir. I'm afraid I don't quite follow.'

'This gaf. That I'm in now, talking to you in. Where's it at on the atlas?'

'Claire Abbey, sir? On the atlas? Let me think: we're one-and-one-half miles north of the village of Aranroe, on the west coast of Ireland, fifty-four degrees north latitude, and I believe eight degrees west of Greenwich, approximate in both instances. Known otherwise, for quite some time, as County Mayo. Should I go on, sir, or would that be – '

'Fucking Mayo?!'

'Eh, no. County Mayo. It is possible, however, that it has on occasion been referred to in the manner you suggest. Perhaps at football grounds, when Dublin were losing to our Mayo men.'

'How'd I get here? Tell me that. I don't live nowhere near Mayo. Somebody's messing with me head. I didn't come here?'

'Perhaps you were brought against your will, sir. Kidnapped?'

Dermot reflected, then shook his head.

'Not kidnapped. Hmm.' The concierge's eyes searched upward. 'Making a pilgrimage to Knock's holy shrine, where the apparitions happened?'

Dermot shook his head again.

'Missing person?'

'What? Nah.'

'Hot air balloonist, came down in bad – '

'Nah.'

'Parachutist? Did us the honour of dropping in, if you'll forgive the pun, sir.'

'Me? Nah. Don't trust them things. Must've been paralytic.'

'I'm afraid that's all that springs to mind right now.'

'You're having me on, right? This isn't Mayo. Mayo's fucking miles away.'

'I'll fetch the manager, sir, if you wish. I'm sure he'll confirm what I've told you, to within a degree or two.'

'Nah, forget it. Just tell me this, do yous have black coffee here and somewhere I can sit down and drink it?'

'I'm afraid the main dining room is closed until 12.30. However, I can have a pot of coffee served to you in the B.B. Bunting Room. That's the smaller dining room, at the east end of the great hall.'

Dermot scanned the interior. 'Down there, right?'

The concierge's eyes swung in the opposite direction. 'And the gentlemen's wash room is directly west of where we're presently standing. Your left.'

'Nah, I don't need to go; I went already.'

'I see. Well then, if there's nothing else, sir, enjoy your beverage.'

'Listen, chief, y'didn't see two girls, did yeh?'

'Hard to say, sir. What sort of girls did you have in mind?'

'A lanky one, snazzy looking bird.' His hands drew curves in the air. 'Know what I mean? Other one's smaller, got a big mouth, a bit fat. See them, did yeh?'

'Hmm. One slender, good-looking lady, and a shorter, somewhat rotund lady with a larger than average mouth.' The concierge stared meditatively. 'No, no, I don't believe I have. Perhaps they went back to work? Or might I say, to bed?'

'Nah. I was with the both of them last night. Least I think it was last night, then I can't remember after that.' He pressed his hands to his temples and groaned. 'Have to get meself a pint of strong coffee. I'm half fucked, so I am.'

'Excellent idea so. I'm told our coffee is to-die-for, as our American guests are fond of saying. I'll have your coffee sent down to you. Enjoy the rest of your morning, sir.'

*   *   *

'We're leaving,' Lenny said, this time getting to her feet and pushing back from the table.

'You'll be back to see us in the afternoon, won't you, before you head off?' Leo asked.

Emer glared again at her friend.

'After Mweelrea we're driving to Westport, then straight to Dublin,' Lenny said.

'Then mind Peggy's words, girls; the mountain's another world.' Leo paused as though awaiting Lenny's eyes, which didn't arrive. 'Looks harmless from a distance, but souls have been lost up there, especially – '

'Dermot!' Emer exclaimed, her attention jumping beyond the group. 'What are you doing alive?'

Rough and grimacing, Dermot halted.

'Come in, son, come in,' Peggy said. 'We've been talking about you and your studies.'

'How're yous,' he said with pained pleasantness, then side-eyed the girls. 'There yous are.'

'Everybody, this is Dermot Connolly,' Emer announced, 'Known as Dermo to his enemies.'

'Join us, please,' Charles motioned to an empty chair next to him. 'How are things in medicine these days?'

A gawky blankness took over Dermot's face.

'Demanding field, no doubt. How are you finding your lecturers?'

Dermot's open-mouthed plea went to Lenny, then Emer. Neither responded. 'Well, eh, like, eh, like I don't really, like – '

'That was a long drive, boy, all the way from Dublin,' Leo said. 'Especially at night.'

'Dublin . . . yeah, was, right. Bumpy kinda, sometimes, was bumpy.'

'We're going.' Lenny spun away from the group just as a waitress arrived.

'That's me black coffee,' Dermot said hoarsely. 'Me, Miss, for me.'

'We are leaving, Dermot!' Lenny said. 'You can get coffee on the way.'

'But I'm dying, I am. I'm half . . . I have to finish me coffee. Don't even know where yous brung me to, and me head, me head's – '

'Guinness flu. Hundred percent incurable.' Emer grinned.

'Dermot!' Lenny snapped. 'We're leaving. Now, please.' She gripped his arm, led him to the side.

Leo got to his feet. 'Princess, wait, hang on.' Leo and Peggy each hugged Lenny, but as before received a lukewarm response.

Emer then shook hands with everyone, talked about seeing them all again very soon and how she and Lenny would stay for weeks, even longer, next time.

Charles had remained outside the farewells, all the time watching Lenny. 'You're not forgetting to give your father a kiss?'

he said. She responded with a peck, not allowing the closeness his arms offered.

'We'll just grab our things out of the apartment and be off,' Emer said as the trio exited the B.B. Bunting Room to a chorus of goodbyes.

* * *

As they readied their bags, a knock came at the door. 'Darling, it's me,' Peggy called out. Lenny opened the door just a crack. 'You're a busy girl, I know you're hurrying to get off. But I want to see you for a wee minute, darling. Just you and me.'

'But we're just ready to go, and – ' Lenny jolted. Emer hovered behind her, threatening a second poke.

Peggy reached in, took Lenny's hand, and led her out.

'The break room's a good spot. Nobody over there now,' Peggy said.

At the rear of the hotel they descended the twisting steps, into an echoey chamber of grey stone and racks of pots and pans. There they sat across from each other at a long bare-wood table.

'Before I say another word, here's a few pounds for you, in case you run short.' Peggy pressed a bundle of folded notes into Lenny's hand and dismissed her protest. 'From Leo and me, to help you get what you'll need. So how have you been, darling, doing well?'

'I'm grand.'

'Remember when you were in St Agnes's, in primary school, how you used to be with us every day?'

'No . . . Maybe I do. Some. I don't know.'

'I told you before the story of how we were all so close, you and Leo and me and your poor mother, Róisín; God rest her soul. You'd play games with Leo the whole day if you could, and he with you.'

'There's lots I can't remember,' Lenny said, staring at the table.

'Up to the time I went into secondary school. Except for a few things. I know I couldn't wait to grow up, get away from here.'

'We've long been praying that all the nice memories would come back to you. Remember the day the three of us went to Donegal, to Downing's Beach, and we lost you?'

Lenny shook her head without looking up.

'Ah, you must. We were in bits, Leo and me. We found you in the sand dunes, staring up at the sky, not a bother on you; you were counting the birds, you said. We swung you around and around till we all fell down. That was 1970. Ten years ago, hard to believe, scorching hot day; you were eleven. You must remember, darling?'

'I think I do, Aunt Peg. But I only think. I can't be sure what's a memory and what isn't.'

Peggy laid her hands over Lenny's. 'We always loved you dearly, you know that; and we're so proud of you. Charles too; he'd tell you that himself if you gave him the chance.'

'Yeah,' Lenny said dismissively.

'Darling, now that you're twenty-one, Leo and I were thinking it's the proper time to talk to you. About your mother. And other important matters. But before I say any more, be sure not to leave here today without giving Leo a big hug. He'll be worried sick, with you off in America.'

'I'll be okay; I told him. He trusts me.'

'He does, of course. And you'll be grand. But keep your wits about you over there just the same.'

'That's what upsets my father. I proved I don't need him; I'm independent now, pay my own way, decide things for myself.'

'You've grown up into a wonderful young woman. You're the star in our eyes, like you always were.'

'Why are you talking this way, Aunt Peg; what are you – '

'When you were a wee girl it was like you were ours; you lived with us for three wonderful years, just Leo and me and you, in the cottage. I wish to God you could remember more. Then

Charles' work changed and he was able to take you back. We had a terrible time getting used to you not being there. Poor Leo was never the better for it.'

'Then my father gets rid of me. Packs me off to boarding schools and private houses. At seven years of age. What a moron.'

'You were eight, darling. And you were away for under two years all told.'

'Because I kept getting myself expelled, that's why.'

'You always knew what you wanted, and you went after it. Not a bad quality in a woman. But there's another matter altogether that we said we'd not tell you till you reached twenty-one. Hard to know when's the best time to tell – '

'Tell me what? More family secrets? I don't need to know those things. I have no family. Who have I got? No one.'

'You've got good people, more than a few, you can count on that, who all love you, who've always loved – '

'Really? Like sisters and brothers I've never met? Whoppee! Can't wait to meet them, be normal.'

Peggy squeezed tighter on Lenny's hand, allowed moments to pass, in which each woman avoided what was in the other's face.

'I sat beside Róisín in St Agnes's, all the way up to sixth class. That's what I want to tell you about. When your mother was seventeen she fell in love.'

'I don't need to know this.'

'You do. It's right you should know. She fell in love with Leo. My Leo, before I knew him, except to see. He adored the ground she walked on. They had you when your mother was eighteen.'

'What? . . . What?!'

'I know, darling. I know it's a – '

'What are you saying?!'

'I'm saying my Leo and your mother, they loved each other. And they had you.'

A torn stillness descended on Lenny; then slowly her features changed as though answers were falling into place.

'When Róisín found out she was expecting, she told Leo. But then she turned him down, didn't want marriage, even though she loved him. But she wasn't without good reason. She'd have been making a quick widower out of him, as it turned out. And only she knew it, poor soul.'

'This is all crazy! It's crazy. I don't believe you. It's not true. It's not. I don't believe you.'

Peggy lost Lenny's hand. 'Listen to me, darling. For eight years, from when she was sixteen, your mother knew her time on earth was to be short; she told no one, not even Leo; only her immediate family knew, and that's God's truth. He begged her to marry him, even before they knew about you. But, no, she wouldn't. She had definite ways about her. When you were four she married Charles, and you took his name, became a Quin. She said she wanted you to have the best of everything, grow up without needing to scratch and scrape, travel, get an education, be somebody.'

'Then she was stupid! A stupid fool! Stupid!' Lenny's head fell into her hands as she burst into tears. 'She was dead, dead wrong,' she cried.

'Yes, Princess, she was wrong.' Leo's voice reverberated from the doorway. 'But she believed what she was doing was for the best.' He moved across the stone floor until he was standing beside her, and he placed a hand on her shoulder.

'Wasn't best; not for me,' Lenny said through sobs.

'That was my feeling too,' Leo said. 'But Róisín was certain. She wouldn't see me or talk to me. Not because she didn't care; she did care, for you most of all. And for me.'

He sat into the bench, looking as though he was inhabiting an old time. 'Way things worked out, I got to see you nearly every day; the old cottage you lived in was beside us, just across the field. Those early years, things were at their happiest. You and I planted spuds together and all manner of greens up in the fields, wet days and dry days; we chopped wood and cut turf in the bog.

You loved the soil. Never mattered what the work was, you'd be there with me. Your mother was always glad about that. You were four when she and Charles married. That was June '63. A few months before that I'd started getting to know Peggy and we were married that August.'

'The Lord didn't bless us with children of our own,' Peggy said, 'When Róisín left us we saw you as ours. And you loved being with us.'

'You could've adopted me; could have easily.'

'We looked to do that; we tried,' Leo said. 'Charles was your legal father, they told us, and that was that. From the start your mother had filled in all the registration forms her own way, even found a way to get them notarised. And she got a solicitor to make certain that her share of what Charles owned would be yours.'

'How stupid. He gave me not one thing I ever needed. I often wondered.'

'To be fair to the man, he didn't know our Irish ways; he wasn't from here. It's a fact too that you weren't the easiest child to rear; all that was hard for him. And none of it was your fault; you'd suffered most in the, the whole – '

'Suffered what? What are you saying?'

'It was hard on you, that's all, you and Charles both,' Leo said. 'Claire Abbey was your home only for four or five months. That's when your mother decided to leave the marriage. You weren't yet five; she took you and herself into the old Tracy cottage across from our own. I got a pair of lads to fix the roof, and I put in a few windows and a good door back and front, and got in the electric. She never went back. That's when Peg and I started seeing you more and more; we were newly-marrieds. Wasn't long before you'd be charging over the back field to us. Braver than any tomboy.'

'There's more you're keeping from me. Isn't there? I know; I can tell. Something else. What is it? I want to know.'

'Nothing else to tell,' Peggy said. 'You can be sure that Róisín Doyle loved you dearly every day of her life. Everyone loved you. Paddy McCann too; Paddy was another fond admirer of your mother's. Poor man was beside himself for ages after she passed away, even gave up the Church. Fr Foley all but did the same; took it very bad.'

'Leo, you tell me,' Lenny said. 'Tell me what really happened. I have a right to know.'

Leo remained quiet, a pause that brought the room into silence. 'Not every man loves the same way,' he said. 'Charles loved you. But his village was the world. He was a businessman.'

'He sent me away to boarding school for his own convenience, and for spite. To get rid of me. Three times!'

'You were a handful of a wee one; y'have to count that too, and he'd be away a lot,' Leo said, then his tone brightened, as though to lift the mood. 'You were the cleverest pupil in St Agnes's; I'll tell you that. One time, on account of yourself, I nearly threw a dig at a school inspector fella. You were about twelve. You told him I was your da. I was working in the patch and over comes this big lad, calling me Mr Quin. Remember?'

'Sometimes I think I only imagine I remember. My brain doesn't work for things that long ago. I don't know why.' Lenny's eyes, without anger, lifted up and went again to Leo. 'Even nice things. I know them only because you told me, some of them. I used to write them down, secretly, in my journal, so I wouldn't lose them. Other memories come to me now and then, and I don't know if they really happened. They used to frighten me. Like films that go on for seconds then stop, except they always come back, at really odd times. Then I started looking forward to them.'

'There were loads of lovely times,' Peggy said, trying hard to smile. 'Leo and I do have a great laugh even now, about you telling all sorts of people that we were your mam and dad and that our little cottage was your home. Could be that you knew something even then, about you and Leo. Strange the way some can know things never told. And you'd no time for playmates, ever. Except for that Emer girl; now there's the nice kind of friend every girl needs; I'm glad you're such good pals.'

'Grand wee lassie, and a grand sense of humour,' Leo said. 'I'd feel happier if she was going with you to America, Princess. No good being on your own.'

Peggy rose from the table. 'I better check the lunch set-up. I'll leave you two to yourselves for a wee while.'

Leo and Lenny sat within their thoughts, shoulder to shoulder. One wordless minute became two. Then Leo's hand drew from his pocket a small brass box which he placed on the table, his fingers caressing it as though it were about to part from him. He pushed it over the wooden boards.

'Belonged to your mother. It should be yours.'

'I don't want it. I don't. I never knew her.'

'From the minute you arrived, all her time was for you. It was you that gave her the extra years they said she'd not live to see.'

'Don't.' She pressed her palms to her ears. 'Please, I don't want to know.'

'All right, Princess, I understand. When you feel ready I have a few of her personal things for you.' He returned the box to his jacket, then from his breast pocket he took a small matted photograph and laid it down. 'Your mother, when she was younger than you are now. I thought you'd want to carry it with you when you – '

'I told you,' she sobbed. 'I told you. I don't know – '

His arms burst apart, accepted Lenny's clutching embrace, and so they remained until their shared disquiet calmed.

'She'll always be mine and yours,' he said. 'When she passed on we had each other, you and me, from when you were five until you were eight. Not a day forgotten.'

She placed a teary kiss on his cheek. His eyes fell to the photograph; a youthful, red-haired woman beaming a mischievous smile. 'When I look at you I see her. Even your voice is hers.'

Lenny sprang to her feet, squealing the bench against the stone floor. She rushed across the room and out into the cavernous hallway, Leo in pursuit.

'Princess,' he called, extending the photograph. She stopped, wiped her sweater sleeve across her cheeks, then turned, sad and glowing. Their matched blue eyes re-engaged, as though sharing the inexpressible, and she tumbled back into his grasp.

Then it was over. Already into her departure, she reached back, took the photograph from his fingers. A moment later she was racing down the long, loud passageway, Leo in witness to her youthful form departing the dungeon-like labyrinth.

'Darling,' Peggy shouted, emerging from a side corridor. Lenny stopped, threw her arms around her, then bounded up the steps to ground level.

*　　*　　*

'Where's Dermot?' she asked, re-entering the apartment.

'The bar, probably. I couldn't stop him,' Emer said. 'You look wrecked.'

'Could you go and get him, please.'

'No, I won't! I want to know: Did you tell them?'

'Tell them what?'

'Stop talking shite, Len. It's Emer O'Hare you're talking to now.'

'You mean about the shrink?'

'You didn't tell them. You're so dishonest. And daft. You promised you'd tell them.'

'The ridiculous things he said? He's a quack, you know that.'

'No, I don't. You're the quack! Think you're intelligent but you're not. You're a coward; you're running away from the problem. Go back over and tell them! I'm serious. Or I will. You're twenty-one, not twelve!'

'Oh shut up.'

'I won't shut up! If you don't tell them, I will! They care about you. They're all really lovely people, nothing like you made me believe. You lied!' Emer, flushed and fiery, stalked after Lenny. 'Don't walk off! Have to get your way, don't you. Not this time. What if you collapsed, or had an attack? Or if something worse happened to you in America?'

'Mind your own business. What do you care?' Lenny shouted. Just then a look of remorse gripped her. 'Emer, I'm sorry. I don't know why I said that. You care more than anybody. I did tell them. I told them. Can we talk about it later; it's too hard right now?'

'You're lying. You're fobbing me off.'

'I told you, I did tell them.' Lenny dropped onto the bed, head bowed. 'I asked Leo and Peg if we could talk without my – without Charles there. That's the only way I wanted to do it. We talked in the cellar, the three of us; it was really hard. Ask them if you don't believe me, the phone's beside you.'

'How did they take it?' Emer asked deviously.

'Made me promise to ring them after I see the doctor in a fortnight, tell them what he says about the tests. They both offered to go with me, but I told them you'd be there. You will, won't you?'

Emer's hug was long and consoling, and vigorously reciprocated. 'Sorry for shouting at you,' she said. 'I just want you to get alright. Know how much I care about you, Len? Do you? Do you really know? Answer me.'

Lenny nodded, sad-faced.

'Hey, I know! Put off America till next summer. I could go with you, get leave or something. We could have great craic. Give yourself time to get a second opinion, or even treatment if they say you need it.'

'I'll definitely think seriously about that. I will.'

'Okay, now the bad news: Wolfman's acting the eejit again. Says he's staying here till Monday; he's off work till Tuesday.'

'Neanderthal. What's the matter with him?'

'Your dad rang and asked if we'd stay for the weekend, as his guests. Dermo told him he would. He said he doesn't give two shites what you say, he's not afraid of you, and that it's his car not yours.'

'He's over there now, stuffing himself with food and drink,' Lenny said. 'We shouldn't have brought him. We should have got rid of him when we thought of it.'

'We kidnapped him, remember? We're criminals. They'll have posters out with our faces on them. Why don't we just stay, Len. Might be fun. You think?'

'I can't, I have the psych prep test on Monday, I need to study. And Tuesday morning we both have the maths test.'

'Could I forget. We better go, you're right. I'm going to fail maths, I know it.'

'I'll help you. How about we work on calculus tonight, for an hour, even if it's late when we get back, and do trig and statistics tomorrow afternoon?'

'That'd be brilliant; I need it. And, Len, I didn't mean to get angry at you.'

'Don't worry. Look, I've a plan for Dermot. You find him; he won't be anywhere except where there's food and beer. Tell him that last night he forced himself on me; he stole my virginity – '

'You mean he . . . you let . . . Len?!'

'No, silly! Just say that. Tell him he forced himself on me and that I'm certain I'm pregnant and I'm up here very upset, and I'm planning to tell my father any minute now.'

'That's shite, I couldn't say that. It's stupid. Pregnant, one day after doing it? Not that you ever did it with anyone. Right, Len?'

Lenny rolled her eyes. Just do it, will you?'

'No. He's a dope but not that big a dope.'

'Men are just big little boys, you know that. They know nothing about these things. And Wolfman Connolly knows even less.'

'Yeah, they think a missed period is when you skip a chapter in your history book. That's one reason they don't interest me: they're stupid. Think he'll fall for it?'

'Wolfman? He'll fall for it. We'll get our way.'

'I'll give it a shot. And, Len,' Emer filled her pause with a sigh, 'I don't like him being with us; it shouldn't be.'

*   *   *

Dermot skulked into the room. 'Y'all right, Lenny.'

On the edge of the bed, Lenny sat bent over, arms across her stomach, rocking back and forth. 'Close the door, Dermot, please, will you,' she said.

'Em . . . I . . Lenny, I – '

'Don't! Don't, please. Saying you're sorry won't make it go away,' she whimpered. 'You're coming with me to speak to Daddy? Or are you leaving me to do it on my own? You need to tell me this minute.'

'Em, eh . . . are you . . . like, are you – '

'Sure? Am I sure?! You have the nerve to ask me that? Am I sure?' She lay over and buried her face in a pillow. 'You don't feel anything for me, do you?'

'No, like I, I do. I didn't mean, I swear I don't even – '

'Emer! Emer! Ring Daddy, please; ask him to come over here.'

'Brute!' Emer snapped at Dermot as she lifted the phone. 'May I speak to Mr Quin, please.'

Dermot's gaping mouth tried to make words.

Before he could give any utterance to his turmoil Emer intruded. 'Len, do you think it'd be better to wait a few days, see how you feel? Or not?'

'Yeah, yeah, like, that's like what I think,' Dermot said. 'That'd be the best thing, what Emer said.'

'Couldn't do that,' Lenny whimpered. 'Daddy should know now. It's only proper that I tell him, out of honour. Oooohh, ooohh. Why did you do this to me, Dermot Connolly, why, why?

Ooooohhhh.'

'Er, y'all right, Lenny; I didn't mean ... are y'all right?' He turned to Emer. 'What'll we do?'

'What will *you* do? Stupid ... man. She look alright to you, does she? I saw you last night. Sick, what you were trying to do to her. Beast!'

'I swear I never meant, I can't even remember. I swear. What'll happen to me? I didn't – '

'Oooohh,' Lenny wailed. 'I was looking forward so much to going up onto Mweelrea.'

'We can go, Lenny, now, we can go,' Dermot said. 'I can bring the car around to the front door for you. And you can even drive if you want.'

Emer put her arm around Lenny. 'Come on, Len, let's go to Mweelrea now, then back to Dublin, and think about things for a few days, see how you feel. Look at it this way: if you tell your dad now, what'll he do? You know his temper. He'll go stark raving mad; probably shoot Dermot in the head with his shotgun, from up close. After all, you are the only daughter he has. What do you say we hold off telling him, wait and see?'

'I don't know. Dermot, what'll I do? What?'

'Ah yeah definitely, definitely what Emer said, do definitely do that, I think.' Dermot's words stole his breath. 'See how you feel next Tuesday, or Thursday.'

'Oh, I need someone to help me. What should I do, what should I do?' Hugging a pillow to her midriff, she whispered dreamily: 'Mweelrea, maybe that would help me; see the mountain, see the water, drive up the back road, probably help me decide.'

Dermot sprang up. 'I'll get the car. Want to drive, Lenny, do you? I'll let you.'

'Okay, we're all agreed, let's go.' Emer turned to Dermot. 'Get Len's bag. And make sure the car is warm and the Neil Young tape is in the player.'

Dermot scurried off. Emer bolted the room door. Then locked together the two girls fell into the bed, in rapture.

'You are rotten to the core, Len Quin!' Emer glared into Lenny's thrilled visage, then pulled closer until her lips kissed Lenny's. 'That's why I love you.'

'You're right, I am' Lenny said. 'Very bad sometimes. And Emer O'Hare brings out the worst in me.'

'And the best. You said so.'

Soon the purple Beetle was rumbling toward Mweelrea, leaving Claire Abbey and Aranroe in its wake. After touring the lower slopes, the trio set out for Dublin. Entirely as Lenny Quin had orchestrated.

15

'Get back! Get back!' His feet and hands welded to the skull of the summit. He pleaded in his mind for it all to be a dream, and pleaded with her. But to her, it seemed, he did not exist.

He shimmied closer, fixated, whispering her name, aware that any move could send them both to the rocks. In this slow dissolution he realised too that there was nothing more he could do. Now his body stopped responding, senses turned off, the furore silenced. And in what seemed like the next moment, he felt again the gale in his face, in his eyes, its racket in his brain. If it was a moment he'd been away, it had been long enough for all the pictures of his life to play out.

Now her beating dress commanded his focus. His body clawed back another foot of rock, a foot closer to her, almost near enough to touch her. If he struck and screwed up, doom. He sprawled lower to the ground, called her name, asked her to come to him.

There was no fear in her, that was clear, just a calm beyond his comprehension. Then cotton whipped his fingers, flew past. He reset his hands, hoping they were still fast enough. And once again, like lightning in mad flight the cloth snapped in front of him, chaotic movement impossible to predict. Second miss. No more deaths to his name, he told himself, nor could he fail to stop one; he owed it to a sixteen-year-old Latino Jesus, even more to Joel Vida. Just one half-chance, he'd take it, go for her, even if life ended for them both. That was the deal.

He braced his boot to a new anchor, set for the final try, and lunged toward her. But the anchor gave way, sent him slipping out slowly, feet first, hands digging against gravel and stone, until his boot found a ridge. He recomposed, looked directly up at her. Her hand opened out, called for him to take her.

With no conscious forethought he pitched forward, clamped her wrist, and crashed back to earth. But he was sliding again, out to the abyss, anchorless, scratching desperately, gaining speed. Could he let her go? Save her? Save himself? He was losing ground.

He let her go.

But in that atom of time, time stopped, and an instantaneous force re-locked him to her. His boot stopped hard against a divot. In reflex, he kicked powerfully, forced his body into an inward roll, still harnessed to her.

Then he saw her cotton dress, felt it in his hands, just the dress, billowing, beating, blowing over him. Was he dead already, gone, he asked, being seduced by a rogue reality? Tumbling toward Atlantic rocks? Already there? Was it over?

But next he was under Lenny Quin, on the ground, weightless, and the wind didn't roar, a state without turmoil or fear, nothing pulling at him, and he heard the words of Joel Vida: *In life, darkness, but in darkness always one star to aim for.* He was ice cold now, spread-eagled, soaked in sweat, the world screaming in his ears once again, Lenny's body manacled to his own. Alive. Secure.

Drained and disoriented, they crawled off the summit, made their way down the trail, stopping frequently to rest and touch the earth. At the Druidic stones they both fell onto the metal bench, a long, trembling silence over them before either found words.

'I don't know why. I don't know. I'm deeply sorry.' Her gaze stayed on the gravel at her feet. 'I felt I was lost for good, that moment.'

'Fuck! A moment?! You don't know? How close that was? We could be stone fucking dead right now. Me too, not just you. Maybe we are fucking dead. Fucking ghosts.'

'I'll never be able to tell you how sorry, how enormously grateful, I am. I think it was the height.'

'Fucking bullshit. What's going on, Lenny? That happened before, didn't it? Don't take me for a dumb-ass.'

She shook intensely, said nothing.

'I'm not dumb. Those things don't just start. You looked like you were out of your fucking mind. What is it? Tell me now.'

'Not now, Tony . . . Let's hold off, please. Till we feel more able.'

He retreated. The bliss he'd seen in her terrified him. As though she wanted nothing more than to go to another world. He'd seen crack addicts the same way. With her it was something else. She knew what it was, he knew that. He'd find out, but could he deal with it, any of this shit, any more of it?

They left the Druidic stones and walked until they reached the Seaview Café, lower down, where they sat in facing chairs and drank tea. Out of fractured intimacy they retrieved a composure of sorts, eventually. But what had happened went on terrorising him. He kept his darkest thoughts to himself, and his words few and measured.

After a while it came back to him that he had begun this day with a mission, to find out if anything was left between them. He could go there. But why? And about what he had done on the summit, when he was powerless, what god gave him that? Worth celebrating. He'd deal later with what he'd learned this day, and consider what he'd lost.

Lenny's voice broke into his thoughts, a new voice that belied the trauma of a few hours before.

'Tony, as I said earlier, I feel it's only fair that you should know what I want to tell you. About me, who I am.'

'If you mean about the guy you're seeing, forget it. Don't need it.'

'There is no guy. How many times do you need me to say this? Why is it you can't trust my word?'

'Little things. Like dozens of photographs of a man, one man, you and him, his clothes on your bed, your secret disappearances, drugs. Simple shit like that.'

'It isn't like that. Not at all.' Her eyes opened wide to him; she held her gaze. 'Just listen, will you.'

*   *   *

Her mother, Róisín Doyle, had passed away when she was five, she said. She had no memory of Charles ever being with them. He had to go away to do business, she was told. Then he disappeared altogether from her life, or maybe that was just how she thought of it. But it wasn't hard to be sure about the real parent figures in her life, the couple who dominated her early years, Leo and Peggy Reffo. Leo had been a close confidant of her mother's, and to the degree that anyone was able to raise her – not easy, she'd been told – Leo and Peggy did that. Peggy died three years ago, in early 1991. Leo was devastated. But he went on managing informally most of what happens in Claire Abbey, and now in his mid-sixties he was nearing retirement. Despite him being the closest thing to a father-figure she had known, as a teenager she directed a lot of loose anger toward him and rarely expressed appreciation for the unconditional love he and Peggy always had for her.

At eight years of age she was deposited in her first boarding school, in Sligo, a fiasco that lasted six months. Then for a short while she lived in Dalkey, in south Dublin, in the care of a live-in housekeeper and Italian au pair. When she was nine-and-a-half her father tried again, she said; he placed her with the nuns at Regis Hall in Wicklow, a boarding school walled in by ten feet of granite and an army of disciplinarians. At least that's how it felt. Two weeks into that experience she earned the first of what became many suspensions. And hated her life.

Before she reached eleven her persistent insubordination succeeded: she got expelled for good from Regis Hall. Charles was abroad at the time, as usual, so once again Leo and Peggy took her in. Three weeks later Charles took her back, screaming and kicking, to Claire Abbey, and hired a governess. When that didn't work he enrolled her with the nuns in Castlebar, which meant a forty-five minute bus ride every morning and afternoon. That went on for a few months, until she got her way, a place in St Agnes's Girls School in Aranroe. She had some difficulties there with people, to do with not fitting in. But she did well academically for the first time, and for a while she was happy and sad, which was an improvement. Otherwise, she suffered and sometimes barely scraped through her early teenage years.

Then, in 1976, when she was seventeen, she escaped again, this time by enrolling as an arts student in University College Dublin. She came to detest the constriction of college protocols but did well and lasted out the four years. That's when New York called, and she didn't hesitate. It spelt ultimate freedom, which she grabbed with attitude and a long-held passion to turn herself into a professional studio photographer. Her one other great dream, cherished even longer, would also be fulfilled: she'd get out from under the oppression of Claire Abbey and all it represented. And one day in the future she was about to march into, she promised herself she'd have her own real family and real home. Neither of which had come about.

The initial narcotic of Manhattan turned slowly into a depressing grind: often decrepit, always requiring compromises that at first shocked her Irish sensibilities. But, after three years of room sharing, learning to recognise the prima donnas and massaging the right egos, her name and talent had won recognition among avant-garde art cliques. She learned to exploit every stare that roamed up and down her body, every flirting comment on her accent, every buy-you-a-drink invitation. Thereby she negotiated the essential imprimaturs, and doors swung open; she was hot, her images and fashion eye in demand. And she grew even more clever at servicing the power set, the royal road to the top. Her credo was compelling: play their game, climb higher. By 1984, her fourth year in the city, she was a minor celebrity, some said major, free to shoot her own style, choose her art directors and contracts. As she saw it, there was no ceiling that couldn't be broken through.

Her commercial work won acclaim in international markets and led to suddenly-huge fees. Hence the framed magazine covers in her apartment. And that's how life went on. Though constantly troubled by it all, she was addicted. She drank up the embraces, the admiration, sank into the anaesthesia and false nurture of it. Being talented had become a means to an end, a path to belonging, to feeling powerful and sought-after, and wanted. She drowned in the elixir of being a social icon, top of the party lists, always ready to hover on regal arms and all that went with that. Looking back now, she said, it seems vacuous and immoral, but it felt better than anything else she could envision, always more than what she had left behind in Ireland, better than anything there to go back to.

She had succumbed to a cult, been blinded, become an insider in a world that was voraciously self-preserving, up-town emperors and empresses flaunting power, exploiting celebrity, turning over lovers as new obsessions arrived, a compassionless game. Penthouse parties, white lines, hugs and kisses, libidinous frenzy. The delusion worked. Most of all the conviction that she was loved, the lie that lasted longest and was ultimately the most damaging.

Except for short periods, the scene had never felt right, she told him. That was not her, in Manhattan; somewhere in her heart she had always known it. In time, the truth began intruding, usually just before she fell asleep, accompanied by an increasingly heavy affliction, the loneliness in her soul. Then full-blown despair set in, and other warning signs she could no longer suppress. Until she felt that life as she had been living it could not go on. And it didn't.

The beginning of the end came in the form of odd social insecurities, then physical spasms and brief mental absences that could strike at any time; she didn't understand what was happening to her, but told no one. Bouts of depression followed, sometimes for weeks.

Then one morning, out of the blue, everything became clear as day: she'd been masquerading, living a lie, a failed way of life, unable to find what she needed, never even understanding what that was.

Nearly a decade after she had kissed the city with twenty-one-year-old lips and impetuous naivete, it all crashed. The struggle stopped at 8.06am on a late-March day: there was no longer any reason to live. No reasons for her for suns to rise. No one real. Nothing to move on to. And not a single love in that decade, not a touch that even fantasy could disguise. All this became clear.

Two hours later, after walking out on an ad agency shoot, she wandered semi-lucid along Fifth Avenue, into Central Park, and a number of times around Columbus Circle. By some circuitous route she ended up on a street bench, trying to make sense of her seemingly disembodied hands and feet that felt somehow not her own. All around her was distortion, shapes fearful and frantic, things dancing, rumbling, whirring. She tried to re-attach to the security of people, cars, buildings, trees, escape a chaos that was urging her to an end. But it felt futile to fight, to return to a life where the meter had already run out.

A while later she forced herself off the bench, trying to win back lucidity. Right then, the world felt like it had become too heavy on her shoulders. On another street, somewhere different, she began winning back willpower and the ability to question her condition. Was she expelling herself again, she asked, from a bigger boarding school? Cutting out from a world she could not relate to? The answer came, clear and certain: it was over. The New York game. The whole game.

A part of her protested, but the depth of loneliness extinguished all argument, blocked all retreat. There was no reason left to wish for one more day. Then, somehow, she was back by Central Park: cars and buildings again, people walking hounds, stick figures, cold-eyed doormen, a hurdy-gurdy grinder, but not one decibel of the clamour entered her ears. All around her, spongy pavements, skyscrapers blowing in the breeze, blues pouring from the sky, green-glowing bodies running through a Dali-like pastiche.

In the midst of this chaos her thoughts jumped to Róisín, her mother, a woman she didn't know, pressing her to find a rationale for living. But other, stronger powers insisted her dreams were hopeless. Time to end time, she resolved. Quiet. Painless. Calm. Fix some things first. She dropped her gold Solvil-et-Titus watch into the gutter. A yellow taxi bounced to a stop in front of her, rocked her back to the pavement, the driver shouting, gesticulating.

Then, on that March day in 1990, one minute before noon on a digital clock bleeding red time, an alien stumbled into her impending denouement. A long-haired Englishman. An accidental bump in a publishing-house doorway, a client's place of business into which she had wandered for no reason known to her then or later. A bump into a funny, intense apostle of good with an electric smile.

Over the next six days he built a new world. On the seventh, on his arm, she walked out on New York City. Restored. Left her studio, everything in it, with her two assistants, for them. Didn't look back. Never went back. His name was Aidan Harper, the man with the short pony-tail whose photographs hung in her bedroom. That was four-and-a-half years ago, she said. She was thirty-one. She had seen his face for the last time three-and-a-half years ago.

Here, her voice dropped, her features turned trance-like. Previous fractures had resolved quickly, as though something in her compelled her to go on. This time, though, her hand repeatedly swept back her blond hair but no words emerged.

Tony's hand reached across the table.

She pulled back. 'I'll lose my . . . I want you to hear.'

'You don't have to.'

'I want to. For me. For you.'

*   *   *

It was incredible and beautiful what happened next, she told him. And terrifying. Like something out of a novel. Those seven days with Aidan Harper took away the city. And took away despair. In an altogether unimaginable way he gave her more faith in attaining joy than she had ever known. They spent every hour of that week in her apartment. Unplugged everything, even the phone, had food delivered, went out only twice, once to the zoo, once for a long stroll. She knew within minutes of their meeting that she had discovered a new reality. And soon to follow was a way of living that was foreign to anything she could ever have dreamed. His untidy, mismatched clothes, his silver mane, his awkwardness at nearly everything, all came with a rare heart. And brought with it, for her, another certainty: her Manhattan addiction was done. From that moment she would live only for what was true; she'd save dying for the day truth left. He brought love and wonders and wisdom from somewhere she had never travelled, never even known; he infused her with life. It was glorious, in all its seconds; not just him, as much as he was glorious, but his world.

Clients were screaming for transparencies, proofs, appoint-
ments. She didn't care, really didn't care. She had found her
heart, maybe her soul, on a day when everything was worth
nothing, no star shining.

By the end of the week her before-Aidan life, the agencies,
magazines, the parties, the favour-takers, didn't exist. Gone too
were the distortions, the delusions, the brief but crazy notion that
her limbs were detached from her body. Real joy had taken her
beyond it all. All because of a silvery prankster who'd approached
her with a British accent and a deadpan face, asking if she knew
where one might buy an African elephant, deceiving her in her
craziness into insisting the zoo was the obvious answer. And, yes,
she did know how to get there; and, yes, she would have a free
hour or two to accompany him. And she did. A funny encounter
on a terrible day.

Unbelievably, she said, the future looked exciting and wonderful. And so it was. It was truly all those things. And that's how it
remained. Until he was gone. The only one who was real.

Her voice sank to a whisper, then silence, for moments. 'Mind
hearing this, Tony?'

He shook his head.

*   *   *

'Aidan . . . He was killed.'

She returned to expressionless staring. His calling was to care
for the poor, she told him, the sick, the down-trodden of the
world. A relief worker, he cared for others like no human she had
ever known. More than he cared about himself. In the pain of
Africa and Central America, he told her, he had found himself.
The day they met, he was in New York seeking funding, but also
because he was ordered to take a break from eighteen-hour days
in drought-ravaged Ethiopia. He held no ambitions for wealth or
status; only higher causes commanded his talents. At the publishing

house at which they'd accidentally met, he was being interviewed about famine and AIDS in developing countries. The media, to him, was a mere vehicle for generating funds for food, water, sanitation, medicines, and saving lives.

In that halcyon week together word came that he was to go to Iraq, not back to Ethiopia. There, in a Manhattan loft, they charted their journey together. It was 1990. Iran and Iraq were counting their dead after almost a decade of war with each other; the region was dangerous, potentially explosive. That didn't bother him. Or her. She'd go with him, no question; she couldn't imagine living outside his world, a world filled with hope, belief, love, the opposite of what had been hers.

At zero hour, flashing a bunch of papers and her out-of-date Irish passport, Aidan rushed them through tarmac security and aboard a chartered relief flight to Baghdad, via Amsterdam. In the air, fellow relief workers Bobby and Kathy Tracy made a Polaroid mug-shot of Lenny and glued it in place on an improvised ID document. And so, high above the earth, *Lenny Quin, Relief Worker, Ireland* was born. On landing in Baghdad, Bobby's take-charge style and knowledge of protocol sailed them through every checkpoint and into the heart of the city.

She accompanied Aidan into village after village of noble people, grateful strangers in need of nutrition and medicines and hygiene systems, and later into searching out the sick in the underbelly of other cities and towns. Never had she felt more fulfilled, she said. Never more frightened. Never closer to being killed. Never more alive. Even the longest days seemed easy because they worked together, she and Aidan, her irreligious but holy English eccentric. Every moment counted, and she counted them. In that desolate land she was reborn. Life gave her back the bright light of day and the stars of night. It was overwhelming at times, in a positive sense. What she had thought of as romance bore scant relation to what she was experiencing. More than once in private moments she wept for having found inside herself what she realised was unconditional love, which she had never previously acknowledged nor felt capable of, and the glories it brought.

As the months passed, the rigging and set-building skills she'd honed in her studio proved invaluable and never failed to elicit Aidan's fascination. Together they made a difference every day, easing suffering, restoring hope to the ill and the fearful, nurturing bodies and hearts that in turn nurtured others, and they kept people alive who otherwise would have perished. In conditions of severe hardship, what they shared lightened all the burdens and led her to her spiritual realisation.

Eleven months, that's how long it lasted, she told him. Then time ran out: February 11th 1991, in Baghdad City, during the Gulf War. American smart bombs crumpled the Amiriya shelter. Eight hundred civilians, maybe one thousand, were gathered inside, praying under the thunder for long lives.

Fifteen minutes before the bombs hit, she and Aidan had finally succeeded in coaxing the last group of mothers clasping children to follow them down into the shelter, to safety. She'd stay with them, she had promised, until the planes were gone, the thunder past, until it was over and they could go back to their homes. But it was never over. Never would be.

The bombs came. First, a flash. Then a sucking roar. The shelter turned white-hot, blew apart. Concrete slabs the size of cars crashed down, mangled everything beneath them, crushed women and babies, men, children, teenagers, left holes to see the heavens through. Then the fireballs, hissing like demons, turning people into puffs of smoke, leaving bits of black flesh where infants suckled seconds earlier, evaporated in a chasm of chaos. Hundreds mutilated, crying, bleeding, dying, dead. Everywhere, parts and pieces of people, clumps of ash.

In the middle of that hell was the face of Aidan Harper. Black, matted, bloody. An image that had not been healed by her surviving, still there in every detail. She saw him as she lay strapped to a stretcher, being carried over rubble and bodies. Just feet from her, his head protruding from under a slab of concrete: black and raw, his silver hair scorched off. A face bearing no anger, for none had ever lived in him. A prankster. Greyed with soot and ash. Her cry, she recalled, drowned out the wailing of that world, a cry of spiritual death, again and again, on and on until it blocked out the whole inferno and accompanied her into delirium.

Now, three-and-a-half years after that violation of innocents she could still smell the burning flesh, taste the soot in her mouth. Up until recently she was sure it would never leave her.

Hours after the bombs, in a hospital on the outskirts of Baghdad, she awoke concussed, heavily sedated, her body bruised, superficially burned and lacerated. Inside her a fierce siren was still blaring, for Aidan. He was with the four hundred and thirty dead, all of whom had been freed from what she had been spared to bear. Evacuation came two weeks later, first to Germany, from there to Dublin, and later to County Mayo.

For more than two hundred of the dead there were no bodies, no identification. Nothing of Aidan's was recovered, no journal or ring or watch. Not even an urn of surrogate ashes was provided to eulogise or scatter.

Throughout the following months she had pleaded with the Iraqi authorities for assistance. Too much annihilation, they said, too much human disintegration to establish that an English relief worker ever entered the Amiriya shelter. Aidan's agency offered their condolences. All they knew about him or could find were the few details he had written on his application thirteen years earlier: Born 1947 in Highfields in the English midlands; moved to Ely to attend Cambridge University, graduated 1970; no current address; next of kin a half-brother, sixteen years older, had been living in Argentina, address not known, no contact information; no other relatives; no assets; no bank account; no will; no last wishes in the event of death. Apart from that, just glowing tributes from colleagues, warm recollections and reminiscences. All unwanted, she said, too unbearable.

*   *   *

Lenny leaned back from the table, opened out her hands. That was it. And here, she said, September 1994, she was alive, able to talk about it for the first time, with a man who had brought this unbelievable lift to her life.

Tony's expression acknowledged her. He offered no words for none felt right or worthy. The horror of his past seemed lighter now, more easily borne. Other innocents had suffered and stayed standing. And, like him, she was a survivor, now setting alight in him a reverence he had denied her. Once again it came to him that fate must have brought them together; perhaps they sensed in each other some parallel of pain or affinity. In both their lives death had cheated them. Only God, if he existed, if he wasn't a murdering sadist, could ever, could ever –

'You okay?' she intruded.

He nodded, suddenly self-conscious.

'Sorry for the tears. I've never spoken of these things, to anyone. Except Leo, just parts of it; he's a good man. Thank you, Tony, for letting me go on like that. You've no idea how relieving, how energising it feels.'

'I do know ... more than you might think. Anyway, I did nothing, just listened.'

'You did an unbelievable amount.'

They agreed to talk later, that they'd said enough for now. In warm sunshine they linked each other down the paved lane that formed the last of the Killadoon trail. Occasionally she stopped and squeezed his hand in both of hers. At the end she wrapped him in a long unexplained embrace.

They lingered for a long while in the grounds of Horslips Hotel, in and out of superficial conversation. He decided against asking the questions he most wanted answered: Why had she gone away? Where to? To whom? Why the medications? A better time would come.

Later, they left the hotel, arms around each other's waist. 'I've got a surprise,' she whispered with a look of mischief. 'Follow me.'

'Where?'

'Just follow.'

*   *   *

She led him into foliage outside the grounds, then under dense overhanging trees. The wind rattling and the sounds of creatures scurrying about brought back the banshee stories of his boyhood, and unnerved him.

'Excited?' she asked.

'Dark in here. Feel better to know where you're taking me. What you're planning to do with me.'

'Don't tell me you're afraid. You are! You're shaking.'

'Not afraid. Just like to know.'

'You can't know. It's a surprise. Soon you'll see.'

They passed through giant ferns and red-berry briar, then came abruptly upon a blue, rippled loch. Five feet below them, three small row boats banged together, tugging at their moorings. Tony's eyes journeyed across the water, beyond a pair of pincer headlands, to a raging ocean, the Atlantic, and to a small green island about a mile off shore.

'Loch Doog,' Lenny said. 'Once sacred to the ancient Druids. Doolough Lake, to give it its Anglicised name. The island is Intinn Island. This is the secret side of the loch. That's how I've always thought of it. And guess what.'

'There's a monster in the lake?'

'Loch, not lake, you're in Ireland,' she said, smiling. 'Keep guessing.'

'There's a monster in the loch.'

'No, that's Scotland. But the brown boat is ours. Let's row over to the island, Tony. It's spectacular. Really superb. You'll love it.'

He stalled, but drawn on by her excitement he suppressed a

strange spookiness in him, dismissed it as one more legacy of a past he had yet to put right.

On the water he found a rhythm for the drop and pull and lift of the oars, and quickly worked out how to point the prow. The boat bore out to the farthest edge of the loch, through the pincer headlands, and into the Atlantic. His physical strength and discovered seamanship managed easily the swirls and currents. At Intinn's wooded shoreline he steered under a canopy of branches, broadsided against the bank, and tied up.

The island was breezy and overgrown, darker than it appeared from afar, gnarled trees and briar everywhere. Close to where they landed he was taken immediately with a railinged square of rampant weed, two mottled headstones standing in its centre.

Lenny took his hand, led him along a shoreline of tide-pools and weed-coated boulders, all glistening in the afternoon sunlight. Farther down the shoreline broke left onto a pristine cove of white sand and turquoise water. Half-way around the cove a rocky promontory jutted out to the Atlantic, and beyond its tip, as though de-coupled by time, a 25-foot-high needle-like rock rose out of the depths. He closed his eyes and took in the dream.

'Wake up.' She pulled on his sleeve. 'What do you think of my surprise? Isn't this heaven. It was here, these waters and islands, that inspired John Synge's plays.'

He hadn't taken in what she said, he realised now. His mind was sailing away still, over alabaster sands and craggy rocks and alcoves into an endless blue; he was being seduced for the first time by the splendour of being alive.

Then intrusions of isolation whipped him back to that long-ago world, an unlit cell, dreaming of escape, of freedom, of a fantasised woman, of Ireland, obsessions that sustained him through more than three thousand days and nights. And by some mystery of fate it had become real. So often he'd seen it in his mind, he'd touched it and smelled it, this very scene. And here was. Freedom. Home. Ireland. A green island. And this woman called Lenny Quin.

'Well, what do you think?' she said, this time calling for a response.

'Totally incredible.' He tried to disguise his introspection, for he carried things she could never know, what she would not comprehend; and he knew that words would never explain the ordeal or the dream that had forged his life.

'Devil's Cove. My safe place,' she said, tipping her face to the sun and salt-laden breeze. 'Out there, the spike, that's Finger Rock. You're right, it is incredible, everything here; my feelings precisely. Since I was fifteen I knew I would always want to come here to die.'

'Die? I don't get it. Everything's alive here. This place is alive.'

'Where better to die than where everything is alive? You die but you don't die. You can't. You stay alive for always in the sand and the ocean and the sky. You never die.'

He arched his eyebrows and waited. Her detached seriousness discomforted him. Then her rich blue eyes re-opened and she smiled as though realising she had let something slip.

'Come on,' she said, playfully pulling him along.

They strolled to the middle of the cove. Away to their left sat the distant hills of Connemara; to their right, twice as far, a faint Inishturk Island. And there they eased down into the sand, soaking up the warm sun on their bodies.

'Let's go,' Lenny said, leaning over him. 'For a swim! Come on.'

'Swim? We've no . . . You mean – '

'Why not!' she said with a thrill. 'Not a soul comes here.'

'Might not be safe . . . It's rough.'

'Of course it's safe. No current in here. You can see where it sweeps past, between the end of the promontory and Finger Rock. We don't need to go near there. Oh please, Tony, come on, it's a wonderful opportunity, come on, please, let's go in.'

Again, his hesitation caused him to question how free he had really become. They'd already slept together; she'd seen the scars, and everything else. Nothing to be embarrassed about. So why, he thought? All that shit in prison maybe. Maybe not. The feeling was strange, like he needed permission. Joel had warned him he'd have to learn to permit himself. He didn't need Lenny Quin for that; this was the original Anthony Xavier MacNeill, not something a stinking penitentiary had shaped. He'd do it.

Her sandy fingers touched his cheek. Then, hair dancing in the wind, she stepped out of her long cotton dress and flung aside her underclothes; and as she ran to the water his eyes ran with her in every slow-motion stride, ran with her all the way, through the shimmering light that mingled her into the scene; she was elemental, she was god-like, as one with the beauty before him as the sand or sea.

He sighed at his whiteness, then followed her, hoping she would plunge under before he caught up. The frigid shallows sent shocks through him. Freezing cold and frontally exposed, he feared, was no sight to show off; so as the chill bit into new regions he surrendered all of him to another chapter in his fateful dream.

He watched in wonder as Lenny moved with the poise she had on land. Farther and farther out she swam until her blond crown disappeared beneath the whitecaps for spells he thought of as much too long. She was a mermaid. Her grace underscored his own clumsiness, his panicky scrambling when his feet lost the bottom. Then after a while together their exertion sent them back to the comfort of the sand, where breathless and gasping they reclined on their stretched-out clothes.

'Are you asleep?' She stroked his hair minutes later as he lay face down. He smiled at her nakedness, then sat up and pushed his legs into his jeans.

'Not as warm now,' he said. 'Maybe you should put something on.'

Her face revealed a different desire.

'Sand all over me,' he muttered, concealing that he had read her thoughts.

She shook out the bright calico dress and stepped into it. 'This place is special, Tony; it'll stay warm for a long while yet; you'll see.' She leaned back against one of the great boulders set into the beach and patted the sand beside her.

As he dropped into the spot he drew from his jeans pocket a tiny gold envelope, which he handed to her.

'For me?' She lavished it with wonder, then kissed him. Her fingers raised up a gold chain with a tiny Connemara Marble cross at the end. 'Tony! I adore it! I'll put it on now. I adore it. I'll always wear it, I will.' She settled in his embrace. 'I could stay here forever like this, just you and me.'

His fingers threaded through her ocean-damp hair. At the same time, his mind wrestled with his uncertainties, and what his destiny might be.

'Remember I mentioned a second surprise?' she said. 'Well I have one. But not yet. First, I want to know about a truly special man. Who is Tony MacNeill, really deep down?'

He shrugged, made a face. 'Like anybody else. Not that interesting.'

'Liar. That's not who he is. Be serious, I want to know.'

'What is it you want to know?'

'Everything.'

'It'll be dark soon.'

'No it won't. Please, be serious. I understand life and how unpredictable it can be; I'm six years your senior, remember. You've had trying times, ups and downs, but so what, we both have. Tell me what happened. Those scars. And about your family.'

Her genuineness induced in him a rare urge to open up. It felt both desirable and dangerous, like the night he spent with her. Foolish to give in to her, he felt, yet he couldn't deny that that was the yearning in him now.

'Six years and eleven months,' he said, and paused as his words hung in the air. 'You're March '59, I'm February '66. Another month, you'd be seven years older.' As soon as his words were out he hated their superficiality, knew that he had carried his avoidance too far. And he noticed in her a hurt, at least clear disappointment. He owed her more, he realised that, especially for fighting through telling him what had happened in New York and Baghdad, re-enduring such terrors so that he could know her. But could he tell her anything? Tell anyone? His heart was beating hard. Where was his escape?

She knelt forward, facing him, knees buried in the sand. 'You're hiding,' she said. 'What makes you so afraid? I care about you, a whole lot. I'd like to know you, your life; you're that important to me. But if you feel I don't merit your trust, then we'll just let it be.'

*   *   *

Though vacillating, he told her how destroyed he had felt when his parents took him out of Ireland. Moving to America wasn't the adventure it might have been for any other fourteen-year-old. And how in Newark things turned bad from the start. Within three months he had sunk into what he now was sure was adolescent depression. He wasn't to blame for that; that's how Kate explained it to him years later, and Joel too. But no one talked about teenage depression then; to some he was just one more moody kid, a trouble-maker. From there he slid downhill but always had one thing going for him: he could fight, better than most. He thought of it as the only thing he did well, not being naturally good at anything else. Dublin had given him a fighting heart, an edge, as he saw it, a way of surviving, the one thing nobody could take from him. In the seediness of Newark, where trouble came free and loose, he would have been dead without that edge. He looked down on the tough kids on the streets, in the housing projects, the jocks in high school. As he saw it, they imagined themselves to be poor, deprived, victimised, but none knew real hardship, nor had ever been really poor or hungry, nor had had to struggle every day because that's just how life was. Only the immigrant kids, and not all of them, knew such things.

It was with these immigrant kids, he told her, with the grittiest of them, who roamed in gangs, that he found a connection, common cause, common enemies, and he took on a new identity. They were not heartless kids, like some; they wanted only what he wanted: to break out of what they'd been forced into, to find a life, a way up, or a way out. His own thing was one-to-ones, being seen as tough, a fighter, so he directed his own private vendetta against bullies, thugs, street punks. For others the lure was drugs, which never interested him, except for weed, which everyone smoked. The really dumb kids became stick-up men; they robbed stores and people, even cash trucks, and always lost. For him it was enough to have fast hands and fighting skill and opportunities to show off. When he grew up he'd figure out what he wanted to do with his life; then he'd just go do that, become something, somebody; that was the plan.

Yet all the time, when he was fourteen, fifteen, sixteen, seventeen, he never wanted to be what he was. A gang member. Because he knew he would never be like them, deep down nothing about him was like them. Only circumstances. His real ambition, he realised later whenever he looked back, was to rise above them, be better than all of them, show friend and foe how superior the Irish were, how superior he was. It was immature and stupid, but that's what he was always fighting for. He understood much later that he was fighting in a way too for the country that had been taken from him. Never just for glory, or power, or to be the leader. Maybe a leader, but never just that. This rage that destroyed his adolescent years and a good part of his life, he was later told, came out of rootlessness.

A year went by, then two, then three. He managed to stay out of serious trouble. Out-ran and out-foxed the cops when he had to. And he out-fought opponent after opponent in the manner that he alone dictated: one-to-one ritualistic battles, tough against tough, fair and square, no weapons, not even brass knuckles. He was skinny, at best a middleweight, but he fought them all, and conquered all who were brave enough to fight clean. And he became a kind of street king, a king for others to de-throne, which meant constant battles, and constant satisfaction. By seventeen he'd given up believing in the future that wasn't showing up, and he was angry and disturbed.

*   *   *

He resettled against the rock and fell into quiet. Lenny hugged her knees to her chest, looking ready to soothe the pain if called upon. A minute passed. Only the rumble of the ocean intruded. Then two.

'Something happened,' she said softly. 'If anyone can understand, Tony, I can.'

*   *   *

He turned to her, as though signalling a breaking-in to an inner place. 'Trouble with the law,' he said. 'That's all over now, a long time. I was seventeen. Eighteen when they sentenced me. Nine years of my life. Taken. I went straight to Arizona when I got out, in February of last year. Maybe Arizona because that's where Joel Vida grew up, the prison psychologist I told you about, always talking about Arizona. Seven months after getting out I met you, last September at the train station. I almost hit Boxer that night; you couldn't have known that. It was that close. Anyhow, I didn't. So I'm here now. Twenty-eight. Guessing every move. Learning how to live.'

'What did they charge you with?'

He sighed, wanted to jump up, go, get away, but the unfairness of doing so kept him next to her. 'Not now,' he said.

'That's fine. We can talk about other things. What would you – '

'Two things.' He searched her face. 'Where did you go Thursday, when you disappeared? And all those pills; are you sick?'

'We'll have time later to talk about all those silly things. And the things you are not comfortable talking about.' She sprang up, reached down to him. 'Come. I'll show you the other surprise I have for you.'

He ignored her request. His eyes lifted to her, her slender form teasing him through a translucent veil. She tossed his hair, moved away gaily. He chased after her, caught her hand, let her take him.

They'd been hiking for five minutes through scrubland when a small stone cottage appeared in front of them. He gazed at it, amazed. Much of the open space around it had been taken over by vegetation. Yet it did not have the appearance of being abandoned.

'Like it?' she asked. 'It's old, we own it. Nobody uses it anymore. Except me. Rarely.'

He trailed after her across the face of the cottage to a giant sycamore whose massive bough curved down to the ground before turning up again. They sat there together, staring out, as the sun descended and Intinn and the Atlantic glowed with fire.

'When I was very young I'd try to come over here when I could,' she said. 'I'd sneak out, implore the trawlermen to drop me off as they sailed out to the fishing grounds. None would take me. When I got to sixteen, those long summer days off school, then it was easy, sometimes a problem. They'd want to hang around me, and the island. They couldn't comprehend that I wanted none of them near here, or me. I wanted no one here. Intinn was mine. For me only. I hated them, those men. Hated them being near me. Hated them stepping foot on Intinn.

'Then one day I figured out how to keep them away. By putting the fear of the banshee woman into them. I made up a story. I swore that I saw corpses here, dead people walking the island, disturbed spirits who talked to me. When word got around, someone in the village reported me to the bishop. I told all of them the same story: this house, Rock Cottage, was still home to the soul of an old woman with sunken eyes, a very tall emaciated woman nearly invisible inside a hooded shroud, an angry spirit with a chalk-white face, ready to devour any man or woman who violated her threshold. A banshee through and through. Her name was Liza Murtagh; this cottage was once her home. Her two children were murdered here in 1920 in the War of Independence, by British soldiers. Their graves, near where we landed, are the only graves on the island. What happened here is well known; poems and songs have been written about it. The Black-and-Tans tortured a mainland couple into betraying Fintan Murtagh, Liza's husband, a rebel, one of Michael Collins' men fighting for Irish freedom. He wasn't here when they came for him, and Liza would never have known his whereabouts. But that didn't satisfy them; they wanted information. They forced her to watch both her children being drowned in a cattle trough. Some said later that they didn't intend to kill the children, that the children were sickly with TB. True or not, they fabricated a story to cover up what they'd done. You probably remember from school, the Black and Tans and the Auxiliaries were British forces sent to Ireland to teach the Irish a lesson; they murdered civilians at random, showed no humanity, and were answerable to no law. W.B. Yeats wrote *Reprisals,* a poem about their brutality.

'I told everyone that Liza told me she would never rest, that her dying wish as I heard her tell it from her own withered lips, was to forever possess Intinn, the holy soil that held her poor innocent offspring, and that's why no one to this day has ever found her body. I swore that she moved through walls and bushes, that she waited for anyone foolish enough to come here, and if a person dared to cross her doorstep she'd very quickly bring that person the most horrible end.

'When someone died in the fields on the mainland, or out of a currach, I'd tell them that that was Liza Murtagh taking revenge

against locals for betraying her, and that she'd go after any tres-
passer even if he fled to England or America, and even the sons
and daughters of trespassers. She'd wait for her victim in the dark
of a lonely lane; the person would hear a cry from hell that would
sink fear into the bravest man, then he'd see her coming for him
in a long burial shroud, closer and closer, until her chalk-white
face floated out of her hood and she tore the soul out of him, then
she'd carry it off with her so that he'd never see the face of God,
or rest in peace. Because that's what she was, the banshee, and
here, Intinn Island, this was where she kept every wailing soul she
had taken. And Rock Cottage would be her home for ever more.'

Her recitation stopped abruptly. 'They said I was mad. But
they were afraid. Superstitious people. Doing novenas, saying
Rosaries. Other girls were forbidden to talk to me. But it worked;
from then on they all stayed away; they knew I hated them here.
None of them belong here. Intinn is for me and Liza and her
children. Now it's yours too.'

An intensity beamed in her, the sight of which chilled him. He
was lost again, he thought. What did he know of such terrors? Cold
sweat down his back caused him to shiver. How could he hide from
her? Where? He needed to breathe. His body was getting beyond
his control. He had to stop acting like a scared child, a coward.

'Tony!' she said with a startle. 'What's wrong? It's not true,
none of it, I made it up. About the banshee. I made up the whole
thing. Are you alright?'

'What do you expect?'

'What do I expect?'

'Think.' He willed his body to be still. 'No evil spirits or ban-
shees where I'm coming from. Locked in every night, all that
time, never needed to worry about things like that.'

'You mean . . . Oh my God, how insensitive of me. I'm so foolish; I'm truly sorry, Tony. I shouldn't, oh – ' Her hands drew him
nearer until their foreheads touched and they settled in to an
edgy embrace.

In and out the silver moon waltzed, large and crisp across his world, brilliant against the always visible blues of the Irish summer sky. For a while his thoughts surfed the unrelenting waves. If only he could rid his mind of Liza Murtagh, the ghost woman, he thought, be certain she wasn't real, be able to think about sensible things again.

'Up there, this morning, on the cliff, what happened?' he asked firmly.

Her expression turned, as though the asylum they were sharing had been breached.

'I need to understand, that's all. You and Aidan, you were up there, I bet, on the top, weren't you? And you came here to Intinn Island too.'

She went on staring into the distance, and with each passing second seemed to recede further.

'Lenny . . . Lenny.'

Her aspect caused him to regret bringing Aidan back to life, especially now, in this ghostly place. But that's what he had done and now could not re-bury him.

'Why is that important to you?' she asked. 'You're supposed to be a present person. Remember? No living in the past for you. Aidan is the past. Dead. I love you. Here, now. Is that enough?'

He searched inside him for how to tell her how much he felt for her. And that his caring for her was real, as were his concerns and hopes. But in the seconds allowed, the right words would not come.

'Yes, I was up on the cliff with him. Once. We stood on the summit. That same day we came here to the island. Is that what you want to know? If it makes a difference, tell me.'

To him it did make a difference, though not in the way she meant. He didn't have the experience to quarrel with a woman this smart. But in listening to her, in dwelling on her anger and her power, he saw her more akin to himself, closer to his own unrequited core. Her tenacity came from a security that is born out of terrible suffering, the bluntness of the survivor, and from spirit. He knew that kind of anger. He could carve it in the dark into cell walls – and had.

'Well, does it?' she asked.

'Not one bit. Not at all.'

As they sat in separateness, incoming clouds obscured the sunset.

'It's just that I was scared up there. Very scared. I thought I was going to die. You too. Without even knowing why.'

'Scared? I've lived with fear every day of my life. Since I was five. I learned to accept it. Then I met Aidan and forgot about fear. Then it came back. I'm afraid now I'm going to lose you. Can't you see? I don't know what happened up there. I don't know. Is it something we can put behind us, move on? Or not?'

'What if it happens again? Ignore it? I've been there, trying to deal with things I knew no one could understand. A year before I got out they offered me counselling. I said yes, to get a break from the low-life I spent twenty-three hours every day with. No other reason. Joel, the psychologist guy from Arizona they assigned me to, it took me months to trust him. He was a jerk, that's all I knew; what could he know. I was dead wrong. He taught me things; taught me that I always had a choice, in everything I did, that nobody could take that away. Stand up, slide down, it was always up to me. He showed me how to think in ways I'd never have known. Joel Vida. Smart man. I was dumb. But for him I wouldn't be here today. Would you talk to someone like that? About what you were feeling up on the summit, what happened to Aidan, the bombs, all that shit in Baghdad?'

'Go on, be brave, say the word. Psychiatrist, shrink, psychologist, witch doctor, shaman. Find out if I'm crazy? Think I'm crazy, do you?'

'No, I don't. I'm not saying that. No one is one hundred percent sane. I'm not. We can all do with help, at times. If you'd met me in Newark, you'd never have wanted to know me. But I'm not that person now. I never was. I just believed I was, so I acted that way. At first, when Joel talked to me, I thought he was a fool. But he got me to prove things to myself, got me to dig out the real me, up out of a grave. When I look back now, he was brilliant.'

She shook her head. 'No shrink did that. You made yourself smart. Prison changed you. You grew up, became an adult. It's that simple.'

'Wrong. You're wrong. You didn't know me then. It's more than growing up. I had to be the toughest, fastest, bravest; nothing less would do. No choice, zero. Maybe I was for a while, all those things, tough. But life was hell. Now, I just want to live a normal life.'

'You're saying a shrink made you what you are. That's juvenile. Give yourself a break.'

'Remember the train station last year, when Boxer gave me a problem? I could have hurt him; I knew I could. But I didn't. Because I'd learned I didn't have to give in to thoughts like that. I decided that. Me. Not Joel Vida, not Lenny Quin, not Boxer Dunne. In Newark I never knew I could think that way, especially when someone was in my face. Just want you to know that. And Kate was good, too; she helped me; you'd like Kate.'

'Aidan talked like that, the miracles of talk therapy. I wasn't persuaded then and won't be now. He'd been through wars, spent every day dealing with genocide, disease, drought, inhuman suffering, thirteen years of watching people die. Told me he'd had dozens of sessions with counsellors, employed by his agency. Maybe people who've spent years locked up need the same type of help.'

'You don't believe that. Not for a second. You're the educated one. It's not about prison or the work Aidan did; it's about being hurt, and we've all been hurt. You and me, Lenny. Face it, we carry scars, we hide away. Everyone needs to get rid of shit like that. If you'd – '

'Stop! Please. Will you. You sound like a damn psychoanalyst I once – I'd be happier if you'd not say another word about it. Your logic is weepy, too self-indulgent for my taste.' She stood up, brushed feverishly at her dress, then stopped mid-motion. 'Come with me. I'll show you inside the cottage. I have a key hidden.'

His unresponsiveness halted her. She leaned toward him. 'Don't start worrying about me. Okay? As long as I have you I'll be fine. Come on.'

She disappeared into the blackness behind the gable and moments later returned with a metal key. The heavy wooden door creaked in. She stood on the step before the threshold, turned, and kissed him. 'Tomorrow, the photographs in my bedroom are coming down. Nonsensical. Surrounding oneself with pictures of people who are dead.'

'Person,' he said.

'What?'

'Person. One person who's dead.'

'That's what I meant. Person.' She reached in through the door, retrieved a small box of matches, struck one and touched it to two table candles immediately inside. She glanced back. He had not moved. She caught his jacket, pulled him in.

In a room full of familiarity he was instantly a child again. His thoughts fled to the tiny crowded rooms where he'd lived every day. Here, in front of a big black hearth stood a pair of old soft-chairs with cratered cushions. Underfoot, linoleum squealed at the press of his boots, and a bandy-legged dresser offered undisturbed dust for fingers to write in. To one side of the chimney breast a line of small photographs faced out, except for two, which seconds earlier he'd glimpsed Lenny turning down. Most noticeable though was a legacy of turf fires and tobacco pipes, and a sense of the lives and stories that were lived here.

As he sat back into one of the soft-chairs he marvelled at the love of simple pleasures that had returned to him. He inhaled the room and eloped deeper into his own unrecoverable past.

'You're somewhere else again,' Lenny said. 'Where are you drifting off to now?'

'When I was eight and nine. Home. Maybe we'll go down to Dublin soon.'

'I'd love that,' she said, holding a flickering candle. 'Want to see the rest of the cottage?'

As the door strained in on a cramped bedroom, his grandparents' wrinkled faces smiled back at him, old hands beckoning him in.

'Same place and time?' she asked.

'No, no, thinking of my grandparents' farmhouse; they died in the seventies. For a flash it was like they were here, in this room. Like they've been waiting for me. For all these years. Strange.'

She coaxed him along a narrow, papered hall to a crooked door. Inside was a cramped kitchen familiar to him in every detail.

'See, there's even logs in the scuttle,' she said excitedly. 'We could light a fire in the main room. I'll do it; I've done it here before.'

He watched her go about setting the kindling and logs into the blackened grate. Her enthusiasm was life-giving, even childlike. Unlike his own, he thought, it showed on the outside, in her smile and beautiful eyes. Even the blushing he'd seen burn her pale cheeks had a youthfulness about it, as did every movement of her fluid body. He loved her sense of excitement, envied the freedom of it. But her moods, her swings, still worried him; they too were real, a part of her, pieces of the puzzle; she could be vulnerable and confrontational at the same time. She also had an earthiness about her, and an omen of danger that could frighten him, and had more than once. And how quickly she could change. Had he met her at any other time in his life – not that there had been any other time in his life – he would never have possessed her, for he would not have had the will nor the way to understand a woman like her. Here, though, on this isolated island in 1994, all that had changed. Sitting behind her as she built their fire, watching her bring light and warmth to their subterranean world, as he took in this whole woman – he knew, despite his fears, that his soul held one certainty: he loved her.

The first jets of flame from the kindling sent shadows dancing about the room. And just then, as if in intimacy with his thoughts, she turned slowly to him, her eyes in his, and in this instant he felt her to be a part of who he was always meant to be. From below she presented her slightly-parted lips to be kissed. Instead, his mouth teased her sea-scented cheek, denying her, but only until he was helpless once again in the ocean of Lenny Quin. He leaned back from their confluence, stared at her fiery nakedness, stared with all his thoughts, all his welled-up hopes and dreams, and he set his fingers coursing through her hair, out over her warm satin shoulders, and with flames now blazing in the hearth he manoeuvred down to her.

16

Shortly after midnight the small boat pushed away from Intinn, into a noisy strait. Tony sank both oars, beaconed through the blackness by the illuminated belfry of St Brigid's Church. Five minutes out rain spat down on them in blobs, and soon the winds attacked. Lenny gripped to the gunwales as the boat shot into the air and smacked down. Half-way across, bursts of water and wind forced them off course. But each time, Tony's strength and nascent seamanship righted their progress. Closer to the mainland, the gusts calmed, he sat up the oars and rested. Lenny's eyes had not left him since their voyage began; now they stared even more intensely.

'I didn't know whether to tell you or not,' he said. 'Yesterday, when you were away, there was someone in your apartment, besides me.'

'Who?!'

'Your father and fat boy.'

'My apartment? Doing what?!'

'Your father was upstairs. Looking for something, I'd guess. Boxer stayed in the hall.'

'You saw this?'

'I was under your mountain bike. Feet from them.'

'What did they – '

A sudden squall spun the boat, broadsiding it to a wave that cascaded over them and lodged in the hull. Tony re-sank the oars and rowed hard for shore.

'I've had enough,' Lenny said. 'I'm leaving there, I mean it, getting far away. Twice before, I thought I smelled cigars in there. Now I know I'm not crazy.'

'Could be he's just worried about you. He is your father.'

She went to stand. The boat tipped steeply. 'Careful!' he yelled, canting his weight.

She grabbed the gunwales. 'I'm getting away. That's it. Damn fool.'

'Calm down! Will you.' He bore down, brought both oars up out of the water. 'I should never have told you.'

'It's alright to be spied on at thirty-five years of age? Is that what you think?'

'Cut the bullshit, Lenny. That's not what I mean; you know it. I'm trying to stop you getting riled up, that's all.'

'Well I am riled up, if that's what you choose to call it. Every right to be.'

'Not with me you don't.. I've taken enough crap in my life. So go easy.' He restarted the sinking, pulling, rising, and sweeping of the oars resumed.

'I'm finished with Aranroe, Tony. I'm telling you, I'm leaving.'

'You belong here. Take a break. Get a train to Dublin. Visit Kate. Stay a few days. Enjoy my city.'

'I don't know Kate; never spoke to the woman.'

'She wants to meet you. Told me she can't wait.'

Lenny's face released its anger, as though assuaged by a forming thought. 'Maybe. Maybe I will. Let's both go. Why not. Get away from here.'

'I can't, not now. You and Kate, you'd get along great. I told her you might visit. She's all for it. She'll tell you about the terrible things I did, when I was young. She used to mind me, when she could catch me. This is Friday; she's free on weekends. Get the early train in the morning, come back Monday.'

'You come too, Tony. Please. Can't you just please me?'

The boat moved through the headlands, into the placid waters of Loch Doog. 'Better just the two of you this time; you'll have fun. I'm heading up on Mweelrea in the morning, really early. The weather's good until Sunday, bad after that. Might not get another chance.'

'Go to Dublin, meet Kate,' she said, as though picturing the event. 'I'll do that. It's okay with Kate, this sudden?'

'Any time, she said, day or night, doesn't matter. Kate's like that, you'll see. I'll call her when we get in. You could catch an early train.'

'No, the quarter past seven bus from Louisburgh is non-stop. Gets to Dublin before eleven, which is perfect.' As the boat grated against the shore there was a brightness in her. 'New life, Tony,' she said, standing in the glow from Horslips Hotel, 'new life.'

*   *   *

The mud-splattered taxi pulled into the driveway of Greyfriars B&B Hotel and beeped twice. Paddy scrambled out, began power-walking around the car. Soon, he flopped against the bonnet. Tony stared.

'The good wife said I've to lose a stone and a half, get meself back into shape. There'll be nothing left of me by the time she's finished with me.'

Tony acknowledged, climbed into the car.

'Two hundred and fifty deep breaths every day,' Paddy said, 'and they say you'll live till the day you die or ninety-five, which-ever comes first. You can tell Eilis McCann that you're a living witness to me doing all that – '

'Everything went okay this morning?'

'Quarter past seven on the dot, put herself on the bus, safe and sound.'

'Sorry about waking you last night, getting you out so early this morning.'

'No harm. I'd be at the Abbey early anyway. Saturdays you nearly always get someone going up to Knock.'

'You made sure with Leo Reffo?'

'Said the very words you told me: had to be private between yourself and himself, I said. And that it was me own suggestion for you to have a chat with him.'

'Then why are we waiting?'

'It's not ten to ten yet. He'll not be at his place for another twenty minutes. It's just over the hill and into The Pound.'

'You know him. What's he like, Leo Reffo?'

'Grand man. And a hard man. Nobody'd ever get the better of old Leo. Sixty-four now, ten years older than meself, and as fit as any forty-year-old.' Paddy's interlocked hands sat on his paunch, his bulky frame reclining into the angle of door and seat. 'Poor man's wife died and left him a few years back. Peggy, nice woman. He's not himself since. Sour too much. Told me he'll retire soon, do a bit of market gardening. But who'd run the Abbey? Nobody else'd know how. Head Waiter is all he calls himself. But I'll tell you this, that VanSant one, she'll be arse-deep in cow shite – if you'll pardon my French – the day he walks out them doors. The whole place'll come down like the Tower of Babel.'

'Lenny told me he's helped her, over the years.'

'Better than that.'

'Better?'

'Them farmer fellas with their hay carts, never occurred to me!' Paddy bounced up. 'It's Saturday. They'll be blocking up the road.' He swung the taxi out of the driveway and started up the hill.

'What did you mean, Paddy, *better*?'

'Ah just that, you know yourself.'

'No, I don't. I don't know.'

'Ah you do. There's more than one kind of friend. Real ones, half-real ones and the other ones. It's only when you're in a ditch, me old father would say, that you get to tell the difference.'

'What do you know about Lenny's mother, Mrs Quin?'

'No harm telling you, no Mrs Quin – only for a short while. Róisín Doyle, that's Lenny's mother, she and meself were very fond of each other. Grandest lassie you'd ever meet. Sickly her whole life, unfortunately. Passed away when Lenny was only a wee thing.'

'I figure Charles Quin and Lenny fell out somewhere along the way?'

'Sure isn't Leo the best man to tell you all that. He knows things I could never swear to.'

'Why the hell does nobody around here talk straight? Any chance you could answer that?'

'Has to be us Irish, the way we're born, sir. Same as your good self, if you're Irish, I mean, like you told me.'

Tony exhaled loudly. It was too much like hard work to figure out what he was or wasn't being told. 'Dublin, Paddy, remember I told you? The heart of the city, born and reared.'

'Irish through and through so.'

Tony pulled back, turned his eyes to the passing countryside. They drove over Aranroe Hill, past the grey fortifications of Claire Abbey, down narrow roads running between lines of birches and breezy sycamores, then into a lush demesne of dairy farms and the smell of livestock.

'This is me own place,' Paddy said, turning into a white-walled yard. 'Have to nip in for a minute. We're grand for time.'

Tony gestured agreement.

'Eilis will have a cup of tea for us. I'm ravished with the walking, the flesh'll be falling off me, no one will know me. They'll think I'm me brother Mick, skinny as a tinker's greyhound.'

From inside the house came the sound of raised voices.

'The young fella and young one, at it again,' Paddy said. 'Bickering like cats and dogs from the time they get up. At twelve and fifteen.'

Tony shrugged. 'Kids fight.'

'*Ciúntas, cuairteoir!*' Paddy yelled on reaching the door, and turned to Tony. 'That was asking them to let on we reared them in a good Catholic home with no insanity on either side that we know of.'

In the kitchen, a long boy with a pimpled face and untidy hair leaned over a bare wooden table. Opposite him, hairbrush in hand, sat a plump teenage girl with a heavily made-up face. By the sink, hands on hips, a small, trim woman smiled in greeting.

'Eilis, this is Tony, Mr MacNeill, from Dublin; he's here to climb the mountain.'

Eilis extended a damp hand. 'I heard. Sit down there and make yourself comfortable. You'll have a cup of tea, you will? And a bit of soda bread?'

Tony started to decline but Paddy intruded.

'Few sambos, Eilis, would be grand. This poor man must be falling out of his standing with the hunger. And I might have a bit meself too. All me exercises are finished for the day, thank God; Tony here is me living witness.'

Tony nodded, then noticed again that the girl's stare on him had not let up.

'Madeleine, Madeleine,' Eilis said, with no response. 'Maggie McCann!'

The girl jumped, then sighed through two-tone maroon lips.

'That's Madeleine,' Eilis said, completely calm again. 'And that's – '

'Ma, Ma,' the girl scowled.

'That's Magdalena, I mean. Sorry, my mistake. At fifteen, these days they can call themselves after whoever they like.'

'Anyway, sure me and Tony know each other already,' the girl said.

Eilis's eyes quizzed the girl. Tony looked at Paddy. Paddy at Eilis. Then all three re-targeted the girl.

"Member, the other day? Cilla and me saw you at the Beehive and you asked us did we want to have breakfast with you.'

'Of course, I do.' Tony smiled, just then realising.

'And that's Pearse,' Eilis said, 'the youngest, twelve on Friday.'

'Hello,' the boy muttered then flung a glance at his sister. 'Tell her, Da, she won't give me the key for ma's bike. I have to go down to Roy's house.'

'Sorry. Y'have legs, haven't you,' the girl said. 'Might be using it meself. Told you.'

'Should go back to the hospital and get them to drop you on your head again,' the boy said, whereupon his sister's face flushed.

'Pearse McCann, you've been warned about that,' Eilis said. 'That's enough! No more!'

'She started it. It's not her bike.'

Paddy pulled the door. 'Out, the pair of you. Now, both of you.' He oversaw their exit before rejoining Tony and Eilis at the table.

'Hear you have an eye for Lenny Quin?' Eilis's tone was sober.

'Nice person,' Tony replied.

'She is that, so are all the Doyles.'

'Lenny's mother's people,' Paddy explained. 'From up outside Louisburgh; there since before the Great Hunger in the 1840s.'

'Lenny sees them, the Doyles?'

'She doesn't, no, not now,' Eilis said. 'She's back here these three years and I doubt she's seen a Doyle in that time.'

'She took off for America, then the Middle East, of all places.' Paddy said. 'Over ten years away. Came home just the one time and brought a friend with her. An English lad, Lord rest him, used to work helping people in poor countries. Killed not long after in Baghdad, when the Americans and Brits bombed the place.'

'She told me. Some of it.'

'Very hard on her, the poor thing.' Eilis's stare held on Tony. 'You've been to war yourself; is it that that I'm seeing in you?'

He struggled to break from the woman's kind eyes. Neither looked away. He shook his head, but she seemed unconvinced.

'Before all that happened she was at the college up in Dublin.' Paddy said. 'Brains to burn. Didn't often come back down to visit, and when she did you'd hardly see her.'

'Dirty business, war. Break the heart of any woman, or man,' Eilis said. 'The agony it leaves after it. Did her not a bit of good. That and the bad luck that bedevilled her as a wee one, poor soul. Not easy to get over that sort of thing.'

'Not at all, she's well over all that, grand altogether now,' Paddy insisted. 'Strong woman. Bore her cross well.'

'Same as did her poor mother,' Eilis said. 'One thing's for sure, that man Leo Reffo is bound for heaven. Looked after her from the minute things went bad with Róisín, and not just that, with all the – '

'Holy God, is that the time it is?' Paddy flicked a look at his wife and pushed up from the table. 'Have to rush or Tony'll be late for where he's off to.'

'Let him finish his sup of tea, man.'

'He's nearly late the way it is. No good all this yak about the past; we have to go.' Paddy steered Tony through the door; a minute later the taxi beeped twice as Eilis waved from the yard.

*   *   *

Leo Reffo moved impassively, austere, waist-coated, arms protruding from roughly-rolled sleeves. He led Tony to a white-walled room with a small square window and said he'd return momentarily.

Tony's searching stopped at a photograph of Lenny, a portrait, black-and-white, and out-of-place, he thought, in what felt like a museum. Opposite, a photo of a bride and groom hung alone. And from the mantle beamed the joyful face of a thin young woman. There was much to learn here, he thought, but the urgency of the occasion did not permit. And he still didn't know what to expect from his host. He sat on the edge of a chair and pondered how he might begin this odd confederation of his own making.

Leo returned, stood before the fireplace.

'Thanks for – '

'First thing you can do is hold your thanks,' Leo said. 'I'll spell it out so you're clear. Fellas that want to sniff around here for what they can take, I've seen off a few. There's any number of women around Westport, and half-a-million in Dublin. Y'understand me?'

Tony stared back without malevolence, his mind turning. There was something to admire in this grey, angry man: directness for a start, and strength, traits he could relate to. But he was here with a mission, he reminded himself, not to admire the man.

'You made your point,' he said. 'Now I'll tell you where I – '

'What business do you have with me?'

'I'm trying to tell you that.' Tony's voice hardened.

'Fire ahead.'

'I'm here, one, because Lenny doesn't want me to contact her father. And, two, because she told me you and her are friends going back a long time. '

'She told you to talk to me?'

Tony's face stilled; he said nothing.

'Then maybe you shouldn't be here. Maybe she's not all that interested.'

'Look, you're screwing this up. She is interested, and I'm interested in her. Right now she's on her way to visit my sister in Dublin.'

'If it's money you're after, you're on thin ice.'

'What the . . . what is it with you?!' Tony got to his feet, moved to the bride-and-groom photo. 'Is this you? Is it?'

Leo's remained unmoved.

'I can see it's you. You loved someone once. This woman. I love Lenny. That's the only reason I'm here. I need you to tell me some things – for her good, her happiness.'

Leo walked to the net-curtained window. Then he turned, leaned over the tabletop. 'What is it you want to know?'

'Lenny goes off for days, away somewhere. Why? Is she having some kind of medical treatment. Do you know?'

'Before I say more, hear me well. The girl's suffered more than her rightful share. Hurt her or cross her and you'll have more than you – '

'Why would I do that?! Tell me. Why would I hurt her? I told you why I came here. I want her to be well, and happy. Like you do. Haven't you figured that out yet?'

Leo slumped into a soft-chair, quiet, preoccupied. 'When she finally made it home to us from Iraq our prayers were answered.'

'She told me about that, and how you helped her recover.'

'Has she spoken to you about anything else?'

'Not much, not yet. But I know she will. I want to know.'

'She can't tell you about the early years. Too young. And she doesn't remember.' Leo straightened up in the chair. 'My generation isn't in charge any more. If you love her, like you say, and if she feels the same – '

'She does! There's no if. None. We know each other for over a year. I know she told you; she must have told you.'

'She didn't. I heard.'

A silence descended between them. Tony's gaze found again the photo of the young woman with Lenny's eyes, then Lenny's portrait nearby. But he let the quiet continue.

'You say you love her,' Leo said. 'Maybe you just think you do but you don't know yet; maybe she'd be a bother to you – so what is it?'

'It's yes. Yes.'

'Yes to what?'

'Yes, I do know. I don't think, I know. I love Lenny.'

'You'll not take her away again; y'understand that too?'

'I'm not doing that. I don't live anywhere else. This is home, for me. Here.'

'I'll tell you the little I know. She gets bothered sometimes, living in a small village. Likes to go to Dublin, places she was fond of once, when she was studying; she walks by the canal and goes to galleries, goes to Bull Island and Iveagh Gardens, all over. Always comes back the better for it.'

'No. That's not it.' Tony shook his head. 'There's more to it. The pills she takes, what are they for?'

'For war.'

'War?'

'Medicine for war.'

'I want to understand. Tell me.'

'To help with the pain of all she's been through. That's what. Might be a doctor in Dublin she sees. That's just my suspicion.'

'Somebody must know more. Would Paddy McCann know? He talks to her.'

'Not things like that. And he'd not be one to break her trust.'

'Somebody has to know the doctor's name.'

'Could be one. A wee girl, a pal from college. Emer, that's all I remember, small Dublin lassie with a sense of humour. She was here once, fourteen years ago, 1980, just before Lenny took off for America. They were good friends, going to graduate together. Only friend I ever knew her to have.'

'They stayed in touch?'

'Possible, maybe not. Back then we all hoped the two of them would travel off together, to work for the summer. But the girl didn't go, instead went to work in RTÉ Television. Might be there still. Or could have emigrated, like so many. She'd be in her mid-thirties now. More than that I don't know.'

'She could be anywhere in the world. Fourteen years, no last name. That's almost impossible.'

'Then that's your task, isn't it: the almost impossible. If you want what you say you want, enough.'

'I told you where I stand. It doesn't change my mind.'

'In that case, prepare yourself to be shocked. When she was in New York she met an Englishman and from what I – '

'Aidan Harper. I know, I know all about that. Lenny told me. Doesn't matter.'

'You don't know.'

'She loved him, for a while, so what.

'Does matter.'

'Not to me. What happened to him, and Lenny, it's sad, but it's years ago, it's gone. '

'They came here. On their way to Baghdad. Bad trouble over there at the time. She was happy, different, like she was contented inside. She couldn't wait to go with him. Then they flew off together, and the next – '

'I told you, I don't need to know. None of that matters. I knew he was here; Lenny told me.'

'If you'll listen, I'm telling you what she didn't tell you. What nobody could tell you. Not even Lenny.'

'What? . . . What?'

'The man's alive.'

Tony sprang to his feet. 'Aidan Harper?!'

'You heard me.'

'That's crazy. He was killed, in that shelter. Lenny saw it happen. Hundreds were killed.'

'He wasn't one of them.'

'This is crazy stuff. Where do you get your information?'

'I'll tell you. Something I'm not proud of. After the bombs, she was here, re-living the hell day by day, every day; you could never imagine what she suffered. We were all afraid for her. Then four months after she got home two things happened: she started to pull out of it, and his first letter arrived to the Abbey. I saw his name on the back of the envelope. A dead man. I didn't know what to do for the best. Right or not, I opened it. He had beaten death, he said, by holding onto a picture of her they found beside him. In all the months in hospital, the hope that kept him alive, he told her, was that picture, and seeing her again.'

'I don't believe this,' Tony said.

'No one knew who he was. He had bad burns all over him, skull fractures, a crushed leg, and other injuries. The doctors put him into a coma for his own good. He said that when he was unconscious he felt she was with him. They re-set his leg a number of times, until they could do nothing more. They told him he'd probably not walk again. The letter said his head was healing and he was learning to walk. It went on that way. I didn't give it to her, or any of his letters.'

'Real fucking crazy shit, this. I can't believe – '

'Peggy and me, we worried for so long that we'd never see her again, when she went to Iraq. A year later she came home. Not well.' Leo's words faded, then came back. 'Sick or not, she was home with us. The photograph you were looking at, that's Peggy and me the day we were married. Our prayers for children of our own never got answered. From the earliest days, Lenny was like she was our own. We'd lost her twice before, but then she was back home from the war. Peggy was two months dead then. I don't know what she would've done: let Lenny go back to him, to war; be killed or tortured, lose her mind? That would be all three of them gone: Róisín, Peggy, Lenny. I couldn't allow that. She had people here who'd love her, who'd make sure she got well. Cilla, Paddy, Eilis, Liam, and me, and others. Even the Doyle boys in England, Róisín's brothers; they never came home but they wrote to her. And Charles too, he was sound enough; Lenny and him just never settled. I decided against war. I hid his letters. To save her. If she meant as much to you, you'd do no different.'

The air in the room throbbed, neither man spoke.

'Maybe I wouldn't,' Tony said, eventually. 'Wouldn't do what you did.'

'Three and a half years I've watched her get well. Said not a word about the letters to a soul. Except Róisín and Peggy.'

'But they're . . . they're both – '

'Souls don't die. You don't talk to souls in America, do you? Maybe you should.'

'Cilla deBurca, she's a friend of Lenny's, a good friend?'

'Since the day Lenny came back to us.'

'She knows all this, what you've told me?'

'No one knows. I told you that. Just me and you, in this world.'

Tony's hands pushed back through his hair. This place, these people, he thought, were stranger than he could ever have imagined. No one here was an individual; no one ever seemed to stand alone, not Cilla, not Paddy, not even Leo, none of them. All were like limbs of the same tree. What they meant could only be guessed at; so often their facts were made up, intended only to nurture how they felt or wanted others to feel. They obscured reality for reasons that were not obvious to an outsider. But he was beginning to understand them, their ways, things he must once have known. What Leo had just told him was true; he felt certain of that. Now he needed to stay focused, learn here what he could, then get out and make things right.

'What else should I be told?' He glared down at the older man. 'Other letters you know about? How about mine, to Lenny, this past year?'

'Are you up to the task in front of you?' Leo asked.

'I faced bigger.'

'A young man's boast.'

'You know zip about me.'

'I know this. If the Englishman is alive, and there's cause to believe he is, you'll never be sure of Lenny. The day he turns up, everything will change. You can handle that?'

'Bullshit. You don't know that. You can't even – '

'Because . . . because, if you can't, better for everyone that you find another woman, don't trouble Lenny, or yourself, any further.'

Tony brooded, face and body tense. Leo's words frightened him: lose this woman to a ghost? Live in fear of Aidan Harper? After making it this far, a woman who'd be his only for safe-keeping? He'd never live on the run, looking over his shoulder for a cripple. No way. He'd fix this, fix it for good, make it permanent.

'Where is he at now?' he asked matter-of-factly.

'I read only one of his letters, the first one. To make the right decision. The other five, I didn't open. He said he was hoping to set up a house for drug addicts. That was over three years ago.'

'Drug addicts? In Baghdad?!'

'Dublin.'

'Dublin!? Dublin!? Where in Dublin?'

'Didn't say that. He was back in Ireland only days when he wrote it. Said he was looking at a situation.'

'Those other letters, the later ones, where are they now? Must be an address on them.'

'Not your property.'

Tony approached. 'I want those letters.'

Leo rose up out of the chair, stood erect. 'Nobody touches them.'

'You don't get it, do you? I need that address.' Tony's bearing caused not a flutter to show in Leo. 'What if I told Lenny, about what you did; what would that do for you, huh?'

'You could do that? And you love her?'

'You used those letters to get what you wanted, to keep him away from her. It's wrong for me to do the same? I care about her more than he ever could!' He broke away, tried to subdue an old fury. He could see it now, see her abandoning him and their new life, for a dead man, the only person who could kill his dream. His glare re-locked on Leo.

'Last time. I'm asking you. I want that address. Don't give me any shit.'

'Over my dead body.' Leo squared his shoulders.

Neither spoke, just stared into each other's eyes. Then Tony pulled out, turned aside.

He'd already fucked up half his life; this wasn't his fight. But live or die, he vowed, nothing would take Lenny Quin from him. No one could want her as he wanted her, or love her as he would. Which meant one thing: Aidan Harper. Find him. Right now though, something else was going on that he hadn't figured. What made Leo so intense, so unafraid to fight? He realised they were alike, him and Leo. Lenny owned a chunk of each of them; she was the brightest flame in both their hearts. Which left him nowhere. This man was too good to go up against, too loved by Lenny, and in his own right not a man to be pushed. No, the real target was Aidan Harper. Sort that out; deal with that. He was no good for Lenny, didn't love enough to go after the woman he wanted. Left her to mourn because his letters didn't get answered. Fuck-all guts. MacNeills were made of better stuff. Almost impossible, that's what Leo had said, almost impossible. But not impossible. Not to him.

He broke out of his thoughts and from the doorway nodded back.

'Wait!' Leo followed after him. 'Too much harm's been done. Make no more.'

'I'll do what needs to be done.'

'Then do it honourably. Make the living and the dead happy.' Leo turned back in toward the hearth; his shaking hands reaching to Róisín.

17

He pushed through the plate-glass doors of the glass façade and all at once came a flood of memories: the big marble-floored vestibule, funny trees growing inside instead of outside, the exuberance of his schoolmates.

He was eleven then, in fifth class at St Eoin's. Mr White had brought all thirty-seven of them here to learn how television programmes were made. Any day off school was great, didn't matter for what, but on that particular day he and his mates couldn't wait to spot the man who read the news on the telly every night, who rumour had it had only one leg. But they never got to see him. Though they did see Bottler, who had his own show, and he shook his fist at them just because Micko asked him to tell them a joke. And Mr White said that Bottler had thumped a couple of smart-arse fellas the week before and would do the same to Micko and the rest of them if they didn't behave. And then Micko got –

'Hello.' A woman's voice punctured his reverie. 'What can I do for you?'

On turning, he found a pony-tailed girl with a face plain and pale and pleasant, almost hidden behind the circular reception desk. 'I'd like to see Emer,' he said, trying to sound business-like.

'Emer Gilligan, is it?' He nodded. 'Who will I tell her?'

'Tony. Just say Tony.'

Seconds later, out loped a tall mini-skirted brunette with a puzzled smile. He apologised for the mix-up. No problem, she said, she was nipping outside for a fag and a bit of fresh air anyway. He held the door and followed her into the exterior breeziness.

'From America, are you?'

'Not anymore; I lived there. The Emer I'm looking for, I can't remember her last name.'

'O God, there's millions of Emers here, four or five at least. RTÉ is a big place. What's she look like?'

'Thirty-five, thirty-six, from Dublin, not tall, wavy hair probably, and – '

'That's Emer O'Hare you want, head of production.'

'Big job?'

'Big!' The girl arched her eyebrows then stubbed her cigarette in the sand pot. 'I better get back or she'll be sending St Anthony after me. I'm in graphic design, if you need any more help; just tell them to ring me.'

Tony collected his thoughts, breathed in the chill Montrose air, then re-entered the building.

'Hello, again,' the pony-tailed pale-faced girl said with a smile.

'Wrong Emer. It's Emer O'Hare I need to speak to.'

The girl delivered the message and rested the receiver on her shoulder. 'She's in editing at the minute. What's it in connection with?'

'Tell her Lenny. Lenny Quin. I need to talk to her.'

The girl did as instructed. 'That's grand,' she said. 'If you walk to the end of the corridor then turn right, Suite 3 will be on your left; you can go ahead in.'

Outside the suite he paused, then knocked and pushed his head in. A voice beckoned him. The attractive woman swivelled out of the blue glare of a pair of TV monitors.

'You're Tony.' She extended her hand. 'Len's been telling me so much about you I feel I already know you. Nothing's wrong?'

'No, no. Just like to talk to you, few minutes. Won't keep you.'

'I can do with a break.' She flipped on a lamp that spread a narrow pool of warm light. 'Pull up a chair. I wondered when we might meet. I hope you won't mind me confessing something right off: Len described you as handsome; I guess I didn't expect it to be quite so true.'

A smile hid his surprise at what he was already discovering. 'You and Lenny, you've stayed in touch through the years?'

'No. Now we do. All the time. Some weeks we're on the phone twice, three times, blabbering for hours; you know women. We're a couple of crazies. Always were.'

'You went to college together here in Dublin. Lots of fun?'

'A world of fun. UCD, just down the road. I was the slow one, Len was the genius. Many's the exam she pulled me through. Best years of my life.' She paused dreamily, then continued with a more serious bearing. 'Len told me she told you everything, the whole story. I'm glad she did. So you know how close we were. Until one day, it all ended. She headed off for the Big Apple and I came here, and that was that: finito.'

He searched for words to respond to her obvious glumness, then gestured to an array of wall plaques. 'You won all these? And you got married?'

'No and No.' She twisted the ring on her marriage finger. 'Friendship. From Len. Doesn't fit any other finger. Some of the awards are mine; majority are shared with others.'

'You guys kept in touch when Lenny went abroad?'

'Not a screed. 1980 to 1990, nothing. Like Moses in the wilderness. At Easter four and-a-half years ago we found each other again. She dropped in, literally, out of the blue. Half-hour later she's gone again, bound for the Middle East, a whirlwind visit if ever there was one. Next time I lay eyes on her – a year later, in summer – she's banging at my door in the middle of the night.

'I know she told you about Aidan, I encouraged her to do that, the unconscionable tragedies in Baghdad. Charles had her flown home two months after the shelter disaster. The embassy hadn't been able to reach him before then. Anyway, that night, from the airport, she made straight for my apartment. Found my address in a directory, she told me. I almost died; she was skin and bone. I tried to get her to eat, make her comfortable. What a task. Her nightmares were horrific, night after night, really frightened me. First it was Aidan; she'd scream at him, words I couldn't make out, except his name. Then it was *Mama, Mama, come down* time after time. I never understood what that was about. Down from heaven to help her, I suppose, in her grief. She'd shoot upright in the bed, eyes bulging, then floods of tears, non-stop. That went on for weeks. In the end I got help for her, after a number of false starts. And things improved, slowly.

'Aidan's death, particularly the way it happened, was a hair's breadth from killing her. It took over her mind. She'd keep describing the scene to me like it was still happening inside her: the noise, the cement ceiling dropping down on them, people being crushed. Balls of flame whizzing around, burning people to cinders in seconds. I listened each time, hundreds of times, and I realised one thing: I will never comprehend what she went through. Never. No one could, unless they'd been there.'

'You did everything you could do. She needed your friendship and you gave her that.'

'The second week, I succeeded in getting her to a psychiatrist, someone I know over in Baggot Street. Managed to get her to agree she needed help, treatment of some kind.' She pressed two fingers to her lips, fell silent for moments. 'Len told me she was up-front with you about all this, that you know the whole story.'

'I still want to hear whatever you can tell me, anything that will help.'

'I hope you won't take offense at my asking this: You do love this tender woman as much as she loves you?'

Tony nodded. 'I want to do everything I can to make sure she gets completely over what happened. Just like you do. Everything.'

'Because she's the loveliest person I've known in my life. Another tragedy could destroy her. You do recognise that?'

'Like I said, Emer, I want exactly what you want, for Lenny to be happy and stay happy, and be well. That's what I want.'

'We're kindred souls so, you and me.' She left her chair, moved wordlessly to the coffee machine. After initial fumbling she held up the coffee pot; he declined. And there, at the dark end of the suite, her crimped hair obscuring her face, she stayed leaning against the counter, hands cradling a mug.

He walked to her.

'We were both just seventeen. When we met. Kids, but we didn't know that then. I needed a flatmate, she needed a place to live, we talked for five minutes, an hour later she moved in. A few months after that I got a fright, the first of many. We were sitting together on a sofa, and it was like she fell into a trance. Not ordinary daydreaming, I mean like a deep hypnotic trance. Then a second time, and a third, within weeks.'

Emer spoke as though re-living the incidents of her story.

'She's taking drugs, I thought, on the sly, like others at the time. I hassled her; I threatened to report her. She swore she wasn't. And she wasn't. Stupid me. Then the following year, things changed; she'd stare at her hands or her feet, push them out in front of her like she was trying to figure out who they belonged to, like they were someone else's. Gave me the chills.

'All that time, she was wonderfully talented. Her passion was fine-art photography. Bill Brandt, Weston, Cartier-Bresson. Diane Arbus, Tony Ray Jones, Robert Frank; I remember all their names, though I'm not a photography buff at all, just that she never stopped talking about them. Then things got even worse; she'd develop a roll of film in the darkroom – she never let anyone breathe near her film – she'd look at the negatives and insist they weren't hers, that somebody switched her film. Her short-term memory wasn't recording, but only now and then; most of the time she was fine. The sheer irony of it is that she went to enormous difficulty in capturing every image; she'd wait hours for a moment, for the light to be just the way she wanted it. I'd insist to her that I watched her taking the shots, I was there, I helped her. That would cause trouble between us: fighting, shouting, and more worry; and that's how it went. In between all that we shared everything, everything, had so much fun.

'It took from 1976 to 1979 before I could convince her to talk to a doctor. She was twenty then; we were in third year. I went along with her; that was the deal we agreed. She told the psychotherapist she had forgotten most of her childhood, remembered just bits and pieces here and there. I had always suspected she was fibbing about that, ashamed of her family. Once again, stupid me. She was telling the truth. Most of her early life up to when she was a young teenager was blurred or gone.'

'Why? How could that – I mean, what could cause something like that? Did they say?'

'Couple of doctors said it looked like panic disorder, probably caused by trauma. But where was the trauma? There was no trauma. Her mother died when Lenny was five, which was heartbreaking, of course, but young children get over tragedies like that. Charles was away on business overseas most of the time. Leo Reffo and his wife Peggy – I met them both – sort of adopted her for a few years, and from all I've seen and heard they cared for her like she was their own child. Uncle Leo and Aunt Peg, she called them; I remember it so fondly, meeting them. There's a couple of old photos that still make me cry: Leo with her on a big black plough horse, and one of him swinging her around on the bog. She told me that the few memories she still has are from that period, of being especially happy; so I keep reminding her of those good times. She remembers sitting in a field, knitting daisies into a chain to give to Leo as a gift, and him wearing it around his neck.'

Emer became silent again. In the low hum of the room Tony re-sank his mind into the puzzle he was slowly piecing together, and the terrible complexity of seemingly simple lives.

'And you're still the best of friends, after all this time, how about that,' he said. 'You're both really lucky.'

A wry smile swept into her face. 'You know something: she has never permitted me go up to Claire Abbey to see her. But I think now I know why. What she always needed was someone to love her, who was just hers, not to be shared with anyone else. Even today, when she feels something is amiss she rings me, asks can she come down. Sorry, Tony, am I going on too much? Just tell me to shut up.'

He shook his head.

'You asked what the problem is. In January of this year, six months or so after she came home, I found her a new psychiatrist, a lovely gentleman on Sandymount Avenue, close to where I live. I go with her, still. We've talked to him together a number of times. He's warm, and he has so – '

'Did he say what's wrong? If it will, if she'll . . .'

'No guarantees; that's all any of them will say. This new man stressed that the way to overcome this is not all at once, but one specific stage at a time. He's the only one who'd venture a diagnosis. It's a mouthful, I know it by heart because I've researched it so much: atypical dissociative disorder with systematised amnesia and depersonalisation symptoms.'

'What does that mean? Did he say what causes it, how to cure it?'

'He's convinced something very troubling happened to her, probably when she was very young, and she suppressed whatever it was. She asked Leo if she almost drowned or got attacked or knocked down or anything like that. There was nothing he could tell her. She did get bounced around: different homes, different schools, after her mother died, but she was always well loved and well looked after, as far as we know. No abuse of any kind, which they told us can cause similar symptoms. Anyway, be that as it may, this doctor has her on a new drug combination. Thank God all is going very well; he says it's time now to start psychotherapy. She's one hundred percent better than six months ago and all the dosages have been reduced. There's just one problem – '

'She goes off the medication.'

'You know about these things?'

'Volunteer work. Did she say anything to you about Killadoon Cliffs.'

'Killadoon, I know. What about it?'

'Oh, nothing, just that we, you know, we went up there, onto the head, saw the views.'

'That's fabulous! I'm thrilled. She's waited so long to feel able to do that. The day she could go back up there, she told me, she'd know her problems were over. She told you the same, no doubt. Well done.'

Tony nodded, tried to look pleased.

'See, Tony, Len is a bit like a street fighter; I felt that from our earliest days together. She's brave, and that's an understatement; she takes things on, is so resilient. She can beat this thing, no question. You can imagine how desperately she wants to be fully well for you. When she feels good for a few weeks, she believes she has it conquered and goes off the tablets. But she's certainly at the final hurdle. And I'll always be here for her, she knows that in her heart, whatever she needs, day or night. And now she has you, strong and masculine. How lucky can a girl be!'

Her awkward smile faded; she looked into Tony's eyes. 'I say this knowing her better than anyone alive. You, you're her cure, the final piece of the jigsaw. I know that.'

He pulled his mind back inside himself, pulled it far, far back. 'I could've done with a friend like you. Often in my life.' He listened to the replay of his words and was reminded that he had not surrendered to circumstance.

'We make our own worlds, they say,' Emer sighed. 'I could get lost in yesterdays. I try hard not to. Today is it. Not yesterdays, not tomorrows. And you have Len.' She fumbled at her wallet, handed him a photo. 'Len and me. At twenty. Kicking up our heels. You can have it.'

'Hey, you were cute. I mean you still are, you look great.'

'Be everything for her. Never let her forget I'm here, even if she doesn't visit.'

'She'd always want to see you; always, you know that.' He savoured the whiff of joy his words brought out of her. 'Know anything at all about Aidan?'

'Just that he worshipped her. I met him in 1990, the time she came to see me before flying to Baghdad. I was dumbfounded, it seemed mad; they'd known each other one week. Seven days! When I got her on her own she told me he had saved her life, in Manhattan; that's how she put it, and that's all I was told at the time. Looking back now, it seems that was his calling, saving lives. A year after that, when she came to me from the Gulf War, I heard the full story, about how they met, how he appeared from nowhere, plucked her out of danger, and how wonderful things were for the next year in Iraq. The whole story seemed surreal.

'Then he was killed, God rest him, and that ended that. I wept when she told me how it happened. Couldn't stop. She tried to get off the stretcher carrying her away so she could die holding him. In the fire and destruction. I just kept crying, I wanted to turn back time, get them both out of there before the bombs, make them not explode, give all those poor people back their lives. But I couldn't do that, could I. All I could do was love her, care for her, hold her close to me. I became a surrogate Aidan.'

Tony grasped both her hands. 'Thank you for telling me,' he said. 'I know it's hard.' Her face pressed to his chest, their embrace soundless but for her distress. She then drew back, pulled a tissue from her sleeve.

'You seem depressed, Tony. Stop. Don't be. Nothing but silly jealousy on my part. It's plain she loves you.'

'She does. I know.'

'Leo's the only one left who might be helpful about the past. But tread carefully. He loves her every bit as much as you and I do, and he doesn't take well to strangers bothering her. Which I admire him for. What do men want with gorgeous women except to use them then ditch them when something sexier comes along.' All at once Emer's look was one of having spoken too transparently. 'I don't mean all men; I'm sorry. Not you, definitely not, not at all.'

They leaned back separately against the counter, the blue of her room over them both.

'Emer, I'm understanding things better now; thanks for filling me in. What about Boxer Dunne?'

'His job is to look out for Len, when he's told to. Otherwise, labourer.'

'Charles' minder for his daughter.'

'Not at all. It's Leo who calls the shots there.'

'But why Leo? I can't figure that. He's so – '

Her frown scolded him. 'Smart man like you?'

His thoughts wandered out beyond the windowless room, to what he had known before today and what he had just learned. Then his face opened up. 'You mean, you mean Leo, Leo is, Lenny is – '

'That's in strict confidence. Because I know you have Len's best interest at heart.'

'I should have guessed. By Leo's first wife, cute girl, short red hair. I saw her picture.'

'Róisín Doyle. She and Leo were in love, I heard, but for whatever reason never married. Róisín took ill later. Leukaemia. And tragically she died. Len was five; she has no memory of her mother. Talk about bad luck.'

Tony pieced together this fuller story in which, as far as he could tell, there were no sinister forces. Except one, Aidan Harper, who could one day rob him of his future, plunge him back into the hell out of which he had risen. He had to find him. Not someday. This day. Starting right now.

'I'll get going,' he said.

'Where do you go from here?'

'Oh, one or two little tasks in the city. For Lenny.'

She followed him to the door. 'I won't be losing Len, as a friend? Couldn't fathom that, her not being part of my life.'

'Not at all. No, you won't. We both owe you a whole lot.'

'You'll bloom, you two. You're both so strong, and brave; I can see that,' she said with effort. 'I hope you decide to live in Dublin. If you do, come talk to me about work. I heard you're a sports writer?'

'Not really. Not there yet. Emer, don't say you saw me, for now. To anyone. No one at all. Please?'

'Not a word; don't worry. She deserves the best, Tony. Always give her that.'

'I will. No fear.'

*   *   *

After he left, Emer's emotions churned in his mind. Was this the other world, he asked, the one he'd dreamed of belonging to? People loving the damaged, the illegitimate, the long dead, even those lost in their own nowheres. People pleading on behalf of others as if for themselves, and expecting that he too was like them, was one of them. Was this what fate had dispossessed him of, this culture of kindness? And if that were so, how big a price had he still to pay to earn it?

The words they had used burned deeper in his thoughts: a decent man, one had said, over and over; a man with power to make the living and the dead happy, said another; a man brave and strong; a man who could love; who could bring healing. But could he? Could he achieve what Leo had said was almost impossible? He wasn't God.

As he crossed the glassed-in atrium the eleven-year-old boy ghosted again. And the plain-faced, pony-tailed receptionist was smiling still. But no, no to all these seductions, he swore. No to the kind smiles and warm hearts, no to his growing sense of home. Not time yet for any of this. Deal first with the biggest threat, Aidan Harper. Then give Lenny back her life. Take back his own. Make it permanent. Make certain.

He pressed into a Dublin spitting drizzle at him.

18

It was a fresh day bereft of vapour and sun. The early autumn breeze blowing down the quays put a chill in the air that hiked up urgency in the narrow streets.

Kate and Lenny, at Lenny's urging, had strolled amid the southside's Georgian architecture. They followed the grey perimeter of Trinity College then along Grafton Street and into a boutique where Lenny purchased small gift items.

Further on, they turned into Duke Street to stare at Davy Byrne's pub, historical haunt of Irish writers and hangout of Lenny Quin and Emer O'Hare in their student days. After passing the arch at St Stephen's Green, they strolled the length of Merrion Street and ascended the steps of the National Gallery. There, over lunch, their conversation continued with the fecundity of reunited comrades.

* * *

SAME DAY, OUTSIDE DUBLIN CITY

A leaden sky hung over the west of the city. It was 3.10pm. Tony had disembarked from the Mayo train minutes earlier and stowed his bag in a locker. Now he hurried out of Heuston Station and along the Liffey toward the city centre, a mile and a half distant. He still knew the city, he complimented himself, almost as well as he did at thirteen. The sensory actuality of Dublin's streets, of being home, sent a surge through him. Beyond the Ha'penny Bridge he turned into Anglesea Street, where he spotted Focus Agency, the social support centre to which his research had pointed him.

The tight wooden doors opened into an interior reeking of cigarettes. The chatter stopped. Around seven or eight timber tables sat a mix of men, some peering over mugs, others minding only their food.

A navy-smocked, weary-looking woman eyed him from behind the counter. 'Y'all right there, son? What can I get you?'

He was off-guard, still mulling on his thoughts.

'If it's a bed you want you'll have to go up to James's Street.' She glanced at the clock. 'Nah, y'won't get one now; they'll be all gone.' Her hand fluttered toward a pamphlet holder. 'The blue sheet; there's a map on it if you want to go over and ask them; maybe they'd be able to look after you.'

A mixture of curiosity and distrust came at him from around the room. 'I'm looking for a guy,' he said to the woman. 'His name's Aidan Harper. English accent. I think he runs a drug rehab –'

'Ah no, son, you're in the wrong place. We only do meals here, and tea, and get people into shelters, that sort of thing. Drugs, y'have to go to the clinics for that, but they'd be closed now, on a Saturday. Monday morning they'll be open.'

'No, no, I'm just looking for this guy; it's an emergency. He has an English accent. Somebody would know him. He'd stand out.'

'Nobody stands out these days, son. Dublin's a different country than it was. Foreigners everywhere y'look. Anyhow, there's nobody here except me and Betty, and she knows nothing, she just started. On Monday there'll be somebody here who might know.'

'I can't do that. I have to find – '

'Er, sorry, Mister.' The voice came from behind.

Tony turned to a man of about forty, dark eyes set deep in an apprehensive countenance. A baggy gabardine wrapped his slight frame, collar pinned high under a chin of black and silver stubble.

'I wasn't listening but I couldn't help it. I think I could know how to help you.'

'Aidan Harper, you know him?'

'I don't meself. See there's this fella and he knows all them fellas. And, like, I could show you where he does have a gargle, if you'd a few bob you could loan me for a hamburger.'

'Michael!' the woman behind the counter said.

'No, no, on me mother's grave, Missus, I swear, it's true. This fella used to be in a squat up at the Park but he's down here now; the coppers flung him out.'

'Who, Michael? What's his name?' the woman asked.

'Don't know for sure. But I know a few pubs he does be in.'

The woman made a face.

'Take me there,' Tony said. 'Or tell me which pubs. What does this guy look like?'

'I wouldn't say that'd work, Mister, doing it that way,' the man said. 'Like, I mean, you couldn't find him like that, y'know. Y'have to know who to ask.'

'These bars, they're near here?'

'Bit down the quays, about five minutes, or ten.'

'You go see where he's at, then come back here and tell me, okay?'

The man made a strained face. 'Suppose I could.'

'Go ahead then. Come back here fifteen minutes from now.'

'Like, it might be more like twenty minutes, or like sixty. Have to scour around, y'know.'

'I'll be here.'

The man delayed. Tony glanced at the weary-looking woman. She fired back a disbelieving frown.

'Thought maybe like, if you, y'know, if you could – '

Tony pulled out a handful of change, picked out three one-pound coins. 'What's this guy's name, and which pubs does he hang out in? And what's your name?'

'Me own name's Mick Quilty. And the fella, they call him Gus but I wouldn't swear that's his right name. He does be in the Tara House and Mooney's, and the Ormond or Hill 16 Bar; could be anywhere.'

'It's ten to four now.' Tony held out the coins. 'You'll be back?'

'Ah, I will, I swear; I'll do me best.' The man moved off, shoulders up, hands deep in his gabardine pockets.

'That's him gone now, off to drink your money; y'realise that?' the woman said. 'Foolish man, giving him anything.'

'Don't think so,' Tony said, barely giving voice to his conviction.

*   *   *

'I want to know, Kate, I'm dying to know: what was he like?' Lenny's face sparkled. She pushed aside the table items and leaned closer.

'What was he like. Oh God. Well, he was the only boy among three very loud girls. Don't know how he put up with us. Funny thing though, we threw away our dolls when he came along; dolls were boring, he was it, the real thing, we couldn't believe our luck. I was ten when he was born, Violet eight, and Pat five. We fought constantly over whose turn it was to mind him, so it usually ended up with all three of us minding him.'

Kate smiled distantly then took up again, with spirit. 'He didn't utter a word until he was three; we yakked and yakked at him. He swallowed up all the attention but he wouldn't oblige. Turned out there was nothing wrong. As he got older I'd read to him most nights; he loved that. And I'd take him into the city with me on Saturdays. He was very good, very kind. And clever in school, always absorbed in one thing or another: bicycles, scouts, chess, boxing, lots of things. He was a tough little urchin, too; scrapes and cuts and black eyes were his stock-in-trade. Very determined, too. Before I knew it, he was thirteen; we were getting ready to emigrate.

'We cried, all three girls, we all cried. I remember once father crying with us and trying to hide it. Usually, Pat would start, she was the youngest, eighteen then, very attractive, and very sensitive; she had lovely friends she didn't want to leave, and I'm sure there was one boy she liked that she wouldn't tell us about. Then Violet would join in; very bright, and quiet like Pat. When the time to leave got close, we were like big babies, tears every day. We wanted to go but we couldn't bear leaving. The closer the day got the more withdrawn Tony became, extremely so in the final few weeks. It was like it took away his personality. My father was very worried about him, even talked of putting off going; father himself was never keen on the idea, we all knew that. It was like a wake in the house for a week before we left. America meant a better life, everyone said so, my mother loudest of all; she was brave and ambitious; I can say that for her. Anyway, off we went. And I suppose we got used to it after a while. Has Tony told you anything about what happened?'

'Just that he hated leaving Ireland.'

'Say anything about over there, Newark?'

'No, he didn't. I know something serious happened. He said he'd tell me later, but you know how private he is, Kate. I do want to know; I want you to tell me.'

'It's a heavy load. You've known each other such a short time. Weeks only.'

'We met last year. He probably didn't tell you. It was brief. But there hasn't been a day since that I haven't thought about him. Did that ever happen to you, when you just knew about someone?'

'Once. I was twenty. So brilliant that I talked myself out of it, after two years of going out together. I heard he moved to London, married a nurse. Still have his poems, every one of them. So, anyway, back to reality. You were saying?'

'Tony and me, it isn't like we're seventeen or eighteen. We each have life experience to call on. Besides which, we know our feelings; we love each other.'

'Lenny, if I can speak professionally for a moment, as a psychologist, I mean. I feel certain he needs time to adjust. He's still vulnerable; he's a stranger to your world. Even to mine. He needs to relearn to believe in his own intrinsic worth, in his potential. And then how to go after what will make him happiest in life.'

'He and I both. We need exactly those same things. That's one reason we've grown so close. And that's what love is, isn't it, helping each other, when the poetry is over and put aside.'

Kate gazed silently through the half-empty gallery restaurant.

'Anything you tell me is just for me,' Lenny said. 'I promise you that.'

'You want to know about the fight, and what followed?'

Lenny's eyes answered.

'It might make you cry. It does me, still, nearly eleven years later.'

'We're women, Kate. We know how to handle these things.' Lenny's hands clasped Kate's. 'Our gift is to be strong, to be nurturers; we heal men's wounds, despite their silence; that's why they love us. One reason. And we cry, as women, but so what; we're brave enough not to have to hide our emotions. None of this made any sense to me until someone caused me to pack in my life in Manhattan and open up to a whole different reality.'

'Maybe we are, as you say, all those things, brave and nurturing and strong.' Kate turned her regard aside, then back. 'But maybe only because we're not really free. Free to show what else we are. We need to take responsibility for that.'

'We're free to fight,' Lenny said. 'Freedom needs to be fought for, right? If not, the power stays with the more aggressive of the species. So, yes, I agree, we're responsible for not falling into acquiescence.'

This time, Lenny's words drew warmth and a smile from Kate, but no elaboration.

'Tony and I have known each other only a short while; you are right about that,' Lenny said. 'But inside me I'm certain he would not intentionally harm anyone.'

'They were my words, almost verbatim, to a nice, respectable, red-faced prosecutor who insisted he be tried as an adult, at seventeen. And called for a life sentence.' Kate's features froze. 'No one would listen to me. Not even Tony's court-appointed attorney, a man – not a man in any emotional definition of that term – a drone going through the motions, padding his own felony trial record so he could move up. Not a trial. A farce. A callous insult to all moral reasoning. A system-conditioned megalomaniac on one side, called a prosecutor, a diabolical fool on the other, called a defence counsel. Both disgracing every principle of justice.'

Lenny rocked Kate's hands within her own and remained silent.

'Tony was a problem adolescent,' Kate said, as though still strained by the fact. 'He'd been in more than his share of trouble. Minor scrapes, all of them, misdemeanours. He was his own person, fiercely self-driven. He smoked marijuana, like most of the kids, but no alcohol or hard drugs, ever. If he was fighting with another kid, which he did far too often and stressed my poor father no end, he fought just with his fists. Unlike some of the dysfunctional kids that hung out all around us in Newark.

'A week before the fight, this Spanish boy, Jesus Pomental – how could I forget that name – a textbook psychopath, he stabbed a girl and a boy, two lovely, sweet neighbourhood kids, Margo and Stewie, boyfriend and girlfriend, in love, Anto's closest friends. Everyone called Tony *Anto* in those days. Margo was sixteen, Stewie seventeen; both wonderful dancers. On Saturday mornings the two of them would put on their own little routine in the square – a flat concrete area behind where we lived, what was left of an old rail yard. They'd spread out flattened cardboard,

turn on their music and do their thing. Gave the local kids something to cheer for. They weren't rough kids like Anto and the
others, just two smitten teenagers. But they came from Witchell
Heights; that was their crime. Turf warfare. Margo suffered a
punctured lung, a knife stab to her stomach, and both collar
bones broken. Stewie lost an eye, got sixty stitches in his face and
head. That was the end of their dancing.

'Anto went crazy when he heard about it. Even my father, who
he was very close to, couldn't calm him. My mother was tran-
quilising herself to the heavens most days so she could deal with
her own things, but that's another story. Violet and Pat had
moved away the year before, in June of '82, to Atlantic City. For
the summer, they said, for work, but they never came back to
Newark.

'That kid who did the stabbings, Pomental, he was known as
Big Blade. Good with a knife. Everyone feared him. He'd
maimed others before, one detective told me. But gang business
stayed on the street; the locals didn't trust the police, or the
courts. Anto couldn't accept the kid getting away with it; it kept
him in a state of rage. So he sent out a challenge: he'd fight Big
Blade in the square, no weapons. The kid wouldn't accept, just
threatened his gang, the Wetboys, on the Witchell Heights kids.

'The following Saturday, we'd just come back from visiting
Stewie and Margo in hospital, it was my birthday: October 22
1983. I was turning twenty-eight. Anto was seventeen. He and
four of his friends were out back playing cards, smoking their
cigarettes. I was single then, upstairs studying for a state test. We
heard screams coming from the square. Anto seemed to know
instinctively what it was. He was over the back wall like a light, his
friends after him. The Wetboys, about ten of them, had brought
their baseball bats and were beating three of the Witchell Heights
kids. I ran as fast as I could to get to Anto; I climbed over the
wall, fell down six feet, got up, kept running. I could see what was
going to happen.

'When I got there, feeling like my hip was broken, all the fighting had stopped. Everyone was deadly quiet, or maybe that's just how I remember it. They were all standing around, in a big circle, watching Anto and this Big Blade guy. They had their fists up, circling each other. Anto was smaller, but his mind was invincible, you could see it in his eyes that day, the way he looked, the way he was boxing. The other guy's nose and face were bloody; Anto was holding back, showing him up, making him suffer; he knew the Spanish kid couldn't beat him; nobody could've beaten Anto that day. He was paying him back for Margo and Stewie. But it wasn't even a fair fight; the Spanish kid had brass knuckles on both hands. They kept going round and round, throwing punches. When the Big Blade guy tried to charge forward Anto made him miss, punched him away, and he was talking to him each time the guy's head snapped back: "For Margo, for Stewie." Blood was pouring from Anto's temple, down his neck, down over his shirt. But it didn't stop him. He had something to avenge and that's what he was doing. A horrible situation. That got worse. Turned into an incredible nightmare.'

Kate interrupted her own monologue. 'Looks like they're closing here. Will we leave this for later, at home, maybe?'

Lenny nodded, delaying in her seat. 'I'm grateful to you, Kate, I am, for telling me. I hope it's not too upsetting.'

'No, no. I'm just thrilled he's out now. Alive. He spent the time reading, he told me. Nine years. Read hundreds of books. Exercised every day, stayed in good physical condition, which was smart. Millions of times I wished the whole thing was just a bad dream, that I'd wake up.'

For a moment they remained detached, as though captives of their own inexpressible thoughts.

'Ready?' Lenny asked supportively. 'Let's walk through Trinity, over the old cobblestones. I love it in there.'

'But, your heels,' Kate said.

'I'll be careful. It'll be a trip down memory lane. My friend

Emer and I, when we were students, we'd often hang out at Trinity's art gallery, eavesdropping on what visitors were saying about my photography. Seems like aeons ago. I loved art, photography especially.'

Both women moved together through the gallery rooms, and finally through an island of Monets and out into the city.

*   *   *

It was 6pm, a grey overcast dulling the city. Mick Quilty shuffled along the narrow footpath of Anglesea Street, past the nine-teenth-century facades of the Stock Exchange and brass-plated solicitors' offices. Just before reaching Focus Agency he cried out with the exhaustion of a returning warrior.

'Fucking brutal hard it was, I'm telling you. But I got Gussie for you, I found him, I did.'

'Two hours, Mick! Two fucking hours!' Tony said. 'It's after six.'

'Yeah, look, I know, but he wasn't nowhere. And I told you I'd do me best to help you, and I did me best. He's down doing the doors in Talbot Street. Down there – '

'Doing the doors – what's that?'

'Only way you get a good one. See, you get a flagon early and get in with a fella you know before the rakers and druggies start to come, and you lock in.'

'He's there now, in Talbot Street? And he knows Aidan Harper?'

'He's just after telling me himself, about ten or twenty minutes ago he told me. He forgot to tell me the door he does be in but that doesn't matter, there's only four good ones and I already know all them.'

'You mean a store entrance, a doorway, for shelter?'

'Yeah, I'll show you. I'll go over with you.'

'No. Just tell me. What does this Gus, or Gussie, look like?'

The man's face faded.

'Mick! What's he got on, what does he look like?'

'I'll hop over with you, show you how to get there. Be no bother.'

'No. I know Talbot Street.'

'I'll just walk you far as the bridge, and I'll – '

'No!'

'Not sensible down that end on your own. Won't know where y'are or where to go. Need a man like meself that knows them areas like the back of me hand.'

Tony's head shook.

The man shrugged. 'Anything happens to you, don't say Mick Quilty wasn't the man that warned you. I'll be in Madigan's, beside where the Pillar used to be, if you know Dublin. Don't forget that.'

*   *   *

Tony scoured the length of Talbot Street, now peopled only by stragglers, and shop assistants fleeing the end of a busy Saturday. Once again he paced up and down, along an avenue of staleness and shabby metal shutters locked down over shop-fronts. None of the half-dozen un-shuttered entrances held any inhabitants, and no loiterers showed except two homeless men sharing a bagged bottle under the pigeon-painted bridge. No man in a big green army coat, wearing long grey whiskers, as Mick had described Gus. Beyond the bridge he wandered into Store Street, a feature-less lane at the end of which was Busarus, Dublin's central bus station. He was about to turn back toward Talbot Street when a sound seized him. He held his breath. Imagination, he thought, and longing. But then it sounded again, distinct, a voice, very near, from beyond the corner next to him. Couldn't be! He hugged the wall, poked his head past the edge, and pulled back. Lenny and Kate! Twenty feet away. Approaching. Almost upon him. No time. No escape. He ruffled his hair, dropped into a squat, collar up, head buried. The click-clacks grew louder. They were laughing, talking, just feet from him, now upon him, in front of him, passing, passing, past. He peeked through his fingers. There was Kate, half-glancing back. And Lenny, blond, blue jeans, hip jacket, tall, shopping bags on arm; Kate shorter, grey skirt, Aran cardigan. They crossed the narrow street to a white Audi, linking each other.

It made sense, he felt: they'd met earlier at Busarus, left the car and went shopping in the city. It was now 7.10pm, which meant they'd spent the whole day together. As they drove off, Kate's eyes glanced back once again but his face was still hidden. The Audi turned toward the quays. He got to his feet, hurried back to the vacuity and litter of Talbot Street.

Just then it occurred to him. Mick had said there were four good ones, meaning they were not obvious. Fuck it, that was it! He'd wasted too much time. Being able to get in behind what looked like a closed shutter, secure it down, stay concealed, that's what made them good. That's what he'd missed, which meant four could probably be pulled open from the outside. But which four? Mick said he'd be in Madigan's, waiting. The crafty little bastard was there now, Tony thought, sure that he'd be needed.

But he didn't need Mick. Not yet anyway. Yank up really hard on every shutter, he figured. Fifty, maybe sixty. Try them all. No quitting now. He'd find the man he'd come for, the man who would lead him to Aidan Harper. Not one doubt about that. Work down one side, up the other. Whatever it took he had it to give.

Just over an hour later he had tried to force all but the last few shutters. Not one had budged. Not a sound or a voice was discernable inside any of them. A patrolling police car made him fade occasionally into shadows or inconspicuous strolling. Now, in a night becoming chillier by the minute, he was nearing the end. At the corner, behind piles of swept-up litter, just two shutters remained.

He squatted down at the first, his back to the latted metal, poked his fingers underneath, and pushed up hard with his legs. It groaned, then gave. Only an inch. But this time there was no clack of steel against steel. Stuck, jammed maybe, but not locked like the others. He tried again. This time crunching something, a stick maybe. And it gave.

Still facing toward the street, he dropped down. 'Gus, you in there?' he shouted into echoey space. He waited. Nothing sounded. Then, from inside, came a scrape. 'Gus, I'm a friend. I'm coming in. Okay?'

He raised the shutter, ducked underneath, pushed it back down. Instantly, he caught the scent of humans, a sensibility nine years of incarceration had gifted him. He readied his fighting brain. Wisps of yellow street light leaked in through slits near the top of the shutter. To his left and right glassed-in mannequins posed in women's clothing. Straight ahead he sensed only an endless passage, and nothing but darkness.

'Gus. Gus, I want to talk to you,' he called out. 'I'm a friend. Mick Quilty's friend.' Only hollow echoes came back. He shuffled his feet, faked his advance, stayed alert, listening. Nothing stirred. Nothing sprang. He started forward quietly, reached to where the passage turned to the right. The stench of urine stung his nostrils. 'Gus, you there?'

A clatter of noise erupted. He broke into a stance, adrenaline pumping. Another eruption. It was coming from behind him; the shutter rattling violently. Voices outside, on the street, loud, swearing, someone or something crashing repeatedly against the metal, an argument, a man saying the cash was short, he was a lying bollox, he'd get a bullet in his head if he didn't cough up fifty-eight quid; he had two days, till three o'clock on Monday, if he didn't get it he'd be in the morgue by four. Then came a final hard thump against the shutter and it was over.

He edged nearer again to where the passage turned, crouched low, peered into the darkness. And he froze. Two eyes were staring at him. Two catchlights. Then four, dead still in this tomb-like chamber, all watching him.

'Gus, that you?' he asked. Then a lighter lit, and shapes began to form. Two men. One with what looked like a scraggy beard, in a bulky coat. The other rounder, also heavily wrapped.

'Gus, I'm a friend. I'm looking for a guy. Mick said you'd know him. I'll make it worth your while.'

The bearded man cleared his throat. 'You're that Yank. I know about you.'

'That's right. You'll help me?'

'I can't do nothing for nobody,' the man said with a phlegmy growl.

'We don't bother nobody, mister,' the smaller said, tipping back his bottle. 'Don't we not, Fergus?'

'Listen, Gus, I'll get you a hamburger and coffee. How about that?'

'Few bob's better.' The man's waxy fingers put the lighter to a small candle. 'Who're you looking for?'

'Lanky fella, about six foot, English guy, Aidan Harper.'

'Know nobody by that name,' he said, then turned to his partner. 'You, Victor?'

'You're the man, Fergus, that does know fellas. Don't know no one meself, except me and you.'

'Kinda grey and black hair,' Tony said. 'Could be long, in a pony-tail.'

'Where does he be?'

'He used to run a place for addicts. methadone clinic, maybe, something like that. Mick said you'd know him.'

'Druggie fuckers. Me and Victor steer clear of fuckers like that.'

'All bolloxes. Telling you, mister, mad lulas they are,' Victor said. 'That's me own personal opinion anyhow. Right, Fergus?'

'This guy's a Brit, probably talks like a snob, maybe walks funny.'

'Only one English fella around here, that's not his name.'

'What's his name?'

'Cyril something. Don't know.'

'Tall, around forty, greyish hair, has a limp?'

'Said you'd have a few bob for me?'

'Take me to this guy. If it's him, I'll look after you.'

'It's him. Has a gammy leg. But his name's Cyril. Tell you that.'

'Fergus is never wrong, mister.' Victor's regard swung to his companion. 'Tell him, Fergus. How you were the head foreman in Guinness's before them fuckers thrun you out. Tell him about when you used to make the stout.'

'Quit it, Victor, fuck sake, will you,' Gus said.

'You don't want a meal?' Tony asked. Neither man reacted. 'How about fish-and-chips, for both of you. How's that?'

Victor shifted noisily on the cardboard, gazing into Gus's bearded visage. Still, neither man answered.

'Okay, a fiver in cash,' Tony said. 'Five quid?'

'I get the fiver now; that's the deal.' Gus's words triggered a smile in Victor.

'How far is it, to this Cyril guy?'

'Gardiner Lane. It's a kip. Up the road. But I'm telling you, I'll show you it, that's the deal; I don't go near it.'

'Yeah,' Victor added. 'Pack of skinheads. Not one of them working-men like meself and Fergus.'

'Gus, tell me this,' Tony said. 'How sure are you that it's him, and that he's there?'

'Me word. Don't know if he's there. That enough?'

Ten minutes later, three blocks away, Gus pointed to two dilapidated buildings, adjoining tenements standing alone in darkness alleviated only by the glow of a solitary street lamp, with mountains of demolition rubble on either side.

Tony took in the scene. A wasteland. He pressed a five-pound note into Gus's hand. 'You never saw me,' he said, dropping two one-pound coins into the same hand. 'Now go.'

Gus stared back, as though perceiving something unstated.

'What?' Tony said.

'I was a fighter, once, in me day. Don't drop your guard, champ. Or the fuckers'll get you. Hear me? Never.'

Their stares engaged for another moment, until Tony's nod conceded a brotherhood, unspeakable as it could only be. Then Gus retreated, see-sawing into the night, bulked out by his coats, outermost the string-tied, brass-buttoned long green of the Irish Army.

*   *   *

He paced back and forth over a strip of waste-ground, monitoring the lane and both tenements. One house had boards nailed across its Georgian doorway. The second seemed in use. To the rear, blocks of red-brick flats dangled washing from lines stretched across balconies.

This was no Aranroe, no Arizona, he thought, more the Newark he'd known, and the penitentiary. The clamour of traffic and headlights shielded his presence from four men loitering on the steps of the tenements. Fifteen minutes passed, a light rain began falling; the men had not moved. He'd wait no longer, he decided. He was ready to deal with this final obstacle. But what exactly would he do here, he asked. Force Aidan out of Ireland? Warn him that over meant over, that Lenny would never again be available? If that didn't work, there was a surer solution. He was ready to fight for a life that was only a dream through nine years in shit-and-piss cells. And if he felt himself shaking now, needing that bit more to fire up, get his power revved, it was only because he'd let himself relax too long. Because normality of a kind had lulled him, Lenny and Cilla, particularly, and the other real people he'd met. At his core, though, certain parts of him hadn't changed, he told himself. Still the guy who'd held his own inside, earned respect in the pit, who'd put pervert Shift Commander

Yablonski in the nailed-shut box he deserved; that's who he could still be, if he had to, the fighter who dropped Rip Wundt on his two-hundred-and-fifty-pound ass with one shot. That's who he was. Anto MacNeill. Psyching up for what he had to do.

The tangle inside him abated. All that was left, he told himself, was to give himself the go-ahead. He stretched high up on his toes, reaching, flexing. And in that instant it came. The uncertainty was over. He drilled his heel into the ground, rubbed damp black earth into his hands and fingers. He was wired now, back on mission, counting down.

* * *

Now settled into an oversize sofa with Lenny close by, Kate brooded, as though reluctant to continue the story she had begun in the gallery.

'The fight turned into a disaster,' she said eventually, 'and I could not do a thing to stop it.' The Spanish kid, when he knew he couldn't win, reached inside his jacket, pulled out a long knife, a switchblade, and started waving it around, just like you see in films. I kept trying to run, to get between them, but someone – I never found out who – was holding me back. All the time, I was screaming at them to be sensible, shouting to people to call the police. I was powerless. And everyone just stared. No noise, no sound. I remember watching Anto back away from the knife each time it swiped at him. I could tell he was waiting for his chance. In my head I was seeing him dying there, bleeding to death. I could barely get a breath. My mouth was wide open but I was getting no oxygen, and my heart was racing. The kid kept making sweeps with the knife, across and up and down, and he lunged it over and over at Anto's face, but Anto was quick; he danced away every time, then suddenly he'd jump in and punch the kid really hard, two or three punches together.

'Then the kid went berserk. He charged at the crowd like he

was going to stab someone. Everyone scattered. Except me. I stood there shouting at him to put the knife away, go home, that it was over. I don't know where I got the courage. He called me all kinds of names. I kept telling him I wasn't afraid of him, that I was ordering him to go home. He was shaking. He pressed the blade under my chin. It was like a razor; I couldn't move. Peripherally, I saw Anto tearing toward us, it was like in slow motion. The kid saw him too, and he grabbed me around my neck, held me in front of him. He began pushing me toward Anto, until there was just a few feet between us. All the time he kept his knife to my throat. The blood from his hands and on his brass knuckles, some of it Anto's blood, was all over me. I'll never forget the feel of the blade against my skin, sticky with blood, and the taste of blood in my mouth. Anto tried talking to the kid, told him to let me go and everyone would just leave; he was begging but his eyes were on fire. I thought the knife was going to dig in to me any second, that I would die there, at twenty-eight, on Witchell Heights square in Newark, New Jersey. I kept asking God to save us all. I commanded myself to be strong. I tried to plead with Anto to go home, leave, but the words didn't come out; I don't even think my lips moved. Then suddenly the kid jerked my head back and pressed the knife high up under my chin. And I fainted. Went straight down. I know what went through Anto's mind, though he's never talked to me about it; he thought my throat had been cut; there was blood everywhere. Looking back, I wish I could have held on, stayed standing. I didn't. Anto went wild.

'What happened next was told to me by my father, who arrived on the scene just at that moment, along with another man. I was out cold on the ground.

'The Spanish kid was standing over me, switchblade in hand. Anto crashed all his weight into him, knocked him over. My poor father and the other man rushed to me, not knowing if I was dead or alive. Anto and the kid were wrestling on the ground. Anto got on top, pinned down the kid's hand with the knife in it, and kept punching the kid in the face. By the time the men got to them it was over. The kid wasn't moving. His eyes were wide open. Anto was straddling him, just staring at him, in shock. My father told me later they knew right away the kid was dead. Jesus Pomental, The Big Blade as he was known, not yet seventeen years of age. It could make you lose all hope.

'Then three years after that I feared Tony was lost to us for good. He was in a fight in prison in Florida. He saved a German boy from abuse, maybe death, an innocent young man who had done nothing wrong, just happened to be in the wrong place at the wrong time. A guard died, a man named Yablonski. It came out that he was a serial rapist of inmates, maybe much worse according to some of the evidence. It was blatant self-defence, just like the first time. But I was sure they were going to do the same thing again: charge Tony with murder. I wrote to President Reagan, the U.S. Department of Justice, senators, congressmen, the Irish Ambassador in Washington. Everybody who could possibly do something. In the end, no charges were filed. But Tony fell into a near-catatonic depression. They had him on suicide watch, for months. But he pulled through. He always pulls through. That's Tony. Always pulling through.'

* * *

Arrows of sleet stabbed into him. But his edginess and hesitation had been conquered. He darted into the glistening road, halted half-way as cars swept past, and weighed up again the four men loitering in front of the tenement. He took on a purposeful locomotion. At the house the raw-faced men fanned out in front of him.

'He inside?' Tony said with an implication of familiarity.

'Can you fucking read,' one of the men said, flicking his shaven head toward the building. 'Get fuck-all in there. Tell you that.'

In the iron-barred window a hand-written sign read: *Not a Clinic. No Drugs on Premises.*

'Get you fixed up in a light.' The hooded man in a nylon tracksuit moved closer. 'Real stuff. Dead clean. Fucking brilliant.'

'Nah. Gotta see this bloke in here.' Tony's shift slipped him between the end man and the railings and onto the bottom of the five steps, which he skipped up.

'Hey, pal, hang on, c'mere.' The man with the shaven head leapt up the steps. 'Ten quid. Fucking brilliant stuff. Not that methadone shite.' Tony's earth-darkened hands distracted him momentarily. 'Have it for you in two minutes, fix y'up, I swear. Right? A tenner.'

Tony's head shook, almost provocatively, drew a dismissive spiel from the trio below.

'Fuck him. Let's go, Skinner,' the hooded man yelled. 'He's a fucking waster.'

'Now, fuck-head,' Skinner said, with malice. 'Give me a fiver for fags. Hand over.'

'Don't have it.'

'Much you got?' Skinner's fingers called for money. 'Hand over or I'll fucking do you right here and take it off you.' He reached for the breast pocket of Tony's half-length army jacket.

Like a viper striking, Tony grabbed the man's wrist while remaining otherwise still. In the spraying rain and the rattle of traffic their faces raged, intimately close. Tony's vise-like clamp tightened, his free hand a primed fist. Skinner's eyes narrowed, his face twitching as his body bent slowly, then sank lower, and his mouth broke open.

By now the trio on the street had drifted away. Tony wrenched the man's wrist back against its joint and released it.

'Fucking pig bollox. Fucking kill you. Kick your fucking head in. You're dead, I swear, fucking dead.' Red-faced and with rain streaming down his skull, he laboured off into the drizzle and dark.

Tony pushed the massive door until it gave way. As it thudded behind him, it isolated him in near-darkness and marijuana air. In the distance, from what seemed like a half-flight down, light leaked from under a door. He moved into the dark bowels of the house, floorboards groaning with his intrusion. His fingers traced along a pocked plaster wall, past two doors, then the wall was gone and at his left was a passageway. He felt his way forward, stopped on hearing faint voices and music; from upstairs, he thought, but maybe from the door he was headed toward. Could be Aidan Harper's flat, he figured. If so, he'd give it to him straight: time to go, get back to England, do his good deeds over there, or Africa or Iraq, didn't matter, just far enough away from Lenny Quin; she had a new life, a better life, didn't need old ghosts – '

'Looking for me?'

He jumped, backed up against the wall. A man. Somewhere near. Where? He stayed still. Five seconds. Tried to quiet his breathing. Then a bulb turned on, a weak light, in the main hall. Still no one visible. To his right, big, hand-painted lettering stood out: DANGER! KEEP OUT, across a boarded-up staircase. Then came a continuous creaking, wheels grinding, and out of the far passageway a wheelchair emerged, a man, scraggy, coming toward him. It was him, he was sure. The face in all those photos. Older by a good bit. But definitely him.

'Cyril?' Tony called out.

'I have one bed left, in the basement. Share with one other. No drugs, no alcohol, or you'll be removed instantly by the police. You want it?'

'Cyril?'

'Do I know you?'

'We need to talk.'

'Who are you?'

'About Lenny Quin.'

'Lenny?!' The man straightened in the chair. 'God, not bad news?'

Tony delayed. 'No. But you and I need to talk.'

The man exhaled loudly, flopped back. 'Follow me, please.' The chair reversed down the passageway until the grinding stopped. 'Come in, please,' he shouted before disappearing through a lit doorway. Tony edged forward.

At the doorway a shirtless man emerged, big, face menacing, arms out-stretched, blocking the entrance. The facts were processed instantly in Tony's brain: size, stance, eyes, butchered nose, age, threat level.

The man jutted his face into confrontation. 'DSF, drug squad fucker; DSF, drug squad fucker.'

'Want to stay breathing, shithead?' Tony's stare didn't waver nor his expression change.

The man's eyebrows jumped, his face sneered. 'Rat's fuck, redneck, prick face. Y'want me, yeah?'

'Fogarty!' The roar came from inside the room. The man in the wheelchair arrived. 'What did I tell you?! Well?! You want the police to take you? Now, this instant? Say the word. Do you?'

The shirtless man glared.

'Or the morgue,' Tony said. 'Take your pick.'

The man skulked to the side. Tony passed him, fully cued.

'Hey, Brit,' the shirtless man plucked a parka off a nail, 'I'm off to Moran's for a few minutes, see Skinner and the lads.'

'You're doing nothing of the sort!' the man in the wheelchair said. 'You're staying right here.'

'Fucking nothing wrong with a few pints. Half hour I'll be back.'

'Inside! Now! Any more of this and the arrangement is off. Try me.'

The man fired his parka into the floor and slumped against the wall, arms locked across his bare, hairless chest.

'Won't be a jiffy,' the man in the wheelchair said to Tony as he got to his feet and manoeuvred through a narrow inner door. Tony took in his surroundings. A huge, high-ceilinged room of stale air and worn-out upholstery, two bulbs dangling on long strings, stuffed plastic bags all about, plates piled with cigarette butts, trash at every turn. A cell. And from somewhere an operatic diva crying out.

He leaned over a large sink to wash the earth from his hands. The shirtless man's eyes had still not left him. Just then the wheelchair returned, its occupant looking fresher, less dishevelled, silver hair tied back in a pony-tail.

'Have a seat, please, please,' he said. 'I'm sorry about all this, you'll have to excuse the state of the place. It's impossible at times, you have no idea. Anyway, you were saying?'

'You're Aidan Harper?'

'Was.' The man paused. 'Aidan Cyril Harper. What's this about? Lenny is alright, isn't she? I mean – '

'She's fine.'

Aidan stalled again, then his tone and demeanour changed. 'Well then, you're the bearer of very welcome news. Which makes me feel almost well again. Is there anything I can get you? Cup of tea?'

'Private talk.'

'Mr Fogarty, take yourself down to the far end, please. You may take one bottle of Guinness from the box.' Aidan fired a warning after his words. 'One. Understand?'

The man grabbed an audio-cassette player and earphones and tramped to the barred window where he dropped into a sofa and wrung the cap off the beer.

'No drugs, no booze?' Tony said.

Aidan acknowledged, then spoke quietly. 'Discretion being the better part of valour, that kind of thing.' He leaned closer. 'Courts waiting for a psychiatric assessment; doesn't happen fast. Ordered to sign daily at police station. Homeless, reformed addict, he claims.'

'What charge?'

'Assault and battery, for now. They know he's a supplier: crystal meth, crack, etcetera. And worse maybe.'

'What?'

'The story going around is that he killed a twenty-year-old man. Could be just talk. No body. Officially still missing. Might be two, the police think. Before that a sixteen-year-old boy, an addict, found with his neck broken; owed money to our friend here.' Aidan glanced in the direction of the shirtless man and tapped his own upper arm. 'Tattoo. Three scimitars. One for each victim is what a former confederate testified. Still just a suspect, though, as things stand. Habeas Corpus, you know, lack of sufficient evidence to convict. The way it works is I can have him locked up immediately if he breaks my rules.'

'He will.'

'Please. You're not a crime investigator, I assume. Unless I'm totally out of touch with what a modern-day Sherlock Holmes looks like.'

Tony stifled his amusement, tried to stop himself liking any part of this man.

'Anyway. Now. About Lenny. Your coming here is clearly important.' He held up a bottle of Guinness. Tony declined. 'A big surprise too, I must say. You're a friend of Lenny's?'

'No.'

'I'm sorry? Oh, I see. I beg your pardon. Husband. Forgive me. She's happy then, Lenny, is she? Doing well, all going well?'

'She's fine, I told you. I didn't come for a chat.' He leaned forward. 'Look, I know about you and Lenny. I came here because I want you to agree to something. It's like this: I'm going to ask Lenny to marry me. She wants to, she told me so. And I don't need trouble; know what I'm saying?' He got to his feet, his focus still fixed on Aidan. 'Put it this way: it'd be better for Lenny, and me, if you went back to England, do you work over there.'

'What? England? That's absurd. Out of the question. I would not consider such a thing. Does Lenny know about this? What you're saying? She would know there's nothing for me in England. Lenny would know that. I don't believe – '

'What's here for you? This shit house?'

'People! Irish people. That's what's here. Whom I care for, counsel, defend, house, who need help every day. Enough?'

'How I figured you. Your work's your god. You can't escape it.'

Both men fell quiet.

'Do you know one single iota about the work I do here?' Aidan asked, sounding less disturbed.

'I know a lot. You run away. Africa, Iraq, doesn't matter. You waste your life in deserts and barred-up kips like this, then all you can do is brag about how fucking great the war was, then, you, then you – '

'Then nothing. You seem to have it all worked out: why I run away, why I approve of this or that. A theory for everything. Life's not that simple, I'm afraid.'

'It is. It's you, how you are. You pull others into your obsessions. You're a misfit. End of story.'

'Excuse me. A misfit, am I?' Aidan hurried his wheelchair forward, came to a stop in front of Tony. 'And you? What about you?'

Tony rounded the wheelchair.

Aidan's stare followed him. 'Mr high-and-mighty. Whatever your name is. You swagger in here like Bruce Lee, into this jungle, ready to fight a psychopath. And I'm the misfit? I'm listening, go ahead, tell me; what about you?'

Tony kept a stoic face, said nothing.

'Let's speculate, shall we? You've risked your life for a cause, something you believed in? Battled against human suffering? Cared for people riven by disease and despair? Paid for your principles with something more precious than your life? You have, have you?'

From opposite points on a circle connecting them, their eyes met.

'Maybe I have,' Tony said with understated conviction. 'Maybe more.'

'Oh, I see. So your life is somehow superior to my misfit life?'

'How could you know what goes on in ordinary people's lives? You couldn't. You only know famines and war zones and refugee camps.'

Aidan's demeanour softened. 'Sit down, please, we're both quite upset. We can talk. You have another reason for coming here. Something else you want to tell me.'

'Can you turn off that squealing?'

'Of course. I'm sorry.' Aidan reached under the table, clicked off the opera singer.

'Tell me what happened in New York, to Lenny?'

'We fell in love. That's what happened. Within minutes of meeting. Sounds juvenile, I know; in love at forty-three. I'd never known it before, I don't mind telling you. Wonderful good fortune, nothing short of, nothing short of miracul – '

'What I'm asking you is – '

'I know. I know what you're asking. You want to know about her illness. She described to me some worrying symptoms she'd been having. I pressed her to consult a specialist, talk to a psychiatrist. She wouldn't. It was obvious she was troubled, she needed someone close who would care for her. There was no one in New York. She was alone and she liked it that way, she told me. In those circumstances I felt any place was better for her than Manhattan. Apart from that, I knew, I was certain, despite having known her just days, that I'd never be the same man without her. That's it in a nutshell. You've seen it in films, in novels, no doubt.' He shifted forward, began pushing up out of the chair. 'Perhaps you've been fortunate enough to experience it first-hand. I hadn't.'

'You can walk?'

'With a cane. Good days, bad days. Last week I had a nasty bone fragment removed from my knee. The chair is just to help it heal.'

'What if you'd never taken her to Iraq? Ever think of that?'

'After the carnage of Amiriya, I never stop.' He dropped back into the chair, interlaced his long knuckly fingers, set his eyes to the ground. 'What was I to do? Think about it. Leave her behind in Manhattan, in crisis? Alone? Who would do that? It's four years since then, the day we literally bumped into each other. Feels like much longer.'

'Since you heroically rescued her.'

'It would be fairer to say we helped each other.' Aidan appeared to retreat, as though indulging what was alive in his mind. When he spoke again his tone had shed its culpability.

'You must understand that she desperately needed to get out of there. She was ecstatic about the idea of doing relief work, ironically just when I thought I might be burning out. I didn't pressure her in the slightest. Lord's truth. Within the week, we landed in Baghdad. And Lenny Quin restored a missionary zeal in me.' He paused, smiling. 'Was she marvellous or what. You couldn't count how many lives she saved, or all the people she brought hope to. Under the most God-awful conditions she had more energy, more imagination, more natural intelligence than I could ever lay claim to, even at my best. Sixteen-hour days, every day, day after day, she answered every call. She was indefatigable.'

'That's what I mean; if you weren't on your way down you'd have had no room for Lenny, or any woman. You needed someone, someone who'd lift you up, prop you – '

'Stop. Please. This combative thing does no good. You and I are not enemies.'

Both men receded, Tony impassive, Aidan clearly disturbed.

A short time later, Aidan rose up out of his chair. 'I wanted to care for her, for her. For who she is. I even asked her to marry me, which you might already have heard.'

'She said no. I know.'

'Not, No! She said she wasn't a believer, had never wished for marriage. Everything for the joy of life, except marriage; that was her credo. Goes back to her childhood, her mother dying so young, maybe. I don't know; I'm no psychologist. But that's who she was then. Not now, from what you tell me, concerning marriage, I mean. For which I'm happy. Truly. We all change.'

'Her answer was the right one. You couldn't have been all that important to each other.'

Aidan smiled. 'What's your name?'

'Anto.'

'I'm afraid, Anto, you don't quite understand. I don't mean to be rude, but perhaps it's best that way, in the circumstances.'

'No, I do understand. You needed to drag her into your world for the relationship to work, and into a war; she didn't want either and that was her way of telling you.'

'I had a dream! You understand? To care for people. You're young; you'll learn what that means. Without a dream what do I have? What do you have? Fantasies, formless hopes, adolescent lusts. Without a dream, some kind of dream, we may as well not live. You and Lenny have that now. Or, Anto, you would not be here.'

'I want what Lenny wants. It's that simple. Ireland is her world, and it's mine. I won't be smuggling her off anywhere.'

'You're so right; she does belong here. I'm so relieved to hear you say that. This whole country is Lenny. The sky, the air, the rain; it's all Lenny. How could I ever leave here? When I met her, Ireland became mine too. So many late nights in Iraq we talked about Ireland, how our new life would be. No flies, no burning heat, no land mines, no dysentery or dying children. Then one day, my malaria flared up. I shivered and sweated for five days and nights with no let-up. Only then I began to understand a woman's love. The power of it. It was like God was tending to me, healing my spirit. She stayed at my side through every minute of that, twenty-four hours a day, even though she herself needed looking after.'

'Lenny caught malaria?'

'Oh, no, not malaria. The same problems she'd had in New York. A lot milder, though: not remembering for a few seconds who she was or where she was, brief delusions. Just two occasions, that I know of. The medics around us were used to trauma, the *Médecines Sans Frontièrers* guys especially – Doctors Without Borders, you've probably read about them. They didn't offer a diagnosis, but they came up with medications that seemed to help. You have to understand, everyone adored her; people would go to the ends of the earth for her. Me, too. I couldn't get enough of her – excuse me, I'm sorry, I didn't mean to sound insensitive.'

'It's all just history. Why are you telling me?'

'I don't know, Anto,' Aidan said with obvious intrigue. 'I never felt able to talk about it before. Who'd understand? Except you. Strange, isn't it. Very strange. We've both loved something truly special. No matter what the future may hold, for you or for me, neither of us will ever go back to being the men we used to be. Quite extraordinary really.'

'Hypocrite. You are, you know that? If you'd any fucking balls you'd have said fuck-off when they told you to go to Iraq. But you didn't. You knew she had problems, and you went anyway, you dragged her with you. Maybe you could've gotten the life you say you wanted, but you didn't fight for it, did you? You played big mister hero.'

'Hero? It's not that simple, my friend.' Aidan's eyes closed. 'That order for Baghdad said: *Mass suffering; innocent citizens dying; children sick, starving.* The night we landed in Baghdad, we agreed we'd give it just six months. Then six had turned into eleven. It was then that war came. Unholy war. The night before the bombs hit our shelter – it was a Sunday, tenth of February 1991 – we made a new promise: we'd work on in Iraq for six more months. Not one week longer. We even set an exit date; we'd fly out, spend a week in England, and be back in Ireland by September 10th. We'd buy a small house, become the quintessential invisible couple. Just the two of us, for a while. Until we started having our own children; two, maybe three, we said, who knows. We'd give them, all our, we said, all our, we'd give them all our – ' Aidan's face dropped into his hands. 'What manner of god do I serve?! What manner of god?'

'So you gave up; you just – '

'Amiyira!' Aidan's eyes searched up into a void stained by the soot of generations, and he went on as though talking to himself. 'Sounds like a young girl's name: Amiriya. Playing in a garden, being summoned to lunch. How many I summoned that day.' A whistling hiss rose from him and climbed to crescendo: 'Booooommmm! Booooommmm! One half minute apart. When the first one hit, I ran. Didn't search for her, didn't try to save her. I don't picture it as much now, a picture of hell. I forbid myself even to think about it. Block it out every time, every time it comes back.'

'Lenny told me.'

'Charred humans. Ghosts. The serpent, turning living souls into puffs of smoke, melting young bodies. Four hundred innocents. Gone in seconds. Grey blood, like pools of mercury. Limbs, torsos, stuck onto walls. And the ones that crawled out, the corpses that went on living.'

'So you came back to Ireland to die?'

Aidan braced himself erect, spoke softly, shaking his head. 'Oh, no. Not to die. No. To be in the same country, treading the same soil, breathing the same air as her. Legs or no legs, I share this with her. Even now. She's everywhere here. Even in this pig sty. In every Irish face, every street, every film – '

'Hey! Hey! I get the picture, loud and clear. Ever think of using the fucking telephone?'

'I wrote letters to her. Several. Before this leg got bad I got on a train to Aranroe. September 10th 1991, the day we pledged we'd be back in Ireland beginning our new life, seven months after Amiriya. I made it up onto Mweelrea, the foothills. Even knelt down and prayed at the Druidic altar. After that I walked around the village. That's when they told me she'd gotten married – '

'Married?!' Tony jumped to his feet. 'Bullshit. That's a lie. Who said that?'

'Does it matter? My faith deserted me. I didn't want to believe it, that it was over, that she could – '

'She didn't! I know she didn't. Someone was fucking with your head.'

'She'd found happiness, had her life back, I told myself. A future to look forward to. Children. Everything I ever wanted for her. What right had I to interfere with her dream.'

'You abandoned her; that's what you're saying. What kind of relationship is that? Dumb-ass stupid.'

'Hey, Brit, want me to mangle the bollox?' Fogo approached. 'Will I bury the fucker for you?'

'Sit down, you uncivilised God-forsaken moron,' Aidan roared. 'Sit down!'

Fogo's hand shot up, middle finger raised. 'Fuckhead,' he said, then retreated to his lookout onto the dark wasteland.

Aidan turned back to Tony. 'I don't know what kind of relationship it was. Not in words, I don't. I never knew. Only what it felt like: everything. In a world better than this one. But I have never abandoned her, not to this day.'

'You're here in Dublin, a hundred and fifty miles from her, and for three years you never phoned her, even to say you were alive?'

'My friend, your mind is too young, too innocent. Look at me.' He hauled his body up out of the chair. 'Look at me!' he yelled, forcing Tony's compliance. 'Would you approve of your beautiful young daughter sharing my life? Would what you see standing here before you be good enough for your precious daughter?'

'You mean Charles Quin; he had a hand in this? Or Leo Reffo?'

'I don't know. Don't know about any of that. I believed Lenny had found love. That's all. In the letters I'd written, before I went up there, I told her how my leg was getting stronger. That the doctors were surprised at how well my skull had healed. I was almost as good as new, I told her. Same old Aidan, almost.'

The air between them turned quiet, interrupted only by the rat-tat-tat of rain. Aidan's hands swept through his silver mane as a wretchedness seemed to come over him.

'I begged her to write back, tell me we could still have our dream, become the invisible couple we'd often joked about. Or not, as the case may be. Whatever she wanted. Just let me know. I heard nothing back. After a while I didn't write any more. Then I realised I was having some kind of breakdown. As it turned out, not too serious. She was praying for me, I told myself. That's when I started pulling myself together. For a long while now I've been really strong again. Over it all. Over Lenny. Finally.'

'You're forty-something and you learned what about life? If you're not brave enough to go all out for what you want, who the fuck's going to give it to you? The god you pray to? Who? Who the fuck'll give it to you? I'm asking you, who?!'

'Anto, that's you. Who you are. Me, I trust in God, and in people. Too much in both at times, perhaps. But like I said, none of that matters now. Really, it doesn't. Even if they lied to me in Aranroe, if Lenny knew nothing of it, now she has you. And I can see you'd let no man change that. So, God bless you both.'

Aidan's chair rolled over the gritty floor, followed the arc of the table until the two men were closer than they'd been up to now. With firmness in his countenance, Aidan rose up, stood unaided.

'No, Anto, I'm sorry. I go on here. I, too, am part of this land, and forever will be. I will never go back to England. Nor anywhere else, ever. Not even in a box.'

*   *   *

Shortly after exiting the tenement he found a phone kiosk by the river. He pulled the brass handle, then stalled, tussling with his thoughts. Two linking girls moved toward the kiosk. He stepped inside. The girls crinkled their faces and waited against the Liffey wall.

'Kate, shhhhh, don't say my name! Is Lenny nearby? Just say yes or no.'

'Tony, where are – '

'Kate!'

'She's in the lounge with Ferdia, playing draughts. Something's wrong, what is it? Where are you?'

'Nothing's wrong. I only have a minute, Kate, I'm in a coin box. You guys getting along well?'

'Everything's wonderful, Tony. Lenny's crazy about you, she never stops – '

'Kate, what are your plans, you and Lenny?'

'We walked around Dublin today. Lenny's staying till Monday evening. She's taking the afternoon bus tour to Kilkenny tomorrow. I've been called in, unfortunately; I have to work, but she said she's grand going on her own. I'm taking Monday off instead; we'll go somewhere nice. Tony, she's really worried; she phoned you earlier, your B&B, and again after we got home. Where have you been?'

'What time is she getting into Aranroe on Monday?'

'The 7pm train, gets there at ten past ten. She was afraid you'd fallen or got lost up in the mountains. What's wrong, Tony?'

'No. Nothing. Just thinking . . . about strange people – '

'Tony, you're not okay.'

'I'm fine! But I have to run.'

'Wait, tell me what you were saying. What strange people?'

'It's nothing, just people, in general, can be strange. Have to run, Kate.'

'Wait, hold on.'

'Can't. Have to go. Something to do. Then I'll – '

'Something dangerous! That's Anto I'm hearing. That's Anto's voice. Listen to me: you have nothing to prove any more, to anyone, even yourself. Are you listening to what I'm saying?'

'Kate, come on, I don't want to hear this. I know, I know who I am. I'm free of all that.

'Think of all you've achieved, Tony. Don't throw it away.'

'Nothing's wrong, Kate! I'm telling you. It's just, just nothing, it's – '

'Stop it! Stop telling me lies. I can feel it. I hear Newark in you. You're angry about something, or someone.'

'Kate, look, I'm dead tired, that's all. I got four hours sleep. That's what you're hearing. Nothing more.'

'Is that so? I all but reared you, remember that. I'm here, now. No judging, no advice, just to listen. Tell me what's wrong, Tony.'

'Have to go.'

'Tony, remember our agreement, last year? The day of your release? If trouble came to either of us we'd trust in each other, tackle it together. Remember that?'

'And a few months after that you said no to Brendan when he wanted you to get back together. You took care of it, Kate, didn't you? On your own, the way you should. You didn't need my advice. Same for me now. Anyway, look, there's nothing to worry about. Now I have to – '

'Have to, you have to. Don't give me that. You don't have to face anything alone. No one does; that's one of those myths. My problems with Brendan started ten years ago; splitting up and staying split was the solution, Tony, not the problem.'

'Didn't mean it that way. You were a hundred percent right. But I'm after a different freedom. Been waiting for it since I was seventeen. Now I'll take care of what I have to to get it. See you very soon, big sister.'

'Wait, Tony!' At that moment she noticed Lenny moving toward her with a conflicted look. 'Tony, Lenny is right here, beside me. I'm going to put – '

'No. Kate, Kate – '

'Darling,' Lenny said, pausing. 'I'm missing you. I kept calling. You've been up in the mountains all this time, the whole day?'

'Good bit of it. Then I was out. Rambling. You enjoying yourself?'

'It's great. Be perfect if you were here. To hold me in bed to-night.'

'Things will be, everything will be fine. Very soon.'

'Tony, is Kate upset? Are you okay?'

'I'm fine, not a thing wrong. Kate just wants me to get down to Dublin sooner. But listen, I'm in a coin box now, people are waiting to use it. I better run. Just called to see how you were doing.'

'Really, really good, Tony, really excellent. Kate's wonderful. I'm taking a tour to Kilkenny tomorrow afternoon, so I won't be back in Aranroe till late on Monday. You're not taking the hiking trail up on Mweelrea tomorrow, I hope? You promised, not without me.'

'Not without you. Not without you.'

'Better not. We're doing it together, like we said, as soon as the weather looks good.'

'Gotta run – '

'Tony, nothing's changed, has it, between us? You sound different, down. If ever something is – '

'Nothing's changed, Lenny. Nothing. Just dead tired, that's all.'

'I love you so much. Get rest, go to bed. Hear?'

He caught himself smiling at how her words stirred him, a brief diversion from the mission spinning in his head. 'I will, don't worry. Have a great time in Kilkenny.'

'Good time. Can't be great without you. You sure nothing's getting you down?'

'Positive.'

'You do love me?'

''Course. Be waiting for you at the station on Monday. Bye.'

'Not bye. Don't say bye. We'll be together in two days. Dream of me.'

'Always do.'

He trudged along the river, past the Four Courts, then turned off into the old-city quarter of Smithfield. The rain had died off somewhat; and now in the puddled gloom, down narrow twisting streets, past raucous pubs spilling out revellers and anthems, he searched for a place to sleep. In a strangely invigorating way he felt part of this dark ward, saw it to be the sinew and bone and blood he was born to. A membership neither Aidan nor Lenny could claim. He belonged to the soul of an ancient capital. But even here, he realised, his Irishness and other passions were all mixed together in a grey-matter mess; he was adrift, raging once again against his dispossession, just as fiercely as in Newark, with still more to learning to do, and more to lose. He journeyed on, deep into the marrow of the original city, into a labyrinth of lightless arteries, a place primeval and womblike.

*　　*　　*

For a while after the call Lenny remained in the kitchen, the bloom gone. Moving back toward the lounge, she paused by the photo-montage she and Kate had earlier shared, a melange of corduroyed urchins and rosetted first-communicants from a black-and-white past. MacNeills all, lined up on Dublin City streets, their innocence captured by a long-gone itinerant cameraman. Ferdia disturbed her reverie, holding out coins, the spoils of a draughts champion.

'Ferdia, love,' Kate called out and waited for the child's attention. 'Go and pour yourself a cup of juice.' The boy bounded for the kitchen.

The two women came together.

'Kate, I'm worried about Tony. I'm sorry, but I feel I should go back tonight.'

'He's just exhausted, that's all. And he misses you; that's also why he's not at his best. I wouldn't worry.'

'Even so. He's been through a lot, and he's such a good person. You think he sounded like he was in some kind of trouble?'

Kate brooded before answering. 'He's fine. At twenty-eight he can take care of himself. Always could.'

'But did he say anything? You know, anything out of the ordinary?'

Just that people were waiting to use the phone box. That's why he was hurrying. He's fine, don't be worrying yourself.'

'Kate, there's a late train; I've taken it before. It's nearly nine now. Could we? I know it's silly, but I'd be –'

'Let's go. You're worried. It's not silly.'

Lenny pushed her arms into her raincoat. 'When I get there I'll go straight to his B&B and I'll phone you. I'm being paranoid, I know; I get that way. We'll come back up very soon, and we'll all go out to dinner together, somewhere really nice, maybe the Shelbourne, or the Westbury, or Patrick Gilbaud's; it'll be my treat.'

A sentient smile lifted Kate's countenance. She opened out her arms; the women hugged. 'We will,' she said. 'Very soon. But we have to leave right now.'

*   *   *

Tony MacNeill pressed further into the darkness, almost marching for no reason that was clear to him. He was unfazed by these bleak streets, at ease in the glances of the stragglers he had passed, among whose kind he felt no blot or blur or stain, no number or shame, where he could flaunt his belongingness or parade in the comfort of anonymity. Gradually, though, this conceit gave way to snatches of the hell that had been his, a life lost to incarceration, soulless and alone, the agonies in holding on, staying human, remaining sane, and the poison of despair. And now, sifting in this night for what was still strong in his core, he was swept forward with no clear purpose.

He drifted through a maze of foreign lanes suffused with the stink of the low-tide Liffey, ruminating among myths and realities, sucking in the night air, demanding lucidity, conviction, and ultimately a decision. And once again he passed a dim window sign that read *Rooms*. From there he skewed off onto Old Forge

Hill, a snaking rise closed in by high, razor-wire walls; and at the top he stopped to curse a turmoil inside him that would not relent.

Then out of this unyielding ether, slowly, something occurred, took shape: a compulsion, a compulsion to actualise the crazy notion forming in him, a lunatic notion, which his internal voice called him to execute. Then, like the stick of a blade, the pick of a sharp bone, the notion became a knowing, and a decision. Firm. Absurd. Impossible probably. And just then a big moon floated free, lit his watching eyes, sealed his resolve, and disappeared.

Time now, he decided, although now he bore no sense of the passage of time, time to find a place, get inside, make peace if he could with what was upturning his mind. He would not be diverted from this, his new mission, for ultimately his life had to have worth. And when the voice inside paused he wondered if his mind was intact. Or gone, at last. Then the hide-and-seek moon re-emerged, luminous, like the shining silver sixpence he'd long ago earn for polishing all the shoes in the house for Sunday Mass. And in this cool blue light it was profoundly clear what he hadn't until now accepted: his love of Lenny Quin had brought an end, and a beginning, clear as day and night. He would stake all on this.

His eyes flicked open. He struggled up off the wet concrete, puzzled at his circumstances, at this place, at the journey that had brought him here, how it had happened. But he'd find his way out; he always had done. He'd get in out of the night, get warm, dry, think himself straight. In the far distance he found a lighted steeple. He steadied his legs, brushed damp and grit off his clothing, and went in search of a window sign he hoped was real: *Rooms.*

19

It was close to midnight when the nearly-empty train pulled into Aranroe's deserted station.

Neither Paddy McCann nor any car waited. Lenny set out up the hill, her breath fogging the raw country air. At Greyfriars B&B Hotel she tapped the metal knocker.

After repeated knocks an upstairs window opened, a head poked out. No, Mr MacNeill was not there, the desk clerk declared. Lenny persisted. It was not his business, he said, to know the whereabouts of guests, and it was late.

'But you haven't checked his room,' she shouted up. 'This is very important. Please. What time did you come on duty?'

The thin-faced man peered over his shoulder. 'Two hours and ten minutes ago. If he doesn't show up, try back in the morning.' He pulled the window closed before she could plead further. But her fingers found the night bell and kept it depressed. The window reopened. 'Look, that's enough out of you,' the clerk said. 'Our guests sleep at night. Now, be off, or the gardai will be here in minutes.

She stabbed the bell again in long bursts. The clerk did not respond. 'Bastard!' she shouted, then laboured up the hill and through the entrance into Claire Abbey.

At first light she confronted the same clerk across the front desk. 'Tony MacNeill; I need you to check his room.'

'All one can do is buzz.' He dialled the room, listened briefly, and hung up. 'Afraid not.'

'Try again, please. Let it ring.'

'If he was there, he'd – '

'Please! It could be a life-or-death situation. Ring again.'

'As I said, if he was there he'd have answered. If he wanted to be disturbed, that is.'

'He's a climber. Be reasonable, will you. If he's not here he could be up on the mountain, hurt. I need to check his room.'

'Out of the question. That's enough now; I have work to do.'

She spun away, pulled open the lobby door, and beckoned. Leo approached.

'I'm sorry, I know it's early,' she said, gripping him. 'Tony's missing. I think he could be hurt, on the mountain somewhere; something has happened to him.'

Leo's eyes deflected, then returned to her sadness. 'Is it, could it be possible that he – '

'No, no, it's not! No.'

'Grand so. What can I do?'

She told him of the clerk's refusal to cooperate.

'Room?'

'Nine.'

Behind the counter, Leo pressed the clerk onto a chair. 'You'll stay there if you know what's good for you,' he said. He took the key from the rack and handed it to Lenny.

'What would it cost you?' he said, glaring down at the clerk, 'Tell me that. What would it cost you to care a bit more? The lad in there, that woman, they're worth your – '

Lenny's cry pulled him down the corridor. In Room 9 she sat on the edge of the bed she had one night shared. Leo's eyes raced around the room; he pushed in the narrow bathroom door.

'He's gone,' she said.

'Not at all, he's not. Just from here. He's off to Achill, hiking, someplace like that. You'll see, Princess.'

'He's gone. Everything's gone.'

'Just moved to a better B&B, and he couldn't reach you, you were up in Dublin.'

Her blue eyes rose up slowly until her anguish and Leo's commiseration convened.

'Let's go now,' he said. 'It's not how it seems at all.'

At reception, the clerk produced the registration card. The bill had been paid daily, one day in advance, he explained, but not for today. And no calls or messages had come in.

'It's that so, just what I told you; he found a new place, nothing more,' Leo said.

'Don't, please, unless you know something I don't. He'd have told me, or left me a note.' Suddenly, her features flashed alert. 'I know! I'm back here one day early. He caught the early train this morning to Dublin, to surprise me! That's what he was scheming on the phone last night. Kate!'

She rushed back to the reception desk.

A minute later Leo's relief ended. Kate had heard nothing, and was now more concerned.

Outside, Lenny insisted Leo should go on with his business. She'd phone later, she told him, as soon as she heard anything. She then hurried away toward the train station.

'Dangerous manner of a morning, Miss Quin,' the ruddy-cheeked female station master called out in greeting. 'You're not at your best at the minute. Something's at you?'

'Mairead, you know Tony, have you seen him?'

'Your young American? When was it now, when did I see him, have to think about that.' She inclined her face to the sky.

'Just tell me, please, can you? This is very, very serious.'

'Yesterday, must've been. Had to be. About two minutes after the Angelus.'

'Twelve noon? Leaving?'

'The 12.05 to Dublin.'

'Dublin? No, Mairead, that's not right, you couldn't have. I spoke to him last night. He was here, in Aranroe. He couldn't – '

'Only know what me eyes saw, Miss. Marched in them doors and onto the 12:05. *Will you be back to see us?* I called to him, thinking he was headed off home to America. All he gave me was a quare look, not even a *slán leat.*'

'You're absolutely certain, Mairead? I need you to be certain.'

'Certain as you and me are standing here getting blown by the same breeze.'

'Did he have anything – '

'Knapsack, big green one. Same as the day he got here asking about the da.'

A whiteness fell over Lenny. The iron gate banged behind her as she left.

'No cause to worry, grand looking woman like yourself,' Mairead said, but Lenny was already well gone. 'Now he'll be writing you them nice love letters.' The station master went on in the empty station. 'Some lads are that sort, they say. Like them Viking fellas with the horns: came to Ireland for the nice Irish Catholic ladies, then ran off and left us. Never met one meself, and don't want to; nothing but trouble, romances like that.'

*   *   *

The muddied yellow taxi came to a stop on the hill. Paddy lumbered out. 'Some place I can take you, Miss?'

Lenny's gaze stayed with the ocean, out toward Inishturk and the deep western waters.

Paddy moved to her. 'I can tell something's on your – ' Lenny's arms gripped him, clung to him. His hands hovered about then became her support.

'C'mon now, c'mon outa that. Whatever it is it'll work out. Not good to be letting little bothers get on top of you, you know that.'

She eased out of his hold. 'Tell me the truth, Paddy. You know about Tony leaving, don't you?'

'A glimpse, that's all I got, truth of God. I was dropping off Chris Desmond, the big actor fella from Dublin, and, and – '

'What, Paddy?'

'And he told me he's making a picture over in Roscommon. Could you credit that, Roscommon, of all places. Couldn't meet a nicer lad. Put a tenner in me hand when he – '

'Paddy. Please.'

'Walking into the station; a glimpse, that's all it was.'

'A little innocent mix-up; nothing more, you'll see, a tiny little mix-up.' As he spoke, his big corpulent frame moved uneasily. 'A pound he went to Galway, and I'll be happy to take your money. Or over to Leenane for the scenery. You know how the lad likes to hike, up and down and sideways all over the place. That'll be it.'

Lenny turned away, gazed inland, to a land of rambling red fuchsia, small cottages and a string of Celtic crosses lording over weathered gravestones, and in the distance a land of valleys sweeping up into green velvet foothills and hard mountain rock, and beyond all these a world beyond Mayo.

'He's gone, Paddy.' She sighed unrestrainedly.

'In the name of God, will you not be saying silly things like that. Took a ramble, the lad, nothing more.'

'To Dublin? No note or call?'

'Probably hopped off at Westport, or anywhere he liked a few miles down the road.'

For a moment nothing in her face moved. 'The 12.05 stops in Dublin. Nowhere else. One hundred and sixty miles away.'

'Look, if you want Paddy McCann's opinion, Tony's a good lad. He'll be ringing you before the day's out and everything'll be grand. Then you can hand over the pound you'll owe me, and if you want to double it now we'll shake on it.'

Over the following minutes Paddy's humour and bravado sought to lift the prevailing mood. After a wordless interlude Lenny reached out and squeezed his hand.

'One thing I have to say to you,' Paddy said, strain in his face. 'All of thirty years ago I stood not a stone's throw from this very spot. With your sweet mother, God rest her soul. Last I saw of her alive. What I want to say is you're every bit as grand a woman as she was. I promised meself I'd get the courage to tell you that one day, and now I did and I don't regret it.' Just then, as though jarred by his reminiscence, a graveness transformed him. He yanked open the car door. 'In you get,' he said. 'I'm running you home.'

'No, no, I'm walking. Fresh air, it'll do me good, it's what I need. Definitely, no.'

'Sorry, Miss, can't let you. Can't. Not taking no for an answer. Not this time, I'm not.'

Lenny's head shook with finality. 'Thanks for caring, Paddy. For so long. But I'll be fine.'

'You're not yourself today and the day's supposed to turn bad: bad thunder and lightning, bad hailstones, all sorts of terrible things. Them clouds'll tell you that. C'mon.'

He waited by the car, holding the door open. Lenny did not move.

'In you get, c'mon. I can be a hard man when the humour's on me.' Before his hand reached her she started forward and sat into the car.

As the taxi laboured up Aranroe Hill his chatter punctuated the mood. 'Have you know I used to be junior cruiserweight champion of all Western Connaught. Could've knocked out all them big black American fellas: Muhammad Ali, George Foreman, Joe Frazier, all them fellas, if I had a mind to, and been the first world champion from tiny little Aranroe, and been famous. So now, aren't you the lucky girl you didn't tangle with the champ . . . '

20

The pounding shot him awake. He tried to remember. These bare plaster walls, bare striped mattress, in this hole, what brought him here?

The raps came again, louder and longer, someone at the door. What time was it? He scanned the grungy room. At one end, high up, were two blocked-up windows, light coming in through gaps at the top.

Another clatter of knocks shook the old wooden door.

'Mr Vida, Mr Vida. We know you're in there.'

It was a woman's voice, sharp, demanding.

'It's Mr and Mrs Kelly, the proprietors. Y'alive or dead in there or what?'

Tony pulled the chair-back from under the brass knob and opened the door just a sliver. Staring in at the little they could see of him was a sixtyish couple, each looking as dilapidated, he thought, as the room in which he had just found himself: a stern-faced woman in a navy housecoat and a headscarf knotted under her chin, next to her a rail-thin, silver-whiskered man in a worn-out suit.

'The daughter said you'd be staying just the one night,' the man said.

'So what?'

'It's twenty past four, that's what!' the woman said. 'You're supposed to be out hours ago or cough up for another night. That's how it works around here.' She banged an elbow into her partner. 'Tell him, Patsy.'

'Yeah, Mr Vida. Joel. But it's grand if you want to shack up for another night. Cosy little room, good bit warmer than down below. Perfect for two. It's just that the rent was to be due at, em, at – '

'At twelve o'clock, same time it's always due,' the woman said. 'But you wouldn't wake up any time Patsy called you.'

'Could've knocked harder but I said no, us men do like a bit of a lie-on when we can get it, especially of a Sunday. If a man doesn't get his sleep, I always say, he's no good for nothing, especially the ladies.'

Tony tried to shake the grogginess from his head. He pulled paper money from his pocket and began unfolding it. 'How much?'

'Seven quid for last night; thirteen for the two, a pound discount,' the man said. 'That be okay, Joel? Run you all the way up till tomorrow.'

'Thirteen pounds for two nights?' Tony said. 'Who was that woman last night; black curls, dark skin, the one I spoke to?'

'That's me daughter, Veronica,' the woman said. 'She's married, for your information.'

'So?' Tony said.

'Very happily married!' the woman said. 'Doesn't want no bother. Get me? You can keep your fancy to somebody else.'

Tony's confusion turned from the woman to her partner.

'So far, so good,' the man said cheerfully, tipping up and down on his toes. 'The marriage, I mean, so far so good. But time'll tell. They only tied the knot on Wednesday. But don't let that stop you, squire; no shortage of women round here.' He swung his forearms in rhythm with his pelvis. 'Tons of sexy birds not very far away, if you get me, Joel. And you with that tan; the birds here go mad for a tan, they do.'

The woman glowered at her partner. His face dismissed her.

'He's not one, I'm telling you, missus,' he said, then addressed Tony again. 'She thinks she's psychedelic. Says she can smell a copper a mile away. Copper me arse, says I; I never laid eyes on a copper with a suntan.'

'Cop? Me? No.' Tony's head was clearer now, but he was still bewildered at the pageant playing out in front of him, wondering if it might all be a delusion, similar to whatever it was that had happened to him hours ago up on Old Factory Hill.

'And you wouldn't be one of them other fellas either, I can tell,' the man said. 'You know them fellas, them other kind of fellas, the homosexual fellas?'

Tony shrugged again.

'Well then, as horny as meself I'd say y'are.' The man leaned forward, massaging his hands. 'Can't get enough of the ladies, am I right? Oh, I am, I'm right, I know I am. I can see you're a man after me own heart, and if you don't mind me saying, very hand-some too, and nicely put together, the bod I mean, nice and – ' With a look of self-consciousness, he fell silent.

'So I'll give you the score,' the woman said, poking at the first of her upstanding fingers. 'You pay up in advance, fifteen quid, no horseplay, no handcuffs or ropes or any shite like that, a half hour and no more under no circumstances, except if you pay more. Them's the rules, and we don't break them for no one.'

'Wait a minute, hold on. You mean this, this is a – '

'Sundays y'have a bigger pick, so you're in luck,' the man said. 'You've Daisy and Caddy and Brett, take your pick, all in the parlour right now waiting only for you to give the nod. And Queen Bula, she'll be over any minute now; a black pearl, I call her, from Zamboraland or some foreign place like that.'

'Memory gone again?' the woman snapped. 'Leaving out your little pet?'

The man rolled his eyes. 'Myrtle's below, too, Mister Joel. Lost her voice a few days back, cold went down on her chest, but she's a fighter, and gor – '

'Stop there! I've heard enough.' Tony braced the door with his foot as he fished in his pocket.

'If you're a bit squeezed, Mr Vida,' the man said, trying to poke his head in the door, 'we might be able to let you off another quid. Daisy's obliging that way.'

Tony dropped coins into the woman's outstretched hand.

'Four quid! Where d'you think y'are? Four quid won't buy you a pack of frenchies.'

'Look, maybe we can do it for ten, Joel,' the man interjected. 'Can you swing ten little smackeroos?'

'That woman, last night,' Tony said, 'Veronica – '

'Told you, didn't I? She's not available,' the woman said.

'Not definitely, definitely not available.' The man talked with the air of someone piecing together possibilities. 'Depends, Missus. That's what she said. Depends. On the cut of the customer and things like that. Wouldn't hurt to ask.'

'That's me own flesh and blood you're talking about, Patsy Kelly.' The woman snarled. 'Them days are gone; she told you.'

'Didn't say she'd do it. Only tell her she's a chance to make a few bob.'

Tony's raised hands forced a respite. 'Veronica told me nine pounds for the room, that's what I gave her. And four makes thirteen, for two days. Now go. Go away. Understand?'

'Daisy'd never disappoint you, Mr Vida, I swear, she wouldn't; does anything you ask. Great value for your hard-earned cash.'

'Fuck it, listen! You want cops all over you? Not cops like me. Unfriendly cops? Then go away.'

The woman side-eyed her partner. 'Told you. I knew it. Y'wouldn't listen.'

The man's face morphed into stillness; he gave a token wave, then he and the woman stole off down the corridor.

21

Gusts blowing in off the Irish Sea were now beating the southerly airstream into a vortex. After Navan and Kells the bus headed directly into the turmoil, made worse by the flatness of the terrain. The reds and russets of early autumn now swirled as debris on the passing bogs, and in the distance spears of sunlight lit up random green patches.

Onboard, an atmosphere of guts had given way to edginess among the two dozen or so passengers, whose hands now locked to metal bars and seat-backs.

Tony wriggled to find comfort, and if he could, sleep. It was already Monday, the insane weekend past but not over. If the bus didn't get blown into one of the lochs, he thought, he'd be in Aranroe by 2pm. Loads of time, right on plan. First thing he'd do was grab four or five hours of sleep somewhere, then clean up and get something to eat; he'd be at the station by ten for Lenny's bus from Dublin, just as he had promised her.

Things would work out, he told himself. But Aidan Harper still hijacked his every thought. He knew what he had to do about that, and how he'd do it. He'd figure himself out too. And maybe come to understand what it was that had taken him to the top of

Old Factory Hill, so much time in the dark, drifting, unaware. What had possessed him? All the silent words then that would not stop streaming through him, a well that wouldn't shut off, and the bedlam in his brain that had left him out cold, a still-unremembered journey that ended in the Kellys' seedy house. He felt exhausted now, too weary to even wonder what it all meant, if he had dreamed it all, if he'd ever know. Time for peace now within the storm, time for rest among these anxious passengers.

Over the following hour he dozed off occasionally but only for minutes, roused each time by the swerving and jarring of the bus. Eventually, he stretched his legs across the adjacent seat and lowered his head onto his rolled-up jacket. Soon he was dreaming, falling back into old darkness, old realities. He forced himself awake, into the yak and hum of half-sleep. But soon he was losing again, slipping back beyond rescue, into the hell of his past.

*   *   *

The buzzer blared, the light flashed red, crimson red, on off, on off, gears clunking, steel shifting. Fear surged in him, turned him cold. He glared as the riveted wall slid aside, not knowing what to expect but certain of whom. King Kong Yablonski. Prison Shift Commander. Abuser of cons. Rapist. Whose eyes had been on him for four nights, since he'd started the library job, midnight shift. All the cells had the talk. All knew Yablonski for what he was, knew that outside he was a dead man, with real contracts on his grey missile head, that his luck and lust and viciousness had run thirty years, that if he dared leave the prison even for a day he could die a hard death, that payback was coming sooner or later. Not soon enough, Tony feared.

Then there he was, black-uniformed, leering, in all his big flesh, tobacco-brown mouth, club thumping against his thigh.

Tony held out both books, books he'd been ordered to deliver.

Right from the start it had felt wrong. Now he knew it was, this big sick shit reading books.

A hand gesture ordered him in.

'Have to get back,' he said, as blank as he could, offering the books again. Yablonski's eyebrows tightened. Tony was certain now, something was going on. The voice in his brain screamed stop, don't go through the door, not with a pervert armed and deadly, cut off by steel. But here no one said no; there was no way to say no, no rights, no recourse, no justice, no escape. After midnight, the only power that reigned was towering over him, rapacious eyes sizing its prey.

'Inside!' Yablonski commanded, the club hot-dogged in his hands. Tony remained still. Yablonski approached, blood in his cheeks. No rights, no choices here, the facts scorched Tony's mind. No opportunity to fight, or escape. He edged forward, crossed the steel track.

*   *   *

The sound of his own outburst shot him upright in the seat, to be met by a busload of staring passengers. Then another gust set them all back to bracing, to navigating the road that was taking them to their destinies.

He tried to slow his pounding heart, settle his shaking. Seven years had passed since that night, since King Kong Yablonski. He was twenty-one then, but it was branded to his soul in all its detail.

Minutes later, he refolded his jacket, lay back across both seats. He'd rest, stay awake, hold Lenny in his thoughts and senses: her *Opium* scent, dancing hair, her smooth warmth wrapping around him, just Lenny and him, their nights together at Greyfriars and Rock Cottage, light at last in the misery he had lived, let it fill his mind.

But hard as he clung to her, his recent experiences in Dublin flooded back: deserted streets, the strangest dark he'd ever known, if his mind was not fooling him; and that voice inside him that had taken over, that he could not stifle, and the endless walking, foreign streets, if it was real, wasn't imagined. And Aidan Harper. And what Tony MacNeill now had to do, his next move, one that seemed unthinkable, but would be done. For he still had hope, hope for the life and love he'd just begun to know.

Each time his eyes closed he forced them open, kept the dark at bay. But now they stung like thorns. Then Yablonski's face reappeared. Soon he'd bury that too, he thought, for ever, in the grave of vampires and tyrants, put a stake through his heart, never to rise again. Yablonski, Yablonski, big battered bastard, Yablonski rot forever. Yablonski. He was fading, falling, back into Yablonski's lair.

*   *   *

Inside the steel door, he froze, mind racing. Can't run or call out, he thought. Nobody near, no guards in the wing. No escape hatch.

'You hearing me, boy?!' Yablonski snarled.

He moved one step forward. The Shift Commander's arm powered past him, fingers stabbing at the code pad.

'I have to get the paper done. It's just me in the shop. Billy Headington got out yesterday.'

The door stopped sliding, clacked shut.

Yablonski glared. 'Don't know no cons read the paper this late. Except pretty little foreign boys, could be.'

'Paper's running late. The front page isn't done.' Tony's voice exposed none of the fear rampaging through him. 'That's why I need – '

'I know all about you. Who'd you think fixed your shift, boy?' Yablonski thumped the club against his own massive chest. 'Because right off I knew I could like you. Cute way you talk. Top of that you're a smart boy; ain't like them dumb fucks you and me gotta live with. Good shape you got there too, real tight; appreciate that in a man.'

The club pointed to the inner office.

Tony glanced to where he was being directed then back at Yablonski. He'd go along for now, had to, but he'd kill the fucker, he swore, if he put his paws near him; take his eyes out first, ram them into his head, do things he never let himself do on the street, then he'd snap the fucker's jugular, rupture his solar plexus, crush his balls.

At the inner office door it was the man's white flesh that jarred him first. A slight man about his own age, long fair hair, wearing only white briefs, perched on the arm of a leather sofa, shaking, trying to cover himself, clearly not a con.

Yablonski locked the inner door, made a show of dropping the key into his chest pocket and buttoned it closed. Tony needed no explanations. His muscles and fists ached. Strike hard, strike now, he felt, he could do that, had to, couldn't let this happen, no fucking way could he let this happen. His eyes scanned for a weapon, anything he could use. Burst the fucker now, he decided, right now, smash his skull.

'Mr Stapf. Come over from Germany,' Yablosnki said, puckering his lips in a mock kiss. 'Town lock-up's full. Station boys loaned us Wolfgang for the night. Obliging of them.'

Tony shifted his weight onto his toes, eyed the club, then saw it was strapped to Yablonski's wrist. Go at him low, with everything, go hard, bring him down, three hundred pounds against hard tile; he could do it, he decided, he could take him down. Pick the moment, set a back-up plan, do what he was better than most at, fight. But not yet, when the distance between them lessened.

'Asleep in an automobile. Believe that? Inside city limits. Violation.' The Shift Commander grabbed the man's blond hair, yanked him to his feet. 'Figure that,' he said, glancing toward Tony. 'No sir, Mr hippie! Bad, bad, bad mistake.' He pushed his face into the young man's face and spoke with cheerfulness. 'For your crime, you get to entertain us right up to 7am.'

'I have to get back,' Tony said assertively. 'Inspection will be checking for me.'

Yablonski released the trembling man, drifted to the side, circled about. From behind, the club snapped like a branch into Tony's ribs. He recoiled. The room blurred, he knew he was going down, banging against the desk, kneecaps thudding, head smacking the floor, no feeling. Then his senses were returning, pain surging. He hadn't seen it, didn't anticipate it, a loser's mistake he never made in Newark. Now the street code kicked in. Get up, he commanded his body. Get up! MacNeills didn't stay down. Get Up! His legs pushed up, but gave way.

*　　*　　*

'Uuuppppp! Get up!'

Something squeezed his shoulder, shook him, shook him again, a voice talking to him, small hands on his forehead, in his hair, tugging at his busted side. His eyes burst open, he tried to make sense of what was happening. A girl. In his face. What was she doing? Huge purple-blue eyes very, like lanterns shining, so close. Who? Why?

'It's alright, you're alright, only a nightmare you were having,' the bright face said. 'Don't be worrying. I've been in far horribler storms than this; believe me, I have, far horribler.'

He wanted to reject her, dismiss her concern, be left alone, but he was in a stall, still muddled. Then all her unpainted naturalness came into focus: beautiful face, perfectly made, thin, kind, warm.

'You okay, are you? You awake? I'm Cáitlín. Hi, you okay?'

'Crazy dream,' he said, pushing his hands through his hair. 'I'm fine, I'm fine now, thanks.'

'You're from Dublin. What part?'

'North side.'

'I'm a Dub, too, Dundrum. I noticed you getting on with your pack. I bet that fella's been all over the world, I said to myself.

Then when I heard someone shout out, I couldn't see who it was, but I guessed it was you; don't know why but I did. I'm off to see the granny, in Carna; she's ninety-one, still galloping around the place. Sure you're alright? Truth is I hate storms; the wind especially, I hate the wind. If you want me to, I'll sit beside you; help keep the nightmares away. Do me good, too.'

He shook his head. 'I'll be fine. I can stretch out here. No sleep in days.'

'No bother. Bound to be over soon.' A mix of pleasantness and disappointment radiated from her. 'Try to get your rest. I'll wake you up if we stop, in case you feel like a cup of tea.'

Once again he pillowed his jacket on the armrest and settled himself. Despite the howling and battering, before long he was capitulating. Back he slipped, further back, deep into sleep.

*   *   *

Down, the voice in his head kept repeating, he was on the ground still; can't stay down, can't stay down. His head was a jangle of noise, body damaged, pain burning in his side. Beneath his face the blood moved slowly, dark purple on terra-cotta tiles. The metal club, he'd been caught by it, sucker blow. The young undressed man was trying to sit him up. Yablonski, legs astride, weapon swinging, was standing over them.

He cursed his disobedient brain. Stay down and you're dead, his street voice kept warning. He made it to his hands and knees, pulled his body up, felt around his side and shoulder. The club was pointing at him now. He straightened into the pain, looked into the Shift Commander's bloodshot eyes, eyes his avenging hands would rip out given one half chance. And he heeded his own code, learned a long time ago: show no pain, dig quietly for strength, be harder than the enemy, be like steel, that was how to stay alive.

'Wipe that look off you, boy!' Yablonski said, unhooking steel handcuffs from his belt. 'Never ever do that, never ever smart-talk me. Y'hear? Said I like you, and I do. You obey me, be my buddy, and no one in here'll trouble you less they answer to me. See, you and me, we can have us a whole lot of fun with our little hippie here. You get me? Huh? You follow me?'

Tony glared at him but didn't answer.

'Putting these cuffs on you because y'aint big but you got yourself a real strong shape, and something I can't figure about you, could be a real wildman for all I know.'

The young man rose off the sofa arm, his body shiny with sweat. 'Sir, I don't know I break the rules to be sleeping in car. I know now, I don't do it again. Never.'

'You're in Florida now, Mr hippie-man; quit your whining. We got ordinances down here for violators, bikers, draft dodgers, communists, long-haired hippies, all kinds low-life. We lock y'up!'

The Shift Commander busied himself about the room, all the time mimicking the man's pleas. Then the sound of scraping metal riveted Tony's attention, a long bayonet being drawn from inside the club. Yablonski held it aloft, sighed reverentially.

'Yes sir, you young boys gotta learn how to show respect. Old momma here's cut real men, cut real good, big men, small men.' He slid the blade back into its shaft and flung it onto a low credenza, where it thudded against the wall and came to rest.

Tony's eyes stayed with it, surreptitiously. He needed no education on what was coming. No sense in waiting, he told himself. Knock him out of the way, get the weapon; any weapon.

As though alerted, Yablonski retrieved the club and made for Tony, now supporting his weight against a heavy desk. Yablonski pushed him aside, threaded a plastic hand-restraint through a hole drilled through the desk's metal overhang, looped a second restraint through the first and secured it around Tony's wrists; only then did he unlock the steel cuffs.

Covert flexing had brought a degree of suppleness back to Tony's hand. Beneath the overhang his fingers found a burr around the hole and started grinding the plastic restraint. He followed every move of Yablonski, watched shirt and shoes being removed, the unbuckling of the service belt. If he could make it to the club, he felt sure he could handle the bastard, best odds he'd get. And what then? Could he kill if he had to, if that's what it took? He hoped he had what it took. Then what? Capital murder, death row? None of that mattered that much any more. He'd lost with life already. Just crack the pervert. Be proud.

Yablonski stepped out of his black uniform pants, draped them over the credenza. Tony dug into his reserves, questioned his body's readiness for what he was prepared to do. He rehearsed strike options, tried to flex and release his muscles, but his lacerated fingers were making grinding more difficult. At times his efforts seemed in vain, but each time he willed himself through, in honour of Witchell Heights he told himself, when he was king on the street, unbeatable.

Yablonski, slapping about in Bermuda-style undershorts, had disappeared for minutes behind a narrow annex door. He returned concealing something within a folded towel, which he laid down. He grabbed the young man's hair, forced him face-down over the sofa-back and held up the bayonet. 'How about that, Mr hippie-man: number fifty,' he said then looked toward Tony. 'Bookworm's fifty-one. Whole lot prettier. And he ain't no pussy. Fact, red-boy could be a problem, shape like that. Come his turn, gotta lock him down good.'

The young man straightened up, tried to speak, but only convulsed.

'Never had me no Nazi, far's I can figure. And ain't had no hippie since Christmas before last, must be.'

'Sir, officer,' the man cried. 'Officer, please, sir – '

Yablonski's hand gripped the man's throat. 'Gimme any shit, your dick goes in my dick jar. Get me?' He forced the man back over the sofa-back, held him down, then scraped the bayonet tip diagonally across his back, releasing a thin line of blood. The man screeched, wriggled violently, until a heavy fist thudded into the back of his skull, dropping him forward. Yablonski flung the unshafted blade onto the credenza.

'Mein gott, mein gott, vater, mutti, nein, nein.'

In that instant it happened. The plastic cuff gave way; just the stringy outer shell was left. Tony hid his shock; his blood-matted hands were almost free. He assessed: eight feet to the credenza, three strides, blade pointing toward him. One chance, that's all he'd get. If he could spring, he figured, get the weapon, he'd have power, adrenaline, new strength, time to breathe; once the blade was his he'd be safe. He'd die before giving it up. Might have to. Die a fighting MacNeill. Not so bad. Maybe this was the day of the end of everything. Though his whole body was shaking now, more than he could ever remember, he'd fight, no question, harder than he'd ever fought.

He pressed all his weight against the burr, bore the pain of metal tearing his flesh. A few more seconds, he told himself, until, unlike the first time, he'd face killing with intent, with someone to save if he succeeded, besides himself. He'd make certain the swine never raped again. This was his sacred oath, and it felt freeing. Then a wave of fear made him think of his parents and sisters, Kate's loving kiss before they shifted him to Florida. But no, no, he had to wipe all that away, couldn't help him now. Stay strong, focus, keep control, be hard, fast, brave, unmerciful, get the weapon!

The plastic skin snapped.

He sprang for the bayonet, three strides, got it, swept immediately to the side, gained balance and leverage. But the Shift Commander's reflexes fired almost as fast. He had turned his prey in front of him, fingers of both hands embedded in the young man's neck.

Tony's attention riveted to Yablonski's face; there he'd read what was coming, as he'd done so often in other battles. He arced to his right, bayonet primed, feet and shoulders poised to drive it. Fighting with a weapon for the first time, at twenty-one, incarcerated; the irony of it flashed through his head. Four years since Margo and Stewie stopped being Margo and Stewie, since Jesus Pomental died and started haunting him. Four years of torture, to this.

'Put it down!' Yablonski roared.

Tony noted each edgy shift in his target. The young man's eyes had begun bulging, gurgling coming up out of his constricted throat. No way he could put it down. Too late to be afraid. Whatever was about to happen, he wouldn't put it down. If he did, he'd die here, today. The German kid too, probably. And the swine goes free: cutting, raping, killing. The young man looked to be losing consciousness, choking, sinking lower, harder to hold up. If he dropped, it would be just him against King Kong Yablonski. One against one. The way he liked it on the street. One would win. One wouldn't. Except here, one could die. Maybe two. Even all three.

'Lay it down and this is over,' Yablonski shouted. 'No charges. Got my word, boy. No charges, no charges. We all walk outa here, all of us. Or you're a fucking dead man.'

TV talk, Tony thought. Nobody talked like that on the street, not on his streets. And with the swine's face pumping sweat, it was clear the fear of death was in him. He faked a lunge. Yablonski jerked back, held the young man farther out in front of him. Tony registered the change; here was the mistake he'd been watching for. For this opponent knew nothing of Anto MacNeill: how his mind worked, what he could do with speed and leverage and fighting skill, what he was willing to risk, and ready to lose. He moved forward, bayonet low and angled, shoulder coiled, studying the Shift Commander's flushed face. Then another step closer to the enemy.

'Kill me or him, you fry, y'hear me? You fry! Y'hear? You fry!' Yablonski's words poured out, his head a damp, glistening ball.

For Tony, rehearsal was over. He'd pick his spot, strike fast, retreat. He had him now; he was street-sure of that. He stalked his retreating target, blade tip four feet from Yablonski, two feet from the barely-conscious kid now drooling spit. Had to go for it, he told himself. At best force a surrender, then make his case. Slim chance. If not, do what he had never done deliberately. Don't get played for a fool, don't fuck up. No backing out now, no matter what. Miss the kid, be sure to miss the kid.

What he'd do he had learned in boxing. The kid could still see, had instinct, which was needed for the move to work; he'd see the bayonet coming for him, he'd collapse, become a deadweight, too heavy to hold up, Yablonski would back away without his shield. The feint-and-hit. Aim directly at the kid, last-second pull back, then the strike, the real one, go all the way, with power and legs, for the Shift Commander.

Go!

The instant the strike started the young man's head fell forward. Inches away, the bayonet pulled back, then lunged explosively forward again, the real strike under way, then a corrective jiggle that slowed the weapon so that it missed the falling blond skull, raw steel still going, slicing through air, still going. Bayonet into chest, into grizzle.

Yablonski stumbled back, stayed up, the blade in him; he pulled it out, barrelled toward the young man now on hands and knees. Tony caught the young man's hair, tried to haul him aside, but he sank flat to the floor. Then a glimpse, the red blade flashed into Tony's peripheral vision. Too late. He felt the metal piercing the flesh of his upper leg, then slashing across his ribcage. He was hit. Hard.

Before the bayonet came again his reflexes shot him not into retreat but forward. He swung a hard fist into the Shift Commander's mouth. Yablonksi reeled backwards, tripping the alarm as his naked, wet mass thudded onto the tiles. Almost immediately he was back up, mouthing vengeance. Bayonet primed, he made for the now crawling young man. Before he could strike, the steel underside of a desk chair crunched into his face, knocked him across the credenza and down, his body a blotched mess. Alarms blaring now, he scrambled up for the third time, this time without the weapon, and with a roar he charged forward. Tony stood his ground, his strike hand ready. He feigned right, jinked left, and with all the leverage his wounded body would allow, he unleashed an upward thrust. The blade drove into Yablonski's middle. His bulk bulldozed on, crashed against a wall. He tried to extract his weapon of forty-nine notches. It would not part from him. Eyes rolling, then closing, he slid down in stages until coming to a stop, seated erect.

Tony MacNeill surveyed the passing. Benjamin Arthur King Kong Yablonski, Shift Commander, State Prison. Pervert, and more.

Dead.

22

To the west, rain clouds still hung over a wild, hissing Atlantic. He trudged along a line of storm-torn fuchsia, battling wind and hill and a weekend that had left him craving sleep. Just before Greyfriars B&B the green Escort slowed alongside him.

'Tony, Lenny's not with you?' Cilla shouted.

For a second he caught himself smiling, a rarity in recent days. He watched her manoeuvre onto the shoulder and into a tight 360-degree turn. The feeling in him, he thought, was something like belongingness; though he wasn't sure that was it. Whatever, he felt taken by the unexpected comfort she induced in him, her unique brand of corny: jeans, boots, curls and ruggedness. And intensity. And looks.

'Where's Lenny?' she asked anxiously.

'Dublin. Coming back tonight, the late train.'

'She's not in Dublin. She was – '

'She's with my sister, Kate, in Dublin.'

'No! No, she's not. She was here yesterday.'

'That's not possible. I saw her in Dublin. I mean I talked to her there.'

'When? When did you talk to her?'

'Night before last. Saturday. I phoned her there. Why? What's wrong?'

'Paddy met her yesterday. Mairead told her you got the train to Dublin. She was depressed, Paddy said, very down. Now she's missing, she's nowhere in the village. Paddy's racing around like a madman.'

'You sure about this?'

'I'm telling you, she was here in Aranroe yesterday; she's not here now.'

Tony sank into his thoughts.

'What? What is it? You know something?'

He shook his head. What was in his mind was too frightening to think.

'Leo's in a state. He went to Greyfriars with her, looking for you. It's just over an hour now since she rang him.'

'She's at the Beehive. Or in the Horslips. Got to be.'

She's not, I told you. I've searched, so has Paddy. We were praying she was with you. The weather's set to turn.'

'Lenny phoned Leo? What are you saying? She called Leo an hour ago, and?'

Cilla's eyes turned away then back to him. 'You ready, for a shock?'

'What?'

'*I love you, dad.* That's what she said, nothing else. Now you know.'

'Father, daughter: I figured that. So what, what does it mean?'

'She never called him dad or da or father, never in her life. And she thinks you took off. I hope I'm wrong, but it could mean she was saying goodbye.'

'Oh Christ. Intinn Island. She told me, she said she, she – '

'What? Say it.'

'She said her soul, her spirit, would always ... Devil's Cove! It's Devil's Cove, I'm sure.'

'Let's hope to God you're wrong. C'mon, get in.'

Tony threw his backpack into the car. Before they could pull out, the blaring yellow taxi drew up alongside them with Paddy, Eilis and Madeleine onboard.

He was the last person to see her, Paddy reported breathlessly. Drove her up yesterday to the Abbey. Should have said to Leo about how she was; thought it was just a little mix-up, be fixed in no time. He was collecting Leo now, to drive along the road to Killadoon. Eilis and Madeleine were hiking over the head, to the beach. Wherever she'd taken off to, she'd a good hour head-start.

'Tell Eilis the wind on the head will be crazy,' Tony said. 'Could sweep someone over the edge.'

'Go, Paddy, you go on. We're going to the loch,' Cilla said. 'If we don't find her, we'll try cross over to Intinn, Devil's Cove.'

The taxi sped up the hill, the Escort in the opposite direction.

Out beyond Loch Doog, beyond the pincer headlands, the ocean roared like thunder, throwing up mountains of white spume. From the mainland they scanned the length of Intinn, a mile offshore but densely wooded. Nothing moved on the island but windblown trees and bushes. They then bustled down to the water, where a cluster of small rowboats bumped together. The brown boat was missing, the Quins' boat, Cilla declared; no one other than Lenny would have taken it, and she was not a strong rower.

They scoured the strait separating them from the island. Nothing but water and a few lobster pot markers.

'It's doable,' Tony said. 'Close enough to get over there.'

'Wind's kicked up in the last half hour; it was calm up to then,' Cilla said emphatically. 'She made it across. Definitely.'

Tony grabbed the line of a tar-black boat and waded out to it, Cilla behind him. He turned, raised his hand. She slogged past him.

'No, Cilla! I don't want you with me.'

'Not your call,' she said, and climbed into the boat.

Standing knee-deep in the slapping water, he watched her ready both oars in their locks, exuding her own stamp of invincibility.

The instant, fleeting as it was, felt to him like it fused their spirits, and maybe their destinies. At her insistence they sat abreast, each grasping a heavy oar.

Out past the headlands the flap and furl of the ocean smacked the little boat high and low, racked the oars against joints and muscle and washed surf over them. Farther out, gyrating air currents sucked them into a swirl. No word was uttered by either, no sigh or cry or curse. Nor did either break from the rises and drops and pulls that kept them stable and lugged the island closer.

Halfway across, something hit their boat, a jarring thud that sent them chasing after their oars. Seconds later it hit again, this time appearing alongside them. The brown boat. Empty. Both oars inside, lying side by side, under water.

'Doesn't mean a thing,' Cilla roared over the hiss and rumble. 'Broke off in the storm. Happens.' She re-sank her oar and pulled harder, forcing Tony to match her, all the way across.

On Intinn Island they slogged up to Rock Cottage. Found it locked. No sign of life. Tony searched around the side. No key.

'Fuck it, don't do this!' he yelled toward the dark clouds now stealing the blue sky. 'Don't do this to me!'

Cilla tugged at him. 'Not your fault! None of it.'

He broke her hold. 'She's gone to Devil's Cove to die.'

'No, she's not. Stop saying that! We'll go there, now. If she's not there, she's back on the mainland.'

He shot away, Cilla at his heels, through ferns and whitethorn, not certain he'd remember the trail Lenny had shown him. But soon they emerged onto a familiar stretch of shoreline; they raced past rocks and tide-pools with never more than a couple of strides between them, until together they rounded the tip of Intinn and onto Devil's Cove, into a vortex of elements.

He halted there and stared as though hypnotised by some invisible force. Everything was intact in front of him: Lenny reclining, beautiful, full of life, full of sun, him beside her, serene in this new world they had brought to each other, each on fire, on the white sand, newly free, she teasing him into swimming naked, then lying together, soaking up the world's warmth. All in a flash, the life he had lived in one single month.

Cilla's shouting snapped him alert. They pushed on, down the curving beach, searching land and the thundering waves.

Nothing here for him, the voice inside his head insisted, no human life, just the Devil's winds and waters, no sun, no child at play, no joy-filled woman; just dreams, hers and his, drowning in a world in which he could no longer believe.

'Look!' Cilla's yell jolted him once again, from higher up on the sloping sand. 'The rocks! The rocks!'

His eyes shot to a cluster of sea-rocks three hundred feet away. In the erupting tide a rose-pink form was beating against the weed-encrusted boulders. They ran toward it, straining to maintain sight of it.

Jesus Christ!' Cilla cried, reaching for him. 'Holy Jesus!'

They raced into the surf together. The form kept tossing chaotically, ballooning, disappearing and reappearing. Now well out of his depth, he battled through walls of water, arms working machine-like, until he reached the rose-pink form.

A nylon jacket! No body. He searched about. Lenny's ski jacket. No body. An empty jacket. He started back toward shore. No reason to believe the worst, he told himself, and he wouldn't, he just wouldn't. She was powerful in any water, he'd seen that, a fish, dolphin-like, a survivor.

But as his feet found the bottom Cilla's face tore at his hope. From twenty feet he saw the agony in her, saw that within her lay something only she knew, the gravity of which he could not undo. He could turn around, swim away, swim out, not face it; the notion overtook his mind; no he couldn't, he couldn't wipe away what Cilla knew, nor turn back time, nor change what was coming.

Nearer to her, her bearing told him she would lead him, that he should follow. She circled around a set of giant beach rocks, toward the spot where he and Lenny had sat watching the red sun sink into the western ocean. He trailed after her, dead to the elements, asleep to all but the beating inside him.

On the sand lay clothing neatly folded, anchored by three sea stones. Cilla dropped to her knees: blue jeans, black turtle-neck sweater, sneakers, and tucked between them a folded white cap. From inside the cap she extracted an empty pill bottle, then a gold chain with a tiny cross of Connemara marble. She held it out to him, kept holding it out. Her hand took his, fought it into shape, and into his palm she placed the chain and small green cross.

'Yours,' she said, squeezing the hand closed. 'It's okay.'

He spun away, thrashed into the surf, and there he stood against wind and rushing waves, staring out along the long black promontory, out past Finger Rock, a twenty-foot granite needle pointing heavenward out of the depths.

In a blaze of speed he took off along the waterline, climbed up onto the promontory, and continued running out. Cilla roared his name, bolted after him, then halted. About two-hundred yards out, at the end of the promontory, a lone figure stood out against the dark rocks, a woman, purple swimsuit, poised above the tempest, about to dive in.

Cilla all but caught up to Tony, now slowed by rock-slime and weed.

'Lenny, it's Lenny!' he shouted, picking his way forward. Cilla followed his course until they came together, breathless, with no safe next step. He stepped back, sprang into the air. His feet hit the landing spot but continued sliding, taking him over the edge and down into a crevice. In two feet of swirling tide, he righted himself, took stock: throbbing shoulder, right thigh hurting, pounding head. With bloody brine washing over him he tested his legs. Nothing broken, he was fairly sure; he'd been worse.

Cilla's arm appeared, reaching down; he gripped it, climbed up. He continued picking his way to the jagged tip of the promontory, where moments before, Lenny had been standing.

But not now.

Then he saw her, a blond head rising and sinking in the surf. But swimming. She was swimming, strongly. Swimming out.

'Lenny! Lenny!' Cilla yelled over and over, waving frantically. Tony did the same, bellowing as loud as his lungs would allow. But the furore carried off their calls. He pressed his palm against the bleeding wound in his thigh, then tore off his boots.

'No! You can't go in there! Oh Jesus, look at your leg!' Cilla's fists held on to him. 'No! It's suicide. You'll die, the current will take you, there's nothing you can do!'

He prised away her grip, discarded his jacket and sweatshirt, then pulled a silver ring off his finger. 'My father's. Look after it.'

'Don't go in, please, don't.'

From an elevated ledge he glanced back. 'I'd do it for you,' he said.

Cilla offered no further protest. He jumped. A big rebounding breaker swallowed him up, carried him out toward the current, nearer to the pitching golden head. He plunged beneath the surface, stroked till his lungs were empty, his sinuses sour with salt. As a wall of water threw him up, he saw her again, caught in the Africa current, but close, so close to shoot new hope through him.

His wounded leg was numbing. But she was almost reachable, when he could see her. Another sustained effort closed the gap even more, to three or four body lengths. Then doubt hit. His clumsiness in the water had burned his energy, had him in oxygen debt. Had he enough left, he asked, to get to her and get them to safety. The only response he heard was that he should go to her. For her, for him, and because it felt like they'd be stronger together. When he caught sight of her she had stopped stroking. And the current now had them both in its grasp.

Just one more burst would unite them, he felt certain. He blotted out the weakness in his leg, fought against the unrelenting ocean, then dipped under the last wave separating them, and resurfaced.

But Lenny Quin, in that spot moments before, was gone.

His body jack-knifed high, plunged down through froth and haze into a muffled, low-buzzing realm. In the greyness, he groped feverishly, coiling, reaching, searching. No Lenny. He pressed deeper, lungs on fire. Nobody, nothing, in this near-lightless world.

And still going down, he had no more air, salt and seawater getting into his stomach. Death, he asked again, death today, with Lenny somewhere near, near him, neither alone?

Then a siren screamed in his mind, branded resignation too comfortable an end, a lie. He halted his descent, turned back up. Left her to her spirit's home.

A rush of adrenaline kicked him higher; then nothing impinged his senses until the dark changed to greys and green frothy chaos, and he broke through into noise and light and oxygen, expulsing brine, still stuck in the current.

He treaded water, twisting and searching for her blond hair, stung by new guilt. On the storm now rode his father's voice, his mother's, then Kate's soft cries calling to him, and flashes of Pat and Violet, all invoking him. And Joel Vida too, the man who'd made him see that the world was inside him if he would look. Then his father's mission face loomed larger, hand pointing, something to be done. And suddenly he understood; it was clear.

He filled his lungs. Another jack-knife sent him down through a womb of echoes and fluid darkness, into noiselessness, his father alongside, still pointing, stroke after stroke deeper into blackness. And two eyes lit up, Jesus Pomental, warm, peaceful eyes passing slowly, eleven years after that fateful Newark day. He kicked deeper, blind hands groping, muscles stinging, as the watching chorus approved, even as he grew weaker. Once again the urge came to suck the brine into his deprived lungs, settle with this strange peace.

Just then it touched him, something physical, along his arm, streaming past, like silky seaweed. His flailing hands found nothing.

But then it touched again, now through his fingers. He gripped it. Hair. A human head. Cold human head. Heavy, limp, in his hands, eyes, nose, lips, a string with a key attached.

A world inside him lit up, brought power, and mysteriously the realm was swirling now, chaotic again, light from above getting brighter, if his legs could keep moving, arms hold on, lungs not burst, brain stay alive, if the force that had pushed him this far could push him farther; then a paroxysm of agony carried him through into the storm, cold head still in his keeping.

Lenny Quin. Beautiful. Blue.

Stealing air from the gale, he breathed into her as though the gale would give her life. But no life came. He roared into her face.

Now at the end of his physical strength, sweeping to the south, he felt heavier, sinking, slowly submerging. There was no rescue, he knew, no miracles. All he could do was hold her to him, try to keep their heads above water moments longer. Then to forever, whatever that meant. He pulled her higher, tighter to him; they'd travel together, paired to this union from opposite worlds; end of loneliness, injustice, all hurt and regret, travelling together. Their heads slipped under. But the last of his heart interrupted their sinking, pushed their faces back into air, for moments. She had become too heavy in his arms, her beautiful purple and blond form; she was taking him under. He'd go with her. Share her wish, Devils Cove. Quit the world of storms.

Without air or strength now. None needed. Locked together they sank. He, into a time of old peace. And the chaos faded.

*   *   *

It jabbed into his back. Sharp. Scraping. A presence. Pulling at his hair, pulling at him, until they weren't sinking any more but moving up, and now the presence was a force beneath them, pushing up, travelling with them, forcing them back to the storm, bursting through with them.

Green eyes, mouth moving, shouting at him, in a world of no sound. Cilla. Cilla deBurca, a blur, slapping his face, slapping his face, slapping. Cilla, soundless, telling him, showing him, hand pumping across him.

'Finger Rock!' she yelled into his ear. 'Can you make it?'

He caught her words, barely, tried to shake his head, didn't know if Cilla was real, if anything was real, if this was the place beyond, or a place along the way to somewhere else.

'Tony! I'll be behind you. Go on!'

His senses sharpened, numbness giving way to pain, remnants of strength returning.

'I have her! I won't let her go,' Cilla yelled. 'You go!'

He released Lenny into Cilla's arms. And after fumbling he got his body working, began moving away.

Cilla waited for a let-up, then propping Lenny's head she started after him. But a cresting wave whipped the pair up and out toward the open ocean. When the crash came, Cilla re-surfaced rapidly, fingers knotted to the purple swimsuit, and once more she pressed her air through Lenny's blue lips. This time the effort drew a rush of seawater out of Lenny and a single loud moan. Cilla battled on until eventually catching a confluence of water and wind that drove them out of the current and deposited them within reach of Finger Rock, where Tony waited.

They got Lenny to a flat table-sized slab above the water level. There they slumped down and huddled over the coma-tose figure, shielding her from the breaking waves. Cilla's trembling fingers probed Lenny's neck for a pulse. And a second time, with increasing distress. Tony intervened, tried to make his breath revive Lenny until Cilla nudged him aside and began pressing on her chest. They worked in turns, persistent, alternating, to no avail. Tony's head and shoulders eventually dropped, his face resting on Lenny's. Cilla stared, motionless but for shivering. Then Tony started again: thirty, forty, fifty compressions, until in the end submitting to Cilla's constraining embrace, and they held each other, still shields for Lenny against the storm.

Then Cilla yelled, broke out of their embrace. 'She's breathing! She's alive! Oh my God.' They grabbed for Lenny, whose chest was now rising and falling, breathing Devil's Cove air. They rubbed her vigorously, tapped her cheeks, hugged her, talked to her, none of which opened her eyes or brought any coherent response.

Cilla untied the key from Lenny's neck. 'She can't last here,' she said above the clamour pounding their refuge. 'No one'll look here for us. Not in time. The tide's coming in. If we could get to the island, we'd get to the mainland.'

'You swim across to Intinn. You're strong enough.'

Cilla glared at him. 'Storm won't pass before dawn. Too long for any of us. Too cold.'

'You go! Save yourself. You know you can do it. Fuck it, just go; I want you to.'

She shook her head, an emphatic negation.

'Go, Cilla! Send a boat for us.'

'Boat? In this?' She pointed to the encrusted spire. 'Top of the weed is high tide. Three foot over us. Could be ten. Two hours, maybe three, it's coming.'

'Wade out. Forty feet, fifty feet, to the promontory. You know you can make it.'

'Beat the Devil? Alone? What if I die, if I'm not able?'

'You know you are!' His words brought no response. 'Fuck it, be smart. Live! I'll be with Lenny.'

'Me too. And with you.'

'That's dumb! You hear me?' She refused to look at him. 'Get to Rock Cottage, light a fire, get warm, get dry. For fuck's sake just go, will you!'

Her head shook again with the same slow certainty, her eyes sad with her thoughts. He grabbed her freezing shoulders, pulled her to him; they clung to each other, a tight, wordless embrace.

'Have Liza Murtagh get me. Old banshee woman owns Intinn. I'll be tons safer with you.'

'No, you won't. Be sensible.' He held her at arms' length. 'You're twenty-three. I want you to go. You hear me? I want you to go!' He shook her until her eyes came back to him. 'Lenny and I will be fine. Now, just go. Right? Go on.'

She wrenched out of his grip, got to her feet, seemed to try to force her thoughts into words, but nothing emerged. He took her back into his arms, felt the pounding in her, felt it flow into him, felt her sorrow, and her sadness for him.

'It's okay to go,' he said. 'You're the bravest girl I've ever known.'

Their sopping, frigid bodies shook in unison. And when her tears became sobs she turned away across their drowning slab. He followed, and from behind he urged her into the water.

'Show me,' he said. 'I'm watching. And don't look back.'

She lifted his hand from her shoulder, held it to her cheek. His lips kissed her crown of wet curls, curls he remembered admiring when he first saw her at the Abbey one long year ago. As they edged out he prevented her from turning around, then gave her a final push. From that point, she did not look back. Her head and black cotton shoulders disappeared quickly in the waves. But then a stroking arm arced up, then another, and another, in fluid motion; she was moving strongly but already being taken south, toward the whirlpool and even wilder surf. And then she was lost to him.

Cradling Lenny's head, he closed his eyes and invented Cilla's progress. Cilla deBurca, this woman of simple certainties, as he had come to see her. He watched her, in his mind, saw her con-quer the devil blow by blow, breaker after breaker; he willed her on, cheered her courage, her fire, her fight against the odds, travelled with her in every stroke, until he guided her up onto the promontory, onto Intinn and safety. In more lucid intervals he was thankful she had not once looked back, that she did not feel his faith dying, that she knew only that he believed in her to the end.

Time passed, unmeasurable time. The swells were crashing over them now from all sides, gradually submerging their ocean refuge. And with dusk not far off and thunder in the skies, the cold wind cut like a knife into his bones and flesh. Still, nothing stole him long away, no pain or regret, no delusion of rescue, for all of his moments belonged to Lenny Quin. She was pallid still but with hints of pink, looking almost content to him, as if journeying within a dream to somewhere warm, even wonderful, a haven not so far away.

For the next while, fighting against numbness, he saw her glistening face become faces from the past, faces appearing and leaving and reappearing, one after another, all merging eventually into a single entity, no separate parts, an everlasting one. Then something brought terror to her features, tore out of her a young girl's cry, and lips that pushed out wilfully to form words.

'Mama, mama, come down,' she sobbed, eyes wide open. 'I'll be the best girl, I promise. Please, Mama, come down.' Just as suddenly, it ended, leaving a dreadfulness over her.

'No, no, no, no, no, no, no,' he whispered to her, 'no, no, no, no, no.' His arms rocked her back into the peaceful place that had been hers.

Then somewhere in his head someone kept calling him back to his childhood, to Dublin, to hills and woods and canals, school friends and his dog, comics and bicycles and birds' eggs, fruit fields and football and red coal fires. All parts of the life he had come back to Ireland not to relive, but reclaim, before fate conspired otherwise.

Time after time his fingers plied the ocean from her eyes, pushed back her matted hair, traced her perfect mouth, pressed goose-bumps from her flesh.

Then her eyes opened again, intense as before, unblinking, peering up at him, this time with recognition and delight; he pulled her closer, smiling, a smile of belonging, as though he lived in the bright blue world of her eyes, in a time outside of time. Her fingers sought to still his shaking face, calm his lips; she clasped his hand to her heart, as though re-indulging ecstasies.

'Darling,' she said, in a voice weak but full of intimacy. 'Aidan, darling, you came back. I'm so thrilled. We lost our baby, darling. I couldn't tell you, couldn't find you. The hospital said you died; I couldn't surprise you. We'll have another baby now, won't we?'

'We'll have two . . . three even.'

'How much I love you.' Her eyes glowed like fires shining through eons of lightless time, as though she had reached the end of endlessness.

He pulled her close to him, hiding his sorrowfulness from her joy.

'Darling, you're real, not a ghost?'

His face stayed in the storm.

'Aidan, darling – '

'No, no, I'm real. Real for always and always.'

'If you're a ghost, I want to be a ghost.'

His head tipped back, and with a long silent cry he tried to purge all that he had saved up, hidden from, fought to overcome, and feared. Then Leo's words echoed; how they had scared him: that she wouldn't be his as long as Aidan Harper was alive. How wrong those words would prove to be; they had no meaning now. Lenny was his. Tony MacNeill's. She was always his, even before he knew her. And forever would be. He straightened out his legs across the slab, wiped blood from his thigh out of her hair.

23

Sometime later he awoke, angry that he had allowed himself sleep, if sleep it was, even for minutes, if minutes it was. The wind felt not so fierce but the clouds were blacker and lower, with booms of thunder shaking the heavens. Lenny was in his arms still, sheltered by his numbed body. But now, with no place higher to climb to, the sea was upon them, striking from below and above. Then from deep in his mind, or maybe riding on the gale, it came again, an echo, distant yet familiar, calling to him from far away, calling his name.

It was this, he realised, that had roused him. And again it sounded, faint, then fading: Tony, Tony. If not delirium, then from within his new-born soul, or a lost spirit whose last wish lived on in the tempest, or a *Titanic* child, or the hymn of an angel calling him home.

Later again, in a lull, it came louder, clearer: Tony, Tony. His head lifted, eyes to Intinn Island. And he strained into alertness. On Intinn's shore something was moving. He disentangled from Lenny, tried to stand, crashed down onto submerged stone. But he was feeling again, feeling cold, stiff, feeling brine in his thigh, and he tried again to stand.

'Tony, Tony.'

It was real, he was nearly sure. From the promontory, from Intinn. Someone. Arms waving. Cilla! Cilla deBurca. Alive. Across the strait. Invincible Cilla. He slid down the rock, braced himself upright in the water, and he tried to read what her gestures were saying. She waded into the surf, waving a yellow rope over her head, then gesturing that he should tie it around himself, she'd pull, pull him, pull them, across the whirlpool.

So that's the deal, he told himself. Wait for the devil of Devil's Cove. Or attack, beat it, as Cilla had done. If he had the physical strength, the mind, if he could keep the water out of Lenny's mouth, keep her breathing as they crossed, if Cilla was strong enough, stronger than the devil. So many ifs. But his hope belonged in Cilla of all people, who he had not known to fail in what she promised, who could do what she said. Trust her. Hand her their destinies. Hope she could pull back two lives. Cancel his own demise, whose terror he had defeated on this refuge. No waiting to die. Not the mark of a MacNeill. Die fighting!

He would.

Cilla waited for gusts to slacken, then whirled the end-weighted rope like a lasso. Throw after throw failed, until one landed near enough for him to snatch it from the water. He wedged the end in a fissure, manoeuvred Lenny forward, harnessed the rope to her upper body, then pushed out beside her. Cilla pulled. They cleared ten feet in seconds, his free hand thrashing at the surf, the other holding Lenny up. Nearer the whirlpool gyrating water spun them about, threatened to separate them, but the harness that secured Lenny also locked Tony to her, by design allowing no division of destinies.

When the water demanded, Cilla relaxed the tension, pulling only when her effort counted, pulling them closer and closer against an ocean that sought to steal them away. Near half-way a surge picked them up, swung them like the hand of a time-clock toward Intinn. Cilla beat at the straining line, desperate to abort a crushing impact; she hung from it, flung her body against it, to no avail, the taut line and its passengers raced toward the rocks.

Just before impact, Tony scrambled in front of Lenny, pushed her underwater. His body bore the hit but was saved from serious damage by the forceful backwash. The following wave carried them to the surface and to Intinn's shoreline.

Cilla untied the harness while supporting Lenny. Tony balanced alongside them, glaring out, as though calling the devil's failure.

'Tony! Get in out of the water! Let's go!' Cilla shouted. He smiled for what could not be spoken. For a moment, she reciprocated.

The trio manoeuvred up to the top of the promontory, resting there briefly with a container of fresh water Cilla had brought. They then set off for the eastern side of the island, battling driving sand along Devil's Cove beach before reaching Rock Cottage.

Within minutes they had Lenny dry and under blankets, a tinder fire burning close by in the bedroom grate. When they had dried off using found cloths and bedcovers, Tony lit a pre-set fire in the candle-lit main room and fell quickly into slumber against a fireside chair. Not long after, despite the clamour outside, Cilla joined him.

'Let me see that leg,' she said a while later, tapping at his shoulder. His expression halted her, but only for an instant. She prised away his hand, undid his rough bandaging to expose a jagged, still-bleeding wound.

'Needs about a million stitches,' she said in a disturbed tone. 'God knows how much blood you lost.' She folded pieces of shrivelled flesh back over the wound, and with torn linen she set about stemming the bleeding.

In his self-induced distraction he stared at a row of standing photos to the left of the chimney breast, some of which, when he was here last, he'd noticed Lenny turn face down. Among them now was a picture of Leo with a girl of three or four, almost certainly

Lenny. Also there, the young red-haired woman, Róisín, a photo he'd seen in Lenny's apartment. And at the end, the picture of himself and Lenny climbing to Killadoon Head, when she had set the camera's timer and run around to get in the picture.

'Agghhhh, fuucck!' he cried out.

'Sorry. You moved. Has to be tight.' She continued wrapping layers of material around the wound.

'Climber,' he said, his voice straining, '. . . climber, racer, life-guard. Now, surgeon.'

'Stop your yak and keep still.'

He squeezed her shoulder as she tied multiple knots in the bandaging.

'That's it now,' she said. 'No good if it's not tight; you could bleed to death. Needs to be sewed up proper, and we need to get someone to examine your side and that bump on your head.'

'Freezing cold in here,' he said, drawing closer to the dying embers. 'Should have lit just one fire; only a few bundles of small sticks left. I'll check on Lenny, see if our clothes are dry.'

'No. Look at you, you're as white as a ghost and you're shivering; I'll go.' A minute later Cilla was back, settling next to him before an improving fire. 'She's rambling, neither asleep nor awake. Not in pain though, thank God. Was good she threw up all that salt water she had inside her, after all those tablets she took.'

'Needs a doctor fast.'

'Dr Lappin's the one that knows all her medicines and stuff.'

'You know about that? How come you –'

'Little bits.' Her features contorted. 'Why are you looking at me like that? Person's word's a person's word.'

They exchanged stares, neither choosing to add to the point.

'Anyhow, we've no boat; I robbed the line off it to make the rope long enough to reach you. All I could think of. Means we're stuck, for now.'

He reclined, reliving what they had come through.

'Why did you do it?' he asked after minutes of silence.

'Do what?' she said with a rebuff.

'No way I was getting to shore with Lenny. We were doomed.'

'You don't know that, you're not God. Don't be saying stuff like that. You're not that bad a swimmer. I've seen worse.'

Again, for another while they remained silent, as though their words were immaterial and what mattered was their thoughts.

'Lenny was next to dead – was dead, I thought. I couldn't hold her up. So why did you risk your life? Why did you jump into the water – twice?'

Disquiet entered her demeanour; she delayed responding. 'Who knows why anyone does things. If it's right, you do it.'

'You do know. You know the sea. You knew you'd probably die. So, why? I'm asking you. What makes someone do a thing like that?'

Her eyes remained large and still. 'You'd do it for me,' she said. 'You said so. When you were diving in to get Lenny. Why'd you do it?'

He joined her in staring into the blazing fire.

'Saw you going down. Looking for her. Gone a horrible long time. Thought you weren't coming back up.'

'All I know is, if it wasn't for you I wouldn't have. Nor would Lenny. We were gone.'

Wind and debris continued beating at the cottage; occasionally shafts of air roared down the chimney, firing sparks into their rest.

It was a while later when Tony broke the séance-like mood. He limped to the scullery and returned with an armful of old newspapers, which he wrung tight and placed on the fading embers. At that moment a burst of noise startled him. Cilla charged into the room, directly toward him, panic over her.

'Something's outside! I saw it, I swear, I saw it!'

'Shhh shhh! What? What? What are you saying?'

'It's big. In the bushes. Swear to God, it's out there. Moving.'

She pulled the bedspread tighter around her. 'I don't imagine things. I'm not – '

'It's an island. Uninhabited, you said so. Has to be an animal.'

'It's not.' She shook her head, cowered behind him, eyes glued to the unclad window. 'No big animals here.'

'Just a bat or a bird; there's bats and birds.'

'Not in storms, never. This is big. I saw it – '

'Saw what? What are you saying?'

Her eyes jumped between door and window. 'Liza Murtagh,' she whispered. 'The banshee woman and her children. Holy God!'

'That's dumb, you know that? I thought you weren't afraid of things.'

She edged closer to him. 'Some things.'

'It's a story,' he said, 'Liza Murtagh. Lenny made it up to keep people off the island.' He limped boldly to the window, glimpsed into the darkness, then returned to the fireside. 'Nothing. Trees, rain, leaves blowing around. Okay?'

'Sure?'

'Positive. There's nothing.'

Cilla freed her breath. 'Wasn't really that afraid. I better go back in, see if she's alright.' As she left, she searched back to his unsympathetic observation of her.

He re-wrapped his makeshift covering and went back to tending to the fire.

'Jesus! Nooo!' The scream shrieked through the cottage. A moment later, Cilla's hysterical form appeared. He was already on his feet. This time he retreated, holding her, toward the back wall.

'It's there, definitely, a dark hood over its head, coming for us, at the bushes. I saw it, Tony; I swear, I saw it.'

'It's trees, and leaves, I told you. You're silly.'

'She's come for us; she's here for us.' Cilla dug her fingers into his arm.

Then it started, at the front door. Thumping, rattling. They slid together along the back wall, toward the scullery. Suddenly, a shape appeared, at the window, a hooded figure, head pressing to the glass, catchlights for eyes; it was looking in at them. They stared back, motionless.

'Open up!' A cry mixed with wind and rain. 'Let me in, let me in.' Then a succession of hard raps shook the glass. 'Open the door!'

'It's Leo!' Cilla rushed forward, then stopped.

'Open up!'

'Sounds like Leo,' she said, searching Tony's face.

He didn't answer.

The steel bolt squealed in her hand, the door swung in. She recoiled. Within its dark hood an old face took shape, eyes flaring.

'Christ Almighty, Leo,' she sighed. 'You put – '

'Lenny. She here?'

'Yes, yes, she's okay, she's here.' She pushed the door shut. 'She's okay, but we need to get her to a hospital, and Tony too. Tony pulled her out of the water, Devil's Cove.'

'Thanks be to Jesus and his Blessed Mother.' Leo made the sign of the cross then dropped his olive-green oilskin to the floor. 'Paddy said you could be here. Where is she?'

'This way,' Cilla said.

'Leo's nod beckoned across the dimly lit room, to Tony. He then followed Cilla into the cramped bedroom where Lenny lay tightly wrapped, breathing normally, her features glowing.

'Princess,' he said, touching her brow, staring into her responselessness.

'It's all thanks to Tony,' Cilla said. 'She took a pile of tablets; I think that's why she's so sleepy.' As she left the room she placed a hand on his shoulder.

Leo's silent fixation went on for minutes, then he leaned forward and kissed her forehead. Her eyes half opened.

'Dad,' she said.

'You're doing grand, Princess. Just grand.'

'Dad . . .'

'Right here, Princess. Right beside you.'

She drifted off again.

'Right beside you. The luckiest man in the world.'

He returned to the main room and the last of the fire. To Tony he extended his hand. 'You're a good man. To the end of my days I'm in your debt.'

'How'd you get over, the water the way it is?' Cilla asked.

'Rowed hard. A nightmare. A lot more than a mile. Paddy tried to talk me out of it.'

'How are we going to get to the mainland?' Cilla addressed both men. 'Get to a doctor?'

'The swells are like hay stacks,' Leo said. 'And worse to come. The island could be cut off for days.'

'With four of us the boat should be more stable.' Tony said. 'Shouldn't it?'

'Seas like that, even the trawlermen won't go out.' Leo paused. 'Boat's too small. Dangerous no matter how you look at it.'

'Two rowing, one holding Lenny?' Tony said.

'We have to!' Cilla said. 'If the island is cut off, with all those drugs in her we just don't know. Probably needs her stomach pumped. And that leg of yours, the way it is,' she said to Tony, 'if it bleeds again, or, or – '

As though suspended in private worlds, all three turned silent, gradually displaying a knowing of what fate dictated they must do. And soon their stares colluded and wordlessly signed the covenant.

'I'll row,' Leo said.

'Me too,' Cilla said.

Tony glared at her. 'I can row.'

'You're not okay. Blood could burst out of that leg.'

Cilla wrapped Lenny in extra linen, zipped her into Leo's big olive-green oilskin and snapped the chin-strap. Minutes later the foursome set out through moonless dark and flurries of rain to the edge of Intinn and the ink-black ocean.

Leo heaved both oars, hauled them away into noise and commotion. Beyond the shield of land, big ocean surf attacked the low-lying boat, dropped it into trough after trough and buckled it off course. Leo jiggled the oars, won back stability, and each time righted the prow to point for their sole marker on the mainland, the lighted steeple of St Brigid's Church.

Low in the bare hull, being flung about like on a carnival ride, Tony cushioned Lenny's body from the boat's hard wood. On the forward plank Cilla scooped the bailer machine-like, firing back the flooding brine with a fury of her own.

On it went, until halfway across Leo stopped moving, his gasping almost as loud as the gale. With the oars tearing at their locks, the boat skewed, caught in a squall of wind and current. Cilla dropped the strung bailer, yanked hard at Leo's slumped form, screeched his name. He stared back with agony. She grabbed one oar, shouted at him to switch places. He moved forward, still welded to the second oar; she prised it free and began fighting to re-set the boat. Braced by the gunwale, Leo began scooping at the ever-rising water.

Each time, Cilla held high the heavy oars as the boat was flung up, re-sank them when it cracked back down, and went on heaving against the force of the elements. As the effort wore on, she moved with expiring strength. With about one-third of a mile to go she began losing the battle with the oars. She recaptured control, managed another half-dozen strokes, and broke again. In a cauldron of noise and almost total darkness the boat whirled wildly. All onboard braced against the constant beating. And now, with a foot of water in the hull, they were off course and sitting perilously low.

Tony pulled at Leo. Leo dropped into the hull, took Lenny, who had been muttering intermittently and opening and closing her eyes. He then scrambled to the forward plank, to Cilla. She acknowledged him only when forced to by his grip.

'Boat's too heavy!' he yelled. 'Have to move fast!' He halted her attempt to re-command the oars. With no further protest she manoeuvred to the aft plank.

Stroking shallow and deep, he set his mind against his objecting body, tamed the wild bucketing of the boat and pointed it back toward the steeple. Before long they were moving again toward the mainland, still more than a half-mile away.

But they were going down.

As obsessedly as Cilla threw back the ocean, the ocean returned in greater mass, wave after wave dumping peril into the boat from all sides. Tony fought on, grimacing through each long stroke of the oars.

Leo struggled up out of the flooded hull, motioned to Cilla to take Lenny. 'I can swim it,' he shouted at Tony.

Tony snarled.

'Fourteen stone lighter. You'll have a chance.'

Tony's head shook. How could he agree to such a thing, his conscience asked. How could he not? He reviewed his crew: Leo, poised in front of him, willing to sacrifice himself; Cilla compulsive, still fighting, probably in shock, unaware of Leo's bargain; neither had surrendered, nor panicked, their wills unbroken still. But it was clear what all three knew: that their battle was lost, that in minutes their small boat would sink and the Atlantic would steal four more souls. How could he say no to Leo's bargain if it offered the other three a chance? Or yes?

Leo turned aside, tipped Tony's hand.

'The rope!' Tony yelled. 'Tie it to you, stay behind us.' Leo twisted the rope around his fist.

Cilla screamed.

But Leo's plunge was over. He was gone, consumed by the ocean. Her tirade cast curses at the powers that demanded such a sacrifice.

Tony thrust his oars deeper, exhaling half-formed words with each stroke. Now, sitting higher in the swells, the boat caught a number of shore-bound breakers, and continued closing the distance to safety.

Then, with just a couple of hundred yards to go, the oars ripped from his grasp, knocking Cilla on her back. She quickly righted herself and grabbed Lenny, who seemed still oblivious of the mayhem. Tony's hands boxed the air for the jumping oars, until he forced them back under his control. But now his self-talk was louder, more fragmented, and his shoulders and arms burned. He'd get them in, he swore in each breath; he owed it to each of them.

Closing in on the mainland his rhythm broke, hand working against hand, matter against mind; his racked body was mixing up strokes, rejecting his orders. He berated himself. Where was Anto MacNeill, he demanded, where was his iron will, the power that got him through the streets, through nine years in the pen? Inside! a voice answered, the same voice that always answered. Inside! Where Joel Vida said it was. Where everything is.

His shoulders won back a slow-firing rhythm, oars cutting deep again; pull after pull he was still driving the boat shoreward, at a cost he feared could not continue. Where would he find the strength? In faith, the voice said, in faith, and only to the extent that he believed. Just then a mountain of water crashed onto them, sank the boat precariously low. His self-talk struck back: one more, one more, one more; and he pulled and pulled, an extra breath always there when all felt used up. Then a mantra took over: forward, drop, pull, back; forward, drop, pull, back. And the voice and rhythm and pain endured into delirium. Until out of the dark a hand shot into the boat, then another, bodyless hands reaching up out of the sea, grabbing the boat, serpents' hands, he thought, now four hands, voices in the tempest, dark figures in the water, and from beneath came a roar, stones, the stony shore, Paddy McCann, Liam Foley, trying to swing them in, oars scraping shingle, arms pumping still, until Cilla stilled him. They were in, in, directly below the steeple of St Brigid's.

Balancing in the flooded boat, Cilla pulled at the rope, rapidly at first, then slower, until the end arrived. 'Leeeo! Leeeo! Leeeo!' she called into the maelstrom through cupped hands.

Liam Foley fought his way to her.

'I'm alright,' she said. 'Someone better look after Lenny. I'll help Tony.'

But Tony's body refused to move, his eyes tightly closed. Cilla and Liam set about easing him out of the boat.

'Leo Reffo. Lord be good to him,' Paddy said. His large frame leaned into the flooded boat; he lifted Lenny over the side and made for the boat-slip, talking continually: 'The Volvo's just beside us, *mo chuisle*; nice and warm and comfy, it's all going to work out grand, completely grand, mark my words, you'll see.'

'Already in heaven, good man like Leo,' the priest said, helping Tony along. 'Looking down on all of us right now. God'll reward you both for all you did this day. We'll get you warm and dry in no time, get a few hot toddies into you. You're home now, son; it's all over.'

Just then the taxi's headlights beamed down the boat-slip, followed by the silhouette of Paddy hurrying back. He and Liam carried Tony to the car and sat him in next to a fidgety but still semi-conscious Lenny.

'Where's Cilla?' Paddy asked with alarm. Liam's gaze shot to the water. Both men charged toward her. Out beyond the boat, defying the treachery, Cilla combed the darkness, still calling to Leo.

Liam reached her first. 'Time to go, child, get us all inside out of this pagan weather.' She stood firm as the surf knocked them about. Liam held on to her, his free hand moving in consecration, sending blessings to Leo, somewhere in the dark Atlantic waters.

'You're a credit to the village, to the whole country,' Paddy said, securing his arm around her from the opposite side. 'You've done enough now, more than any human could be asked to do.'

'More than Christ would ask of you,' Liam said as they shepherded her past the boat and toward the boat-slip.

Then above the roar of wind and sea came a call, a cry not of the elements. The trio turned in unison. Out of the black ocean a form splashed toward them. Then an old watery baritone boomed.

'Here I am! I'm here!'

It entered the spill of the car lights.

'Lord Almighty!' Paddy said.

'Holy Jesus!' Cilla cried.

'Suffering God!' said Liam.

Leo's stout frame grew bigger, clearer, face glowing. Paddy and Liam made signs of the cross. Cilla just stared. Then all three made for him.

'Took the da,' Leo said, breathing hard. 'And two of the brothers. The bitch. She wasn't getting another Reffo.'

'Mother of God, I don't believe it,' Liam said. 'Jesus of Nazareth, Lazarus of Bethany, now Leo of Aranroe.'

'Saw the lights, saw the lights and kept going,' Leo said. 'Blessings on the work.'

'Y'can't kill a good man. Can't kill a good man . . .' Paddy's words ran wild, as did his tears.

The men circled their arms around Leo's sopping bulk. Then Cilla joined in and all four clutched for a moment, knee-deep in the raging surf.

*　　*　　*

From Horslips Hotel above the loch, Cilla called Dr Lappin, arranged for him to meet them at Lenny's apartment, then drove on ahead of the others.

With Paddy and Liam up front and Lenny between Leo and Tony in the back, the taxi careered out onto the road. Throughout the short journey Paddy chattered and hummed, mostly to himself. And from the front seat, Liam's lustrous face distributed joy to all. At the crest of the hill the taxi turned onto Claire Abbey's meandering drive and crunched to a stop. Cilla's Escort was waiting for them, as was the doctor.

A short while later Dr Lappin emerged from Lenny's bedroom, informed the five storm-beaten figures that she was doing fine; he'd be staying with her another hour, for observation. It would be best, he stressed, if the ordeal was not mentioned to her; there was a distinct likelihood that her brain had not recorded the trauma. Leo and Cilla offered to relieve the doctor. But no, he responded, he had brought the woman into the world thirty-five years earlier, as a consequence of which he saw it as his responsibility to administer to her well-being. Notwithstanding this, he said, he would relinquish responsibility temporarily to Fr Foley while he tended to the others.

In another bedroom he inserted thirteen stitches in Tony's thigh, praised Cilla's bandaging for stemming the bleeding, and advised staying off the leg as much as possible for at least two or three days. He then rubbed ointment into Tony's raw, swollen hands and dressed a half dozen less serious lacerations to his back and shoulders. The ribs, he said, appeared intact, probably just bruised, but should be x-rayed at Castlebar Hospital. On looking into Leo's eyes and listening to his chest, the doctor pronounced him in need of a good night's rest but not a whit the worse off for all the wear and tear he'd been through.

By this time Cilla had returned in a grey tracksuit retrieved from her staff locker in the hotel, bringing with her Tony's backpack of dry clothing from the car. She declined to be examined, citing only sore hands and icy fingers and toes, no more than she was used to as a hiker, she declared.

'There'll be a grand fire tonight up beyond,' Leo said. 'Whether I'm really still here or only think I am, that's where I'm off to, to sit in front of a bit of heat and raise a glass in thanks.'

'You'll need getting out of them wet clothes first,' Cilla said. 'Paddy and Fr Foley too.'

'I'll drink a toast first,' Leo said. 'To us all. One glass.'

'A hot Tullamore Dew; that'll do the trick.' Paddy rubbed his palms together. 'A drink, Liam, drowned as we are, or need I ask?'

'A toast to life should never be turned down. Let's wet our lips, lads and lassie, and let the fire do the drying.'

They ambled out into the castle grounds, all linked together, rounding big sycamores dropping globules of rain, blithely crunching gravel, and arrived at the Abbey's rear entrance. There, pulling five wooden chairs together, they sat around a log fire that drew musty steam from their clothing. In this almost empty lounge, all but Tony recounted the terrors and triumphs of the day.

Then Paddy got to his feet and saluted the group. *'Sláinte to gach ceann acu, mo cháirde, ar oiche seo faoin shonas.* Here's to good friends,' he said, his glass high. Then he grimaced, as though interrupted by an unseen intrusion, but pressed on. 'Tell y'all a true story. Thirty years ago, couple of days before Christmas 1964, the bitterest cold day, Leo and Liam and meself, the three of us, we got out of the car outside Concannon's Bar. But we didn't go in for a pint, as was our custom. We didn't. We walked down to where the five of us stood not an hour ago – '

'The day we buried Róisín,' Liam said. 'Lord rest her.'

'The very day.' Paddy's voice weakened. 'And the very spot.'

'Aye. A toast, *mo chairde,*' Liam said, punctuating the lull that had fallen. Leo rose to join him, followed by Cilla, and finally Tony. 'To wee Róisín Doyle. And to her da, my old pal, Tommy.'

All responded in chorus and clinked their glasses.

'Will y'ever forget the time we were trying to kidnap Dan Dinny Roe's champion bull?' Liam said, pausing in a smile that foretold devilment. 'The ring slipped out of the bugger's big snotty nose and there we were, weeing in our trousers, Leo and Paddy and meself, inches from the horns that would soon turn us into three dead matadors. I knew then that if that big bastard didn't get me, life would turn out grand. And here we all are, all hale and hearty.'

Amid the merriment, Paddy alone held a melancholic bearing.

'Dan Dinny Roe?' Cilla said. 'That must be a hundred years ago.'

'Nineteen forty-nine, forty-five years exactly?' Liam slapped Paddy's knee. 'A right pair of urchins we were, Leo and meself; isn't that right, Paddy? Paddy here was a wee *garsún* at the time; we were supposed to be teaching him how to hit the *sliotar*. Long before you young people were even – '

Liam broke off on Paddy's doleful sigh.

Paddy lifted his face to the group. 'No harder day. Day we buried Róisín.'

'Come on now, Paddy, that's a long time ago.' Leo's hand squeezed Paddy's shoulder. 'You've no call to trouble yourself. Wasn't one of us could have changed what happened. Not you or nobody.'

'Cruel world . . . when you think about it,' Paddy said. 'How them things come back at you when you nearly lose someone else.'

'Paddy, Paddy,' Cilla said spiritedly. 'What about the time those Yanks wanted to know about your college degrees? Remember that?'

'How could I not. I was showing a bunch of politician fellas from America around, when one of them says to me: "And tell me, Pat, what did you major in?" The Salvation Army, says I. Well, they fell out of their chairs laughing at me. A natural born comedian they said I was. So I asked them did they not know about Major Barbara, and they all just looked at me and laughed even more. Right, says I to meself, pack of eejits, I'll get me own back on you. It's a play, I told them, Major Barbara, by our own George Bernard Shaw, a true account of history if ever one was written, about a lovely local Aranroe lassie with a flair for battle, Barbara Murphy, a relation of me own from just over the mountain, and honoured in history books ever since as Major Barbara. But the real reason she's famous, no lie, is because she was Napoleon's mother, an Irishwoman, something people outside Ireland are never told about. And that's not all; she was the brains behind all fifteen of her emperor son's military victories, and he loved her very much, as any good son would. And that's not even the best of it, not at all, I told these Yankee hot-shot fellas: Major Barbara Murphy Bonaparte is buried under your feet, under the very floor you're standing on, an ancient burial chamber for Celtic chieftains. So, tread carefully, I told them, she's known to come back on occasion, and that's all I have to say about that. Well, I ended up with more free pints of porter than was good for me, lined up from one end of the village to the other. And there's not a word of a lie in that.'

'You doing alright, Leo? Liam whispered under the chorus of cheer.

'Never better. What I did today might've helped save a few lives, mine included. Not many days a man can say that.'

'And Paddy,' Liam asked, turning the other way, 'everything alright now?'

'Dripping wet but well blessed,' Paddy said. 'Lot to be said for old pals sitting down before a good fire.'

'And more to be said for standing up to the rattling sea as we did, the sea of life, no less.' Liam slipped into melodrama, capturing the attention of all. 'On a devilish freezing night, in the year of our Lord nineteen hundred and ninety-four, in the wickedest storm of the decade, and a bitter north-westerly snapping and bashing and thrashing, enough to blow the balls off Dan Dinny Roe's big fecking champ of a lump of a bull, and here we all are, the five of us, despite all that, still here, all alive. What about that! We should never be off our knees thanking God.'

'Are you a man of the Cloth or what?' Paddy said above the merriment. 'Drinking like a bishop and cursing like a common curate.'

'Talking of storms, Liam,' Leo said, 'how's the good bishop these days?'

'As smug as St Paul before his hiccup on the way to Damascus.'

'Never learn to open their eyes,' Paddy said. 'Nothing new in that.'

'Wait! That's it! My sermon for Sunday.' Liam's dramatics again held the group. 'How easily we reject others, even poor old Bishop Buckley, because of what we see as their limitations, when we should be seeking out the virtue in every soul we meet.' He paused, turned more serious. 'It's a hard station. But that's Christianity, isn't it. What the Sermon on the Mount is all about: compassion, do good to your fellow man. Well, what do you think? Too much Mother Teresa? Or bloody brilliant?'

No one answered.

'A man could waste his life in thoughts like that,' Paddy said. 'Or he could go by what his granny taught him and turn out a better man. It'll take more than fancy sermons to bring Paddy McCann back.'

'Does that imply, Patrick,' Liam asked warmly but without a trace of humour, 'that there is something that would return you to the fold?'

Paddy's face worked over the question. No one spoke.

'Thirty years,' Liam said. 'Too long to stay angry. You know that.'

A quiet stayed over the group.

'To Cilla deBurca,' Leo said, rising to his feet, 'for all we owe her.'

'Aye, aye,' Liam and Paddy called out.

Tony struggled up, indulging Cilla's gaze, then thrust his glass into the centre.

'And let's never forget,' Leo said. 'To Tony MacNeill. No better man or braver man walked the roads of this county.'

When the toasting ended, Cilla's private smile turned to Tony. 'What's the matter?' she whispered. 'You're quiet.'

'Tired, I guess.' He grimaced unconvincingly.

'Time for me to be getting home to a warm bed,' Leo said. He turned to Cilla: 'You're alright staying with Lenny?'

'I'm grand, I told you, no bother at all.'

'To bed it is, and a story to be told,' Paddy said, reanimated, and now a little unsteady. 'Can't wait to tell Eilish how Jaws nearly got me, ready to have me for his supper he was, but Patrick McCann, once uncrowned champion of all Connacht, boxed the arse off him, and that's how I'm still alive, Eilish, *mo chuisle mo chroí*, so thanks be to God for all that exercise you made me do.' His face asked for a verdict.

'Sure aren't we all witnesses to every last word of it,' Liam said.

'Enough, I'm off.' Leo's hand asked for Paddy's. 'We'll talk tomorrow,' he said. He then reached to each of them. 'We all have tomorrows. Let's remember that. And get together again soon, the lot of us.'

'Taxi's waiting, Liam; y'all set there?' Paddy said.

The priest held up his glass, and in the other hand an untouched pint of stout.

'Can you credit that,' Paddy said. 'The Cloth counts for nought any more. All that bad language out of you, then you guzzling back the demon drink.'

Liam made a show of knocking back what was left in the nearly empty glass. His hands then moved in blessing over the new pint of black-and-cream porter, before he slid it in front of Cilla.

Then Paddy, Leo and Liam, their clothes steaming, headed for the exit, tangled in banter.

Cilla and Tony pulled closer to the fire, remained quiet for a while and restrained in their expressions.

'How are you feeling now?' she asked.

He shrugged, kept his eyes on the fire.

'Exhausted, I'm sure y'are, after . . . after everything.'

He sank back in the chair, expressionless.

'Tony, I want – '

'I don't want to be thanked,' he said. 'You don't know me. No one does. Not what's inside me.'

A minute later she turned back to him with unconcealed

warmth. 'I do know one thing. I know if you didn't do what you did, none of the four of us would be alive. I mustn't thank you for that? It's only me who knows what you did, no one else at all. In the water, at Finger Rock, in the boat. I saw you. Your face. The pain in it. I was crying for you inside me. When we got to shore, that was better than getting into heaven.'

'I did it for Lenny.' He pushed up off the chair, stood in front of the fire.

Cilla's face held its strength, her eyes staying on him. For a while they remained detached.

'Want to walk over with me, see how Lenny's doing?' she asked. 'Let that poor Dr Lappin go home to his bed. Is your leg up to it?'

'I need to see Lenny alone. Follow after me in a few minutes, if you want.' He limped off, leaving her alone at the hearth.

At the apartment the doctor was ready to leave. There was nothing to be overly concerned about, he told Tony. Lenny was sleeping soundly and should feel better after the rest. However, someone should ring him in the morning before bringing her to his surgery for tests.

Minutes later, in search of a bathroom, Tony pushed in the door of an adjoining parlour, Persian-rugged and rich, it was a room he hadn't reached in his break-in. From the head of a long table he surveyed the setting: antiques, plush sofas, cabinets of crystal, abstract sculptures, paintings. He ejected himself abruptly from his reverie.

At Lenny's bedroom door he listened, looked in, then tiptoed in. Gone were all the photographs that had filled the room previously. Just the picture from their day at Killadoon remained, atop the wicker stand. Here was his Lenny, he thought: asleep, peaceful, beautiful, her face and hair goldened by a bedside lamp, a healthy blush in her cheeks, eyelashes dark and long, her slim form seductive even now. The woman he loved. Who, he knew, he'd go through it all again for: Lenny, alive, well, with a future.

What more could he ask? He leaned closer until his face felt the warmth of her breath, and he placed the lightest kiss on her temple. The rare highs and many lows of his life paraded before him, and all the lessons he had learned, particularly in the past year. Out of this reality, he stared into her with all his feelings, with all their hopes and dreams of togetherness, then he closed his eyes and withdrew.

From the wicker stand he lifted her straw satchel and stole out of the room. In her wallet he found ninety-five pounds. He took seventy. As he replaced the satchel he kept from looking at her, or at their Killadoon photo.

Outside, in spitting rain, the wind rattled the trees all around the grounds. Cilla stepped out of the shelter of her car. 'Everything alright?'

'Sleeping. Doctor left, said she'll be fine. He'll run tests in the morning; you need to call him early.'

She moved into the glow of the hall light. 'Where are you going now?'

He stared at her.

'Something wrong? What is it? What?' By degrees her features tightened. 'You're leaving! You're not leaving! Tony!'

His eyes fled to a starless sky.

'Bloody idiot! Eejit! Open your mind. Everybody here loves you. Can you not see that?' Her voice then changed. 'Lenny loves you. I've known that from day one. You can't just go and leave us.'

'Things I have to do.'

'That's stupid. What do you have to do? Just stay, that's all. This place needs you, you changed things here. Before you know it, it'll feel like home. You'll never want for friends, or work, not after today. Please, Tony.'

The silence between them endured moments longer. Then his head shook. 'Things I have to do,' he said, slipping his backpack onto his shoulder. 'Told you you don't know me.'

'Don't you try that on me. Your face is a dead giveaway. You're afraid, Tony MacNeill. What are you afraid of? What? Why won't you trust me? I trusted you, didn't I? Didn't I?'

He walked away.

'Wait! Tony!'

He pulled up but didn't turn.

'Let's talk. I want to talk. That's all I want from you. Stay to-night, please.'

His head shook again.

'Tell me we haven't been friends. Go on, say it. I bet you can't. I've been your friend, haven't I? Tony?'

He drew the night air into his lungs. 'Just let me go, Cilla.'

'No, I won't. I'm not like that; I thought you knew. Stay down at my place. You know where the key is; you're the only one who knows.'

He strode away from her.

She ran forward, caught his arm. Their eyes engaged intensely. 'What's turned you like this; what are you angry at? I want to help. Let me help. You trust me, don't you?'

'You risked your life,' he said. 'Remember? At twenty-three. Something felt worth it. You're okay now. I'm not. Not till I do what I need to do. Nothing will stop me. No one.' He shrugged out of her reach, limped away.

She watched until the dark consumed him. Then she watched the dark. Later, inside the apartment, she found a folded note with her name on it.

Cilla:
Doctor said call him in morning.
If I don't see you, I had to leave tonight. I hope to come back in two or three days.
Please be sure to tell Lenny. Anto.

24

He had thought long and healed well, quiet and alone at a small farmhouse B&B on Achill Island. Now, after almost three days of wilful recuperation, he was ready. His well-strapped thigh felt safe. His bones and muscles had lost nearly all their soreness, though not yet his blistered hands, but even this could no longer curb his compulsion, or his urgency.

Under an overcast sky he moved through streets of intent Dubliners, faces that he imagined had been chiselled by the city, made raw by its roughness. But it would always be his, this city. Down the breezy quays he paced, green army jacket flapping. After O'Connell Bridge he cut through an alley, came out by the Abbey Theatre, and entered the tiny and time-worn Flowing Tide bar.

In its sole toilet cubicle, amid the hiss of cisterns and the stench of porter, his pocket knife sliced six feet off a new roll of stretch bandage. He split the strip down its length and began wrapping his hands. Right first, then left, his ritual as a teenage fighter at the Railways Boxing Club, less than a half mile from these scrawled walls. Today, trainerless, his teeth tightened the knots on both wrists. He broke into a fighting stance, chin tucked in, jabbing straight, throwing hooks, uppercutting. And once again he waited to be called, hanging for the cue to start his journey to the ring, through the racket of a raucous audience fanatical for their man. And soon it came: Anthony MacNeill. Head up, arms loose, shoulders rotating, in the rising din he started out, hardened by the hoots of abuse, the boos and cheers, faces of scorn and awe and envy. Now climbing up, padded canvas underfoot, in through the ropes, into an over-bright ring, and the bell sounded, and out from his corner he pushed, out through the glass-and-brass door of the Flowing Tide bar, into Dublin city.

Along the river his locomotion eased. He tested the suppleness in his legs, shook out his arms and shoulders, leaned into upper-body arcs, while at the same time battling conscience, and questioning this new mission driving him this hard.

Minutes later he stood glaring across traffic, into Gardiner Lane, the mostly demolished street with just two nineteenth-century tenements still standing, one his target. But the newish navy car stuck out, its interior stuffed with still figures. Police. Watching for someone. He moved off, up the hill of North Great George's Street, then a turn at the top and back down to the rubble and ruin of Gardiner Lane. No sign of cops now, no sign of Skinner and his pack.

He slipped inside the echoey house, across a dim hall with a big boarded-up staircase he hadn't noticed last time, and down the passageway to his right. A note was pinned to Aidan Harper's door: *Back later. For urgent care go any time to rehab clinic in Hayde Lane, behind Pro-Cathedral. Cyril.*

He'd wait, he decided, the dust of decay in his nostrils. He began stretching tendons and muscles, pushing forward and back against a wall, squeezing creaks into the foul air. Sore still, all over, he thought, but in good shape, feeling strong again.

The scrape at the front door stilled him. Footsteps. More than one person in the main hall, voices, the scuff of feet coming nearer. Two figures passed across the top of the passageway, unaware of him. He crept forward. A boy and a girl. No more than fifteen or sixteen. The boy roughly dressed, long wavy hair. The girl bulkier, in a windbreaker and short skirt. The boy pulled knowingly at the board blocking the staircase. Next to him, stiff and jittery, arms stitched to her middle, the girl urged him on. The board swung free. The couple ducked inside and pushed it back into place. Tony listened as their feet scraped the stairs.

Seconds later he followed, kept to the side as he ascended. On the half-landing he stopped. Above him, out of view, the couple were muttering plaintively, rapping against a door that wasn't being answered. He climbed higher, surveyed the rot. To his left and right ran a long bare-board hallway strewn with wreckage, wind and street noise blowing in through shattered windows at both ends. One room was opposite him, another ten feet to the right, both doors open on crumbled interiors. Another step took him to the landing, into view of the murky corridor from which the racket was coming. In a burst of commotion, the boy and girl scrambled up off the floor, speechless.

'What you want?' Tony said.

'Shit, man! For a minute I thought you was the cops.' The handsome, slightly-built boy exhaled dramatically. 'Skinner or Fogo around? Wanna get some stuff.'

'Get what?'

'Horse, you know; two bags this time,' the boy said with an affectation of casualness.

Tony moved closer, switched his gaze to the girl, then back to the boy.

'Kinda in a hurry. Get fixed up. Y'know.' The girl spoke assertively. She unzipped her jacket, searched down her top, pulled out folded notes. 'Ready to go.'

Tony continued staring at them.

The teenagers' faces grew troubled. The boy opened out his hands. 'We're clear, we are, I swear, we don't owe nothing now. Fogo'll tell you; we cleared it; we're clear.'

'You paid Fogo?'

Neither teen answered. Eventually the boy's features refocused. 'No, like, not cash, like. But like, I swear, we don't owe a penny now.'

'Said you paid Fogo.'

'We did! He told you we're clear. And we are.' The girl's voice boomed in the cavernous interior. Then a convulsion shook her body. Her arms pressed into her stomach, her shoulders bent as though fighting a gale.

'Paid when? How much?'

The boy looked to the girl as a new torment twisted her face. He took her into his arms.

'How much?'

'Me and Siobhan, like . . . like we, we – '

'Fuck it, Larry, tell him!' The girl wriggled free. 'I let Skinner poke me. Okay? Now will you take the money and give us the stuff. Need to get fixed up real fucking bad.'

'Get out, both of you. Get home. Now!'

'Hey, mister; mister, look, y'don't understand.' The girl shuffled forward, forlornness in her face. Despite Tony's initial resistance she took his strapped right hand in both of hers. 'We need real bad, get fixed up, y'know, really bad, y'know. Okay?'

He started to move toward the boy. She moved with him. He stopped, allowed her soft sweaty hands to keep their hold.

'Okay, mister? Please . . . Okay? Okay?' Her body jerked again like it had been pierced. It seemed to pass within seconds but left her violet-painted lips twitching. She squeezed his hand, tried to snuggle in to him. He restrained her.

'You will, mister, won't you? You'll help us. Alright?' Her voice took on a quality of sweetness. 'I know you will. You will, won't you? Please? Won't you?'

He tried to detach; she refused to release his hand. The suffering in her face caused him once again to relent. Suddenly she pulled his hand between her legs. He broke away.

'We can do it. I won't tell no one. Swear I won't. Larry won't either, I swear. Just get us fixed up, mister; please, please, won't you?' Tony gripped her roughly, overpowered her protest, forced back both her sleeves. A mass of bruising and purple tracks scarred her pale flesh.

'We can do it here, me and you; I can do it real good, do everything, I can,' she said. 'I want to, I like you. You can keep the ten quid too. Here, take it, keep it, go on.'

He pushed her aside, made for the boy. The boy squirmed.

'Don't you touch him. Fucker!' The girl screamed, sobbing fitfully. 'I'm warning you, don't put your hands near him.'

Tony seized the boy's left arm, then his right. One bore a few feint blotches, the other nothing.

'Only done it a few times, ages ago,' he said. 'Tried to get Siobhan off of it. She won't get off. Said she wants to but she can't.'

Tony looked back at the girl; her face re-signalled her availability. As he turned toward her, his thoughts travelled through her. She was Margo, in Newark, coming on to him in Witchell Heights, trying to get off, turned on, fixed up, trading her body for a high, willing to lie, cheat, go down, do it all, just to feel able to dance with Stewie on Saturdays in the square. Margo, dying to live, living to dance, dancing to escape, until a street knife ripped it all away, an act that somehow had led him here, Tony MacNeill, to this lousy tenement in Dublin, to another Margo, another Stewie, someone else's best friends.

He shook out of his distraction, forced the boy against the wall. 'You love her?' he shouted. 'Do you love her?'

The boy cringed, then nodded.

'Look at me! You love her, yes or no? Yes or no?!'

The boy's face broke before any words emerged. 'I do, I love her. I tell her. Plenty times.'

Tony let him go, turned to the girl. 'You love him; I can tell. You willing to fight for him?'

Her mascara-streaked face affirmed, then more vigorously. As she stared at him a look started to form in her, as though she were sensing something in her questioner.

He gripped them by their jackets, drew them in until the young worn-down faces were breathing into his.

'Know what it's like to die? Have any fucking idea? No one to love you or hold you. People like you – and me – die every day, and they don't need to.'

The boy's eyes fell away; the girl's stayed riveted to him.

'You told her you love her,' he said to the boy. 'But you're going to put her in a hole in the ground. Too bad for her, right? The fuck it's right! You listening? You love her, you save her; you got that? You do everything you have to do. Everything! She worth keeping alive, is she?'

'I told her, I did, to get off it, always tell her. Hundreds of times, I did.'

'Tell her she's murdering you. Because she is. Tell her you want to stay alive. You want her to stay alive. She needs to hear you say that! Follow me?'

The boy's tears spilled through his fingers. The girl held him.

'You,' Tony said to the girl. 'A girl I knew once, like you, loved my best friend the way you say you love this guy. What do you want from him? Want him to die for you? Tell him that! Tell him you don't care; you only care about yourself, your fix. Tell him he doesn't matter, go on.'

'I won't let him die. I don't want to die.' She wiped her cuff across her cheeks then threw both arms around the boy, kissing sloppily at his mouth. 'Nothing bad's going to happen to us, Larry. I won't let it, I won't.'

'Hey, save it!' Tony pulled them to him. 'Know the place in Hayde Lane, the clinic, at the back of here?' Both nodded. 'I want you to go there, right now. Understand? They'll help you, no cops, no questions, no money; they'll get you clean. Deal? Right now? Go on!'

In a fusion of sniffling and hugging, the teenagers started toward the stairs. Tony's hands seized them, ordered them silent. From downstairs came the squeal of a door, and now male voices inside the house.

'Any other way out?' he asked.

There wasn't, they said, the back stairs were gone, and it would definitely be Fogo and Skinner, no one else was allowed to come up.

The pull-out board sounded.

Tony crept forward, crouched low, peeked down through the missing banister rails. Two men, one in a parka, and one tartan-shirted heavyweight. Skinner and Fogo. Coming up. He ushered the teens toward one of the derelict rooms. The boy responded. The girl froze, then fought against moving. He back-pedalled with the boy into cover, urging the girl to hide. Moments before the men turned on the half-landing she scurried out of sight. Skinner and Fogo reached the top. They stopped, waited. From behind the door, ten feet away, Tony watched, the shaking boy crouching below him.

Shirt sleeves high on his biceps, Fogo's big shaven head turned left and right, eyes combing like a hunter's.

In a burst of noise the girl bustled out onto the landing, obviously flustered but with an air of matter-of-factness. 'Hi'ya, waiting here for you,' she said.

'You!' Fogo said. 'Y'doing up here? Come to rip me off, yeah?' He made for her. She backed away.

'No way. Only waiting for you, that's all. Just to buy stuff.'

He sneered. His fingers locked onto her throat. She groaned, tugged at his grip from both sides; then he let go and seized her by her hair.

'Big bone's what she needs.' Skinner cooed, air-jerking at his groin. 'Fuck that skinny prick she hangs around with.'

The girl fought at the fingers embedded in her stringy brown mane. 'I'm telling you, we were just waiting – '

'We?!' Fogo roared, pulling her closer. 'We, junkie? We who?'

'Nobody. I mean me, I was, me. I was, I want to – '

He bumped his forehead into hers. 'Fucking warned you never come up them steps.'

'Strung the fuck out,' Skinner said. 'Gobble, gobble, cold fucking turkey.'

'Hey, Skin, what about this.' Fogo groped for the end of the girl's short skirt. She pulled back, held it down. He groped again, forced his hand further and held her, letting out a string of guffaws. 'Y'had your go, Skin,' he said. 'What's under here's mine now.' His tongue licked across the girl's face. 'You're gonna blow me off till I tell you to stop. All fucking day if I tell you to. Right?! Better be fucking right; let's go.'

The girl refused to move, defiance filling her face. Fogo dropped down in front of her, clamped his tattooed arms around her thighs, lifted her straight up so that her head and shoulders wavered above him. He carried her to the fractured banister, leaned her out over the void. 'Y'ready? Wanna go? Wanna get splattered? Wanna? Wanna?'

Her blood-filled face craned back, small fists locked to the collar of his tartan shirt. He moved closer to the edge, leaned her farther out.

'Think I wouldn't? What? Fucking would. Ready to get splattered? One, two, y'ready?'

Tony tried to stop his body shaking, his judgment on a blade edge. He wanted to pounce. But he knew that could cause her to go over. He fought hard to control what came instinctively, a gut screaming to attack. What he was watching was giving him license to strike, and he would, with no holding back.

Just then the girl cried out, a cry of fear but also of anguish that seemed older than the danger she was in. Then her flushed face said yes, she would do what Fogo wanted. He turned away from the stairwell, nuzzling at her breasts and howling as he carried her down the passageway. Inside the room, still high in his arms, the girl writhed and pushed, tried to force her front back from him. He dropped her onto a cushionless sofa. She curled up, letting out a long, high-pitched wail.

Outside, jacket discarded, Tony swept quietly from his lair, his bandaged hands blackened with soot from a fire grate, a ritual of his he'd never understood. He ushered the trembling boy to the stairs, commanded his descent. The boy hesitated, then obeyed.

Tony stretched his lean muscled arms high above his head, winged his shoulders side to side, pushed his physique into resistance. He could walk away if it weren't for the girl, he told himself. But maybe not. This was his world after all, the arena of scum and brutality, in which he had triumphed, and knew he could now. Because he was smarter, faster, because he had hardened in the pit. Because he could read opponents, could see the twitch before the strike. Because he risked more and had less to lose than all the others, even now. Had he ever left this life, the rush of it? Would it ever leave him? He didn't even know these kids, he thought. But he did know them. Knew them well. No time now. The girl was inside. He was on. Up. Dressed for war. Once more.

*   *   *

He put his ear to the door, loud music, no voices, pushed it open just enough to see in. A huge, broken-down room. Twenty-five feet or more in the distance Fogo and Skinner, their backs to him, stood over a table. He slipped inside. The girl was closer, hunched on the sofa. He signalled her to stay quiet. She jumped up, rushed toward him. The men wheeled around, stared, then sniggered to each other, and they began slowly advancing.

'The clinic,' Tony said. 'Larry's there. Go!'

'The cops, I'll get the cops, will I, I'll get – '

'No! No cops.'

'Run! Run!' She tugged at him. 'Mister, c'mon, will you. C'mon!'

"Go now,' he said, his face alight, as though resigned in a holy mission.

'Mister, will you c'mon!' She pulled at him. 'Run!'

His hand shunted her backwards, pushed her out of the room. He kicked the door shut. Drove home the dead bolt. The men halted.

Balance low and square, feet anchored, Tony MacNeill held still, almost placid. The soot-blackened hands floated up as if in sacred rite, into combat pose. Inside him, his old battle cry resounded, something he'd learned in history: woe to the defeated. No reins now. No cuffs. No prisoners.

Fogo's small eyes glared, his face a sneer, showing not a hint of fear.

'Crackhead fucking bollox,' Skinner called out, a shiver in his voice. 'The bollox is back, what Fogo?' From the hearth he grabbed a long iron poker.

Tony's right hand swept around to his back, lodged lightly in his belt.

'What he got, Fogo? What?' Skinner asked. 'Got a Glock, what?'

'Whoooeeeee! Fucking lucky day.' Fogo hissed a jet of air through his teeth. 'Stone deeeeaaahhdddd, Red. Whoooeeeee!' He held out an upturned hand, accepted Skinner's poker. 'Don't need it. Do the fucker.'

Skinner's stare rose up to his partner but received no acknowledgement. 'Fucking right. You get the fucker that side; I'll get this side.' He shuffled to his right, took a half-step forward, then glanced again at his partner. Fogo hadn't moved, just stood sneering. Skinner retreated.

'Broke into your flat,' Fogo said. 'Y'can kill burglars. Burst the fucker!'

'He got a gun, Fogo, a Glock what? Why's he looking at us like that, and them karate gloves? Fucking escaped maniac. Should be fucking locked up, what?'

'Do it!' Fogo commanded.

Skinner recoiled, white-faced, his hairless head dripping sweat. He slid another half-glance at Fogo. Then his shoulders jinked; he jutted out his chin, bared his teeth. And with a street roar he sprang into attack.

Tony's first strike, a long, poking left to the mouth, was meant only to set up his second. It did. In a cloud of soot a right cross thudded into Skinner's face. Sank him with a crash. Seconds passed before the whining began. Skinner came to, floundered about the floor, struggled up, face bloody, and tumbled out of the room.

Fogo's features contorted; he stared.

Tony waited, ready, his gaze fixed to his foe. In this time-slowed standoff he weighed what might happen. The teens were gone, safe at least from the devastation to come. He was giving away maybe sixty pounds, four stones in the way he once counted weight. That wouldn't matter, he told himself. The burn in him counted for more; on the street it had always been his edge. The spring was coiled now, irretrievably, set to unleash. Just like Newark all those years ago. And again now, here, because he wanted it. Because that's who he was, who he had to be one last time: Anto MacNeill, immigrant, Irish, not to be fucked with. After this he'd complete his mission, the new one, the one he'd come back to the city for, Aidan Harper. Cyril, as he now called himself. What he had to do there, he could do, he felt certain, extreme as it was. First, he'd bury this big scumbag psychopath. Like Yablonski, like Rip Wundt, like all the others. He'd fight without pity, be as good as he'd ever been: alert, fast, powerful, merciless. Unbeatable. For the boy and junkie girl. For Margo and Stewie. For Lenny Quin and what he had to do next. That's why he'd get through this, be okay.

Then both faces took on colder convictions, like gladiators at the gate readying for inescapable war.

He'd been watching for a flicker, a tinge, a twist. And now it came. Fogo's eyebrows narrowed. Then like a man possessed, he attacked, upturning the big wooden table between them. Tony backed away, out of reach of the first sledgehammer blow; he stayed low, moving, gauging his range, figuring the next strike.

This one he saw even earlier, a wide roundhouse punch ripping through the air. He ducked easily under it, spun left, and an instant before Fogo's bulk rebalanced, Tony's boot smacked like a hammer into his opponent's kneecap. Fogo's mouth broke open, he let out a chilling yell as his massive shoulders bent forward. But he stayed on his feet.

'Tear your fucking heart out!' he said, setting for another attack.

But this time, Tony exploded toward him, kicked for the groin. Missed. A fraction short. Fogo's fist thudded into him, knocked him across the upturned table, breaking off two of its legs. He found his feet quickly, but another blow pounded into his forehead. He was down again, head spinning, almost out. He compelled his eyes to stay open, his head to stay clear. Now Fogo's hobnail boot was coming for his face. He spun away. The boot caught his shoulder, though by then had lost most of its power. But he was still on the ground, Fogo grunting and swearing, stumbling forward. He scurried to the side, on his back, kicking up, watching, anticipating, too dazed to stand, become an easy target. Another stomp missed his groin but drove hard into his damaged thigh, sent him into near-delirium.

Fogo, red-faced and sweating, steadied his limping mass as he closed in from the opposite side. He stopped, yanked upward on his shirt, drawing it over his head. Tony shot across the floor feet first. Like a pliers, his legs trapped Fogo's ankles, toppled him backwards into the hearth, body and bones cracking against marble and a scuttle full of black coal.

Tony jiggled his neck and head, tried to rise. Get up, his mind ordered; get off the ground! Blood on the floor caused him to lose his footing, but he was back on his feet, holding on. His hand went to his thigh, bleeding heavily, down past his calf. And now he was down again, face against grimy floorboards, dropped by something he didn't see or feel. He'd been here before, he reminded himself, down but still functioning, strong, senses okay. He back-pedalled along the ground as a ranting Fogo came for him. His dodging and forearm swipes fended off the stabbing boots. As the attack slackened, he lashed out with his good leg, striking his almost breathless foe repeatedly.

He could feel the strength in his body again, better coordination, though the ringing in his ears had muffled his hearing. He knew he'd been fighting on instinct, for how long he couldn't tell, but no question now he was fighting for his life. He needed to believe, needed to keep trusting his gut, get to his feet, see if his leg would bear his weight.

Just then the long, black poker appeared in his vision, above him, in Fogo's hands. His body jerked into a roll an instant before the poker smashed into the floor, inches from his head. Then once again it came, as a lance toward his throat. His wrapped hands deflected the weapon and grabbed it. Fogo yanked hard. Tony let go, sent the sweat-drenched man tumbling back.

On his feet now, he went quickly after his would-be killer. Fogo thudded to a stop against a peeling wall. At that point, Tony was already in the air, powered by one good leg, a flying kick with his weight behind it. His boot cracked against the same knee as earlier. Fogo's roar reverberated through the tenement as spit spilled from his lips. In that moment he presented an undefended target. Tony's left fist drove with all that was in his shoulders and hips. It pounded into Fogo's jaw, mangled his face into distortion and demonic rage.

'Fucking pig; dead fucking pig,' he lisped. 'I'll smash your fucking skull in.'

Tony backtracked, conserving strength for the move he hoped would end it. Fogo, faltering badly now, fired blow after futile blow at a harder-to-hit target. Then an opening came. Tony flashed forward, hands blazing, one, two, three, four straight jabs to the head. Fogo squirmed but barrelled forward again through the wreckage, bracing against whatever support was closest. Tony veered into clearer space. And stopped. He dropped to his knees. Ready for what he knew would come. And it came. He locked both hands onto Fogo's face-bound boot, wrung the foot viciously against the ankle joint, made the man squeal, then snapped it again and pushed him backwards. Fogo's massive body slammed to the floor, smashing the remains of the table.

Tony's hand reached again to his bleeding thigh. His jeans were now a bloody mess, blood squelching in his boot. But Fogo was up, somehow, almost on top of him again, swinging blows. Tony evaded each of them, bobbing one side then the other, staying behind long left strikes that snapped Fogo's head back when they landed. Then he attacked, feinted a left, threw a powerful right cross that missed and crashed him into Fogo, sending them both toward the back wall where they came to a stop, still on their feet. Tony's head shot forward like a demolition ball, cracked into skull bone, sucked a howl out of Fogo. As if in reflex, Fogo's head rebounded into Tony's. Both men sank to the floor, unconscious.

Sometime later the pain in his ribcage tortured him awake. He glimpsed a figure and a weapon set to strike, tried to shimmy out of its path but found it impossible to move. The shiny black bat cracked the linoleum beside him. Meant to kill, he knew. And knew it would have. But his body was not obeying. Then up again rose the bat in Fogo's hands. Tony managed a twist, all his pain threshold would allow. The bat followed him, swung down, glanced his left shoulder. Carried aside by his own leverage, Fogo straightened up, headed back toward his prey. Tony was back on his feet, stumbling over the remnants of the table. He tried to find the willpower, tried to move farther away. His legs would do no more. He dropped. Fogo towered over him, raised the bat as though for a beheading, lowered it down between his shoulder blades, and re-set his stance. The bat launched, swept up over his head.

With all the upper-body strength he could call on, Tony's shoulders and arms had taken off like a single welded cog, through a long horizontal arc that gained velocity by degree, and he let out a rising groan that stopped on impact. The heavy wooden table leg clunked against Fogo's shins, sent him into a choking inhalation. He toppled back, two golf-ball-size kneecaps protruding from his upper legs, the metal bat quivering in his hands.

Tony hauled himself up. 'You lose, fucker,' he said. 'Because y'don't know what dead is.'

Fogo's agony allowed no response.

Tony straightened his body, glared down at the three scimitars on the man's biceps.

In the wrecked room, he prepared. 'Don't know what dead is, fucker,' he said, straining for breath. And in his bloody, bandaged hands the weighty table leg hung over the paralysed man. Fogo's eyes widened, pleaded.

Tony steadied into strike position.

'Anto! No!' The shout came from the door. Aidan Harper moved into the room. 'Anto!'

Tony's face and body remained unchanged.

'Your business is with me. Not him. He's sick, Anto. A street louse. You're a good man.' Aidan's hands reached out. 'Don't sacrifice yourself. Do not do this. He's not worth it! He's finished, for ever.'

The shaking in Tony's body worsened.

'Anto, listen, please, do not do this. The courts will deal with him. I swear to you they will. He'll hurt no one ever again.' Aidan moved closer, paying no heed to the wailing coming from the floor, until he and Tony stood facing each other. 'You and I can settle our differences. I'm on your side, Anto. I am. Much more than you realise.'

The table leg fell to the ground.

'Your two young friends, they came to see me,' Aidan said.

Trance-like, Tony's eyes remained on the three scimitars.

'Anto,' Aidan offered his hand, got no response. 'Listen, I've re-thought things. I'll be leaving tomorrow. Leaving Ireland, for good. Nonsense really, my being here. I see that now. Arrangements all made.' He offered his hand once more, and again let it drop away unanswered. 'It's okay, Anto. Really it is. You and I, we both know this world, what it can do to innocents, we're not so different.'

Tony's head lifted. His bloodshot eyes set on Aidan, a menacing glare, then his hands shot out, grabbed Aidan.

'Anto, no! Anto! Anto!'

25

'Aranroe Hill,' the driver called out. The nearly empty bus pulled onto the gravel shoulder. Tony buttoned his army jacket up to his chin, pulled his ski hat down to eyebrow level, then dragged his backpack toward the exit.

The driver rose out of his seat. 'I'll get that for you, son; you fire ahead.'

Tony alighted into an air of freshness and sudden memories. His green country of fierce seas and songbirds, as he thought of it throughout his long incarceration, the loss of which he'd so often listened to his father lament; land of sky and islands, of lochs and bogs and cliffs, and comfort. Now, here he was, back again, hours before dusk, a mission still in his hands.

The driver's gaze flirted with the bruising in Tony's face. 'Always know a climber. One look's all it takes,' he said, appearing pleased with his own perceived perceptiveness. 'Travel here from all corners of the world, young and old, climbers like yourself.'

Tony gave token acknowledgement.

'All set to beat this mountain of ours, you are?' The driver pointed inland. 'That's her, the biggie. Can conquer it this late in the season, can you?'

'Can try . . . Never know.'

'Has a mind of her own, we say around here. Most years she steals a soul or two. Climber goes up, doesn't come down. Have to watch yourself.'

Both men gazed out to the pastures and the heavens, and in the distance Mweelrea, lording over of the land, side-lit and sharp in the evening light, green-golds lower down, blue-greys nearer the cerulean sky.

'Treacherous, I'd imagine, climbing to the top of that.' The driver's bright moon face came back to Tony. 'One slip and that's it; you're gone for your tea.'

Tony hoisted up his pack, eased it onto his shoulder.

'Not for me, not in this life anyway,' the driver said. 'If I get re-incarnated, you never know.'

Now, once more, Mweelrea held all of Tony's considerations.

'Right so,' the driver said, rubbing his hands together. 'Know how to get to where it is you're going?' He waited for a response. Then the spell seemed to break; Tony's eyes returned to him, along with a nod.

'Right so. Time I brought these poor weary people home.' He started up into his bus. 'Next stop Killadoon,' he announced then turned back. 'Watch yourself up there, son. God bless.' The big white bus headed up the hill.

* * *

At number 9 Connemara Court the door opened before he reached it.

'Tony! Why? I thought – '

'You called Lenny?'

'Come in. Look at you! What happened to you?'

'You made the – '

'I did! Yes! The minute you rang me. I told her you banged your leg climbing but you're alright, like you said. But, Tony, what – '

'How is she? What did she say?'

'She's happy. Really happy.' A sad pleasantness afflicted Cilla. 'Don't be worrying, will you not; she'll be at the station. Probably there now. Problem is you won't be on the train. I don't get it; you said – '

'I will. Catch it up at Killadoon. Lots of time.'

'No, you won't. It won't stop at Killadoon. Westport, then Aranroe.'

He shook his head.

'Westport, ten past nine, skips Killadoon, Aranroe twenty-five past. I'm telling you.'

Alarm shot into Tony's bruised face.

'Quarter past eight now,' Cilla said.

He remained solemn, ruminating.

'If it's that important to you I'll drive you up to Westport. Catch it there; there's time.'

'The late train stops at Killadoon. I've taken it.'

'Listen, will you! After summer nothing stays the same. Not around here. Everything changes.'

'Fuck it!' He leaned over the kitchen counter. 'Fuck it! Fuck it!'

'Tony – '

'Life and death, and I fuck up – again.'

'How?' Cilla demanded. 'Why do y'have to come in on a train? Walk down to her at the station! Ten minutes. Tell her you took the bus. For God's sake.'

'Can't do that. You don't understand. Have to get on that train.'

'Why? What's the big mystery? Not a bit of difference to her how you arrive.'

He did not respond.

'Look, I told you, I'll drive you up to Westport. Okay? Let's go.'

His tired eyes stared past her, then refocused on her, then drifted away again. Neither spoke. Until Cilla's face turned tragic.

'You're hurt!' she cried out, as though noticing a gravity that had eluded her.

'You're positive about the train?'

'You're hurt. Tony! For God's – '

He began unbuttoning his jacket.

'Nooo! Nooo!' she cried. 'This is madness.'

The black cotton of his shirt glistened purple; blotches smeared his neck.

'Why, Tony? Why this? The second I saw you I had a feeling something terrible happened. This is mad; it's stupid. Christ almighty.'

He let his jacket fall to the floor, his eyes avoiding her anguish. Then he eased off his ski hat, revealing a crimson-stained bandana.

'What've you done?!' She caught his arm, tried to get him to look at her. He shrugged aside. 'You've got yourself into trouble, haven't you? What happened? Tell me.'

'Can I clean up or not?'

'Look at your leg! All down you jeans. You're bleeding. You could die.'

'Old blood. It's stopped.' He stared at her, his face frail yet still with determination. 'Fix it for me. Like before.'

'I'm not a doctor. I told you. I can't; I can't do that. You need to get to a hospital. This minute.'

He stood wordless before her, face stoic.

'Who did this to you? Who? You got into a fight. Is somebody else hurt?'

'I need you.' His voice carried all his trust of her. 'You're my friend, you said. Do this for me.'

With a disturbed intensity she gazed into his eyes, then touched lightly his bruised cheek. For moments, all that moved or sounded was their heaving chests. 'You're going to kill yourself,' she said. 'You know that? Y'hear me?'

He pulled out of her reach. But her sadness stayed in his face, and it halted him. 'What do you want from me, Cilla?' he said, grabbing his jacket. 'I have to go. Can I count on you or not?'

'Wait! Sit down,' she said. She hurried away and returned quickly with folded towels. 'I'm a woman, Tony MacNeill. That's all I am, whatever else you think. I only hope they don't put you in, put you – '

'In prison?' He shook his head. 'Not a chance.'

'Keep you in, in hospital, I mean . . . when you go.'

Without further comment he limped off to the herbal-scented bathroom, where on a brass hook the blue terry-cloth robe still hung. As he watched the blood swirl away, a memory flooded back, the night he and Cilla got drenched in the summer rain; and then here, how they had gazed out at the stars, and her nearly-forgotten, as she had put it, goodnight kiss.

Three bangs on the door jolted him. 'The da's robe's on the door; put it on till I bandage your leg, then you can get dressed. And throw away them jeans.'

Armed with ointment and a cut-up pillow case, she set about sterilizing and wrapping his deeply ruptured thigh, offering no conversation as she worked.

'Your father stays over?' he asked after a while.

'When he's too drunk to walk home to my mam. The lads in Concannon's ring me.' She cut long strips of medical tape from a spool, winding them around the first layer of bandaging. 'Next morning he always thinks he walked up the hill to me. I don't tell him.' She pressed the final strips into place. 'That's the best I can do; it was still bleeding and it's got far worse. I should bring you to Castlebar Hospital, not Westport train station, get it stitched up again.'

Minutes later, smelling of antiseptic, and in fresh denims and a tan leather jacket, he posed in front of the hall mirror, shaping his still-damp hair.

'Thanks,' he said without looking at her. 'Feel better. It'll be okay.'

With an air of forbearance, she handed him a comb, then attempted unsuccessfully to dab cream on his forehead. 'It's only concealer,' she said, 'to hide the black and blue, make you look like you're civilised.'

He fussed with his collar and with the fit of the leather jacket on his shoulders, then he turned to her.

'You look nice,' she said without enthusiasm. 'The big day.'

His hands re-shaped a floppy tweed cap. He put it on, pulled it down, then took it off and tried it on again.

'Hurry, will you. Look at the time.' She rattled her car keys. 'I'm busy. I have a life too, things to do; I don't have all night to spend.'

He turned to her once more. This time she said nothing. He returned to contemplating her quicksilver image in the corner of the glass.

'Cap's fine!' she said. 'You going or not?'

He continued peering into the mirror. 'Got it in Dublin. In a market. Donegal wool.'

'Adam Clayton's got one. That real handsome U2 fella. Looks better on him.'

'Seven quid they wanted,' he said to her reflection. 'Got it for two. Goes with the tan jacket.'

'Dark red hair's nicer with no hat.' She made her words sound entirely without compliment. 'And tweed doesn't go with leather. Not in Ireland it doesn't.'

He considered her again, directly this time, with an honesty that had been absent previously. 'Hides my forehead, that's all. Only reason I bought it.'

'What are y'doing? I need you to tell me. It's nearly a quarter to nine. Takes a half hour to get there, driving fast. You've missed it now, that's it!' She sighed loudly, thrust both hands into her pockets, turned aside. But his brooding stare continued, and recaptured her. She indulged it, then broke it off.

He lifted his pack. 'I'm ready,' he said, almost inaudibly, and pulled open the door. 'The big day.'

'Tony – ' She stopped half-way to him, her green eyes serious and engaging. 'Look. Look, I know the minute could be better. And I know, I know you know what you're doing. But, you're sure, are you, about things?'

A brief silence followed, through which her stare held firm.

Yes, he nodded. Yes, his lowered gaze said, he was sure.

The light in her retreated like a string of pearls sinking into a dark pool. 'It was just, you know, just thought I'd ask. So that's good, good.' She bustled past him, raincoat in hand. 'Pull the door after you.'

Over hillocks and farm roads the Escort raced. She rammed the gear stick up and down, left and right, navigating one blind bend after another. Past Killadoon, through Louisburg, past Croagh Patrick, past Liscanvey, then outside Murrisk, with four miles to go, her blaring horn scattered a bunch of black-faced sheep that dared to steal her road. By then, what time they had in hand, little as it was, had been lost. The car raced faster and faster along the narrow winding ways. Then entering Westport she veered onto a traffic-free side road that at the end brought them back onto Altamont Street, to a screeching halt outside the station. At that moment the shrill of a whistle sliced the air. It was 9:12pm.

Cilla leapt from the car, sprinted up the ramp and onto the platform. The black-and-orange train was moving out.

'Matt! Stop it! Stop it!' she yelled through cupped hands.

The young uniformed porter returned a cheerful wave from thirty yards.

'Stop it! Stop it!' She stabbed at the train.

His hands shot into the air, waving wildly. The train continued. She stuck her fingers into her mouth and blared out a long whistle, then a second, and a third. The train squealed and clacked until it stopped with just the tail of the last carriage adjacent to the platform.

Tony limped toward her, grimacing.

'Sure you're feeling alright, your leg?' she called out.

'My backpack, it's heavy, it's at the car.'

'Leave it. I'll get it. C'mon.' Cilla urged him forward. And as he passed her she blushed triumphant and tragic.

Then he stopped. Turned to her. His extended hand was instantly enfolded by both of hers.

'Thank you; I mean that,' he said. 'More than you could know.' She started into a lean toward him. He pulled back, then moved away over the grey flagstones and vanished through the last door of the end carriage.

The porter's flag rose. A hard blast echoed across the lonely countryside.

'You'd do the same for me,' she said as the train departed. 'You said so.'

26

From the west, beyond the station, the late-setting sun painted orange light over heather and hill and sky. At the call of the train a foursome of blue-black crows came cawing from the trees to perch under the canopy. Then out of the dark hole it emerged, headlight burning, and slowly rumbled to a stop. It was 9:25pm.

In blue jeans and an oversize Aran sweater, she stood alone, alert, by the gate.

The first carriage door cried open. Then another. And another. A small group of passengers streamed toward her. In ones and twos they passed, until the last had gone and the station fell quiet again. But, resplendent still, and with her crimped blond hair tossing gently, she recomposed her svelte frame and stood erect.

And waited.

Then, hands intertwined in front of her, she eased forward, glaring along the length of the train. Nothing moved, nor sounded. She retreated to where she'd been waiting by the exit. And moments passed. And then more.

'Princess,' the voice called out.

She jumped.

'Princess, we'll go home now.' Leo's warm face loved her from the doorway. His hands beckoned her to his care.

She shook her head.

'I'll be in the car so, whenever you're right.' He retreated, out through the stationhouse, and sat into the yellow taxi beside the doleful figure of Paddy McCann.

And suddenly the night made a noise. From behind her. The clack of a carriage door. It lured her eyes through a slow arc and brought the day-end sun into her face. The last door of the end carriage stuck out. Nothing else moved. Then slowly down he climbed, and he began moving toward her, limping, silhouetted against the western sky.

She twitched, fumbled, her face on fire.

Then he was closer, ten paces closer, floppy cap distinct, and tan leather jacket, moving brisker now.

Spellbound, she watched, staring into the light, her hands as though self-restraining, eyes full.

'Tony!' His name rode out on her breath. And again on new oxygen: 'Oh Tony, you're safe.'

Rimmed in light, he shuffled toward her with growing urgency. Now just one carriage length away. Now thirty feet. Now twenty. Still she did not move. And then he stopped. Stood motionless. Almost reachable. Fixated on her sunlit form. His hand reached up to his floppy tweed cap.

A silver ponytail sprang out.

Her scream, piercing and out of control, filled all the dark and empty places, an incantation that scattered the band of blue-black crows. And when it lessened, when it transformed into sound-lessness, her face reflected the heaven that hides inside impossible dreams.

As he started again toward her, her body pitched forward, shaking, then pulled back as though not to submit to what could not be true.

But Aidan's arms burst wide as the sky behind him, wide as his teary smile, and his embrace reclaimed her, lifted her up into the trainy air, and he kept her to him, his sobbing buried in hers, and they clung as one.

Eventually they disengaged, just enough for their lips to touch in brief stabs. And when their breaths came back they just held, faces touching, belonging to each other again.

So joined, like the halves of an Intinn Island oyster shell, they swayed in the light of the late-summer night, on Ireland's western shore.

27

From the shadows, Leo and Paddy watched, openly tearful. And at the far side of the station Cilla deBurca turned away from the railings through which she too had been watching.

And she froze.

Before her stood Tony MacNeill, pale and still, in a baggy green jacket. Her features contorted; she gestured toward the train.

'Aidan,' Tony said. 'I got out the other side, crossed the tracks – '

'Aidan?! Aidan Harper?! Can't be.'

'Some come back from the grave.'

'It can't be. You mean . . . It can't be. You're saying – '

'I am. A long story.'

All that had been, and all the unknowns, and all that now might be, seemed to reflect in each of them. They moved off together, unhurried, along the lane.

'I would not have believed it, not for a second' Cilla said. 'That you'd do that, what you did. I just, I just can't – '

They stopped, stood within each other's reach.

Tony's eyes climbed a fading Mweelrea, to its top. 'No way I could be sure he'd get on that train. Half expected he wouldn't.'

'If he hadn't,' Cilla said, not looking at him, 'been on the train, when you got on, then, then you'd have . . .' Her voice trailed away, like she was watching a different story in her head; then her eyes came back to him. 'Done what?'

He shrugged, tried to blank his mind to what in fact he had done, an act too present to comprehend, if ever he would.

They strolled on without speaking.

'Must be jaded,' she said. 'And that leg needs a doctor.'

He held up a sports bag. 'Aidan's. Have to get it to him. Told him keep the jacket and the cap. Leather and tweed, not cool together, I heard.'

She chuckled at the echo of her own words of an hour earlier, but she seemed still lost in her thoughts. 'The car's just here,' she said.

'Big, big day!' he said, looking to the sky.

'Sorry about what I said, at my place, the things I was thinking, I mean.' She paused, then smiled. 'Didn't mean any bad things about you. Very important you know that.'

He nodded.

'Tony . . .' Her inflection of his name suggested feelings about to find words. She looked at him directly, and confidently. 'I was wondering, if there was any – '

'There y'are, Tony!' Leo's jubilant voice exploded. 'Thought it was yourself, from across the way.'

'I'll wait in the car,' Cilla said, acknowledging Leo as she left.

Leo's face beamed. His hand gripped Tony's and held on as all his attempts to speak failed. With a final squeeze he retreated into Paddy's waiting friendship.

Cilla reclined against her Escort, thumbs hooked in the waistband of her jeans. Tony rested beside her. They remained silent. But all around them the chorus of twilight had begun, the frogs and owls, the ocean, the wind in the trees, a melody of air and land and sea.

Her gaze returned to his marred face. 'Where now?' she asked.

'Home.'

'Home?' she said with surprise.

'Dublin. Tomorrow. See about a job in media. Big maybe.'

'I mean . . . I meant right now. You hungry? You feeling okay?' He gave a strained smile.

'You know, you look totally worn out. You must be in pain.'

'Bit zapped. Sore. Be okay.'

'I know a couch that's free. And it's comfortable. And guess what: my telescope, I have it set up. It's not often a night this clear.'

'Eyes in the sky, you called them. I remember. All those stars.'

'I have your dad's ring put away safe. We still on to climb, you and me, when you're healed up? Or are you still afraid a girl might show you up?'

By now the light in his eyes had died.

She waited. 'Yes? No? Don't know?' She tugged at him. 'You okay?'

'Don't have to now. Climb. Odd, but that's how . . .'

Like turf smoke in a gale, his words dissolved. He laboured away from her, around the car, to the passenger door. She dropped into the driver's seat, smiling. He stalled again, seemed to jar. He reached for his backpack on the rear seat, but stumbled hard against the car.

'Heyyy!' She rushed around to him. 'What is it? Tony! Tony! Talk to me. What is it?' She tried to get him to release his grip on the door frame and sit down. At first he was unresponsive. Then his eyes flickered, struggled open; he winced, braced back against the car, then toppled to the side until her hands caught him and held him.

'C'mon, we're going to the hospital. Sit in, sit in the car. Tony, sit in.'

'No. No. I'm okay.' He pulled away from her, vigorously rebuffed her protests, seemed to recover, and he lumbered out onto Aranroe Hill. There he gazed up at the mountain. And in an avalanche of fuchsia his body slid down to the pavement.

And in falling he floated up, felt himself floating over old William's train station, up over Aranroe Hill, over Claire Abbey's warm glow, and further up until before him stood the mountain; then up over the whole western shore he soared, higher and higher into a new starlit sky, into the afterglow, and the elements turned and turned, mixing everything into one, him fusing with meadow and hill, him and fern and foxglove, man and soul merging into rock into wild rose into loch and noble clay into primordial sacredness, all one, worryless, blissful, home, hugged once more in original arms.

Fists down.

28

'Cilla.'

No one answered in the painless room. He absorbed the silence. Echoless silence. Felt the brightness. Took in the strangeness all about him, the strange feeling inside him.

'Anyone here? . . . Cilla?'

He tried to remember. There was no memory.

'Cilla? . . . Anyone?'

'Here, I'm right here.'

'Where? Where's here?'

'Right here, beside you; you're grand.' Her words arrived before she appeared with joy in her face. 'You're doing grand.'

'Where? Where's here?'

'Where's here? You're with me, that's where; that's all that matters. I brought you to Castlebar Hospital. Where I was brought into the world. And all that red stuff, that's holy wine they were putting into you to make a new man out of you.'

He gave her a woozy smile, or thought he did. 'You stayed? How long?'

'For ever.' She drifted to the foot of the bed, then floated off soundlessly.

'Cilla, Cilla,' he called faintly after her.

'And they sewed you up, sewed up that leg of yours, and, and –
' Her hands fought with the window blind until little by little it
started travelling higher. 'And they mended your ribs and your
forehead and your back and a million other things that were
broken on you.'

'So bright. Why is it so bright?'

'Sunrise,' her voice said.

'You stayed through the night?'

'I thought you learned, time's different here.' Her voice was
soft and sounded like it was coming from afar. 'Y'have to make all
the minutes long.'

Suddenly, her porcelain face reappeared, smiling, kissing him,
ebony ringlets swaying, green eyes shining.

Without breaking from worshipping her, he ordered her stay.

'Time enough for that,' she said. 'You'll be getting out of here
soon. But you'll not be able to be on your own for a good long
while. The head fella told me not to let you. Said you'll need a
guardian angel and he picked me. Because you have to get better
some place proper. Where I live is best, he said. Anywhere else
wouldn't be right, make you worse – '

His smile seemed to stop her; he summoned her closer.

She stayed away. Until her tears burst and she leaned over and
held him.

He felt the touch of her lips, instant by instant, felt a kiss salty
and light and tingling, deep and oceany and new, a kiss of heart
and soul, earthy and soft and warm, felt it grow lighter, turn
spiritual, a kiss elemental and endless.

Very sleepy now, he thought, and thought he whispered the
words as his grip on her tightened; then he hugged her even
closer, or felt he did, drew her into his spirit, into all he had once
been, all he had salvaged, into all he had set free. And he felt her
fuse into him, every atom and essence of her, and he saw her spill
moon and stars all across the heavens.

'Sleep now.'
'See you in a little while.'
'Little while.'

- THE END -

TRANSLATIONS FROM GAEILGE
(THE IRISH LANGUAGE)

These words and phrases from the story are mostly greetings, pleasantries, and endearments, along with a few common terms. It isn't necessary to know any of them to follow the story.

A bhuachaill: My boy (addressing).
A ghrá mo croí: Love of my heart.
A mhuirnín: My sweetheart.
A stór: My love.
Amadán: Idiot.
Banshee: Old spirit woman who haunts.
Boreen: A small road.
Bucko: A troublemaking boy or man.
Caointe: Lament, wailing.
Caoine: Gentle, gentleness.
Céili: Irish music and dance session.
Ciúnas, cuairtheoir: Quiet, here's a visitor.
Craic: Fun, merrymaking.
Culchie: A country person.
Currach: Large sea canoe made from skins on a timber frame.
Dia dhuit: God be with you (a greeting or blessing).
Dia is Mhuire duit: God and Blessed Mary be with you (greeting).
Divil: Devil (fondly).
Eejit: Idiot, sometimes said light-heartedly.
Feis ceoil: Music festival.
Gaeilge: The native Irish language.
Garsún: Young boy.
Gobdaw: Foolish person.
Is fearr ná bac léi: It is better not to bother with her.
Jackeen: A Dubliner.

Maidin breá: Good morning.

Mo chairde (dílis): My friends (loyal).

Mo chuisle (mo chroi): My darling; my treasure ('beat of my heart').

Ó cailín caoine dearg: Gentle red-haired girl (addressing).

Ráiméis: Rubbish.

Sliotar: A small ball used in the Irish sport of hurling.

Sláinte go gach ceann acu ar oiche seo faoi shonas: Health to you all on this happy night.

Slán leat: Goodbye.

Author Special Request

Now that you have finished reading,
will you please take a few minutes and
post a short review of this book.

It doesn't need to be elaborate or stuffy;
all you need do is go to Amazon.com or GoodReads.com
and say what you liked or found moving or intriguing.

It's that simple.

As an independent author I rely on readers like you,
who appreciate literary fiction, to let like-minded
readers know about this book.

Simply go to my book page on Amazon: OntheEdgeoftheLoch

Sincere thanks for doing that.
I value your interest in my work,
and your feedback.

JÉC

BOOKINGS, EVENTS, LECTURES

To check on my availability for workshops, conferences,
or speaking engagements, please email me with your details at:
JEamon1998@gmail.com.

You can also connect with me at http://JosephEamonCummins.com
or by searching my full name at: Goodreads, Twitter, and Facebook.

On the Edge of the Loch
A Psychological Novel set in Ireland

A Guide for Book Clubs, Teachers and Writing Students

On the Edge of the Loch explores a range of themes, both contemporary and timeless. Each theme can be a separate focus for discussion, or two or more can be combined for a more in-depth session. Whether you are an avid book club member, a writer, writing teacher, or a student of literature, you'll recognise issues humans have been grappling with – and debating – since the time of Socrates, and probably much earlier.

Themes you might discuss include: love, identity, belonging, resilience, justice, suicide, self-regulation, passion, childhood vulnerability, rebirth.

In the category of serious fiction, what a book 'means' is rarely told to us directly; we dig out meanings by going beneath the surface, by noticing clues that tell us more than is on the page. Reading like this enriches our appreciation and increases our enjoyment of a story. In fact, the biggest reward we get from literary work comes from this 'subtext' and our associated interpretations. You move beyond being an observer when you bring to a story the qualities you use to navigate your way in the world: your wisdom, life experience, discernment, and emotional intelligence, to name just a few.

But don't for a moment think you need to notice all the subtleties or interpret the story exactly as someone else. You don't. Within any book club or study group you'll have a range of viewpoints. This is what makes exchanging ideas and insights so enjoyable and instructive, and why literature is such a precious gift. Books, like people, are infinitely variable and intriguing.

Below you'll find lists of questions I created to help you to think about particular aspects of this novel. These are largely the questions that occupied my mind as I wrote the book. Focus on those aspects that seem most relevant, pose your own questions, and explore your hunches. Most likely, you'll find connections and allusions that I did not even recognise. After all, all writing connects to the author's unconscious, usually without the conscious mind being aware of it. This is what Picasso was getting at (though he may not have realised it in the moment) when responding to a questioner asking what one of his paintings meant: 'My job is to create,' he reportedly said, 'the viewer's, to interpret.'

If your assignment is to write a book report, I suggest you create first a broad story summary, then identify the plot points (events that initiate or change the direction of the story). This way, you have a framework that links the major events before exploring the nuances of structure, setting, characters, relationships, plot twists, dialogue, exposition, and so on.

And finally, if you're a book club chairperson, teacher, or study group leader, you'll create the richest possible experience for all concerned if you invoke a simple set of discussion rules, starting with acknowledgement of all participant viewpoints.

On the Edge of the Loch
Suggested Discussion Points

Let's not be stuffy about this; it doesn't matter very much where or how you begin a book discussion. The most important thing you can do is express your views, then be willing to listen and learn from others. And keep in mind that it's not about another person's opinion being 'right' or 'wrong'.

Saying what kind of story it is, is a good place to start, and what genre you feel it belongs in. Then perhaps commenting on the structure, settings, time period, the main characters and their goals and relationships, etc.

Or, begin with exploring broader aspects of the novel, such as the impression or effect the story had on you. You decide: work with my suggestions below or develop your own approach. And remember, you'll encourage others if you begin with questions rather than opinions.

THE STORY AND THE WRITING

- What are two or three themes in this book that stood out for you? (Themes are important ideas that repeat in the story.)
- How is the story structured (chronology, tense, narrative, style, etc)?
- Which character or characters are most responsible for driving the plot?
- What is clearly different about this story from other books you can compare it with?
- How would you categorise this novel (in which section does it belong in a library)?
- What did you discover or learn from reading this book? Identify three things.

- What recurring metaphors did you notice, and how did you interpret them? (A metaphor is a word or phrase used to stand for something else. For example, a mountain might represent a challenge).
- Why do you think the author used flashback chapters?
- What did you notice about the dialog, how people talk?
- What did you learn or feel about the geographic cultures featured: Arizona, Aranroe, Baghdad, Dublin, prison, etc?

- Could you picture Aranroe village? Claire Abbey? Mweelrea? Intinn Island? Rock Cottage? Devil's Cove? Finger Rock? The

water scenes? Yablonski's prison office? The Amiriya shelter?
What was easiest to visualise?

- What stood out particularly about village life in Aranroe?
- Could you see the characters, how they looked and dressed
  and moved? If so, why was that?

- How do Tony, Lenny, Cilla and Aidan compare? Do they have
  traits in common? Elaborate.
- Which character was easiest to picture, and which was hardest?
- Tony's was the only mind you were allowed to see into directly: his self-talk, memories, dreams, fears, hopes, ravings,
  mental stability, etc. With all other characters you were asked
  to try understand them based on what they did and said, or
  what someone, accurately or inaccurately, said about them.
  How did this contribute to the story?

- Did sound help you experience particular scenes? If so, pick
  out one. For example, could you hear the ocean and storm?
  The sliding steel door of Yablonski's prison office? The train
  station? The sound of footsteps?
- Significant events in Tony's and Lenny's pasts are not revealed
  until later in the story. How did this affect your experience of
  the book?
- What similarities, if any, did you find between particular pairs
  of characters? For example, Emer and Tony? Tony and Leo?
  Emer and Cilla? Gussie and Tony? Aidan and Liam Foley, or
  any other pairs?
- What specific emotions did reading the story arouse in you?

- Which character did you care most about?
- Which character caused you most negative feelings? Identify
  the feelings and say why?
- Was Róisín's suicide justified, given her grave illness? Why do
  you think as you do?

- Was anyone else responsible, even partly, for Róisín's suicide? Why do you think as you do?

- In what way was Lenny's childhood abnormal? What do you feel was lacking? Elaborate.
- Did one or more characters who did not actually appear in the book have a bearing on events? Elaborate.
- Is Liam Foley what you see as a typical cleric? If not, how is he different?
- How did you interpret the final chapter with Tony and Cilla? Did you notice anything 'different' about it? Should you re-read it?

THE MAIN CHARACTERS

Tony
- Why do you think Tony, at fourteen, was so disturbed by the idea of emigrating?
- What traits characterised Tony's pre-prison period in Newark?
- How would you describe Tony's personality?
- In your opinion, what drove Tony so hard?
- How would you describe Tony's state of mind? (pick any stage or time period)
- What do you think was Tony's most redeeming quality?
- Why did Tony seem afraid of intimacy?

- Which of Tony's strengths might also have worked against him?
- What was Tony's biggest weakness or flaw?
- Why was it that Tony found Cilla so attractive?

- Would you have made a friend of Tony. Why? Explain your answer.
- In what major ways did Tony and Aidan differ?
- Can you identify similarities between Tony and Aidan?

- Which character did Tony learn most from?
- How did Tony view Aidan?

- Which events in Ireland caused Tony, in his adult years, to grow as a person?
- Describe how and why Tony's thinking in relation to his mission changed late in the story?
- Did Tony sacrifice his dream to allow Aidan to recapture the love he, Aidan, had lost? Explain.
- Where did Tony 'end up'?

Lenny
- What factors or events had the biggest bearing on how Lenny saw the world?
- How would you describe Lenny's behaviour as an adult? (pick any stage or period)
- What did Lenny want most in life? If you feel this changed along the way, please explain.
- What reasons caused Lenny to want to escape Aranroe?
- Why did Lenny get into so much trouble as a child in school?
- Why was the relationship between Charles and Lenny so problematic?
- Lenny and Tony made a perfect couple: what do you think?
- Looking at Lenny's whole life, who let her down most?

- How did you view the friendship between Lenny and Emer?
- How would you characterise the relationship between Lenny and Cilla?
- Why was Lenny eager to abandon everything in New York and go to Iraq with Aidan?
- Who was Lenny's best friend(s)? Give reasons for your answer.

- What qualities did you admire most in Lenny? Explain.
- Why were people generally so loyal to Lenny?

- Given that Aidan was 'dead', why did Lenny keep visiting the train station?
- Why do you think Lenny acted the way she did toward those closest to her?

- What was Lenny's biggest flaw or weakness (pick any stage or time period)?
- What was Lenny's strongest trait?
- How would you characterise Lenny's mental state (pick any stage or period)?

Cilla
- How would you describe Cilla to someone who never met her?
- What feelings did you have for Cilla?
- What did you admire most or dislike most about Cilla?
- What do you think Cilla found hardest about living in Aranroe?

- What do you think would be Cilla's idea of an ideal life?
- What were Cilla's strongest traits?
- Why did Cilla project an air of independence and capability?
- At times Cilla seemed fearless; but what made her feel insecure?

- In what significant ways did Cilla and Lenny differ from each other?
- Did Cilla have a closeness with anyone apart from Tony?
- What changed about Cilla when she had drunk a few glasses of wine?
- What was it that made Cilla's attraction to Tony so problematic for her?

- What action or scene revealed most about Cilla?
- Did you see Cilla as an outsider in her village? Explain your view.

- Despite conflicting objectives, Cilla and Tony got along well. Why was this?

- What drove Cilla to risk her life more than once? Foolishness? Bravery? Or some other trait?
- Cilla sometimes seemed like a simple country girl. Did you see her that way?
- What do you imagine Cilla would have done if she and Tony hadn't met?

Aidan
- How would you describe Aidan to someone who hadn't met him?
- In what way did Aidan differ from other main or secondary characters?
- How would you explain Aidan's life in Dublin?
- Were particular traits lacking in Aidan? Explain.

- Was Aidan justified in giving up on Lenny?
- What strengths did you see in Aidan?
- What was Aidan's greatest flaw?

- What psychological factors caused Aidan and Lenny to fall in love in New York?
- What needs did Aidan and Lenny have that made their connection so strong?
- What values motivated Aidan most in life?
- How would you describe Aidan's decline from who he had been in New York and prior to that?
- How would you have advised Aidan in his Dublin period, before he and Tony met?
- Did you consider Aidan brave? Explain?
- Did you see Aidan as naive or compassionate, or either? Explain.

- How do you think Aidan viewed Tony?
- Did you see Aidan as a misfit?
- What was it about Aidan that you feel impressed or affected Tony most?
- Were Aidan and Lenny opposites or similar? Explain your view.

SECONDARY AND MINOR CHARACTERS
(Secondary characters can affect the direction of the story; minor characters rarely do)

- How did you feel about the female characters: Eva Kohler? Kate? Róisín? Emer? Peggy? Eilis? Siobhan? Caitriona? Mairead? Etc.

- How did you feel about the male characters: Old William? Charles Quin? Ravarro? Paddy? Fr Coy? Liam Foley? Leo? Tom Quilty? Gussie? Dermot? Fogo? Larry? Etc.

- Which secondary characters did you find most interesting or likeable? Select two and say why.
- Which two secondary or minor characters did you dislike most? Say why.

- How did Paddy, Liam and Leo differ from each other, and what did they have in common?
- Did one minor character intrigue you more than others? Explain.
- Was there a minor character you'd have liked to see more of in the story? If so, explain.

MISCELLANEOUS 'IF' QUESTIONS

- If you could invite any four of the characters to dinner together, who would you choose? Why?
- If you could interview one of the characters, who would you choose? Why?

- If you were shipwrecked, which character would you wish to have with you? Why?

- If you needed advice about life or achieving a big goal, which character would you consult? Why?
- If you could choose just one of the characters as a friend, who would it be? Why?
- If you could discuss this book with author Joseph Éamon Cummins, what three questions would you ask?
- If you could discuss just one main character with the author, who would it be? Why?
- If you could discuss just one secondary or minor character with the author, who would it be? Why?

Final Note: AUTOBIOGRAPHY OR NOT?

Here's my take on a particular question that arises at workshops and seminars, often from philosophy enthusiasts.

I am asked if I believe that all fiction is, in a certain sense, autobiographical. It's not a silly question. Writers are constantly recording impressions from their personal interactions with life. Some of these impressions are factual: the behaviour of the old guy on the bus, the passionate language of the hippie hiker. But even a whiff or a whisper can flower into utter fantasy, the human imagination at work. Consciously and unconsciously the storyteller works this mix of impressions into a coherent narrative soup. In this act of creation the events of a story can indeed be said to be experienced, felt, and lived through by the author. Therefore, some ask, isn't this, by definition, autobiographical? The point can be argued, but until we agree a broader definition of 'autobiographical', I think no.

Joseph Éamon Cummins

INTERVIEW WITH JOSEPH ÉAMON CUMMINS
For more interviews and resources see: JosephEamonCummins.com

Why did you write *On the Edge of the Loch*?
Sometimes a story, or an article or piece of music, demands to be written. It bangs the walls and won't stop. That's what this book did.

What is the significance of the title?
In Gaeilge, Ireland's native language, the word 'loch' means lake. And when someone is 'on the edge', it usually spells danger. So it is with the two main protagonists; they've been on the edge of disaster for way too long. As the story begins they're strangers, they meet by accident, in circumstances that could lead to new lives, but life is seldom that simple. And here it certainly isn't.

Is the story entirely fictional?
No story is fabricated entirely. What a writer creates originates in 'events' that happen within the mind and outside. These actual and mental events are the seed of all art. An abstract painting, for example, is born of real experience. The sequential events in *On the Edge of the Loch* are not factual; neither are the characters. But then true and factual are not the same. A well-told story is always 'true', as the old Irish storytellers would claim, and as did Ernest Hemingway.

Are you saying that actual events sparked the story?
One event. In a remote train station, I noticed an attractive woman who seemed to be waiting for someone to arrive. Over the next week I revisited the station many times to photograph it. I was an avid photographer then, always searching for the perfect shot, the best light. Each time I went to the station, the woman was there – still just waiting.

On the day I was leaving she smiled at me. I smiled back. Our eyes held in a sort of silent conversation, just for moments. Then she gestured like she was about to talk to me, but suddenly her head dropped, she turned away.

I left on that train, never saw her again. I sensed that she was waiting for a dream that would never show up. But what if, I thought. What if that dream could come true. And what if that changed her whole life, and other lives. I built the story from that idea.

Tony's singularity and complexity make him seem like a real person. Is he based on someone you might have known?
He's a composite character, with traits borrowed from real experience.

Unlike in popular fiction, there are no traditional hero types in your story. What's your thinking on this?
The hero has a place in folklore and in certain fiction genres. The story I'm telling here is about 'real' people, how low they can sink, how high they can rise. Each of the main characters is flawed, yet each might be capable of greatness, which they don't see until circumstances turn dramatic.

Emerson said: *Circumstances don't make the man, but reveal him.* Interesting, but misunderstanding this idea can lead to harmful self-limiting. A person is never wholly revealed in any particular moment in time. Failing precedes winning, invariably, people change and grow, become more than they were, discover their potential. The past is not a prison, nor is it destiny. Too many fail to grasp this fact; they surrender to circumstance, don't honour their potential. Abraham Maslow, one of the founders of humanistic psychology, believed that most people sell themselves short for an entire lifetime. I agree, but it doesn't have to be so. This is at the core of my work with clients.

For a long time I've been guiding students and business professionals on achievement. Ironically, some opt out out of fear of how good they might be – the Jonah Complex. Tony MacNeill, the protagonist in the story, damaged as he is, refuses to surrender to circumstance, or let circumstance limit him or define him, and all is changed by this mindset.

What are other major themes in the story?
There is always the overt story, what happens on the surface. But in literary fiction this is never as important as subtext, what's going on inside the characters, what they really think or mean, which the writer can hint at, imply, or conceal. This means the reader is asked to work, to rise above being an observer.

To answer your question, there are many themes in the story: identity, obsession, mental illness, home, family, justice, belonging, the nature of love, the sacredness of childhood, to name just some. And at the core of the story, there's that resilience that leads to growth and achievement.

Is there a lesson the reader can learn from the novel?
Most authors hope the reader will feel enriched. *On the Edge of the Loch* contains a multiplicity of themes, any one of which might carry a catalytic message for a particular reader.

I wanted the reader to understand mental illness better, and to contemplate the futility of war; these are big messages. I wanted the concept of justice to stand out. And the vulnerability of humans in relation to childhood trauma. Other themes relate to the preeminence of family and the enabling power of friendship.

Also, as I mentioned, running through the entire story is the learnable quality of resilience, the 'not giving up' response when no light is visible at the end of the tunnel. I'd like to think too that the book elucidates the supreme quality of love, not just intimate love but the love of any one person for another: parent for child, sister for sister, friend for friend – the key to everything.

Some reviewers said they see Ireland as a character in the work. Is this what you intended?

I understand what they mean, but I don't see it like that. Ireland is a critical plot element. The environments depicted and their associated atmospherics (storm, sea, fog, heat, sky, wind, rain) facilitate the story's development.

But my characters are all psychologically complex individuals, even secondary characters like Leo and Emer; it's from this mix of personalities, from their minds and interactions, that the story takes its life. Environment is always important in fiction, but I see it as quite distinct from character.

Nonetheless, the use of personification, metaphor, and motif can imbue inanimate objects – a mountain, an island, countryside – with human-like qualities that make them seem like characters. We routinely say 'the sun won't shine' or 'that mountain steals lives' or 'that devil whirlpool' as though the sun or mountain or whirlpool possesses intention, a human mind. This attribution of 'character qualities' to non-human elements is part of the richness and colour of our language, especially in writing.

Apart from the main characters, which other character are you most fond of?

Keep in mind that writers love villains as easily as saints. But, more important than simple badness or goodness is credibility and depth: is the character believable, palpable, breathing, motivated to act.

In terms of fondness, Leo Reffo is absent from the story for long periods but his influence hangs over all thirty-five years of the novel period. He is powerful and quiet, and like others has made big mistakes. Lenny's friend Emer, appears in only two chapters but it's hard not to like her neediness and warmth, and her wittiness as a younger woman.

Paddy McCann is a rich character; he's charming and has a silver tongue but is fundamentally a brooding type. Paddy's wife, Eilis, is a minor character I would have been happy to develop had the story required it. And Gus, the old down-and-out guy in Dublin, is one of my favourites, for his heart.

The women in your story drive much of the action. Is there a message in this?

Not a political message, no. I set out to reflect female nature as I see it. And to be loyal to the female characters I created. In life, though maybe not so much in literature, women are often the stronger sex, despite not having the platform men enjoy. Their strength is often missed in the day-to-day grind, but is nonetheless catalytic.

Characters like Lenny, Róisín and Cilla, even Kate and Peggy and Emer, may not seem like role models to some readers, but each is decisive, each makes things happen, and so they shape outcomes in the story, as so often women do in life.

Tony is obviously searching for redemption. But what does this mean?

We can see living as having three possible conditions. One is existence, where people acquiesce and rationalise and never commit to worthy goals; many get stuck here.

The second is conviction, when people strive to grow, to express their talents and skills; a minority commit to this.

And finally there's redemption, when conscience or courage drives the person to atonement or fulfilment, respectively. For most of the story, Tony is in this last category, driven by conscience. He might not agree, but that's not for him to say; that's for the reader to judge.

You let the reader see inside Tony's mind but no one else's. Why did you limit point of view to this one character? Did it make the book more difficult to write?

For readers, a single character point of view is least confusing; it feels authentic, truer to how they experience life, through just one perspective. And yes, it's harder to write this way because the author must put all the other characters on stage and get them to do and say things that reveal who they are and how they think; he cannot tell their inner stories. When it's done well, this method allows for better control of pacing and helps build suspense.

Interestingly, I wrote the early drafts almost entirely in Tony's stream-of-consciousness, just to get to know his mind intimately. Stream of consciousness, similar to interior monologue, is the voice we each speak to ourselves with, the voice no one else hears. But I always knew I would limit the novel's point of view to Tony. It's his story, after all.

Had I let the reader inside Lenny's head, into an often chaotic mind, it would have become her story. As I've written it, the reader's challenge is exactly the same as Tony's, to understand Lenny from her behaviour and her words, and from sketchy details others provide about her that may not be reliable. Reader understanding is meant to come incrementally as the pieces fit together. Therefore, the reader gets to figure things out only as Tony does, not before.

On the other hand, it's relatively easy to write using the omniscient or 'God' point of view. Most fiction writing students begin this way; some are totally unconscious of the concept of point of view in literature.

Omniscient point of view is where the reader is a fly on the wall, potentially inside the heads of any or all the characters, knowing their innermost thoughts, past and present. So, the writer can reveal hopes, secrets, memories, the characters' loves, hates, and deepest feelings. In the past this was popular; today it is less common in serious fiction.

But, remember, point of view is a writer's tool, readers do not need to know anything about it to understand and enjoy a novel.

The main characters are atypical; at times they're clearly unbalanced, except for Cilla, perhaps. They're also all psychologically different. What was your thinking on this?
Flawed, unbalanced, yes; in given circumstances each is a misfit, as

Tony accuses Aidan, ironically. Yet each protagonist is extraordinary in at least one positive way. In real life it's no different, though many don't see it.

For authenticity, I built a psychological profile for each protagonist. Ninety-five percent of this information was not intended for inclusion in the book. For the characters to be credible, I needed to know their intimate backstories in detail, so I did a case study analysis of each.

Lenny's condition, for example, as presented, is clinically accurate, with its origins in trauma. The mentalities of Tony and Aidan are just as true.

The message is that it's time to normalise and better treat mental ill-health. Few people get through life unscathed.

Why did you end the story the way you did, the final chapter?
This is a question I prefer not to answer. In one sense it is the chapter I am most happy with, the way in which it achieves what I set out to write. The first critic to review the book saw exactly what I intended, which delighted me because I knew it would not be obvious to all.

What I am alluding to is something the reader will sense by carefully reading those last few pages. I am being vague now because there is something in the final chapter that is best discovered rather than being told about. The emotional overhang from the previous chapter, the final train station scene, leaves the reader in a mild state of shock and with a lot of mental pictures. Consequently, for some, the 'secret' of the final chapter may be too much to take in on the first reading. So, re-read. I don't want to say more than that, for the readers' benefit.

You are sending the reader back for a second read?
Yes. At least of that final chapter. Many readers re-read literary novels anyway. One critic commenting on *On the Edge of the Loch* said he would enjoy the second read even more than the first,

that he'd still feel anxious but a little more relaxed, and this would enable him to notice more. There's a hint in that in relation to the final chapter.

What are you planning next?
A number of reviewers have suggested Book Two of the story. That was never my plan. Others said they see it as a film or TV series. I created a pared-down film script as I wrote the story, but only to embed the pictures in my brain and thereby add vividness to my writing. I do agree though; it is a visual novel.

But the answer to your question is, I don't know what will have my priority next. I am always working on more than one project.

Let's wait and see . . .

JOSEPH ÉAMON CUMMINS

Unlike many writers, Joe has carved out a life of diversity and adventure, living in three continents and earning qualifications in different fields.

A Dubliner, he started a diary at thirteen, was published at seventeen, and the writing bug never left. In his early twenties he travelled extensively 'on the road' in America, living and working where he stopped. During long spells with a touring carnival he bought a Nikon camera and began capturing images of a continent that fascinated him, while also documenting his adventures in a journal.

Eventually though, he was drawn back to his interests in psychology, entrepreneurship, and the arts. This led him to Arizona, to study under distinguished teachers Roger Hutt, Bill Jay, Art Christiansen and Ross LaManna, each of whom he credits with influencing his thinking, an education funded by his work as a photographer.

He next moved to Dublin, starting his own company in the then emerging field of video/film production and winning a number of national awards. Concurrently, he co-developed a seminal college program in that field and took over as editor of the leading professional journal. In fine-art, he created and exhibited the world's first collection of photographic portraits of centenarians (17 in total, all Irish), captured on large-format cameras, a show that featured in the Boston Globe and Chicago Tribune.

Then adventure called again, this time taking him to Australia and into real estate, another of his long-term interests. Later, back in the US, he wrote *Not One Dollar More!*, a how-to book on negotiation that sold over one hundred thousand copies (John Wiley & Son, NY), founded a micro press for emerging authors, and published articles in leading US magazines.

At this point, however, an older passion led him back to academic study and post-graduate qualifications in psychology and human learning.

As an adjunct professor he taught creative writing and psychology for over a decade in New Jersey, earning multiple Best Professor citations from student bodies. At the same time, he was consulting and coaching private business clients and lecturing on Modernism and Irish Studies in the Road Scholar program at Stockton University.

Subsequently, he returned to Ireland and set up his own organisational psychology and performance management practice. Today, he travels widely, leading seminars on resilience and human achievement topics. He also lectures occasionally on 'psychology in fiction'.

'Loch' is Joe's first novel. More adventures to come, he says.

Acknowledgements

All artists – fiction writers, painters, poets, sculptors – function on more than talent and imagination, not least on the friendship, encouragement, motivation, input, love, kindness, and support of others. While writing *On the Edge of the Loch*, I was fortunate to have these, and more.

Above all, my deepest gratitude goes to my wife, Kathy, a gifted stained glass artist and teacher in her own right, for her love, her ever-astute reading of my countless drafts, and her invaluable editorial input, all of which made this a better book.

My thanks also to my brother Desi, a writer and thinker of rare insight, and an early beta-reader of this novel, for freely sharing his intellect; to my sister Ann for encouragement, caring and belief I can always count on; to Paddy for his reliability and longest friendship; and special love and gratitude to my parents Joe and Bridget for their dreams and dedication.

And, importantly, ovations to: Karen, Carol, Eileen, Dawn & Bill; Brigid, Christina & Eric, Eamon & Hallie, and Mary Jane & John. And similarly to: Aran, Claire & Phil; and Frank and Lori. Also, warmly, to K and S and GFC. And to Bernadette, Andrew, Roy, Colin, Eoin, and the clans in Ceannanus Mór and Broadwater, WA. And remembering joyfully Mr JR Poly.

Remembering too with deep affection, Isabel and Tom Argenti, for their gracious embracement and generosity of spirit. And very specially, my friend Anthony (Hop) Cardelli, a man and writer of high sensibility.

Also, not forgetting my good friend Harvey and our many adventures along the highways and byways and midways of the USA.

Plaudits also to my colleagues, students and clients on both sides of the Atlantic for their constant willingness to commit to 'new learning'.

For kind assistance with my research on County Mayo and the west of Ireland, special thanks to: Ireland's National Tourism

Development Authority (Fáilte Ireland), DiscoverIreland.ie, Mayo.ie, and Mayo-Ireland.ie.

For help with my US prison research, I am indebted to Arizona Dept of Corrections and California Dept of Corrections and Rehabilitation.

Finally, I extend much-deserved acknowledgement to all those who work for peace, justice, human rights, human development, prison reform, mental wellbeing, addiction prevention and rehabilitation, early-life trauma and PTSD relief, and healthcare as a basic human right.